PRAISE FOR KATE WHITE'S
BAILEY WEGGINS NOVELS

LETHALLY BLOND

The *New York Times* Bestseller

"It's *Murder, She Wrote*—with a much hotter cast of characters!"
—*Star*

"White has the ideal background to write about her heroine, Bailey Weggins. Weggins may get involved in more dangerous adventures than the average journalist, but that's all just part of the fun."
—*Chicago Tribune*

"Smokin' hot…as much fun as your favorite celeb-studded tabloid."
—*Town & Country*

"As a modern-day caper novelist, Kate White reminds us that Nancy Drew is alive, well, and possibly living in New York."
—Gothamist.com

"Whenever I learn that Kate White has a new Bailey Weggins mystery on the shelves, it's an automatic buy for me. LETHALLY BLOND doesn't disappoint. Bailey is fun and trendy and deals with life, love, and work just as all women do today. She manages to get into and out of hot water faster than a tea bag, and it's always fun to see what she's going to do next."

—BookReporter.com

"FOUR STARS! Bailey is a likable, spunky heroine…White's interesting, rapidly developing mystery more than holds the reader's interest."

—*Romantic Times BOOKreviews Magazine*

more…

OVER HER DEAD BODY

The *New York Times* Bestseller and
A *Harper's Bazaar* Red-Hot Read

'TIL DEATH DO US PART

more…

A BODY TO DIE FOR
The *New York Times* Bestseller

IF LOOKS COULD KILL

The *New York Times* Bestseller and
The First Selection of the "Reading with Ripa" Book Club

"Delicious...inspired [and] breezy...a delight. White shows she has plot-spinning skills and a self-mocking sense of humor...[Her] knowing references add insider zing."

—*People*

"*Sex and the City* meets the murder mystery, and Bailey Weggins is a sleuth a girl could love...What wicked fun!"

—Lisa Scottoline, author of *Courting Trouble*

"A page-turner...keeps the reader guessing...[You'll] devour the dishy magazine-world details."

—*Chicago Sun-Times*

"First-rate...feels like a rich dessert...It's impossible to outwit White."

—*Entertainment Weekly*

"White is scathingly observant, capturing the mood at a glossy magazine with a verisimilitude some of her peers might recognize."

—*New York Times*

"It's like devouring a box of chocolates."

—*Los Angeles Times*

"A must-read mystery."

—*Good Housekeeping*

"Fast-moving and gutsy, this first novel delivers excitement with a confidence usually missing in first attempts."

—*Dallas Morning News*

"Wonderful...peeks between the lines of America's glossiest magazines from the very top of the masthead...a deliciously deadly glimpse at an insider's world of fashion and style."

—Linda Fairstein, author of *Killer Heat*

Also by Kate White

Over Her Dead Body
'Til Death Do Us Part
A Body to Die For
If Looks Could Kill

*You on Top: Smart, Sexy Skills Every Woman Needs
to Set the World on Fire*
The Nine Secrets of Women Who Get Everything They Want
Why Good Girls Don't Get Ahead but Gutsy Girls Do

LETHALLY BLOND

KATE WHITE

GRAND CENTRAL
PUBLISHING

NEW YORK   BOSTON

Grand Central Publishing
Hachette Book Group USA
237 Park Avenue
New York, NY 10017

Visit our Web site at www.HachetteBookGroupUSA.com.

Printed in the United States of America

Originally published in hardcover by Hachette Book Group USA.

First Trade Edition: April 2008
10 9 8 7 6 5 4 3 2 1

Grand Central Publishing is a division of Hachette Book Group USA, Inc.
The Grand Central Publishing name and logo is a trademark of Hachette Book Group USA, Inc.

The Library of Congress has cataloged the hardcover edition as follows:
White, Kate
    Lethally blond / Kate White. — 1st ed.
        p. cm.
    ISBN: 978-0-446-57795-3
    1. Women journalists—Fiction. I. Title.
PS3623.H578L48 2007
813'.6—dc22   2007000447

ISBN 978-0-446-19690-1 (pbk.)

To Laura, wonderful
friend and fabulous blonde

ACKNOWLEDGMENTS

First and foremost I'd like to thank my wonderful editor Karen Kosztolnyik for her guidance and my fab, gutsy agent Sandy Dijkstra for her support, as well as her amazing team, including Taryn and Elise. And then there were the people who were so generous in helping me with my research, which is one of the best parts of writing: Kate Carcaterra; Barry Cunningham, television journalist; Barbara Butcher, director of forensic investigations, NYC Office of Chief Medical Examiner; Brad Holbrook, actor; Mark Howell, psychotherapist; Angela Jones, aerialist; Paul Paganelli, MD, chief of emergency medicine, Milton Hospital, Milton, MA; Trinka Porrata, drug consultant and retired LAPD detective; Richard Spencer, editor in chief, *In Touch*; Sheila Weller, author and journalist; Lt. Gene Whyte, DCPI, NYPD.

CHAPTER 1

It all started with a coincidence. Not one of those totally creepy coincidences that make you feel as if someone has just walked across your grave. In fact, later I could see that the phone call I got that late summer night wasn't all that unexpected—but at the time it made me catch my breath. And, of course, it was the start of everything horrible that happened. . . .

I'd decided to stop by the office that day, something I rarely do on Tuesdays. It was crazy hot for the middle of September, and it would have been nice to just hang on the brick terrace of my apartment in Greenwich Village, chugging a few iced teas. But a new deputy editor had started recently—Valerie Crowe, a hyper, edgy chick who left you overwhelmed with an urge to shoot a tranquilizer dart into her ass—and I thought it would be smart to give her some face time. My copy goes through the executive editor, but it's one of the deputy editors who assigns me most of my stories and often suggests leads for me to follow up on. Since Tuesday is the day after closing, I knew she'd probably have a few minutes to spare. Most of the staff never even gets in before noon that day.

My name is Bailey Weggins, and I'm a reporter for *Buzz*, one of the weekly celebrity gossip magazines that have become like crack cocaine for women under thirty-five these days. Unlike most of the staff, I don't cover the botched marriages and bulimic ordeals of the stars. Instead, I report on celebrity crime—like when an A-lister hurls a phone at a hotel desk clerk or hires a hit man to shoot his wife.

It's not something I'd ever imagined myself doing. I was a straight crime writer for the ten years after college graduation, but when the job opened up early in the summer, curiosity and the need for a regular gig prodded me to take it.

"Celebrity crime reporter—are you saying it's some sort of specialized area of journalism?" my mother had asked at the time, as if it were on a par with becoming a pediatric neurosurgeon or astrophysicist.

Initially, I was at a disadvantage because I didn't know—excuse the expression—jackshit about celebrities. Oh, I'd picked up tidbits about the really major stars—you know, like Brad and Angelina and Gwyneth and TomKat—from listening to friends dish as well as perusing gossip magazines during pedicures. But I was clueless about most of the other stars in the celebrity universe. In fact, until two weeks into my job at *Buzz*, I'd thought Jake Gyllenhaal and Orlando Bloom were the *same person*. But I caught on pretty quickly, and to my surprise, I grew to really enjoy my two-to-three-day-a-week arrangement. Celebrities not only live large, they misbehave large, too. Covering their crimes, I discovered, could be awfully entertaining.

One more plus. In November, a small publishing house was releasing a collection of my crime pieces, *Bad Men and Wicked Women,* and the job would be leverage for PR.

The *Buzz* offices were practically tomblike when I stepped off the elevator, though it was mercifully cool, as if the low body count had prevented the air from rising above 65 degrees that day. I nodded to a few people as I walked through the huge cube farm/bullpen that constitutes a major chunk of our offices. I'm in a part of that area nicknamed the Pod, which abuts the art and production departments and houses many of the writers and junior editors. The senior editors are in glass-fronted offices that rim the area. My workstation is right next to that of a senior writer named Jessie Pendergrass and behind Leo Zern, a photo editor they couldn't find room for in the photo department.

"Hey," I said to Leo as I tossed my purse and tote bag onto my desk. He was the only one in the general vicinity. He tore his eyes off his computer screen and swiveled just his head in my direction.

"To what do we owe this honor?" he asked. "I thought you weren't coming in today."

"I had a few things I wanted to take care of. Jessie around?"

"She's not in yet. I heard her tell someone on the phone yesterday that her bikini line was a disaster, so maybe she's having it administered to."

"Anything going on here?"

"Not really. Oh, there was a little bit of a dustup this morning. You know how we said Britney Spears looked like a Smurf?"

"No. Okay, I'll take your word for it."

"Nash got a phone call today, and the fur was flying." He was talking about Nash Nolan, the editor in chief.

"From Britney's publicist?"

"No, it was from a *Smurf* representative. They don't want to be compared to her."

"Very funny. So what are you working on?" I sidled over to his desk and checked out the computer screen. There was a grainy shot of a blond starlet type I didn't recognize sitting at an outdoor restaurant, jamming half a dozen French fries into her mouth as if she were stuffing dirty clothes into an overfilled hamper. "God, the paparazzi don't let these chicks alone, do they," I said.

"The ones who take these shots don't consider themselves paparazzi," he said. "They're *snackarazzi.*"

"You're kidding, right?"

"Not at all. These are the real money shots these days. They're almost as good as one of a star scratching her ass."

"Remind me not to order a double bacon cheeseburger the next time I'm at a sidewalk café."

"I think *you're* safe, Bailey," he said, smirking.

I checked my e-mail and then a bunch of Web sites to see if any A-listers had landed themselves in hot water that day, but things seemed fairly quiet. After grabbing a cup of coffee, I wandered down to the office of the new deputy editor.

"Hi, Val," I said, poking my head in the door and forcing a smile. I've always wished I were good at office politics, but fawning and bullshitting just don't come easily to me, particularly if the person at the other end is a real jerk, which I suspected Valerie was. A guy I used to work with at the *Albany Times Union,* when I was a newspaper reporter right out of college, said that I butt-kissed about as well as a blowtorch.

"What can I do for you?" Valerie asked without enthusiasm. Her dark hair was slicked off her face today, accentuating the large sharp nose she sported between brown eyes. She reminded me of how our family dog used to look when he emerged sopping wet from a pond.

"Just thought I'd check in—see if you needed me for anything," I told her.

"What are you working on now?" she asked, a thin layer of impatience coating her question.

Gosh, I thought, you just don't like me, *do* you? But I couldn't tell why. She'd arrived at the magazine not long after the previous editor in chief, Mona Hodges, had been killed in her office by several blows to the head. It had been a tumultuous time, particularly for me, for not only had I found Mona that night, but I also had later figured out who had murdered her, nearly getting killed myself in the process. Nash, the number two at the time, had been named editor in chief shortly afterward; a deputy editor had taken over for Nash, and now Valerie had the deputy job. I sometimes wondered if she resented the fact that Nash and I were tight and that I had plenty of autonomy.

"Nothing major at the moment," I told her. "Just following a few leads. I probably won't come in again this week unless something breaks."

"Just let Aubrey know," she said, referring to the managing editor. Then she glanced over at her computer screen as if she were dying to get back to work.

"Sure," I said, and walked off. How nice that I'd bothered to take the subway up from the Village.

As long as I was at the office, I followed up with staffers on a few matters and polished off another cup of coffee. And then, with nothing more to do, I stood up to go.

"Oh, Bailey, I know what your favorite TV show is going to be this season," Leo said as I was shutting off my computer. "Have you seen the fall lineup?"

"No, but let me guess, *Survivor—The New York Singles Scene?*"

"Nope. A new show called *Morgue*. It's about investigators from the medical examiner's office. Sounds perfect for someone with your grisly interests."

"Aren't there a million shows like that already?" I asked.

"I guess the public can't get enough of them."

Just to humor Leo, I sauntered over to his desk and glanced down at his computer screen. Along with the description of the show, there were a few shots from episodes and a group photo of the ensemble cast, all perfectly coiffed and smileless, their eyes burning with desire to see justice done and have the show win its time slot in the ratings. Suddenly I felt my jaw drop. One of the actors I was staring at in the ensemble cast was Chris Wickersham. He was a model and actor I'd had a short fling with last winter.

"Oh, wow," I said.

"What—you think you're really gonna like it?"

"No, the guy on the far left. I know him."

"Really?" he said as he glanced back at the screen. "You mean—Chris Wickersham, who plays Jared Hanson, the sometimes moody but brilliantly intuitive investigator? Is he straight?"

"Very. It says it's about the New York City Morgue. Does that mean it's shooting here?"

"Not necessarily. Lemme see . . . Yes, shot entirely in New York City. Was this guy your boyfriend?"

"Sort of. For about four seconds. Is there anything else?"

"No, just that it premieres in two weeks."

"Look, I'd better fly. Tell Jessie hi for me, will you?"

I grabbed my purse and tote bag and headed out of the building. My mind was racing, thinking of what I'd just learned about Chris. The last time I had laid eyes on him was right before he'd struck out for L.A. last March, hoping like millions of other guys with dreamy eyes and perfect jawlines to be cast in a pilot for the fall. We hadn't promised each other anything about staying in touch (though early on he'd sent two e-mails and one goofy postcard of the Hollywood sign), and I'd just assumed he hadn't met with any real success yet. But he had. And based on the public love of carnage and corpses, there was every chance the show would be a success. I felt happy for Chris; he deserved fame and fortune. But at the same time, there was something vaguely disconcerting about the whole thing that I couldn't put my finger on. Maybe it was knowing that a guy I'd locked lips with was now poised to become the kind of hottie women across America drooled over and dished about the next day at the watercooler.

I took the subway to 8th and Broadway, hit the gym for thirty minutes, grabbed a few supplies at the deli, and then headed to my apartment at 9th and Broadway. Though I'd left home only a few hours earlier, my place was stifling hot. I turned on the AC, fixed an ice water, and flopped on the couch. As I took the first sip of my drink, I let memories of Chris Wickersham run roughshod around my brain. I had met him a year ago April, at a wedding, where he had worked as one of the bartenders, supplementing the money he made from modeling and small acting gigs. He was absolutely gorgeous, the kind of guy it almost hurt to look at.

Though he took my number and called me, I'd blown him off. He was ten years younger than me, and though that kind of age gap hadn't bothered Cameron Diaz or Demi Moore, I just couldn't imagine having a boyfriend I was old enough to have baby-sat for. Then, nine months later, we'd reconnected when I'd needed his help during a murder investigation. I was dating a guy named Jack steadily by then, and I tried not to send any of the wrong messages to Chris, but one night he had kissed me and I'd felt it all the way to my tippy toes. It was the beginning of my doubts about my relationship with Jack. Soon afterward I was single again. Chris and I had a few dates and some serious make-out sessions, but I'd been unable to take the relationship—sexually and otherwise—beyond that. One of the last things Chris had said to me was, "Jeez, Bailey, what *is* it with you—yes or no?" In the end, it had been no. In hindsight, I thought my doubts might have been due to guilt. I always associated Chris with my breakup.

If I met him today, would I still feel those doubts? I wondered. What would it be like to date a guy millions of people watched on TV? Christ, Bailey, I thought, you're starting to sound like a star fucker.

I drained the last of my water. I'd planned to stay in tonight to work on a freelance article. Plus, ever since I'd had my heart bruised during the summer by a guy named Beau Regan, I'd been lying low. But thanks to the heat wave, the idea now held nada appeal. I wondered who I might be able to drum up for companionship on short notice. My seventy-year-old next-door neighbor, Landon, who I sometimes palled around with, had said he was heading over to the Film Forum on West Houston Street to see a German flick. A college pal of mine from Brown had recently split with her husband, and she was game for anything that provided escape from her apartment, but an evening in her company could be exhausting. She tended to ask an endless series of borderline-hostile questions that were impossible for me to answer—like "Are all men dickheads or just the ones I meet?" "Who would *drink* a prickly pear martini, do you know?" and "Do *you* think I'm brimming with anger?"

Maybe I would just head out alone and eat a quiet dinner outdoors at one of the restaurants over on MacDougal. As I padded toward my bedroom to change, my cell phone buzzed from my purse, making me jump.

"Hello," I said after digging it out.

"Bailey?"

"Yes."

"Hi, it's Chris Wickersham."

For a moment, I thought it was Leo playing a practical joke. But he wouldn't have been familiar with that deep, smooth voice—so I knew for certain it had to be Chris. I caught my breath, stunned by the eeriness of the timing.

"Oh, my gosh," I said. "I—I was just reading about you two hours ago. Congratulations—I, er, heard about the show."

God, Bailey, this is why you *write* professionally, I thought. You shouldn't be allowed to open your mouth.

"Thanks," he said. "The opportunity kind of came out of nowhere. I've been planning to call you—I mean, just to say hello."

"So you're back in New York?"

"Yeah—I've got a studio in TriBeCa. I don't want to overextend myself until I know if the show is going to take off or not."

"Is the shooting schedule as brutal as you hear?"

"Fourteen-hour days, sometimes. But this is what I wanted, and I've got no complaints. The show kicks off in a couple of weeks, and then we play the ratings game."

"It sounds like a super idea for a show—I'm sure it will be a hit."

"Kind of your type of show, huh?"

"You're the second person who said that today."

"Well, look, the reason I called . . . I mean, I wanted to say hi, but—is there any chance you could meet me for a drink? There's something I need to talk to you about."

"Sure," I said. His tone didn't suggest a man who'd been pining for me for months and had decided to make one last stab at winning my heart, but I was still curious. "When were you thinking?"

"I know this is short notice, but I was wondering if you could do it now. It's really pretty urgent. You're the one person I can turn to on this."

"What is it? Are you in some kind of trouble?"

"No, no. But a friend of mine may be. I need your advice."

"Can you give me a hint?" I asked, though I figured that if a guy he knew was in trouble, it had to involve drugs or money or both.

"It— Look, would you mind talking about it in person? I hate the idea of starting to get into it on the phone and then having to cover the same ground again when we meet."

"Well, I *could* do it now, actually," I admitted. "I was planning to stay in and work tonight, but it can wait."

"That's terrific," he said. He suggested we meet in an hour and asked me to recommend a place near me. I threw out the name of a bar on Second Avenue between 9th and 10th. It would take me less than five minutes to walk there.

After signing off, I walked distractedly into the bathroom and splashed cool water on my face and in my armpits. I couldn't believe what had just happened. Maybe it was my destiny that Chris Wickersham would pop into my life every nine months or so. I wondered if there was any chance that he was using a so-called problem with a friend as an excuse to make contact with me. It had been hard to tell on the phone. And I wasn't at all sure how I'd feel when I saw him. I had never once stopped finding him staggeringly attractive. Perhaps now that I was no longer guilt stricken—and my love life was currently in the Dumpster with a capital D—I would feel the urge to go for it this time.

Covering my bets, I wore a pair of tight jeans and a flowy turquoise baby doll top with a V deep enough for me to flash some cleavage. I smoothed my blondish brown hair and applied just enough eye shadow, mascara, blush, and lip gloss to keep from looking as if I'd tried as hard as I had.

He wasn't in the bar when I arrived. I found a free table by the front window and ordered a Corona. Taking a sip of the icy cold beer from the bottle, I watched people stroll along the pavement in the September dusk. A couple of guys stared through the glass at me, and one even shot me a flirty smile. I realized suddenly how nice it was to be sitting in a slutty top, waiting for a hunk—even if it wasn't really a date. Along with my heart, Beau Regan had bruised my ego. This was the closest I'd felt in ages to being a bitch on wheels.

"Hey, Bailey, hi."

It was Chris's voice behind me. He must have entered the bar without my seeing him.

As I shifted in my chair, I caught two women gazing behind me, their mouths agape. As soon as I spun around, I could see why. Chris Wickersham had somehow managed to become even more gorgeous in the months since I'd last seen him. There were the dazzling green eyes and the intriguing cleft in his chin. But he'd gained a few pounds, filling out his face in the nicest of ways. His sandy brown hair was a little longer and tinged with blond highlights. The biceps were the same, though. They cockily stretched the sleeves of a gray T-shirt he wore over tan cargo shorts. Had I been the stupidest girl in America to reject him?

I stood up to greet Chris, and at the same moment he leaned forward to kiss me on the cheek. Because of the awkward angle of our bodies, the edge of his full, lovely mouth touched mine, and I felt the same rush I'd experienced the very first time he'd kissed me in Miami. Take it down, way down, Bailey, I told myself. I had no idea what Chris's intentions were—or mine, for that matter—and I didn't want to get ahead of myself.

"Hey there," was all I could muster.

"God, it's great to see those blue eyes again, Bailey. You look amazing."

"Well, I'm not the one with half the bar staring at me."

"I'll start describing what we do in the morgue with a Stryker saw and let's see how they like that," he said, grinning. He created a dead-on whiny saw noise that made me laugh out loud.

He ordered a beer for himself, and we talked for a few minutes about the series. It was being shot entirely in New York City, with all the interior morgue shots done on a soundstage at Chelsea Piers. He interrupted himself at one point to ask how my work was going, and I told him about losing my old arrangement at *Gloss* magazine and miraculously finding the gig at *Buzz*.

"Gosh, is it dangerous for me to be talking to you now that you work for a celebrity rag?" he asked, his eyes playful.

"Only if you hurl your cell phone at someone or try to bring a half kilo of cocaine through customs at JFK." I took a swig of beer, thinking of a zillion other questions I had about the series, but before I could ask one, Chris switched gears entirely.

"Like I said on the phone," he said, lowering his voice slightly, "I wanted to talk to you about this friend of mine. I really appreciate your meeting me."

Omigod, I suddenly thought, the "friend" is a girl. He's got chick trouble, and he wants my advice, like I'm some sort of big sister. I felt a flush of embarrassment begin to creep up my chest.

"Okay, tell me about it," I said awkwardly.

"It's about this actor I know—named Tom Fain. We met doing an off off Broadway show a year or two ago, and he ended up in *Morgue,* too. He's got just a small part, but he's generally in every episode."

"Is he in some kind of trouble?" I asked, feeling oddly relieved that it was a guy friend after all. I waited for a tale of woe that would probably include at least one long weekend in Vegas.

"I guess you'd call it that," Chris said. "He's missing."

"Missing?" I exclaimed.

"Yeah, he disappeared off the face of the earth a week and a half ago."

"Have you talked to the police—though they're usually not much help with young guys."

"The first person I called was this guy Tom had mentioned— Mr. Barish—who handles his money. He said he'd get hold of the cops. This detective called me a day later. He looked around Tom's apartment and said he'd make a couple of inquiries, but there was nothing more he could really do. He told me a lot of guys just take off. But I don't think that's what happened. This was Tom's first regular TV gig. He's a couple of years older than me, and he's been praying for this break even longer than I have. I just don't believe he would have walked away from it."

"Is there a girlfriend in the picture?" I asked. "Could he have had a blowup and gone off to lick his wounds?"

"There's a kind of girlfriend, a chick named Harper Aikins he's been seeing for about a month and a half. She's a former actress who does PR for the show. But it's not some major love affair, and she's just as clueless as I am about where he is."

"Parents?"

"Both dead. You ready for another?" he asked, cocking his chin toward my beer.

I'd noticed that he'd chugged down his own beer quickly, feeling churned up, perhaps, from talking about Tom. I was only halfway through mine.

"I'm set for now. So tell me the circumstances. When did you last see Tom? When did *anyone* last see him?"

"I talked to him the Thursday before he disappeared. We were on set together. He plays—or I should say *played,* because they've canned him now for being a no-show—this guy who mans the phones at the morgue, the one who's always handing someone a message or announcing that so-and-so is on line four. I'm not sure what he did the next day because they didn't need him on set, but apparently on Saturday morning he picked up his car from a lot downtown and took off. Harper was out of town that weekend, but she talked to Tom Friday night and he didn't mention anything about a trip. *Originally* he'd been planning to head out to the Hamptons to see this buddy of his, but the guy told me the plans got bagged late in the week. When Tom didn't show for work on Monday, I kept trying to reach his cell phone and finally went to his apartment. As far as I know, no one's heard from him since that weekend."

"Was he depressed—or in any kind of trouble that you know of?"

"Not that I know of. He's a helluva nice guy. He actually suggested I audition for the show."

"Aren't the producers worried about what happened to him?"

"Apparently not. One of the ADs—assistant directors—told me that Tom was apparently miffed about how small his part was. He'd also been having a little trouble on set. The rumor is he just bolted."

Chris drew his fist to his face and blew a stream of air into it. I waited, thinking he was going to say something else, but he only stared at me expectantly.

"How can I help?" I asked. I had no idea what I could possibly do, but I assumed that was the question Chris had been waiting for.

"I want you to tell me how I can find him. You solve mysteries, right? I just want some direction."

I sighed. "When I'm writing a story—or when I'm working on a case like the one I needed your help on last winter—I find that the best approach is to just methodically turn over every stone, one by one. It's not very sexy sounding, yet it's usually the best way. But I don't know anything about Tom's life, so I wouldn't know which stones to start with."

"I can help with that. I can tell you everything I know about him. Plus, I have a key to his apartment. He was nice enough to let me bunk there for a few weeks this summer before I got my own place, and I thought if you looked through it with me, we might find something—a lead."

"Uh, sure," I said. It would be more than providing a "little direction," but I was intrigued, and I liked the idea of being with Chris. "That would certainly be a start. When?"

"How about right now?"

"*Now?* Well, why not, I guess. Even though you've got a key to the place, is there anyone who could make trouble for you if they caught you in there?"

"No. Like I said, the parents are dead, he's got no siblings, and the super is used to me being around."

"Okay, then, let's do it."

He waved for the check, paid, and three minutes later we were out on the street. He said Tom lived on Mercer, so we headed there on foot. While we walked, Chris provided more details about Tom. He'd grown up in Manhattan, gone to private school, and then majored in theater at Skidmore College. Whereas Chris had used modeling as a potential springboard for acting and had eventually headed for L.A., Tom had plugged away mostly in the off off Broadway world, performing in many small "black box" theaters, once totally nude.

I was curious, I told Chris, about the guy Tom had said he was going to see in the Hamptons. Was there a chance Tom *had* headed out there and the guy was denying it? Perhaps he and Tom had ended up in an altercation, or at the very least this dude was covering up something. Chris didn't think so, based on his conversation with the guy. He was an old high school friend of Tom's.

His apartment was in an older, kind of grand-looking building that had obviously been renovated into living spaces. There was no doorman, but the lobby was nicely decorated with an original limestone fireplace mantel. Not exactly what I was expecting for an actor who until recently had done ten-dollar-a-ticket theaters and let his schlong dangle in front of an audience. Reading my mind, Chris explained that Tom had purchased his place with money from the sale of his parents' apartment on the Upper East Side.

We took the elevator to four, and I followed Chris down a long hallway, the walls painted tobacco color and hung with brass sconces. From the pocket of his shorts, he pulled out a set of keys and thumbed through several until he found the one to Chris's place. He turned the lower Medeco lock and, when that was unlocked, a top one. I was right behind him as he pushed open the door, and no sooner had he stepped into the vestibule than I felt his body tense.

I soon knew why: In a room at the very end of the hall, probably the bedroom, a light was glowing. Someone seemed to be home.

CHAPTER 2

I s it Tom?" I whispered.

"I—I don't know," Chris said, his voice as low as mine. "I don't think I left a light on."

I waited for him to make a move of some kind, and when he failed to, *I* did.

"Tom?" I called out. "Are you here? . . . *Tom?*"

There was no answer.

Chris patted the wall with his right hand and found a switch, flooding the vestibule with light. Side by side, we started down a long hall on the right toward the room where the light was burning. Once more I called Tom's name, and once more it was met with silence.

We reached the room, a bedroom, and stepped quietly through the doorway, Chris just ahead of me now. The room was empty. The lamp throwing off the light was on a wooden, antique-looking table by the window. I glanced instinctively toward the bed. There was a hunter green duvet across it, slightly askew and rumpled, as if the bed had been hastily made.

I jerked my head back toward Chris. "Has somebody . . . ?"

"No, it was that way when I came in before," Chris said, guessing my question.

"What about the light?" I asked. "Are you sure you didn't leave it on?"

"I thought I'd switched it off, but I guess I must have forgotten to. According to Tom, I'm the only person with a key besides him. He wanted me to keep the spare in case he lost his."

"Of course, *Tom* could have come back and turned the light on," I said.

"I know," he acknowledged. "But it doesn't make any sense. Why come back but not tell anyone—and not show for work?"

"I wonder if he's in some kind of trouble and feels the need to lay low for a while. Let's check the closet."

Chris slid open the closet door, which bounced on the tracks, making my heart skip. I waited silently as he made a mental inventory of the contents.

"It looks about the same as it did," he declared. "I'm just not familiar enough with his stuff to tell what's not here. The only thing I'm sure about is that there's still no sign of his duffel bag. He has an old leather one—the kind you use for short trips. I figured it meant that when he left that Saturday, he was planning on at least an overnight."

"His parents didn't leave him a condo in Florida along with the apartment, did they? I mean—"

"Not that I'm aware of. I know that they used to have some kind of weekend place in the country, but Tom sold it earlier in the summer. He said it wasn't the kind of place you'd go to if you were single."

"Let's look around the rest of the place," I said.

Chris led the way back down the hall toward the living room.

I noticed this time that the walls were lined with nicely framed architectural prints. The living room was even more of a surprise. It was spacious, with windows on two sides and an expensive-looking couch and two armchairs flanking a brick fireplace. There were several antiquey pieces in there as well. The one incongruous touch was the large empty pizza box strewn haphazardly on the coffee table with a pile of dried crusts in the center of it.

"Was . . . ?"

"Yeah, that was here when I checked this past weekend," Chris said. "So far, nothing looks different."

"I thought you said you were here over a whole week ago."

"I came back—just to double-check."

"This is quite the place for a struggling actor," I observed. "Were his parents well-off?"

"Apparently not as much at the end as they once were. His father played the market, and he was pretty good at it. But Tom told me that he made some bad investments a few years before he died and lost a lot of what he'd saved. His parents weren't destitute. They had their apartment in New York and some savings—and they had put a decent chunk of change in trust for Tom—but they didn't have the *big* bucks anymore. Tom said he thinks the stress contributed to his father's heart attack. His mother died of some kind of cancer about two years later—a year ago this summer."

We moved on to other areas in the apartment—the bathroom (toothbrush missing), the small eat-in kitchen (nothing in the fridge except a few bottles of beer and a quart of milk, which stank to high heaven when I beaked the top part to take a whiff), and then a room off the kitchen that must have once been a maid's room and now held a single bed, a desk, and several bookshelves mounted on the wall. Chris explained that this was the room he had crashed in before he'd rented his own place.

"What is it?" I asked. Chris had suddenly pursed his lips, perturbed.

"That copy of *Backstage*," he said, pointing to the newspaper on the far left side of the desk. "I know it sounds crazy, but I could swear it was in the middle of the desk when I was here before. But I'm probably wrong. Just like I'm wrong about the light. Because why would those be the only things that have changed?"

"Well, if he came back to pick up just a few things like clothes, he might not have disturbed much." I glanced instinctively behind me. If Tom—or someone else—had dropped by once, they could drop by again and catch us snooping around. I really didn't love being here.

I slid open the single drawer of his desk and glanced inside. There were pens, pencils, envelopes, odds and ends. I slid the drawer shut. On top of the desk were a few pieces of mail, which I thumbed through. Nothing more than bills and nothing dated later than right after Labor Day. There was one bill from a parking lot on Houston, and I jotted down the name and address.

"What kind of car does he have?" I asked.

"A black Audi."

"And what about a calendar? I don't see anything here."

"He uses a Sidekick—and I assume he took it with him."

"Computer?"

"There's a laptop over there in the corner," he said, pointing. "I tried a few passwords to see if I could get into his e-mail but nothing worked."

At the very back of the desk was a pile of papers, which I grabbed next. On top was another copy of *Back Stage* and underneath four or five head shots with the name *Tom Fain* printed on each of them.

"So this is what he looks like," I said, staring down at the shot.

If the picture was true to life, Tom was as great looking as Chris, but in a totally different way. He was brown-eyed and very blond, his hair long enough to be worn tucked behind his ears. His skin was incredibly smooth, almost embryonic looking, but his features were strong enough to prevent that from being a negative. If he'd passed me on the street while I was standing next to a girlfriend, I probably would have muttered something short and simple, like "Oh. My. God."

It wasn't simply his stunning looks. In the photo, he had that air of easy sophistication and casual disregard that New York private school kids always seem to possess, resulting perhaps from the strange convergence of growing up with all your needs provided for but also learning to rough it in the city, like riding the subway solo at fourteen.

"Yeah, that's a recent shot," Chris said.

"Did they make him cut his hair for the show?"

"No, they wanted it long. They thought that's what you'd see on a New York guy who worked the front desk at a morgue."

"Do you think it's okay if I keep one?" I asked. "Just for—"

"It's fine. He probably has a huge box of them somewhere."

I felt staples on the back of the photo and flipped it over. Attached to the back was a résumé. It listed not only stints on a few shows like *Law & Order*, but also lots of plays.

"That's where we met," Chris said, jabbing with his forefinger at the name of one of the plays. "Like I said, Tom did a lot more theater than me, but I did this one play with him at Stage Right Productions."

"*Julius Caesar?*"

"Yup. But mostly he worked at this small theater in the Village. Here it is," he said, pointing. "The Chaps Theatre. They put

on over a dozen plays a year—some classics, some written by
new playwrights. He was a member of the company."

I tucked one photo in my purse and let my eyes peruse the
bookshelves. There were books on playwriting and acting and
a few old college textbooks. On the top shelf was a big plastic
tub.

"What's in there?" I asked Chris.

"Photos. I looked inside when I was here last but didn't go
through them."

Assuming I'd want to investigate, Chris lifted down the plastic box and set it on the desk. There were some loose pictures,
stacked sideways, others in wide envelopes with dates. Most
seemed to be family photos, which Tom had probably taken possession of when his mother died. I leafed through them quickly.
Many featured Tom with his parents in various locations around
the world. There were Tom, at about twelve, and, I assumed,
his attractive blond mother on the long green mall in front of
the Eiffel Tower. On the back, in a woman's handwriting, was
the date 1990 and, unnecessarily, "Paris." Another shot showed
Tom and his father standing on a white-and-blue glacier, with
"Alaska, 1991" on the back. And there was one shot of all three
of them in long-sleeved shirts and jeans, a stacked stone wall
behind them. On the back: "Andes, 1994."

"They clearly traveled a lot," I remarked.

"Yeah, Tom said his father loved seeing the world. That
was one of the toughest parts about losing the money. His parents were going to have enough to live on, but not the extra to
really travel well—and that had been something his parents had
planned to do after he retired."

Without warning, I felt a swell of sadness. The family Fain
looked happy, and you could sense the love they felt for one another—in one photo, Tom's mother hugged him in a gesture of
pure adoration. How painful it must have been for Tom to lose

both parents. My father had died when I was twelve, and I knew something about the ragged hole that the early death of a parent leaves in your heart.

I dropped the snapshots back in the box, and Chris returned it to the shelf. In unspoken agreement, we wandered back through the kitchen and out into the hallway.

"If you had to make a guess," I said, "do you think Tom has been back here?"

Chris let his eyes wander around the hall, as if the answer lay on the walls. "I don't know," he said finally, his brow furrowed. "I probably left the light on. And the magazine—it was probably there before, but I hadn't noticed. But why does it matter, anyway? Tom is still missing. He's AWOL at work."

"I know, but if he came back here, it means that he's basically okay. He just doesn't want anyone to find him. And that means we should probably just let sleeping dogs lie."

He shook his head. "Then if I had to guess, I'd say no. Tom's the kind of guy who tends to leave a trail. Like the pizza box."

"Okay, then, let's proceed from there. Tom went someplace a week and a half ago, and we need to figure out where."

"So what do we do?"

"For starters, I want to talk to the guy Tom was supposed to see in the Hamptons. I know you said he doesn't seem culpable in any way, but Tom might have said something relevant to him. I want to talk to his girlfriend, too. Is there anyone else at the show who might know something?"

"The show? That seems like a dead end to me. There's Harper, of course, and he was kind of friendly with some of the crew, but I'm pretty sure there was no one else he palled around with."

Simultaneously we both shifted our bodies, ready to leave. I was thrilled to be getting out of there. But just before we reached the doorway, I stopped dead in my tracks.

"Hold on for a second," I said. "Let's just check the clothes hamper. It's a tip a cop once gave me. If Tom did come back, he might have dumped clothes there."

It was an old wicker basket in the bedroom with one of the hinges missing from the lid. I flicked it open and we saw a pile of smushy-looking clothes reaching three-quarters of the way to the top. Chris reached his hand in, and as he rifled through the clothes, the smell of sweat wafted upward, but it was an old, stale smell like the kind that greets you in a locker room after the season is over.

"Nah," Chris said. "These are mostly running clothes that . . ."

"*What?*" I asked. I could tell by the expression on his face that his hand had touched something unexpected.

"There's a hard thing at the bottom." He tossed several T-shirts and pairs of running shorts onto the floor and then slowly lifted out a plastic storage container, this one the size of a shoebox. We could see through the transparent sides that there were envelopes inside. I felt a weird tingle go through my body.

We glanced at each other, both of us nearly bug-eyed.

"We better take a look," I announced. "Since he's hiding it, it could mean something."

As we carried the box across the hall to the living room, I felt dread gaining on me. Could the contents be tied to Tom's disappearance? Was I about to find records of cocaine deals carried out throughout Manhattan?

With the box on his lap, Chris lifted the lid and flicked through the envelopes.

"It's mostly from chicks," he said. "Jeez, we've found his love letter stash."

"Okay, we better put it back," I told him.

"Hold on," he said, lifting out one parcel of at least thirty cards bound by a fat rubber band. He tugged an envelope from the pack and drew a card from the envelope. "That's what I thought," he said, glancing at the few words scribbled at the bottom. "These are all from this actress he was seeing before Harper—Blythe. Blythe Hammell or Hamlin, I think. She used to call a ton when I was staying here, and it drove him nuts. After a while, he just started letting all her calls go to voice mail or his answering machine."

"So he just wasn't, as they say, into her?"

"He was *initially*, I think. Tom's a pretty private guy overall, so I don't know everything that went on between them, but I take it they had a fairly fun romp in the beginning. But she started getting real possessive after that. He tried to break it off, and she just kept hounding him. She sounded like a bit of a whack job to me. Of course, half the actresses you meet are—and besides, Tom has this way of seeing everybody's good side."

"Is that how they came into contact—through an acting job?"

"Yeah, she's part of that theater company he's involved with— the Chaps Theatre."

"Well, if she was a wack job, we'd better check her out," I said, sitting next to him on the couch and pulling a few of the cards out of their envelopes. Some of the ones from Blythe were greeting cards—silly ones with kitty cats and monkeys as well as sexy ones loaded with innuendo—all signed "Blythe" or "B." Others were just note cards with simple messages in a bold, dramatic script: "I'm missing you," for instance, and "Let me cook you something *delicious* tonight." According to the postmarks, a card had arrived every couple of days through the summer up until about six weeks ago, which meant about a month before Tom had disappeared. The last card had a picture of a pug on the front and was blank inside except for "Why don't you call anymore? B."

"July thirty-first," I said, pointing to the postmark. "Do you think she gave up the fight then?"

"Yeah, that sounds about right. I remember him saying something about finally having her out of his hair."

I took out my notebook and jotted down the return address on East 5th Street.

"By the way, where's his mail from the past two weeks?" I asked.

"Huh?" Chris asked distractedly. He was staring at something still in the box. "Oh, the post office has it because it was starting to pile up. Of course, they won't release it to anyone but Tom."

"What are you looking at?" I asked quietly, aware suddenly that something was up.

"This," he said, picking up a blue envelope. It was made of really heavy stock, the kind of stationery you buy at Cartier. He flicked up the flap and withdrew the note card inside.

There was just one sentence written in blue black fountain pen: "When you fuck me, it takes a week for my toes to uncurl." And then the name, "Locket."

"Obviously a woman who doesn't beat around the bush," I said.

"It's Locket Ford," Chris said soberly. "The star of *Morgue*."

"Oh, *really*. Locket? Is that some kind of nickname?"

"No. And it's not a stage name, either. She came from Appalachia or some other dirt-poor place, and apparently her mother gave her that name because she wanted her to grow up to be special. She was on soaps for twelve years, and this show is her big break into prime time."

"Could it be bad politically for her to be involved with Tom?" I wasn't sure how it worked on sets, but surely it wasn't the coolest thing for the star of the show to be bonking the actor whose part involved handing the morgue staff their paperwork.

"*Bad?* Well, her live-in boyfriend—Alex Ottoson—is the producer of the show, and he's the one who got her the part. *I'd* say that's pretty bad, wouldn't you?"

"Wow. Maybe this guy caught wind of it and that's why Tom split. He may be hiding out."

We took another few minutes to glance through the correspondence. At the very bottom were letters from Tom's mother in shaky handwriting, probably shortly before her death, but we didn't look through those. When we finally put the box back in the hamper, I felt ashamed for having been such a snoop—yet I was glad we had found the stash. The note from Locket could be significant. But now it was time to go.

The minute we stepped out onto the street, I felt a rush of pure relief. Mercer Street was crowded with people headed off to bars and parties and Starbucks, and we were jostled several times as we stood there decompressing from our foray into Tom's apartment.

"Why don't I walk you back to your place," Chris said.

I sensed by his tone that there was nothing loaded in his comment. There wouldn't be any expectation on his part to come up and wrestle with me on my couch for old times' sake. I suspected he was mentally fatigued from our search—just as I was—yet I felt a twinge of disappointment.

On the way over to 9th and Broadway, I told him my game plan for the next day. I would start making calls stat, but there were phone numbers I needed first—Tom's Hamptons friend, the cop, Harper, Blythe. He tugged the cop's business card out of his wallet and also scrawled down the name of Tom's friend, John Curry, as well as the number at the bank where he worked. He didn't think he could locate a number for Blythe but thought I might find it through 411. As for Harper, he'd arrange for me to talk to her.

"Do you think Locket has any idea where Tom is?" I asked.

"I haven't a clue," Chris said, "and there's no way for me to come right out and ask her. I want to find Tom, but I also don't want to shoot myself in the foot."

When we reached my building, Chris gave me a hug the way he had earlier in the evening, though this time the gesture felt more abrupt and awkward. He seemed distracted suddenly, as if thoughts were racing behind those beautiful green eyes. He might have once had the hots for me, but his blood seemed to be running lukewarm tonight. I wondered if a second search of the apartment had left him even more agitated about Tom than he had been before. Or maybe he was discombobulated by the fact that Tom had secretly bedded the star of the show.

I watched him as he hurried the short distance to the corner and then sprinted across Broadway. He may have been just catching the light, but it seemed almost as if he were in a hurry. I turned and entered my apartment. The doorman Bob was on duty tonight, and he gave me a pleasant, almost approving nod, as if he were happy to see that I was heading in alone again tonight. Bob never made me feel skanky, but I also sensed he kept tabs on the traffic coming in and out of 14B.

I popped open a beer as soon as I got in and carried it out to my terrace along with a bag of tortilla chips and a bowl of leftover, slightly tuckered-out salsa. I guess you'd have to call my apartment the spoils of my two-year starter marriage, and I never stop feeling . . . well, *spoiled* by it. Though it's just a moderately sized one-bedroom with an itsy-bitsy kitchen, it has two drop-dead features: the large brick terrace and what I behold from it. There's no glimpse of landmarks, but nonetheless it's a gorgeous, quintessentially Manhattan view. It looks to the west, toward a skyline of nondescript redbrick and limestone apartment buildings topped by nineteen wooden-shingled water towers. At night, when the sky is inky black and there are lights dabbled in different apartment buildings, it seems almost fake, like the backdrop of a Broadway musical.

I took a long swallow of cold beer and then leaned back in my chair, encouraging my mind to idle for moment. Though it was warm out and the red geraniums in my clay pots were still blazing with color, I could feel a touch of fall in the air. Just like cold spots in lake water, there were cool ribbons threaded through the breeze that hinted at the not-so-balmy October and November days ahead.

I should have been happy about the imminent arrival of fall. First and foremost I would be an author, with the arrival of *Bad Men and Wicked Women* late in the season. In addition, I'd just bought a pair of black suede boots that were so snug and gorgeous, my calves had nearly orgasmed when I'd tried them on. And last but hardly least, it had been a bitch of a summer, something worth distancing myself from.

Yet all of a sudden I felt overwhelmed by melancholy. Maybe it was because I'd had such high hopes for the summer, and it was tough to consider how pathetically they'd unraveled. My initial plan had been to write a few gripping articles, spend as many weekends as possible in the sun, take Rome by storm, and have a fling that would leave *my* friggin' toes curled. I know you aren't supposed to bank on anything in life, I know that "shit happens," but *nothing* had worked out as planned. What I'd anticipated as a Gorgonzola soufflé kind of summer had ended up resembling a grilled-cheese sandwich made with one of those individually wrapped singlets that taste like socks you've worn too many days in a row.

For starters, there was the humiliation of being bounced from the gig I'd had for several years at *Gloss* magazine. When the editor, Cat Jones, had confessed that her newsstand sales were plummeting and she was morphing the magazine from a sexy, edgy read for married women into *Take-a-Chill-Pill Monthly*,

I'd tried to be sympathetic to her plight. But that didn't make it any easier to know my crime pieces were going to be replaced by stories along the lines of "The Secret Power of Bath Salts" and "How to Cure Mild Depression by Organizing Your Shoes." Fortunately, I'd found my way to *Buzz*.

The worst thing about the summer was what had happened with Beau Regan, documentary filmmaker and documented heartbreaker. At first I'd thought he was the fun, sexy summer fling I'd been longing for, but I'd ended up falling hard—hard as in onto a car hood from a tenth-story window. I'd come right out and told him that I couldn't see him if he was sleeping with anyone else. I'd thought for a moment that he was going to give up the one chick he'd been seeing casually on the side. But then an assignment had come through out of the blue and he'd taken off for Turkey, saying that he felt he couldn't make a decision until he returned—in mid-September. There'd been one lousy postcard with the breathtaking message "Hope your summer's going well. I've been thinking about you."

My co-worker Jessie had suggested I read a book about the failed patterns of love and see if I could learn how to stop falling for the wrong guy. But I didn't think Beau had been the wrong guy. It had just been the wrong moment.

Something else was making me blue: Tom Fain. The fact that he'd lost two adored parents so young gnawed at me. And where the hell *was* he? Had he just hightailed it out of town on an adventure? Or was he staying below the radar as the result of a mess he'd made? And if so, what kind of mess? Money? Drugs? Or the kind you make for yourself when you fuck the producer's live-in girlfriend? And there was one other question to consider: Had something *terrible* happened to him?

I knew right then that I was going to do what I could to make sure Tom was okay. It was partly because I wanted to help

Chris, just as he'd once helped me, but also because of the lost parent connection I had with Tom.

Suddenly a scraping sound startled me out of my thoughts, and I glanced left. A dead leaf, broken off from one of my geraniums, scurried across the stone floor of my terrace, driven by a gust of wind. Fall *was* coming. That meant crinkly brown leaves, suede boots, and wool coats. But I could only wonder what my search for Tom would bring.

CHAPTER 3

I was at the desk in my home office before nine the next morning. Calling it an office may be slightly generous on my part. It's really just a large walk-in closet that I converted into a work area with a few bookshelves and a built-in desk where I set my laptop. The whole space is about the size of the crisper drawer in my fridge, but the upside is that there aren't any distractions. If I had to work in my bedroom, I'd be getting up constantly to defuzz my sweaters or trim the pad peeking out from under the area rug.

Fully caffeinated after two cups of coffee, I was nearly ready to focus my attention on Tom. First, though, I checked some Web sites—CNN, TMZ, Perez Hilton, the Smoking Gun, Gawker, and so on—to make sure nothing was brewing crimewise in the world of celebs. You never knew, for instance, when there'd be newly posted mug shots of someone like Nicole Richie, and I'd have to spring into action. Once I was sure that *Buzz* wasn't going to need me today, I wrote out a list of calls to make and started in.

The first one was to a cop I knew named Gina who had once worked in Missing Persons. I was hoping she still had buddies in that department and would call the cop Chris had talked to—Kevin O'Donnell was the name on the card—and grease the wheels for me, encouraging him to be forthcoming. I reached only her voice mail, and I asked her to call me.

I had better luck reaching John Curry, Tom's buddy with the Hamptons house. I called his line at the bank, and he answered himself.

"Curry," he said in a voice suggesting that though the day had barely begun, he was already bored to tears with it. I introduced myself, explained that I'd been enlisted to help look for Tom, and said that I was hoping I could meet with him as soon as possible.

"*Meet* with me?" he exclaimed with borderline irritation. "How's that supposed to help?"

"You were one of the last people to talk to Tom," I said, trying to submerge my own annoyance.

"Look, I've already talked to that friend of his and the cop. Besides, this week is a real bear for me. I'm up to my ass in about twenty different things here."

"Could you at least give me a few minutes on the phone?" I asked. "I'm sure you're as concerned about Tom as we are." I was hoping the last comment and the loaded way I'd delivered it would goad him into agreeing.

He sighed loudly, as if he were blowing out candles on a cake. "It's just that . . . Look, I've got five minutes now. Go ahead and ask what you want. And just so you know—I don't happen to be all that worried about Tom. He's been known to pick up and leave before."

"For what reason?"

"Tom's always been a little bit restless, even before his parents died. He's got a love for the open road."

"Did he say anything to you that suggested the open road was beckoning him right at this moment?"

There was a long pause.

"What?" I urged.

"Nothing really. You just put it in a slightly different way than the cop did. I mean, he asked if I knew where Tom might have gone. But I hadn't thought about it in a more general sense— about whether Tom was especially restless these days. I just don't know. Tom and I weren't in touch very much the last couple of years—I've been in Singapore, doing a stint for the bank there. We reconnected a few months ago, but I haven't seen a huge amount of him."

"Why didn't you two end up getting together on that weekend?"

He exhaled loudly again. "Totally my fault. I wanted him to come out and see our new house. But I hadn't let the wife know, and when I told her at the last minute, she got all pissy because she'd already invited her mental case sister and brother-in-law. I asked Tom if he'd mind taking a rain check."

"Go back to what you said about his parents' deaths. Was Tom pretty affected by that?"

"I was away when they both died, so I have no idea what it was like at the time. He didn't go all emo when he told me about it, but I could sense it was tough for him."

"You guys met in high school?"

"Yep. I was a year ahead of him, but we played baseball together. Then just by chance he ended up at Skidmore, too. He was in the theater department, which was a whole different world— but I saw a fair amount of him up there."

"What do you know about his love life?"

"He had this one chick he was seeing earlier this summer, but he wasn't that interested and she finally took the hint. Lately he's been seeing someone who works on the show—not an actress, but someone behind the scenes. I guess he likes her well enough, but the problem is, Tom isn't ready to settle down—despite how much these babes like to pressure him."

He let out another sigh. "Look, my boss has walked by twice and given me the evil death stare. I gotta get movin'.'"

"Just one more question, I promise. Can you think of anyone else who might have a lead on Tom? Someone he might turn to if he was in any kind of trouble?"

"There was a guy from Skidmore he was pretty close to—a professor named Alan Carr. Tom mentioned him lately, in fact. He had this big old house where a lot of the theater kids would hang. But like I said, I doubt Tom is in any kind of trouble."

"Okay, thanks. If you think of anything else—"

"Yeah, sure," he said, and hung up before I could give him my number.

I pulled up the White Pages online and found a B. Hammell at the return address on Blythe's cards. I left a message saying to call Bailey Weggins, that it was important. I *didn't* say it was about Tom.

Next I went on the Skidmore College Web site and found both an office phone number and e-mail address for Professor Carr. I left him a message on his voice mail and also shot him an e-mail. Thinking that the semester might not have even started yet, I tried directory assistance for Saratoga. There was an Alan Carr on Broadway. His answering machine picked up and a laid-back voice announced, "Hey, you've reached Alan Carr. Leave a message if you want, but I don't check this machine regularly, so if it's urgent, try my cell." But he didn't leave a cell number. I left a message on the machine just in case he *did* check it today.

No sooner had I ended the call than my phone rang. It was Gina. The clanging in the background suggested she was in a diner or coffee shop. Talking loudly to be heard over the din, I explained that I needed info from a detective in Missing Persons.

She said she knew O'Donnell and that she would speak to him on my behalf. "He's good people," she shouted. "I'll tell him to call you, okay?"

Moments later, my phone rang again. It was Chris—with an update on his end.

"Good news," he said. "Harper's on set with us. If you can get here quick, I can introduce you."

"Are you shooting at Chelsea Piers?"

"No, we're on location—in Tompkins Square Park."

I slipped on a pair of black leggings, a khaki-colored tunic, and black flats and headed toward my destination on foot. The park—an actual *square* oasis of green between 10th and 7th streets and Avenues A and B—is in a gentrified area of the East Village known as Alphabet City. In the 1980s, it had apparently been filled with homeless people and heroin dealers, but it had been refurbished recently and now held a dog run, handball courts, and a table designed with chessboards. Beneath the old elm trees you could find not only old women speaking Yiddish and men wheeling shopping carts filled with used soda cans but also hip young families with pound-rescued mutts and kids dressed in black instead of pink and powder blue.

Chris had told me to make my way to a long row of trucks and trailers on the eastern side of the park, to look for people with earpieces and then ask for Harper. The directions had sounded kind of vague, but as it turned out there was no way to miss the trucks. There were about eight of them in different sizes parked along Avenue A. Just inside the park was a large cluster of guys in jeans and T-shirts bustling about, setting up lights and other equipment. On the sidewalk outside the park were what appeared to be other crew members, drinking coffee out of cardboard cups. I informed one of them that I had an appointment with Harper Aikins. Speaking into a walkie-talkie, he delivered the message to someone and then told me she'd be right with me.

It was a good ten minutes before she walked up behind me and introduced herself. She wasn't at all what I'd expected. My imagination had conjured up an L.A. type—tiny, thin as a breadstick, with long, sleek hair—but Harper was about five nine or ten, with broad shoulders and wide-ish hips. Her dark blond, slightly wavy hair was cropped very short and brushed back hard from her face, drawing attention to coppery-colored eyes that were so round they looked like two pennies in her face. She was wearing a boatneck pink top with three-quarter sleeves, a tan skirt, and, despite the warm weather, a pair of cowboy boots. Though she lacked an L.A. aura, she exuded confidence. She was the kind of chick who you knew immediately had 1600 on her SATs and had probably gone to Princeton or Yale.

"Hi," she said, shaking my hand firmly, though it was one of those drawn-out hi's that never really sound happy to see you. "Shall I take you to Chris? He's in the honey wagon."

"Actually, Chris thought it would be helpful for us to talk. He told you, right, that I'm trying to help him look for Tom?"

"Yes, he told me. Though I'm not going to be much help. Tom didn't give me the slightest clue where he was going that day."

"Well, it would still help to talk."

She lifted her shoulders in a "whatever" shrug. "But let's get one thing straight," she said. "I know what you do for a living, and I need your guarantee that this is all strictly off the record. Our producer, Alex Ottoson, doesn't like outsiders. And Locket's been burned by *Buzz*."

"How so?" It was hard to imagine a soap actress like Locket even being on the radar at *Buzz*. The magazine, particularly the gossip section called "Juice Bar," focused on the hot young celebs everybody was, well, buzzing about. The sort-of-famous like Locket, as well as the used-to-be-famous and the never-gonna-be-famous-no-matter-how-they-try types made it into the pages only when they overdosed, had a boob break free from a dress on the red carpet, or went through a butt-ugly divorce, the kind that generated language like "Defendant repeatedly demanded that plaintiff engage in three-way sex with prostitute named Glamour."

"They make fun of her mouth. They once wrote that her lips had so much collagen, they should have a stamp on them that said 'Not to be used as a flotation device.'"

"You've got my word I won't feed any gossip to the magazine. I'm only here because of my friendship with Chris—to help find Tom."

She set her mouth in something between a pout and a grimace and glanced around. "Why don't we go over there," she said brusquely, indicating an empty bench just inside the park. As we sat down, she called someone on her walkie-talkie and told the person in a clipped, no-nonsense tone to let Chris know I was here and would stop by his trailer in about ten minutes.

"This must be pretty upsetting for you," I said as soon as she finished.

"I don't know *what* to feel," she said. A tear welled in each eye, but she hurriedly dabbed them away. "One minute I'm freaked that something has happened to Tom, and then the next minute I'm furious because I think maybe he just took off. I've only been dating Tom about two months, so I don't really know him *that* well. Maybe he *did* just blow town."

"Chris says he can't believe Tom would bag a job on a network show after working so hard to get here."

"Chris doesn't know as much as he thinks he does. Tom had *very* mixed feelings about being here."

"You're kidding?" I said, taken aback. "Why?"

"You can't say anything to Chris because I don't think he knows, but originally Tom was up for *Chris's* part. Tom's a nice guy—too nice, if you ask me—and as soon as he heard he was being considered for one of the main roles, he told the casting director about Chris for a smaller role. The next thing you know, everything ended up flipped. Tom never resented Chris—like I said, he's not that kind of guy—but he resented the outcome."

Her revelation threw a new light on the situation. So maybe Tom *had* just bagged it.

"And that's not all," she said. "Alex is *very* powerful—he created about twenty percent of what you see on TV—and he's exerting a lot of control over this show. A couple of days before Tom took off, Alex lit into him after a scene. Said he was 'working too hard.' That's something that actors with a lot of stage experience are sometimes guilty of—they tend to overact in front of the camera, when what you want to do for TV is keep it really small and natural. But from the cuts of the show I've seen, it wasn't true in Tom's case. It was almost as if Alex were just busting his chops for nothing."

So this must be the trouble on the set that Chris had mentioned. "Was Tom pretty upset?"

"It was hard to know because I was in L.A. most of that week and wasn't due back till Sunday. I talked to him on my cell whenever I could grab five minutes, and he did seem fairly bummed—though not I'm-going-to drop-off-the-planet bummed."

"When was the last time you actually talked to him?"

"I called him on Friday night. He'd had weekend plans with this guy he knew at school, but the guy ended up bailing on him. We agreed to get together for dinner Sunday night after I landed. Then I never heard from him. At first I thought maybe he'd just forgotten about the dinner. It wasn't until he didn't show at work on Monday that I realized something might be the matter."

"He didn't say anything about what he was going to do instead that weekend?"

"No, he just said he'd be fine. There was one weird thing— just a little thing that at the time didn't seem odd, but I've wondered about it since."

"Yes?" I prodded.

"He said he had work to do."

"Work?"

"Right. When he said that his buddy had blown him off, I'd suggested half-jokingly that he fly out to L.A. There were some loose ends I had to tie up for work, but I had a nice room at the Mondrian and he could have chilled at the pool. He said no, he'd be okay. And then he said, 'I've got some work to do.' It's just an expression, and I didn't think anything of it at the time, but afterwards, after he just fell off the face of the earth, I wondered what he'd meant by it. We weren't shooting that weekend."

I didn't say anything, just tossed the words over in my mind. I didn't know Tom's life well enough to have any sense what he might have been talking about.

"Speaking of work, was there anyone besides Chris that Tom palled around with?" I asked.

She did that pouty thing again with her mouth while she reflected. "He was kind of friendly with these two grips named Danny and Deke, especially Deke. Since he had a fair amount of downtime, he'd play cards with them. Once, back in July, he and Deke even went to Atlantic City for a weekend. I told him it wasn't smartest thing in the world to be hanging with those dudes, but Tom has a hard time turning people down."

"And he got along with the other actors—Locket and people like that?" Clearly, she didn't know he was making Locket's toes curl up like Froot Loops, but I wondered if she'd had a hint of any flirtation.

"Yes, Tom is just one of those easygoing guys that everybody relates to. I . . ." She hesitated. "Why don't I bring you to Chris now. I've a reporter coming from *Time Out* in a little while, and I need to get myself in gear."

"What's your best guess about where he is?"

"Off licking his wounds. As soon as you find anything out, let me know, will you?—so I can wring his neck."

She rose abruptly then, making it clear that I could either follow her or sit by my lonesome and watch the ratty squirrels chase one another. I trailed behind her to the fourth truck, which behind the cab had a big silver trailer with several doors on the side, all in a row. She rapped efficiently on one, and Chris opened it almost immediately.

"So there you are," he said warmly. "Thanks, Harper."

She headed off with a backward wave and a brusque order into her walkie-talkie.

Chris took my elbow and pulled me gently into the truck. We were in a small room strewn with clothes, magazines, Styrofoam coffee cups, and cardboard food caddies.

"Welcome to my humble abode in the honey wagon."

"Is this room just yours?" I asked, glancing around.

"Yeah, though when you're a star like Locket, you get a whole damn Winnebago."

I pulled my gaze away from the interior and turned to him, smiling. "It must be thrilling, though—isn't it?" I said.

"Yeah, I keep thinking that maybe I won't have to pour another Scotch on the rocks for another asshole for the rest of my life. So how was your talk with Harper? A bit of a bulldozer, isn't she?"

"Seems so. Does Tom find that appealing?"

"Once she set her sights on him, I don't think he knew how to get out of her path."

"By the way, I talked to his pal John, and he isn't worried at all. He says Tom has a love for the open road. Do we have a whole head of steam up over nothing?"

"I don't know," he said, shaking his head. "One minute I'm worried, and the next minute I'm pissed, thinking that he just took off."

"That's exactly what Harper said." I wished I could share Harper's revelation, which gave Tom an even greater motivation to take off, but I'd given my word—and it would probably only upset Chris more.

I took a minute and a half to fill him in on my morning—the rest of my brief convo with John Curry, my discovery about Tom's friendship with Professor Carr. Chris said that they'd moved up the time for his next scene—it involved the discovery of a scantily clothed dead woman in her twenties (natch) in the park—and he would be pulled away at any moment.

"I might as well split now," I said. "I'll call you later if I learn anything."

As I descended the steps of the trailer, Chris, following behind me, squeezed my elbow.

"Check it out," he whispered. "There's the infamous Locket. She's talking to the first AD."

She was just inside the park in the area where I'd seen the crew setting up, an itty-bitty thing no more than five feet two, platinum hair in a bedheady kind of do, and gleaming, porcelain-like skin. Even from where I stood, I could see how big her lips were. They looked as though they'd burst if they came even near a pair of pincers.

Everyone behind her seemed frozen in place, waiting while she hashed something out with the AD. There were two guys with handheld cameras and two other guys with their hands on the lenses, as if to steady them. Also cooling their heels were two patrol cops who I assumed must be actors *and*—I suddenly realized—either a dummy or a person under a white sheet on the ground.

"Locket looks vaguely familiar," I whispered. "Did she once have longer hair?"

"Yeah. Apparently she fought like hell to keep it, but they told her that someone with her job as an investigator would never run around with Cher hair."

As Chris and I stood watching, a tall man in his forties strode toward Locket and the AD. He had tightly cropped gray blond hair, receding from a high, tanned forehead, a mustache, and a short beard, all very Nordic-looking. He was dressed in a black Armani-style jacket.

"That's Alex," Chris whispered. "Producer—and cuckolded boyfriend."

"He looks—how shall I say—stern?"

"Oh yeah. I wouldn't be surprised to see him in horned head-gear one day. A real Viking warrior."

Chris explained that he had to get back to his trailer, and we hugged good-bye. Before leaving, I joined a group of rubber-neckers near the park entrance and took a closer look at Locket. She was talking intently to both the AD and Alex now, looking slightly peeved but obviously trying to keep her cool. "If you think it's really, really necessary," she said at one point, the only thing I could make out. Since this was her big break into prime time, she seemed to be doing her best to be cooperative, but it was probably hard to keep her raging diva side at bay. How was a guy who found Harper appealing also drawn to Locket? They seemed so wildly different. Did Tom just have a hard time saying no to *any* woman? And what had Locket seen in Tom? She had Alex, after all—so why run the risk of blowing that arrangement?

As I hoofed it back west in the heat, I checked my voice mail. There was a call from Gina saying she'd talked to Detective O'Donnell and he'd be willing to speak to me. I found a stoop on a nearby building, plopped down, and phoned him. There was a tiny suggestion of an Irish accent in his voice, the subtle kind someone gets when he's raised here but his parents were born over there.

"I wish I could devote some more time to this one, but the

particulars don't warrant it," he admitted after I'd introduced my-self and explained the reason for my interest.

"Because he's a twentysomething male and there's no reason to suspect foul play?" I asked.

"That's part of the reason," he said. "But there's something else. It turns out he withdrew seven thousand dollars in cash the day before he picked up his car. That sounds like a man with a plan."

CHAPTER 4

With that one statement, everything came into focus, and I felt a wave of both relief and irritation. Tom was probably perfectly fine, speeding his car along a highway at least ten states away, his blond hair whipped by the wind that blasted through the sunroof. Yet he hadn't cared a damn that there were people worrying about him. Or perhaps he'd convinced himself that no one cared all that much.

"So you're thinking he took off somewhere, then?" I said. "Any ideas?"

"Not a clue. He made one call from his cell phone about an hour after he picked up his car. Right near Newburgh Junction. We picked that up on the cell site record. It was to the second assistant director on the show. I checked with the guy, and the two never actually connected. Fain just left a message saying he'd call back later."

"Maybe to tell him he was quitting the show?"

"Could be. But Fain hadn't worked on Friday and so he didn't get the Monday call sheet. This guy said he assumed Fain was calling to check whether he had a scene to shoot on Monday. That part doesn't make sense. Why call for his schedule if he was bailing? But as you say, maybe he was calling to quit."

"I wonder what's in Newburgh Junction."

"He might have just been passing through."

"And that was the last call?"

"Yeah, I don't like that part, either. Maybe he lost his phone. The trouble is, there's nothing I can do. Gina said you're a friend of a friend?"

"Uh-huh—Chris Wickersham, the actor you spoke to. I'm a reporter, and he asked me to help follow any leads. But so far I haven't turned up anything."

"Well, look, would you call me if you hear anything? The money seems to point to him just splitting, but I don't have a good feeling about this one."

"Will do, and I'd appreciate being kept abreast of anything *you* hear. Can I ask why you've done as much as you have? Missing twentysomething guys usually *don't* warrant it—unless there's some evidence of foul play."

"The executor of the parents' will—a guy named Robert Barish—made a call to someone he knows higher up, pulled a few strings. They told me to follow up. But since the money seems to point to a split, there's really not much more I can do."

After hanging up, I flagged down a cab, my thoughts jostling around in complete confusion: Tom was okay—he'd withdrawn a large amount of cash so he could just take off and leave everything behind him. Tom *wasn't* okay—even if he'd decided to split, why wouldn't he have used his cell phone for nearly two weeks? Tom was okay—he wasn't playing the role he wanted on the show, plus the producer had chewed him out, so he'd obviously decided not to hang around. Tom *wasn't* okay—he'd been acting since college, so why burn bridges even if he hadn't been thrilled with his part?

Rather than go directly home, I took the cab to Tom's car lot on Houston—between Essex and Ludlow. There were two Guatemalan attendants on duty. They spoke broken English, but with the help of my rudimentary Spanish, I figured out that one of them had been on duty when Tom had driven off on Saturday. He said that Tom had left very early, at around eight o'clock. He had not mentioned where he was going or when he was coming back.

Five minutes after I returned home, my next-door neighbor, Landon, was knocking on my door. He was wearing a pair of khaki pants and a cerulean blue Ralph Lauren polo shirt. With his compact body, light brown eyes, and close-cropped silver hair, he's one of the best-looking seventy-year-old men I know.

"I heard you come in, darling. You're not at *Buzz Kill* today?" That was what Landon had taken to calling the magazine after the editor in chief had been murdered in July.

"There seems to be a moratorium on celebrity misdoings this week."

"Oh dear, is that going to pose a problem for you? If they stop misbehaving, you'll be out of a job. Maybe you should call Winona Ryder and casually mention that a new shipment of Marc Jacobs pieces has just arrived at Saks."

"Brilliant," I said, laughing. "What about you? How was your date the other night? Did you like the guy?"

"I did until he opened his mouth over dinner. Speaking of which, I stopped by to inquire if you wanted to come face-to-face tonight with the most delectable lamb chops you've ever seen in your life. I invited a client to dinner, but he's just canceled."

"I'd play second fiddle to score one of your lamb chops any day. I've actually got an interesting story to share, but I'll fill you in over dinner."

After throwing together a sandwich, I found a map of New York State online and looked for Newburgh Junction. It was, just as O'Donnell had said, about an hour north of New York City. But even more interesting, it was close to the New York State Thruway. I let my eyes run up the map. About two hours farther north was the town of Saratoga, home of Skidmore College. Bingo. What if *that's* where Tom had been headed? To hang with his old professor. To ask his advice on what the hell to do with his life.

I tried Professor Carr's office phone but once again ended up with voice mail. Next I tried the college switchboard, asking for the theater department and not Carr. A motherly-sounding woman answered.

"Is Professor Carr there?" I asked.

"No, dear, he left about twenty minutes ago. Would you like his voice mail?"

"I left a message earlier. Do you know if he picked up his messages?"

"I believe so. I'm sure he'll be in touch."

I'd indicated in both my voice mail and e-mail messages that people were concerned about Tom and asked for a reply right away. Carr hadn't obliged. Could that mean that Tom was there and Carr was protecting him? It seemed that the only way I would be able to learn if Tom Fain was now in residence in Saratoga was to get my little butt in my Jeep and head up there. I calculated the driving time—about three, three and a half hours each way. It meant investing a whole day and would also mean that I'd be a lot more invested than "making a few calls" for Chris's sake. But I didn't have a ton on my plate reportingwise this week, and besides, I felt a growing compulsion to find Tom, even if he had no regard for his friends. I called the garage and ordered my Jeep for nine the next day.

For the rest of the afternoon, I camped out on my terrace,

reading through clippings for a freelance article I needed to start sooner or later. Often my thoughts flew back to Tom.

At seven that night, I tapped on Landon's door. When I'd first moved into my apartment, not long after my wedding, I'd exchanged only neighborly pleasantries with Landon, but after my marriage had crashed and burned and my ex had fled his law firm job and the city, Landon had invited me in for a drink, and our friendship took off.

"Your cheeks are pink," he said as he ushered me into his apartment. Landon did not believe in gas grills, and from the open terrace door wafted the intoxicating aroma of burning charcoal briquettes.

"I caught a little sunshine late in the day. Here, some Pellegrino. I hear it's an excellent year."

The dinner was to die for: the aforementioned delectable lamb chops, haricots verts, roasted new potatoes sopping in olive oil and mint. Over dinner I shared the whole saga about Tom, beginning with Chris's phone call and ending with my decision to head to Saratoga tomorrow.

"Now that you've heard all the details, give me an objective opinion," I demanded. "Do you think something's terribly wrong?"

"Well, he may have just taken off, but there's something about it that doesn't feel right. You know what intrigues me even more? All this interest on *your* part."

"I've been wondering about the same thing, actually. Believe it or not, I've developed a soft spot for Tom. From everything I've heard, he seems like a really nice guy—and I feel bad that he's sort of alone in the world."

"What's up with you and Chris? Are sparks starting to fly again?"

"He's as hot as I remember him being, but I think he came to see me just as a friend."

"What about *you?*" he asked, his eyes twinkling in the amber light from the citronella candle.

"Well, things never got airborne the last time, so I suspect it's probably not meant to be. Plus, for all I know he's got a girlfriend now. But there's a part of me that thinks it would at least be a distraction from stewing about Beau Regan."

"Oh dear. Can't kick him out of your head?"

"It's getting better. Like today I've only thought about him forty or fifty times so far. He's due back soon, and it's torturing me. I keep wondering if he'll call as soon as he's home, and then realize that if he was interested in pursuing things romantically, he would have stayed in touch while he was away."

"You have the kind of problem that calls for more claret," he said, reaching for the bottle of Bordeaux.

"Nah, I'd better not," I said. "I need to get an early start tomorrow."

I was in my Jeep by exactly nine the next morning. As I pulled out of the garage, it struck me that this would be a good chance to swing by Blythe's apartment. It might be smarter to surprise her with a visit than leave a bunch of messages. The building on 5th Street turned out to be a brick tenement midway down the block. The kind of place that probably held a mix of artsy types and people down on their luck, typical for the neighborhood. Blythe's name was on the mailbox along with an apparent roommate, T. Hardwick. I rang the bell.

A female voice asked, "Who is it?" sounding both groggy and wary.

"Blythe?" I inquired.

Long pause.

"Who wants to know?"

"My name is Bailey Weggins, and I'm a friend of a friend, and something's come up that I think she'd want to know about."

"Blythe isn't here."

"Is this her roommate?"

"Yes, and I'm trying to sleep."

"When do you expect her?"

"I don't know. Maybe never."

The hairs on the back of my neck shot to attention, as if they'd heard a loud bang.

"Look, is it possible for me to come up? This is a fairly urgent matter."

There was another long pause. Finally, she announced that she would come down and I should wait in the foyer.

I was expecting another struggling actress, but the nebbishy, irritated-looking chick who pushed open the door into the vestibule was so lacking in charisma that it was pretty obvious the biggest part she'd ever played was a farm animal in a fifth-grade show. She was dressed in a pair of saggy jeans and an oversize mustard-colored T-shirt. Her blue eyes were nearly obscured by a pair of dark-framed glasses, and her hair, a reddish brown you see only on horses, was pulled back in a low ponytail under a baseball cap.

"What's so important?" she grumbled.

"You're T. Hardwick?" I said, smiling pleasantly.

"Terry Hardwick. What's this about?"

"Like I said, I'm Bailey Weggins and I'm looking for Blythe."

"You're the one who left the phone message."

"That's right. It's really important that I talk to Blythe."

"She owe you money? Good luck getting it."

"No, I just want to talk to her. Has she moved out?"

"That's one way to put it," she said scornfully. "I think the term they usually use is *skipped* out. She took off with a guy, saying they were doing a movie together. Not only does she owe me rent money, but she stole every tube of sunblock I had and this white eyelet bathing suit cover-up that cost me seventy-five bucks."

It sounded as if I might have just solved the mystery of Tom Fain.

"Was it about a week and a half ago?" I demanded. "With someone named Tom?"

"You a girlfriend of Tom's?" she asked, narrowing her eyes.

"No, but I'm a friend of a friend, and I'm trying to locate him. He's missing."

She scrunched up her mouth. "No, it wasn't with Tom—though he was here once or twice. This new guy had a foreign-sounding name. I think she met him in Williamsburg. And they took off longer than two weeks ago—around the first of August."

That was right around the time the cutesy Hallmark card campaign had come to an abrupt end. So she wasn't with Tom. She had obviously cooled on him once she'd found another dude to go apeshit over.

"Do you know where they went—and if there's any way I can reach her?"

"I don't know *where* she is," she answered with disgust. "She called a few weeks ago for her messages and said she was in the Miami area, but she's such a liar, it's hard to know. I can't believe I ever trusted her. She'd get all teary-eyed and ask if I could pleeeeease give her just one more week on the rent because she'd just done this commercial for Burger King and would be getting a big check. Between the rent and the food and all the clothes of mine she took or wrecked, she owes me a thousand dollars."

"That's a shame," I said, finding it hard to be all that sympathetic. Terry looked like the type of humorless chick one might relish torturing. Maybe Blythe had stolen her sunblock just for fun. "How did you two hook up as roommates, anyway?"

"I put a sign up. My mother said I was stupid sharing my place with an actress, and I should have listened to her. I may not work with people as thrillingly exciting as Blythe, but at least they wouldn't eat a whole bag of someone's miniature Snickers and leave all the wrappers in the bag—like you're not supposed to *notice* there aren't any candy bars in there anymore."

"What do you do, anyway?" I asked.

"I work in health insurance. So how you going to find this Tom guy?"

"I'm heading upstate today to follow up on a few leads. Do you think Blythe will call back?"

"Well, she left some of her shit here, so maybe she'll be back. If she doesn't, I'm seriously thinking of calling the police."

I offered her my business card, which she accepted with all the enthusiasm of someone being presented a dead eel, and asked her to have Blythe get in touch if she called again. Yet it didn't seem likely that Blythe would know Tom's whereabouts. She'd apparently found someone more receptive to her charms than Tom had been, someone willing to keep her in Snickers for the unforeseeable future. My best lead now was Skidmore, and it was time to haul ass and get up there.

I'd missed most of the commuter traffic, but there were still bumper-to-bumper patches on the Major Deegan, and by the time I reached the New York State Thruway, I'd been warming the seat of my Jeep for well over an hour. As I pulled away from the tollbooth, I experienced a moment of brain spritz—why in God's name was I spending an entire day in my car looking for a guy I'd never even *met*? Because I'd promised Chris I would help. Because I was moved by Tom's story. If the good professor couldn't help, though, I didn't know what else I could do.

The second half of the trip turned out to be relatively pain-less. I stuck in a CD of Maria Callas arias, and since there was nothing complicated about the route—New York State Thruway to Exit 24 and then the Adirondack Northway to Saratoga—I lis-tened to her haunting voice and kept my speed at around seventy-two most of the way. The suburbs fell behind me, and before long the Catskills rose in shades of blue and lavender off to my left. I passed stretches of woods and marshes, interrupted periodically by giant eyesores, like mini self-storage units that seemed to go on for miles. When I passed the first Albany exit, my tummy did a weird nostalgia flip, as I remembered my job as a beat reporter for the *Albany Times Union* my first two years out of Brown.

It was just after noon when I pulled off onto the main exit for Saratoga. Though my stomach was starting to rumble, I figured food could wait until after I'd located Carr. I'd visited Saratoga a few times when I was working for the paper—to take in the races, to hear concerts at the performing arts center—and I didn't need to ask directions. The road off the exit turned into Main Street, which I knew led through the town center, and then flowed right into Broadway. As I passed through the downtown area, I checked out the scene. Though Thoroughbred racing season was over, the town was bustling with people. They strolled along the street in shorts and tank tops and formed bunches in front of the shops and cafés in the five-story brick buildings, which dated back to the 1800s. Some of the buildings displayed American flags, which snapped in the end-of-summer breeze.

I decided I'd stop first at Carr's house, and if he wasn't there, I'd proceed down the road to Skidmore. Broadway was an amazing little street lined with glorious old houses that had once been owned by rich horse-loving families like the Vanderbilts. The owners would arrive in August for Thoroughbred season and then depart immediately afterward, leaving the servants to recover the furniture in big white sheets. Carr's house wasn't one of the near mansion-size places, but it was a nice big yellow one with a wraparound porch. Chances are he'd bought it run-down and had worked to restore it to its previous glory.

I was in luck, it seemed. An old Volvo sat in the driveway, and I could see that the front door was wide open to the day. I hopped out of the Jeep and scampered up the steps. Somewhere deep inside, classical music was playing, the perky sounds of Mozart, from what I guessed.

I peered through the screen door and, not seeing anyone, rapped on the frame. Nothing. But someone had to be here. There was the music, after all, and besides, there were cooking smells, something cuminy. I rapped again, louder this time.

"It's open!" a man yelled over the music. "I'm in the kitchen."

I stepped inside and adjusted my eyes now that they were out of the glare of the day. I was standing in a hallway with a parlor on either side, the one to the right set up as a study/library. Dark wood antiques filled the rooms, but they seemed mostly of the flea market variety, and the art on the wall was mainly framed museum posters. I followed the cooking smells and music to a kitchen in the back, a room that looked as if it hadn't been over-hauled since at least the 1970s. A tall, lean guy with a dark brown beard, who could have been anywhere from thirty-eight to fifty, stood at one of those rolling carts with butcher block on top, chopping away at a red pepper, with a pile of ten others await-ing execution. He glanced up when I entered, a look on his face of expectation that was immediately chased away by puzzlement. Clearly, I wasn't who he'd been waiting for.

"Can I help you?" he asked, pausing midwhack.

"Sorry to barge in like this. I did try to call you a couple of times. I'm Bailey Weggins. Are you Alan Carr?"

He scrunched his mouth over to one side and mentally tossed around what I'd just said. "Oh, you're the one with a question about Tom. Sorry not to get back to you—I'm serving chicken chili to twenty tonight, and I'm about an hour behind schedule. You're not a student, are you?"

"No, I live in New York City, and I drove up this morning. Why don't I get right to the point. Tom seems to have dropped off the face of the earth. A friend of his asked me to try to find him, and since I heard you stayed in touch with Tom, I was hoping you might be able to help."

"Dropped off the face of the earth?" he said soberly, wiping his hands on the red cook's apron he wore. "What do you mean by *that?*"

"There hasn't been any sign of him at his apartment for nearly two weeks, and he hasn't showed up for work on his TV show. He did withdraw a large sum of money, so it seems as if he may have wanted to take off for a while. I'm wondering if you've seen or talked to him lately."

There was a telling beat before he answered.

"No, I haven't."

"You hesitated."

"That's because I *did* talk to Tom fairly recently, but now that I think about it, it was probably more like a month or two ago. Not long after they starting shooting this show he's in. He called to give me an update." Pensively, he strode over to the CD player and killed the Mozart. "When was the last time someone actually saw him?"

"The last person who saw him that *I* talked to was a guy at his parking garage. Tom picked up his car early in the morning two weeks ago this Saturday. The last time he used his cell phone was that morning, and it was from a place downstate not far from the thruway. That's what made me think he might have been heading up to see you."

"No, there weren't any plans for him to come up here. Jesus, I don't like the sound of this at all."

"Is there any chance he could have just taken off for here, planning to show up unannounced?"

"You mean and then run into trouble. God, what if he's had an accident and gone off the road and no one has spotted the car?" With one hand he squeezed his cheeks together and shook his head. "Tom never showed up unannounced before, but who knows, maybe he *was* headed here. He wasn't thrilled with his part, that much I know. He was supposed to have had a much bigger role, and then all of sudden, bam, the rug got pulled out from under him. And yet, I can't see him just walking away from the job. It was a start in TV."

I massaged my temples, trying to think. I'd half convinced myself Tom was here or that I would at least walk away with a clue to his whereabouts. But I'd driven all this way simply to face another dead end.

"Is there anything, then, you can tell me that might help me find him?" I asked, looking up. "Anyone he knew in the Northeast that he might have decided to hole up with? Any secret problems in his life?"

"You want a cup of coffee?" Carr asked, yanking open a hulking old refrigerator that was the yellowed hue of old piano keys. He withdrew a carton of milk and set it down next to the peppers.

"Sure," I said, using the invitation as a sign it was okay for me to take a seat on one of the scattered stools in the room.

Carr took his time—filling the mugs slowly from the coffeemaker pot, pouring sugar from a yellow sack into a chipped bowl—and I sensed he was deliberating whether or not to make a disclosure. After he'd set everything on the butcher block, he wiped his hands again on his apron and looked me straight in the eye.

"Do you know or *not* know about Tom's stint in rehab?" he asked finally.

Oh wow, I thought. "When was this?"

"About a year ago."

"Are we talking coke?"

"Nope, antidepressants. He started taking them last year right after his mother died, along with sleeping pills, and he just got hooked. He did two weeks at a place in Massachusetts and then crashed here afterwards for another couple of weeks. It was actually great. He helped me on a project, and he worked in my garden every day. And he seemed in great shape when he left."

"Could he have relapsed?" I asked, reaching over and helping myself to a mug of coffee.

"I suppose it's a possibility, but Tom's not really the druggie type. I saw his situation as an isolated incident, all tied in with the depression he felt over losing two parents so close together." He shook his head hard in a gesture of frustration and worry. "No, that's not what concerns me. I keep seeing a car wreck in my mind. And we've got to do something."

"Okay, I'm going to explore that end next," I said. "I'll contact the state police. And I promise to keep you posted."

My stomach was churning when I left a few minutes later, a combo effect from downing an entire mug of coffee in two minutes and the new concerns I felt about Tom. What if he *had* had an accident? I was anxious to be on the road again, but I also needed to eat—and to think. I found a parking spot downtown, and before heading into a small restaurant, I picked up a New York State tourist map at the shop next door. After I'd ordered a Caesar salad, I spread out the map in front of me.

Tom's call to the assistant director had been made when he was less than an hour north of the city. If Tom had indeed had an accident in the hours after that, locating his car would be tough since we had no idea where he was actually headed. He might have been going to Saratoga, in which case he would have stayed on the New York State Thruway. But he could have gotten off onto a smaller road or picked up the Mass Turnpike in Albany to head to Boston or someplace else in New England. He could have even been on his way north to Canada for all I knew. I let my eyes roam the map. North of Newburgh Junction were Ulster and Greene counties. North and to the west was the Catskill

Mountain region, with old-fashioned-sounding towns like Margaretville and Loch Sheldrake.

And then I spotted it. I nearly gulped. A town called *Andes*. Like a flash, I saw in my mind the photo of Tom and his parents, with "Andes" written on the back. Because of their many travels, I'd instantly assumed Peru. But what if it was *this* Andes? According to Chris, the family had a weekend home, and Tom had been in the process of selling it this year. But what if he hadn't done so yet? The turnoff for Andes was right near Newburgh Junction.

My salad arrived, and I wolfed it down while I simultaneously phoned the intern ghetto at *Buzz*. I asked the chick who answered to pull up a Web site we used to check property records and told her to find anything belonging to Tom Fain. She promised to call me back in a few minutes.

"No, I'll hold," I told her, totally wired. I could hear the tap of her computer keys as she worked.

"There are a few Tom Fains," she said. "I'm not sure—"

I interrupted, giving her the address on Mercer.

"Okay, I see it," she said after an agonizing minute. "There's another place, too. Do you want it?"

"Yes!" I nearly screamed.

"Dabbet Road, Andes, New York." She pronounced "Andes" like "Ands," but I forgave her. I couldn't believe it. Mentally, I calculated how long it would take me to drive there. Just a couple of hours—south and west.

As I raced along in my Jeep minutes later, I considered the likelihood of Tom going there. Though earlier he had told Chris he was unloading the place, the sale might have fallen through, or he might have changed his mind. This could also explain why he hadn't made any more phone calls from his cell. Reception might be bad in the mountains, and he could be relying on a landline for any communication. I tried 411 and found a listing for Fain on Dabbet Road, but no one answered when I called it. *Why* would he have gone there? I wondered. Was it to chase the boredom because his weekend plans had fallen through? He'd told Harper that he had work to do. Was he working on the property? Getting it ready for a sale? Then why not return? Or let anyone know his whereabouts? Maybe his real goal had been to place himself far from the madding crowd for an indefinite period of time. Or maybe something had happened to him.

It was nearly six by the time I arrived in Andes, and the sun was sinking in the sky. Though it was still technically summer, the days seemed so much shorter now. I rolled down my window and felt a blast of cool mountain air. Figuring I'd probably be back in the city by this time, I hadn't brought along a sweater or jacket.

The town of Andes was small and charming without trying too hard. Along the main drag were a few little shops, a general store, and a little café where a few people still lounged at tables on the porch. I pulled into a parking spot, looking for someone to ask directions from. A tall older woman, her gray hair pinned up dramatically on top of her head, was sweeping the sidewalk in front of a red-painted antiques shop, with a sign that read NEST OF TREASURES.

"Excuse me," I said after climbing out of the Jeep. "Could you please tell me how to get to Dabbet Road?"

"You're looking for the Fain house?" she asked in a husky, cultured voice that suggested she might have packed up her life in Manhattan and moved here for a simpler existence.

"How did you know?"

"It's the only house on that road. Are you a potential buyer?"

"Buyer? No, I'm actually looking for Tom Fain. My name is Bailey Weggins. I'm a friend of a friend of Tom's."

"Oh, I didn't realize he was up here this week. Okay, then, you're going to have to head back the way you came and make a left on Harrow. Just before you reach the outskirts of town, you'll see Dabbet on your left. Tell him Beverly said hi, will you?"

"Sure thing."

My whole body was buzzing as I jumped back into the Jeep. I hadn't wanted to be too nosy with the woman, but it sounded as if the deal for the house, the one Tom had told Chris about, *had* fallen through and the house was once again for sale. Maybe that was why Tom had come to Andes—to goose the sales process.

It was no problem finding Dabbet. As Beverly had told me, it was only a short hike from the center of town, and I bet myself that as a boy Tom had probably walked it. Dabbet Road, a dirt one, was longer than I expected, maybe half a mile, and before long I was being jounced along the deep gouges under a dense canopy of maples and giant firs.

The first thing I spotted was a barn, a low, long gray one at the very end of the road. Then suddenly the house appeared, off to the right, a big old clapboard. Beyond that on the road was a small white cottage, probably a guesthouse, its back to the road. And right in front of it was a black Audi.

CHAPTER 5

I turned off the ignition and just sat in my Jeep for a minute, feeling my heart thump. I had found Tom. In the end, it hadn't taken all that long or been a particularly wearisome quest, but as of yesterday it had seemed it might be impossible. With the only clue being a single phone call from along the thruway, I had felt as if I were searching for someone lost on a catamaran in the Atlantic. But now here he was, just yards away from me.

I felt relief and an unexpected prickling of tears in my eyes. I also felt weird as hell. What was I supposed to do *now*? Wouldn't Tom be pissed that I'd just shown up out of the blue? What if he was holed up with some new chick, working his way through the *Kama Sutra*? But I couldn't turn around and just head back to Manhattan. Not without telling him that Chris and Harper were concerned about him. Not without making sure he was okay. Because there was still the chance that something wasn't right.

I slid out of the Jeep and slammed the door hard. Better, I

thought, to make noise and not catch him totally unaware. Because his car was pulled up tight to the cottage, I figured he must have been staying there. I wondered if the main house seemed too big to him or if it was too full of memories. I took a breath and started down a slate path that ran along the side of the cottage, its blue gray slabs almost obscured by yellowed tufts of grass.

Rounding the bend in the path, I saw that the front of the cottage faced the woods. It looked like something out of a storybook, with a narrow porch running along the width of the house and white curtains lining the windows on either side of a blue Dutch door. But as I stepped closer, I could see that the cottage was slightly worse for wear. The gray paint on the porch floorboards had mostly worn off, and the two wicker rockers were badly weathered and saggy in the seats. I glanced over toward the main house, whose front also faced the woods. It seemed even more forlorn than the cottage. The shutters had all been removed and lay stacked against the side of the house. Even from where I stood, I could see that it was in desperate need of a paint job.

I turned back to the cottage and mounted the steps, which creaked with each footfall. I rapped on the blue door. Once, twice, three times. No answer. Off in the woods, a bird screeched—a hawk, I thought—but no sound came from within the cottage.

"Tom," I called out. "Hey, Tom."

Still no answer, just a screech from the hawk again. I glanced behind me. The sun had begun to set, and the woods were becoming a smudge. It would be dark before long. I wondered if Tom was over in the big house—playing Mr. Fix-It.

Before heading over there, I gave the door one more rap, and then purely owing to my can't-keep-my-damn-nose-out-of-anything instinct, I tried the handle. It was unlocked. I gently pushed the cottage door open and stepped inside.

"Hey, Tom," I called out again. "Tom, are you around?" Nothing. Just the hum of a refrigerator off in another room.

The inside of the cottage had the same storybook quality as the outside. It was the kind of space that would be great to curl up in on a rainy fall day. I could see a small kitchen through a doorway on the far side, but most of the downstairs space was made up of a living room with a chunky gray stone fireplace. It was filled with an eclectic mix of dark wood tables and chintz-covered furniture begging to be flopped in. My eyes roamed the room and quickly fell on the coffee table. Several grease-stained pieces of sandwich wrapping paper lay on top, practically declaring, "Tom Fain ate here." I stepped closer and peered at the paper. In one of the folds was a small scrap of curled dried meat—it looked days old. An open newspaper next to it was dated the Saturday he disappeared. Dread swelled in me, and I found myself thinking of something an old reporter I once worked with used to say on such occasions: "I don't like the fuckin' looks of this."

"Tom," I called out almost frantically, but not even expecting an answer now. A partially enclosed staircase led up to the second floor, and I sprinted up the steps. There were two bedrooms on either side of the small hall at the top. The one to the right was empty; the one to the left, decorated all in white, showed signs of recent occupation—a pair of large hiking boots lying sideways on the floor and a man's shirt tossed on a chair. The white matelasse spread on the bed was rumpled, as if someone had made it hurriedly.

I glanced behind me and saw a brown leather duffel bag on the floor in back of the door. It was open but full, with a pair of jeans poking out from the top. Why, if Tom had been here for twelve days, had he worn so few of the clothes he'd brought? Just as with the sandwich paper on the coffee table, it was as if time had stopped days ago.

I flew back down the stairs and ducked into the kitchen, where the fridge hummed quietly, clueless to the fact that something was horribly wrong. On the counter I saw the plastic bag that must have once contained the sandwich and, incongruously next to it, an empty bottle of Veuve Clicquot champagne.

I hurried outside. As much as I dreaded it, I was going to have to check the main house now. When I stepped off the porch, I swept the woods with my eyes. Off to the left I could see a ruined stacked stone wall, the one, perhaps, that Tom had posed with his parents in front of. Behind it, through the dense trees, something glinted, and I realized that it was a sliver of silver pond. What if Tom had gone swimming and been stricken with cramps, incapacitated? What if he was lying at the bottom of that pond? Conjuring up that image made me want to hurl.

As I crossed the grass, I saw that the main house was even wearier looking than I'd realized earlier—peeled paint, flower beds long gone to weeds, drooping steps to an open porch along the width of the house. Please be alive, Tom, I pleaded to myself as I crossed the lawn. To my surprise, the front door, inside a screen door, was wide open. Maybe everything was all right after all. "Tom," I called out as I made my way to the steps.

But then the smell hit me like a bulldozer. I had smelled death on more than a few occasions—the first time as a reporter in Albany, watching as a body was hauled from the Hudson and being greeted by that ripe, nauseating whiff from twenty feet away. But this was more putrid than anything I'd ever experienced. It seemed to pour from the door like a force, and it was mixed, almost incongruously, with the awful stench of charred wood. I retched and covered my nose and mouth with my hand. Someone was dead inside the house.

I could see from the outside that the front hall was almost dark, illuminated only by the remains of daylight that seeped through the porch windows. Pulling up my shirt against my face, I stepped inside and fumbled for a light switch. I found one finally to the left, and as I flipped it, an overhead chandelier lit up, flooding the space with too bright light. I was in a large center hall, totally empty of furniture, and from what I could see, the rest of the house was empty, too, except for an odd piece of furniture here and there. The smell was nearly overpowering now. I retched again and forced myself to breathe through my mouth.

What I wanted to do was leave—no, let me rephrase that: I wanted to tear ass out of there so fast that I'd leave a trench in the lawn. But I had to know about Tom, no matter how horrible the truth was.

I did a fast sweep of the downstairs rooms, fighting the unrelenting urge to dry heave. Though the rooms were spacious, there weren't that many of them—to my right a big dining room, kitchen, and mud room; to the left a living room and screened-in porch; and behind the living room what must have once been the library, though the bookshelves were all empty now. Against a wall in the library was a large push broom, a mop, and a two-gallon plastic bucket of dirty water. Someone was housecleaning—or at least had been.

What I didn't find was the source of the smell. Which meant I was going to have to go upstairs.

I swung back to the hallway and began to mount the stairs. I knew I was breathing the scent of death, but what confused me was the burned notes of the smell. There'd been a fire of some kind, but *where*? At the top of the stairs, I discovered that two hallways led off from the landing. One led directly to the left. The other ran perpendicular to the stairs, toward the front of the house. The smell seemed to emanate from that direction, so that's where I headed. Frantically, I searched for a light switch, but when I found one and flipped it, nothing happened. I kept going, though, through the fading light of the afternoon and the upward glow from the chandelier. The first room I reached was huge, perhaps once the master bedroom. Enough daylight spilled into the space for me to see even into its corners. The only objects in the room were a small table lamp sitting forlornly on the dusty floor by a telephone and, near the window, several paint cans and a paint tray. And the smell. It was huge now. There was nothing in the room that could be producing it, but on the far left wall was an open door to what had to be a bathroom. The smell from hell had to be coming from there.

I glanced reflexively behind me and listened. Then I turned back and forced myself to walk to the bathroom. Despite the fabric against my face, the smell fought its way up my nostrils, making me retch again. I noticed the Knicks cap first, lying on the old white tile floor, the window on the right opened a crack, but then my eyes flew to the sink and the mirror above it. They were spattered with what looked like dried blood, as if someone had sprayed a canister of it. And then a movement caught my attention, yanking my eyes to the other side of the large bathroom—to the tub. I turned and gasped. It was the length of a body, partially charred and decayed into a toxic soup. But the face was moving. Terrified, I stepped closer and saw that the movement was coming not from the face itself but from a swirling mass of white maggots feeding on it.

On legs nearly limp, I backed out of the bathroom, my heart beating wildly with fear. It had to be Tom in the tub. Whatever had happened to him clearly had happened days ago, yet the whole house seemed ominous at the moment, as if someone were hiding in there, watching me. I grabbed a breath through my mouth and shot out of the bedroom. I took the stairs two at a time and practically threw myself onto the lawn.

The sun had set now, and I could barely find my way as I raced across the grass. Just as I reached the side of the cottage, a light came on over the porch. I jerked my head fearfully in that direction. It was obviously hooked to a light sensor. I scrambled to my Jeep and propelled myself inside.

Locked in the car, I breathed deeply and willed myself to calm down. I had to call 911, yet I couldn't bear the idea of waiting by the house for the cops. I decided to make the call from the place where Dabbet met the main road.

After I backed out of the driveway and began to make my way jerkily over the bumpy road, my fear gave way to grief. The body had been unrecognizable, but it had to be Tom. Had he *burned* to death? The tiles behind the tub had been singed gray and yet the tub had obviously managed to contain the fire—along with help from the slightly opened window. Was it some kind of freak accident—triggered by a combustible substance he was working with? But then why the blood near the sink? Someone must have murdered him. Bludgeoned or stabbed him and then set the body on fire with something nearby—like paint remover. Or had Tom killed *himself*? Slitting his wrists and then, when that didn't work, setting himself on fire? What if that was the whole reason he had come to Andes to begin with? Perhaps his parents' deaths had caught up with him again. Had the champagne been part of his suicide ritual—a toast to his life? A way to dull the pain? My stomach was sour, and I knew if I didn't stop picturing the body, I would puke all over my car.

The road seemed even longer on the way out, but finally I spotted the main road running in front of me. I hit the brake, put the Jeep in neutral, and dug my BlackBerry out of my bag. The 911 operator picked up after two rings.

"I need to report a dead body on Dabbet Road, in the town of Andes," I said. "It may be a homicide."

"Is there any chance the person is still alive?"

"N-no," I said, my voice nearly choked. She might as well have asked if there was any chance that Coldplay was about to do a concert on the lawn that night.

She asked for the exact address of the house, my name, and where I was calling from. Then she told me that she had dispatched a car from the county sheriff's office and that it should be there within ten minutes. She advised me to stay on the line.

"No, my battery's low," I lied. "I'll wait right here at the entrance of the road, okay? I'm in a black Jeep."

I didn't want to hold. I needed to call Chris right away and break the news to him. I had programmed in his number the other night, but my fingers fumbled like crazy just trying to bring it up. Part of me wanted desperately to hear his voice, to share my grief, and another part dreaded telling him.

He answered just as I thought his phone was about to go to voice mail, his "Hello?" barely climbing over the restaurant or bar sounds behind him.

"Can you go someplace quiet?" I shouted. "I need to talk to you."

"Gimme a second, okay?"

I could hear the noise diminish gradually as he walked, until finally it was totally muffled, as if he had found a spot in a back corridor or down a flight of stairs.

"There, that's better," he said finally.

"Where are you, anyway?"

"Just a bar with one of the guys in the cast. What's up?"

"Chris, I've got awful news. I think—I think Tom is dead."

"What? What do you mean, *think*?"

"I'm at his parents' old weekend home. Tom apparently hadn't sold it yet. There's a body here, in the main house. It's not recognizable, but I'm pretty sure it must be Tom."

"Jesus Christ, you're kidding."

"I'm so sorry, Chris," I said. "I—"

"Wait, where are you, exactly? Where is all this happening?"

"I'm in a town called Andes. It's in the Catskills, a few hours from New York."

"Oh God. What happened to him?"

"Chris, I hate doing this over the phone. The body was burned. I'm not sure how he died, but it's possible someone killed him. Like I said, I think it's Tom, but I'm not a hundred percent sure.

I'm waiting for the police to show up now, and maybe I'll know more in a little while."

"Oh God, this is awful," he said, his voice tight with anguish. "I need to tell Harper."

"Why don't you hold off for tonight, at least? There's no point in upsetting her if it turns out not to be Tom. In fact, it's probably better not to say anything to anyone yet. There's going to be a police investigation."

"Are you all alone there, Bailey? Are you okay?"

"Yes, I'm alone but I'm not in the house anymore," I said, touched by his concern. "It was just too awful. I'm down the road in my car, waiting for the cops."

"How did you end up there, anyway? I mean, I didn't even know where the house was."

"One thing just kind of led to another. I think I see the cops. I'll call you back as soon as I have a sense of what's going on."

What had caught my attention through the fir trees was a vehicle slowing down along the main road, just before the turn onto Dabbet. But it turned out to be a tow truck, headed to a breakdown somewhere. I waited in the car, restless and anxious, trying to banish the memory of the horrible ooze in the tub. It was another ten minutes before a Delaware County sheriff's car finally made the turn and pulled up beside me.

There was only one officer in the car, a woman probably in her mid-thirties. She rolled down her window.

"I'm Deputy Sheriff Sue Dannon. Are you the person who called 911?"

"Yes, I'm Bailey Weggins. I found a badly decomposed body in the house up the road. I think it's Tom Fain, who owns the house."

She eyed me warily. "Is there anyone else in the house at this time?"

"There doesn't appear to be. Tom's been missing for almost

two weeks, and it looks as if he might have been dead about that long. Do you want me to show you?"

"All right—I'll follow you."

She waited while I turned the Jeep around, which was no easy feat on the narrow rutted road. As we neared the property, my heart leapt. Light was now seeping out of one of the windows along the back of the main house. But then I realized it had to be the light from the chandelier spilling into the rest of the house.

Dannon pulled up her vehicle right behind me, and we both climbed out. As she approached me, I noticed that her hand instinctively touched her gun. She was about five six, probably just a few years older than me. If she was attractive, it was hard to tell because her hair was all under her big black hat and she had that tough-as-nails expression that cops are trained to wear.

"The body's in the big house?" she asked, cocking her head toward it.

"Yes, in a second-floor bathroom off one of the bedrooms. I don't think I can go in there again," I said.

She started to say something, and then I actually saw her nostrils flare. The breeze had shifted direction, and a hint of the putrid smell had found its way to us. The expression that suddenly crossed Dannon's face suggested that someone had just offered her a slice of grilled river rat.

"Jesus," she said.

"It's pretty bad. Do you have a mask?"

"Please stay right here," she said, ignoring my question and heading off across the lawn. I guess she didn't want to appear wimpy by taking me up on my suggestion, but as she walked I saw her yank a white handkerchief from her pocket and squash it against her face.

I jumped back into the Jeep and turned the AC on high. I knew she'd said to stay right where I was, but I wasn't going to take her literally. I couldn't stomach breathing in that smell and knowing it was probably Tom.

Less than ten minutes passed before I saw Dannon emerge like a specter from the darkness of the lawn. She was talking into a walkie-talkie, clearly calling in reinforcements. As soon as she'd attached the device to her belt, she dabbed at her mouth with the hankie. Something told me her last meal was somewhere back on the grass.

I jumped out of the Jeep again and discovered that the wind must have shifted because the smell wasn't as horrific now.

"Please get back into the car," she said. "I'd like to ask you a few questions."

She slid into the passenger seat next to me. Up close, I could see that her brow was damp with sweat. I knew from covering crimes that cops could work a lifetime without seeing body soup. This very well might have been the worst, most retch-worthy thing she'd ever laid eyes on.

"You think the body must be this fellow Tom Fain?" she asked after drawing a long, deep breath.

I told her yes and then offered a shorthand version of the story, leaving out details about the various players involved—like Tom shagging the star of the show. She listened thoughtfully, taking notes, but retained that wall of wariness she'd displayed from the first moment we'd spoken. To her, my tale probably sounded oddly far-fetched—I didn't even know Tom personally, yet I'd been out searching half the state for him. As far as she knew, I could have killed him myself and then returned to the scene of the crime.

She was still peppering me with questions when I heard the rumble of a vehicle above the AC and lights pierced the back window of my Jeep. We spun around in unison. Reinforcements had arrived.

"Please wait here," she told me. In my rearview mirror, I

watched her hurry toward the sheriff's car that had pulled up behind us, and then I lost her in the glare of the headlights. For ten minutes I waited, wondering if she'd been beamed up, and then suddenly someone killed the high beams and I could see her in discussion near the car with two men in sheriff's hats. Soon, several other vehicles arrived, and people in uniform began tramping back and forth across the lawn, barking comments to one another. Despite all the activity and how rattled I felt, I almost nodded off a few times. I felt exhausted, achy, heartsick. Thirty minutes later, I was still by myself in the car, and despite all the excitement outside, things on my end seemed to be moving at the speed of melting ice.

Finally, Dannon rapped on my window and asked me to follow her. There were more lights on in the big house now, illuminating a huddle of several people in uniform outside, but she led me instead to the porch of the cottage, where she introduced me to a Sheriff Schmidt—a guy with a torso the size of a redwood tree and a thick, wiry mustache that looked as if it would hurt as much as a bitch slap if you tried to kiss him. He was probably fifty and appeared far less shaken than Dannon.

"Thank you for waiting, Miss Weggins," he said. "Have a seat, please."

With my butt perched on just the edge of one of the old wicker rockers and my arms wrapped tightly around me against the mountain chill, I went through a slightly more expansive version of my saga than I'd given earlier: who Tom was, why I was looking for him, how I'd ended up in the town of Andes. He nodded politely, less stern looking than Dannon, but his next question proved I wasn't going to get an easy ride.

"Quite a bit of trouble to go through for someone you don't even know," he said.

"True, but I do know *Chris* well—he's a good friend," I said.

"And since I'm a freelance writer, I had the time to check out a few leads."

Though he observed me expectantly, waiting for something *more*, I forced myself to stop. What I'd learned about cops—both as a crime reporter and having been interrogated by them myself—is that overexplaining makes them *real* suspicious. Plus the more you say, the greater the danger of becoming tangled in your own words and blurting out the wrong thing. All of a sudden, you're confessing to setting a string of warehouse fires or having helped Lee Harvey Oswald escape from the Texas School Book Depository.

"So you never met Mr. Fain personally?"

"Never, no, but I have a picture of him," I said, drawing the head shot out of my purse and handing it over to him. "Of course, it won't help with the identification, but you might want it for your inquiries."

After studying the photo, he flipped it over and read the résumé with furrowed brow, as if I'd just handed him a clue to the three secrets of Fatima. I took out a pen and paper from my purse and jotted down Tom's address and also Chris's phone number. They would want access to Tom's apartment to search for clues. It wouldn't be long before they'd be stumbling onto Locket's note.

"As you've been following up on your so-called leads, Miss Weggins," Schmidt said, looking up from the photo, "have you found any information that would be relevant to our investigation? Was Mr. Fain depressed, for instance?"

"Are you thinking suicide?" I asked. "The thought crossed my mind—but then how do you explain all that blood?"

"Just answer the question, please, Miss Weggins."

"Apparently, Tom was depressed at one point. After the death of his mother. But there wasn't any indication he'd been upset lately."

"Any enemies you're aware of?"

"No, not that I'm aware of. There is one thing you should know. Tom had apparently withdrawn seven thousand dollars in cash before he came up here. I don't know why or what for."

He considered the info wordlessly. I sensed he had something else to ask me, but suddenly he announced that I was free to go. He added that his office might be in touch with me over the next few days.

Dannon walked me out to my car, which gave me an opportunity to check directions back to the highway with her. As soon as I reached the end of the pitted road and turned onto the main drag, I rolled down all the car windows and let the wind blast away at the interior. The cool air whipped my hair around my face so hard that it stung, but at least I could breathe again.

The ride back to Manhattan was god-awful. My head had started to throb, along with my legs, and I could find only one Advil in my purse, a quantity that proved to be as useful as swatting at a fly with a rubber band.

Each time my mind found its way again to that horrible mess fermenting in the tub, I'd force myself to focus instead on the overall situation. During the next few days, forensic evidence would surely confirm that it was Tom lying dead in the house. I supposed there was a remote chance it could be someone else—a workman, for instance, who'd been painting the bathroom—but why would Tom's possessions and his car still be on site? It also seemed pretty obvious from the evidence that Tom had died the very day he'd arrived. His last phone call, after all, had been made that day, he'd barely unpacked his bag, and the one newspaper had been from that Saturday. I tried to re-create part of the day in my mind: He'd picked up a sandwich—perhaps at that little café in town— chowed down while reading the paper. Had he washed it down with champagne? That part was hard to explain. Had someone shared the bottle with him? Perhaps after lunch he'd taken a walk around the property (the muddy boots) and squeezed in a nap (the rumpled bed). Alone?

At some point before dark, he'd headed over to the main house, most likely to tackle the bathroom. This may have been the work he'd been referring to when he'd spoken to Harper. And then probably not long after he'd started, someone had shown up and killed him. Was it a burglar who had thought the house would be empty? But what had he been hoping to steal? Maybe Tom had an enemy in Andes, someone he'd enraged during one of the summers he'd spent there. Or maybe it was someone from the city who had known where he'd be or had followed him up there.

Of course, there was also the suicide theory. It had occurred to me and to Schmidt, too. But it didn't make a whole lot of sense. Stab yourself and then light yourself on fire? And there was no evidence that Tom had *recently* been depressed.

As I neared the city, I realized I'd been so roiled up, I'd never called Chris back. I punched in his number.

"You're not still there, are you?" he asked tensely as soon as he heard my voice.

"No—I'm about thirty minutes from home. How you doing?"

"Not good. But what about you? You're the one dealing with all this firsthand. I can't believe I got you into this." There was a note of real tenderness in his voice.

"I'll be okay. The police talked to me, and it's clear they don't know anything yet. I gave them your name and number because they need access to Tom's apartment."

"Um, okay," he said.

"Any chance we could get together first thing in the morning and I can go over everything?"

"Yeah, I really need to see you. I'm not shooting till ten, so I could come around eight," he said.

As soon as he hung up, I realized how quiet the car was. I hadn't played any CDs on the ride back because I'd thought the noise would drive me even crazier. The only sound now was my breathing and the whirring of cars outside. I was startled when my cell phone went off again. I figured it had to be Chris, calling back with a question.

"Hey," I said.

Nothing. And then the sound of someone—it was hard to tell whether it was male or female—crying with hard, anguished sobs.

"Who is this?" I asked, my voice catching.

Then there was only silence.

CHAPTER 6

W ho is this?" I asked again, my voice catching. Nothing. When I glanced at the phone to see the number, the words announced "Caller Unknown." A second later, I was disconnected.

Hesitantly, I rested the BlackBerry on the seat next to me, troubled by the sound that I'd heard, wondering if the person would call back. Had it simply been a wrong number—or perhaps an obnoxious prank? For a split second, I considered whether it might have been Chris. Had he broken down after he'd called me, phoned me back, and then hung up out of embarrassment?

My attention was yanked back to the highway. The traffic was picking up now that I was approaching the Tappan Zee, demanding my full attention. By eleven, I was finally back in the city, and the first thing I did after stepping into my apartment was strip off my clothes and stuff them into the hamper. Then I limped into the shower. I needed to get the smell off me—out of my hair, off my skin, out of my pores. I shampooed my hair twice and used a loofah to scrub my body so that it was flushed red by the time I was finished.

Wrapped in a towel and with my hair sopping wet, I traipsed to the kitchen in search of nourishment. I hadn't eaten since lunch, and I was ravenous, yet the thought of most food still made me gag. I settled for toast and tea. Just as the teakettle squealed, my intercom buzzer went off. I had no idea who would be stopping by out of the blue at nearly midnight on a Thursday night.

"Chris is here to see you," the doorman said as soon as I answered.

"Um, okay," I said, surprised. "Send him up."

I was anxious to talk to Chris, yearned, for that matter, to share the whole awful story with him, yet I hadn't prepared myself mentally to do it *tonight*. I threw on a pair of jeans, a tank top, and a pair of flip-flops and warned myself not to start blubbering. It would only make it worse for him.

Chris was in jeans, too, and a dusty green polo shirt, almost the color of his eyes. The look on his face said that the news about Tom was eating him up.

"Sorry to barge in like this," he said soberly. "I just couldn't wait until tomorrow to see you."

"No, I understand. Do you want a beer?"

"Definitely."

He was standing in the middle of the room, staring at the old kilim rug on my living room floor, when I returned a minute later with the bottle of beer and my mug of tea. There was only one lamp lit in the room, the one on the wooden end table by the couch, but it was enough to see his face by. He looked heartsick.

"Any developments since I talked to you?" he asked as I handed him the beer.

"No, and I'm sure the sheriff's department isn't going to want to share anything with me as things move forward. It's going to be tough to get news about the investigation."

"You said the body was badly decomposed. What makes you think it was really Tom's?"

"For one thing, his car was there, and his duffel bag was in the guest cottage."

I described the setup of the property, as well as some of the details of the scene, leaving out the most gruesome parts. He absorbed it all, his mouth clenched.

"Is there a chance that he died of some kind of freak accident?" Chris asked.

"I don't think so, though I wouldn't have any way of knowing from the brief glimpse I got of the scene. The sheriff who questioned me even suggested suicide, but—"

"*Suicide?*" he exclaimed.

"I just don't buy that, though. There was blood all around the sink and on the mirror above it. My guess—and it's just a guess—is that he was attacked with a knife or some heavy object and set on fire afterward." I didn't add, *Possibly while he was still alive.*

Chris shook his head in utter disgust. "Do you think—do you think someone from the show could have killed him?"

"It's a possibility." Alex Ottoson's name flashed across my brain suddenly. What if he'd learned of Locket's affair with Tom?

"I hate the fact that I got you involved, Bailey," he said. "But at the same time, who knows when Tom would have been found if you hadn't started looking."

I explained how I had made the connection to Andes and tracked down Tom's address through the Internet.

"He never mentioned to you that it was in the Catskills?" I asked.

"Uh, not that I recall. I mean, he might have, but if he did, it went in one ear and out the other. I do remember him saying that it had gone to seed after his father had died and that he was relieved to have finally sold it—this was in the beginning of the summer, when I was living with him."

"It seems like the deal fell through. I'll see what I can find out about it." I hesitated. "It's funny that he never told Harper about it, either. Or at least she never mentioned it as a possibility for where he might be."

"Speaking of Harper, do you still feel I should keep her out of this for now?" he asked.

"Actually, I've been rethinking that. Since it may be a few days before anything is confirmed about the identity, news is going to leak out. It's better for Harper to hear it from you than thirdhand. Why don't you tell her tomorrow?"

"I should probably tell the executive producer as well. Better he hear it from me, too."

I sipped my tea and thought a moment. "You know when we spoke earlier—while I was driving back?" I said. "You didn't call me right after that, did you?"

"No—why?" he asked.

"The phone rang, and someone was crying. It was a wrong number, obviously. At the time, though, I just wondered . . ."

"No, it wasn't me. But I've *felt* like crying."

"Gosh, Chris, I'm just so sorry."

I set my mug on the coffee table and squeezed his arms. Through the soft cotton fabric I could feel how hard his biceps were. Late last winter, those arms had wrapped around me on several occasions. I'd engaged in some pretty heavy make-out sessions with Chris on my couch, his jeans bulging and my bra bunched around my waist. But I had never gone to bed with him. It wasn't because that gorgeous face and awesome body of his had failed to make me crazy with lust. They *had*. But I could never stop associating my breakup with Jack—and *hurting* him—with my attraction to Chris, and every time I was about to urge us off the couch and into the bedroom, I would find this weird guilt dousing my desire. Tonight, though, Jack seemed like a long time ago.

"I just feel lucky to be with you tonight, Bailey," Chris said, and offered a grim smile. "This would be awful to handle alone."

He set down his drink then and pulled me into his arms. It was a friendly, caring hug, like the one he'd given me the other night. But as he held me, he sighed and his body relaxed into mine. He lifted his right hand and stroked my damp hair, softly at first and then with firmer, more urgent fingers. I felt something stir in me.

Chris pulled back slightly and stared into my eyes. Then his mouth found mine. I was instantly reminded of how good his soft, full lips could feel and taste. He kissed me hungrily, and I kissed him back with the same urgency. As I relaxed into his body even more, I couldn't help but notice the hardness between his legs.

"God, Bailey," he said. "I want to consume every inch of you."

"Okay," I whispered without any hesitation. I realized I was saying yes for a whole bunch of reasons—because what girl could resist a line like that one, because I *wanted* Chris and there was no guilt this time, and because I felt, as he probably did, that sex would chase away our sadness for a while.

"Why don't we just go to bed, then," I said.

I turned off the lamp and walked with him to my bedroom. I kicked off my flip-flops and found a stretchy to tie back my wet hair. When I turned around, Chris was pulling off his shirt. He was less tan than when I'd seen him before—perhaps from working all summer—but the color he did have accented his well-defined abs. He had two Chinese characters tattooed on his right arm, meaning good fortune, something I'd nearly forgotten about. I reached up and stroked his chest with my hands.

He leaned down and kissed me, his tongue in my mouth. He

laid both hands on my breasts and, through the fabric of my tank top, circled my nipples with his thumbs.

"You know what the first thing you ever said to me was?" I asked. "When you were tending bar at that wedding?"

He shook his head almost imperceptibly, his eyes squinted.

"You asked me if I wanted a buttery nipple."

He smirked. "I couldn't disguise my fascination with you even then."

With both hands, he pulled my tank over my head and took my breasts in his hands, stroking and massaging them while he kissed me again. My heart was racing now, and my legs felt all rubbery.

Still kissing me, he laid the heel of his hand against my groin and pressed, released, pressed, released. I let out a moan, not meaning to. He yanked apart the top snap of my jeans, pulled down the zipper, and then tugged off both my jeans and under- wear. I tried to reach for the button of *his* jeans, but he lifted me and laid me back on the white duvet that covered my bed. He took off his own jeans and stepped out of a pair of gray boxer briefs. His naked body was as gorgeous as his face. It seemed almost illegal that I was about to have sex with someone who looked like that.

For the next hour, he did what he had promised—consumed me. His fingers and mouth explored every inch of me, making me writhe with pleasure. I could see that he was being driven in large part by his despair over Tom's death. Was this what you'd call a grief fuck? I wondered. Maybe, but it felt too good to worry about. By the time he finally entered me, I was barely thinking straight anyway.

I fell asleep almost instantly in his hard, strong arms, totally spent. But an hour and a half later, I woke, needing to pee, and then there was no going back to sleep for me. After pouring my- self a glass of milk, I absorbed the view beyond my terrace. Even at this hour, buildings were dabbed with lights—suggesting party animals and floor pacers like me. For two years after my divorce, I'd been dogged by merciless, unrelenting insomnia, which had finally abated about seven or eight months ago. Any bout of sleeplessness put the fear of God in me. I hoped tonight was a fluke, a response to all the thoughts bubbling in my head—about Tom's ugly death, sleeping with Chris, thinking about Beau the moment Chris had thrust himself into me. From my coffee table, I picked up *The New York Times* that had been delivered the day before and skimmed through it. At about three, I dozed off on my couch and then at five crawled back into bed with Chris.

"Where'd you go last night?" Chris murmured when we both woke at about seven.

"Just a little floor pacing—due to everything that happened. Want a bagel? They're frozen, but if you slather them with raspberry jam, you can hardly tell."

"Sure," he said, slipping his hand between my thighs.

We made love again, quicker but just as urgent on his part as before. While he showered, I made coffee, dug the bagels from the freezer, and scraped ice crystals off them.

"So what do we do from here?" Chris asked, plopping down at the old pine dining table at the end of my living room. For a second, I thought he was referring to *us*—where did *we* go as a couple from here—but then in relief I realized he was referring to Tom's death. Because I wasn't at all sure where we should go from here.

"Well, as we said last night," I said, "you should tell Harper—and the executive producer. I'm going to break the news to this guy Barish. I'm not sure how close he and Tom were, but it will probably be upsetting."

"But how are we going to know if it's really Tom or not—like you said, the cops have no obligation to tell us. We're not family."

"I've got a few ideas on how to stay on top of this," I said. "Leave it to me."

Chris took a final slug of coffee and raked his hand through his hair. "Listen, Bailey," he said. "A bunch of us from the show usually get together on Friday nights at this pub in Chelsea—the Half King. It's mostly crew members and minor players, but everyone will be buzzing tonight about this. Do you want to come? Maybe we'll learn something about Tom we didn't know. Plus— I'd like to see you tonight. Every inch of you again, if it's okay with you."

"Sure, that would be great," I said, smiling—and meaning it.

"I'll call you when we finish up—it could be as late as eight tonight. If it's all right with you, I'll just meet you at the Half King."

After he'd left, kissing me gently good-bye, I grabbed my phone and called Detective O'Donnell.

"Goddamn," he muttered after I broke the news. "I said I didn't have a good feeling about this one."

I described the whole awful situation to him, and he pressed me for even more details. I sensed him silently calculating whether he could have done anything to prevent Tom's death.

"I'll touch base with the sheriff up there," he said, "and see what I can find out. The state troopers will probably get involved, too, and I've got contacts at their headquarters down here."

"I was thinking I'd better phone Mr. Barish as soon as I got off with you."

"Why don't you let me do that for you?"

"Great, thanks. But tell him he's welcome to call me if he'd like." I also asked if he'd call Professor Carr and break the news to him, since that was about the last thing in the world I wanted to do. He agreed and took down the info.

"May I call you in a day or two, just to see what you've learned from the sheriff's office?" I asked in closing.

"Sure. I'll tell you what I can."

After obtaining the number from directory assistance, I phoned Nest of Treasures, the antiques store I'd stopped in front of in Andes. I wasn't sure anyone would be in yet, but a woman answered and it was the same husky voice that had given me directions to Dabbet Road yesterday. I asked if it was Beverly.

"Yes, this is she." She sounded positively grim. Something told me the news had found its way to her.

"This is Bailey Weggins, the woman who asked directions to Dabbet Road yesterday. Have you heard about Tom Fain?"

"Good God, yes. Someone called me just a little while ago. You're the one who found him?"

"Yes, right after I left you. I wanted to call and let you know since you seemed to be a friend of his family."

"That was very kind of you. I'm devastated, of course—we all are. They were such a lovely family. You'd think there'd been a curse against them."

"In what sense?"

"The father dying, then Margo. And now poor Tom. They say they don't know how he died. That someone may have killed him. Or it may even have been suicide. What—what do you think happened?"

"I just don't know. Did Tom have any problems or issues with anyone up there?"

"Goodness, no. He'd actually spent very little time here after he started high school. Kids always feel there's nothing for them to do up here. Margo let the place go after her husband died, and once she became ill, she was rarely here, either. Tom only came back recently to sell the place."

"Tom told a mutual friend of ours that he'd actually sold the house earlier in the summer."

"Supposedly, yes, to some yuppie types—of course they don't call them that anymore. But in the end, the couple couldn't get a mortgage and had to pull out. There were no other bites this summer, apparently, and the real estate agent told Tom he'd have more luck if the house was in better shape."

"So he was trying to do it himself?"

"He was doing an odd job here and there from what he told me, but he'd hired Barry to do the bulk of it."

"Barry?"

"Barry's a kind of handyman/contractor up here. Tom had asked him to do some work on the house. Barry was waiting for the go-ahead two weeks ago but never heard from Tom."

I thought of the $7,000. "Would he have expected an advance?"

"I imagine so. That's how it usually works."

I asked her then if she would be willing to check with this Barry dude and let me know if he'd definitely been expecting a cash advance from Tom. She seemed hesitant, as if suddenly second-guessing her forthcomingness.

"Beverly, Tom apparently had a lot of cash on him, and I'm wondering if he may have been robbed. My goal is to find out who did this to him."

That seemed to reassure her. I promised to call back in a day or two. I had the feeling she was going to prove to be a good source for me.

Since the *Times* was predicting another day of warm weather, I threw on a tan-colored miniskirt, a sleeveless black top, and black slingbacks. Ten minutes later, I was on the train to *Buzz*. Tom Fain was no A-lister, but he was nonetheless an actor in a big new show, and Nash would probably want a small item about his death.

Fridays are always a pretty happening day at *Buzz*. Monday is the big closing day, when the cover story ships along with the other major "news" stories—about who dumped whom, who's shagging whom, and how many kids Angelina Jolie is thinking of adopting *this* week. It's also when the nasty gossip section "Juice Bar" gets written. (Never—let me repeat, *never*—get on their radar.) But many of these stories start coming to a head on Friday, and writers and editors start racing around out of their minds, as if we'd just landed a man on Mars.

I dumped my stuff on my desk and surveyed the scene. Leo was tapping away at his computer. Jessie's desk was empty, but there were corn muffin crumbs on the top of it.

"Jessie get her bikini line taken care of?"

"Yeah, but she's been in and out today. Something to do with Usher." Part of Jessie's job was to cover the music scene.

"You seem crazed."

"Yeah, well, I'm supposed to be doing a whole page on guys with back fat, and so far I've got only four. Any ideas?"

"No, but I'll keep my eyes peeled."

I glanced down toward the glass-fronted office of Nash Nolan. He'd be busier than hell today, but I needed to see him. Though the light was bouncing off the glass, making it hard to see, I discerned movement in there and headed off in that direction.

Nash *was* inside, talking to Mary Kay, the sixtyish former gossip columnist, West Coast based, whom the late and much-loathed Mona Hodges had brought on as a consultant. According to all reports, the last truly pertinent piece of celebrity news she'd broken was Liz Taylor's remarriage to Richard Burton. She seemed to rub Nash the wrong way, but since shows like *ET* loved her sound bites, and that was good for the magazine, her job seemed secure for now.

I tapped on the frame of the open door. Mary Kay glanced over and shot me the kind of look she probably reserved for times when someone came down hard on her instep.

"Got a minute?" I asked Nash. "I have some news I want to share."

"Yup. Why don't we finish up later, Mary Kay."

"All right, Nash, but we need to move quickly on this," she said, and bustled past me, glancing disapprovingly at my outfit. She was in a lightweight peach wool suit, her champagne-colored hair up in a French twist and her legs swathed in white hose that vaguely resembled mosquito netting. She probably considered it a style sin that I was sporting summer clothes in mid-September.

"What's up, Bailey?" Nash asked as soon as Mary Kay was out the door. "Tell me you've got something good, okay? I don't have jack for the cover this week."

I liked Nash. He was in his forties, with a handsome, rugged face and stocky build, barrel-chested. He wore his gray-tinged streaked hair slicked back on the sides, and there was always a pair of reading glasses perched on either the top of his head or the middle of his nose. Rumor had it that he'd had more than one fling at work—which once resulted in his wife dropping by and hurling her purse at his head—and now and then you caught him staring at your tits. But he was a great words editor and easy to get along with.

"It's not cover-worthy, but it's interesting. There's a new show being shot in New York called *Morgue,* and one of the young male actors with a small part on it has been killed, probably murdered."

I explained my own involvement and provided the Cliff Notes version of the situation.

"Jesus, what is it with you, Bailey? You give new meaning to the word *deadline.*"

"Do you want a short item?" I said.

"How'd he die?" he asked, peering at me over the reading glasses.

"Stabbed or bludgeoned. Then burned."

"All your favorite things. Tell me he also dated Lindsay Lohan at some point and then we're golden."

"Not that I know of," I said, ashamed suddenly of how I was bantering about Tom.

"I'll give you a column."

"Fine."

"And Bailey," he said as I moved out the door. "Try to keep your rear out of trouble this time, okay?"

Before talking to Photo about calling in a shot of Tom, I sauntered back to the kitchenette for coffee. Up ahead of me I saw Mary Kay, chin in the air, making her way toward one of the back offices that was reserved for L.A. staff when they came east. She was probably in town for a few days visiting contacts, something she did every month or so. Leo once told me it was so she could blow through the spa services at her hotel and let *Buzz* pick up the tab. I remembered something else he'd once told me about her. She used to write a column for *Soap Opera Digest* and loved that whole world. I grabbed a cup of coffee and poked my head in her office.

"Sorry to barge in on you back there, Mary Kay."

"Obviously it couldn't be helped," she declared in a tone that said she thought it certainly *could* have.

"I'd love to ask your advice if you've got a minute."

"All right, but please be quick about it, Bailey. I'm doing a TV segment in half an hour."

As I stepped into the office and closer to her, I could see that she was already made up for her appearance. Her face was covered in so many layers of Pan-Cake makeup, you'd half expect to find the fossilized remains of early life forms in there.

"What do you know about Locket Ford?" I asked.

"*Locket?*" she asked in surprise. "If *you're* interested, it means she's been up to no good. What did she do—test positive for Botox?"

"I'm simply curious," I replied. "A friend of mine is working on her new show. Has most of her career been in soaps?"

"Yes—and she had an enormous following. I believe she fancies herself as the next Demi—leaving the soaps behind for major stardom. And then there's the book."

"Book?"

"*Locket Ford's Guide to Beauty.* It's a fall book—and there's a party for it at Elaine's tomorrow night. Alex is giving it for her."

I filed away that info for later.

"What buzz do you hear about the show?" I asked. It was a selfish question—I was curious what was in store for Chris.

"Well, everything Alex Ottoson touches is a hit. Locket's always been known as a real fame digger, and hitching her star to Alex's wagon was a brilliant move on her part, professionally. But if you ask my opinion, nothing could be worth *that.*"

"What do you mean?" I asked. I felt a tingle at the back of my neck.

"Oh, he's a nasty man. He's all debonair when you meet him, but he's got a cruel streak. And there's a rumor around that he likes to slap when he's mad."

CHAPTER 7

Do you think it's true? Do you think he's abusive to her?"

"Don't tell me you want to run with this, Bailey. I was speaking off the record here."

I suppressed a sigh of exasperation. "Like I said, I'm just curious. I have a friend on the show."

"Well, for God's sake don't attribute anything to me when you're speaking to this friend of yours. And of course, if you pick up anything yourself, I hope you'll pass it on to me. Now, if you don't mind, I do need to freshen up for my segment."

As I walked back to my desk, I mulled over her revelation. Alex was nasty. Alex was possibly violent. What if he had gotten wind of Locket's toe-curling fling with Tom? Could he have followed Tom to Andes and killed him in a rage?

Tonight, there'd be a chance to chat with people from the show—though according to Chris, probably only minor players would be there. What I needed to do was crib an invitation to the party at Elaine's tomorrow night—for a firsthand look at both Locket and Alex. I certainly wasn't going to ask Mary Kay for help. She'd probably do her best to have me barred at the door. When I returned to my desk, I called the chick who oversaw the beauty coverage at *Buzz* and asked if she could get me into the event.

"You can have *my* invitation. There's a party for Jessica Simpson's beauty products I'd much rather go to anyway. Just let me know if anything good happens so I can file it."

Over the next hour, I drafted a brief write-up on Tom's death, knowing I'd have to flesh it out once I learned more. As promised, the beauty editor dropped off the invitation. Just as I was packing up my stuff to leave, Jessie strode in and plopped down at her desk.

"What's up?" she asked, her caramel eyes curious. "No offense, but you look like you haven't slept in four days."

I suggested we secure some coffee, and after grabbing two cups, we settled in an empty conference room, where I shared everything that had happened.

"Gosh, that's grisly," she said, frowning. "Any ideas about who did it?"

"Not so far. But you can help if you want. There's a book party for Locket Ford tomorrow night. It would be great if you could come with me. Having two sets of eyes and ears will be an advantage."

"Sure. I've got a date, but I've been looking for an excuse to bail. When this guy hits the dance floor, you worry the paramedics are going to show up looking for the person having the seizure."

After we finished talking, I headed home. As soon as I entered my apartment, I staggered toward my bedroom and fell on the bed, wasted. I craved a catnap, yet sleep eluded me. I kept seeing that horrible maggoty mess in the tub, and then my mind would ricochet to the lovely face of Tom Fain from his head shot. His family *did* seem cursed, just as Beverly had suggested. I also couldn't stop thinking about Chris. Had it been dumb to go to bed with him considering the circumstances? Would I soon regret the "we're both really sad so let's fuck" sex? But my interest in Chris had been rekindled *before* I'd found Tom's body, and there had to be more to our encounter than shared grief. I still missed Beau, ached for him, really, but it wasn't as if he were pounding at my door. For all I knew, he might even be back from Turkey by now. Stop thinking for one goddamn minute, will you, Bailey, I begged myself. Finally, from pure exhaustion, my mind shut the hell up. When I woke, the room was dim and the clock read 6:30.

At around seven-thirty, Chris called to say that they'd finally wrapped for the day and I could head over to the bar in about an hour. After speaking to him I left a message for Sheriff Schmidt, saying I'd like to touch base with him. Then I phoned Beverly, just to check in.

"I was just going to call you, dear," she said. "I hung up with Barry only a minute ago—it took me all day to get in touch with him. You were right. Tom asked Barry to do some work on the house, and he was supposed to give him a cash advance."

"What kind of work was Barry going to do?"

"Put in a new kitchen. It wasn't a total overhaul—just some new appliances and a new floor. He was also going to oversee the painting of the exterior. Apparently, Tom was trying to do a little bit of interior painting himself."

"Okay, thanks, Beverly. Let me know if you find out anything else, will you, please?" I wondered if she had really been planning to call me.

There was a long pause.

"They apparently found Tom's wallet in his pants," she said finally, her voice choking. "And there was a lot of cash."

"So I guess there's very little doubt now," I said quietly. "I'm sorry, Beverly. I'm sure this is hard for you."

After I hung up, I sat on my terrace for a while, watching the dusk turn to night. I was glad I was going out tonight. I was glad I would be having sex with Chris later and could push thoughts of Tom out of my head.

Just as I was heading out the door, my cell phone rang.

"Is this Bailey Wiggins?" a man asked in the no-nonsense, authoritative tone of someone used to getting his way.

"Weggins, actually."

"It's Robert Barish. Detective O'Donnell gave me your number. He said you found the body, but it's not a hundred percent clear that it's Tom," he said. "Please tell me everything you know."

Conscious of his need to know but also of the fact that I was now running late, I spelled out everything as concisely as possible—and shared the news about the wallet. He immediately began lobbing questions at me—how did I know Tom, why had I gone to Andes?

"Mr. Barish, I want to be of help to you, but I'm heading off to meet Tom's friend Chris right now. Actually, I'm going to be with some people from the show—and maybe I'll learn something. I could give you a ring tomorrow."

"Are you going to the set?" he asked agitatedly, "Is that what you're saying?"

"No, to a pub not far from there on Twenty-third Street. Do you want to talk tomorrow?"

He said he'd prefer to meet in person and suggested four o'clock at his office in midtown. I hesitated, not overly eager to drag myself up there on a Saturday, but I also knew that having him as a contact could prove useful. As soon as I'd agreed and signed off, I flew out the door, grabbing my jeans jacket as I left—it was supposed to be cooler tonight.

I'd heard of the Half King but had never been there. It turned out to be part neighborhood hangout/part Irish pub/part trendy night spot. And it was already packed. The bar in the main area, lit by several orange-coated hanging lights, was lined about three to four people deep, and the wooden booths across from it were all filled. Chris was nowhere in sight. I could see a back room from where I stood, as well as a brick-walled room on the side, filled with tables. That seemed the most likely spot for a large group to congregate. As I began to muscle my way into the side room, I spotted Chris edging through the crowd toward me. He held my eyes intently.

"Hi," he called over the din as he drew closer. His face looked freshly scrubbed of makeup, and he was wearing just jeans and a gray T-shirt. Wrapping one of his taut, muscular arms around my waist, he planted a soft kiss on my cheek. I felt myself stir from his touch.

"The gang all here?" I asked.

"About fifteen of them. Some crew, the second ADs, a few of the actors . . ."

"Locket, by any chance?"

"No, but there's a rumor she's stopping by. Let me get you a drink at the bar. It takes forever to flag down a waitress in there."

He grabbed my hand, and we snaked our way over to the bar. A spot opened up miraculously just as we got there. Chris ordered us two draft beers. As we waited side by side, I realized for the first time that there was music pounding underneath all the voices. U2, maybe. It was hard to tell. What wasn't hard was noticing all the chicks checking out Chris.

"How *are* you tonight?" I asked him as he passed me my beer. Since he wasn't budging from the bar area, I had the feeling he wanted to talk alone for a few minutes.

"Not great. My scenes today all called for me looking as grim as possible, so that made it a little easier."

"I've got a bit of news," I said. I told him about the wallet.

"So that pretty much confirms it, doesn't it?"

"I'd say so—though the final verdict will come with the DNA. What about Harper? I assume you've told her the news."

"I wanted to do it in person, and I certainly didn't want to do it on set, so I called her at her office and asked her to grab coffee with me during one of my breaks. She figured something was up, so she just kept demanding that I tell her why I was calling, right then and there. She was practically shrieking at me. And then when I told her about you finding the body, she just went totally silent—for like thirty seconds. I think she'd convinced herself that Tom had just taken off. And then she started to bawl. I felt really bad for her."

"Has word spread?"

"Oh yeah. I told one of the supervising producers, and Harper told people—and then the cops showed."

"From the sheriff's office?"

"No, these guys were state police. I guess the downstate part of the investigation has been turned over to them. They talked to me for about a half hour. I could tell from their questions that they'd been to his place—the super must have let them in—so the issue of me having to turn over my key never came up."

"Could you get any sense from their questions what they're thinking?"

"Not really. They asked if he'd been depressed—and whether he had any enemies."

"Be prepared for things to get ugly when they find Locket's note."

Chris pursed his lips and looked away.

"What?" I asked.

"I went over there after I left your place this morning and took the note."

"Chris, why would you do that?" I exclaimed. "That's evidence."

"Oh, come on, Bailey. We both know Locket didn't drive up there and set Tom on fire. I doubt she even knows there's an upstate. I just didn't want to cause trouble for her—and the show—unnecessarily."

"Maybe she didn't do it, but you can still end up in a lot of trouble for removing evidence. Promise me you'll think about it. You can still hand it over to them."

"Okay, I'll think about it," he said, flashing me one of his dazzling smiles meant to quell further protests from me.

"As long as we're confessing, I need to tell you that I filed a short story on Tom today—I would have been covering his death even if I'd never heard of him. But I included nothing the two of us discussed. That's between you and me."

"Wow, I never even thought of that. I guess I'm going to just have to trust you," he said somberly.

"You can," I assured him. "It's probably best not to tell anyone here what I do, but I also don't want to out-and-out lie. You could just say I'm a writer if anyone asks."

"Don't worry. People in show business *rarely* ask what other people do."

"Why don't we head into the other room?"

The group from *Morgue* was at the far end of the side room, at seven square tables they had apparently dragged together. Chris led me to the closest and pulled over a chair next to the one he'd obviously been sitting in. A few people farther down the table glanced in our direction. The mood seemed awfully somber, though there was enough conversation going on that Chris managed to introduce me only to the people right around us—a line producer named August who looked as if he were no more than twenty-one, a guy named Steve who Chris said played Brad on the show and had teeth as white as a new Sub-Zero freezer, and a gorgeous young black woman named Amy, wearing an off-the-shoulder rose-colored sweater and dangly gold earrings.

"Is Deke here?" I whispered into his ear.

"Deke? Why?"

"Harper said Tom palled around with him."

"Yeah, he's the beefy dude, the one in the T-shirt that says Mudfest 2004," he said into my ear, indicating with his eyes a guy way down the line. Deke was hoisting a glass mug of beer to his mouth and nodding to a fellow next to him, who looked as if he were crew, too.

Aware that several people at the table were watching us whisper, I turned my attention back to the group immediately around us and offered a smile that I hoped seemed friendly and inviting.

"You guys were smart to get drinks at the bar," Amy said. "I'm nursing my martini because it took about an hour for it to materialize."

"Amy works in PR—along with Harper," Chris said. I figured that was code for "She's in the loop on everything that's going on."

"How has response to the show been so far?" I asked.

"Great. We did our press party on the set—you know, in the morgue—and people went nuts."

"It must be an interesting show to publicize," I said.

"It has been—at least up until today. If you're a friend of Chris's, you must have heard the news about Tom Fain."

"Yes—have you already started to get calls about it?"

"A few—the word is just leaking out. What I'm waiting for is someone to start implying there's a jinx of some kind—you know, 'Work on *Morgue*, end up in one.'"

"Did you know Tom?" I asked.

"Not all that well. But Harper told me what a nice guy he was."

I was aware suddenly that Chris, who had been talking to Steve, had stood up and pulled a cell phone out of his pocket. He listened for a moment and then threaded his way toward the rear of the room, near a doorway to the outside garden area.

"That's what Chris told me—what a nice guy Tom was," I said. "It's so hard to imagine someone killing him." I let the remark just hang there, hoping she had an insight to share.

She shook her head, her dangly earrings flopping back and forth with each turn. "It's all just unbelievable—but you know, the weekend he disappeared, Harper had almost a sixth sense about it. I mean, she *felt* something was wrong."

So Amy *did* have an insight worth sharing.

"How do you mean?" I asked as nice and easy as I possibly could. I was afraid that if I got too pouncy, she'd drop the bulletproof shield PR types have practically trademarked.

"You know the stories about how people get a weird vibe before they get on a plane and end up changing their flight? It was kind of like that. We were out in L.A. meeting with folks from the network, and after Harper talked to Tom on Friday, she just got this really funny feeling something was the matter. She ended up taking the red-eye on Friday night instead of coming back Sunday."

I flashed back to my conversation with Harper. She might not have actually *said* she'd returned on Sunday, but she'd told me that was the plan and had *implied* she'd followed it. Liar, liar, pants on fire.

"Oh, so she got to see Tom before he left," I said, again all nice and easy. I felt like someone trying to pluck a dropped earring from the edge of an open drain.

"No, he was gone by then, I think."

As I offered a benign, bewildered-by-life's-injustices expression, my mind began to race. What if Tom had been less vague with Harper about his plans for Saturday and had told her exactly where he was going? She might have been aware of exactly what kind of "work" he had to do. She could have taken the red-eye home from L.A. and then hopped in a car and headed for Andes. Perhaps she'd learned about Locket. She may have exploded in jealous anger at Tom and hit him over the head with something— like a tool he'd been working with. Or stabbed him. Then set his body on fire. The info was too slim to take to the police—it might land Harper in trouble for nothing—but I needed to talk to her and determine why she'd misled me.

Chris returned just then and plopped back down in his chair.

"That was Harper," he said, sighing. "She says she's out just wandering the streets not far from here. She sounds totally wigged out."

"Is there anything we can do?" Amy asked.

"If there is, she doesn't seem to know how to articulate it. . . . Oh wow, Locket and Alex are here."

I looked up to see a couple standing at the farthest table— they'd obviously come in from the door closer to that end of the room. Locket looked hip and cool despite what a long day she must have had. She was wearing skintight black jeans, boots and a hot pink turtleneck (also skintight) and was carrying a pink Birkin bag. Alex took a seat, but Locket began working her way down the row of tables, saying hello to people one by one. If she was overcome with grief, she wasn't giving it away.

Her scent arrived at our end about four minutes before she did—an intoxicating blend of what I guessed to be patchouli and vanilla. When she finally reached us, Chris stood up and gave her a kiss on the cheek. I was closer to her than I'd been the day before, and I could see that though there were fine lines around her face, they did little to detract from her other attributes—the platinum hair, the large blue eyes, and skin as white and luminescent as the inside of a scallop shell. And then there were the lips. In some ways, they were like fake boobs—they might be absurdly larger than normal, but you couldn't peel your eyes off them.

"Bailey," she said after Chris introduced us. She let her eyes roam over my face, as if she'd been given permission to search it. "How does one end up with a name like that?" There was an edge to her words, and she looked intently into my eyes. The thought that bounded instantly through my mind was: Does she *know* me somehow?

"It's just one of those old family names that you end up with regardless of whether you're a girl or a boy. I believe it means the wall of the castle."

She wrinkled her nose in a manner that suggested my answer didn't smell right to her.

"Your name is quite unusual, too," I added, hoping to engage her a little in conversation. "Where does it come from?"

"You'll have to ask my mama that," she said, dismissing me, and then rounded the corner to greet Amy. When she moved past Chris, she gave his arm a squeeze.

As we sat down, she worked her way up the other side of the table, back toward Alex. I leaned toward Amy again, hoping to restart the conversation, but Chris's cell phone rang. All I heard him say was, "Okay, I'll meet you right in the front." That didn't sound good to me.

"That was Harper again," he said into my ear. "She's outside the bar. I'm going to meet her for a minute, maybe take her out in the garden and see if I can talk her off the ledge. Are you cool with that?"

"Uh, sure." I didn't like it, but what was I going to do? I had my own questions for Harper, but this wasn't the time or the place.

"Are you going to be all right hanging here for a while?"

"Actually, I'm done with my beer, and I think I'll just grab another at the bar."

Amy had ambled down to the middle section of the *Morgue* tables, and it didn't look as if she'd be missing me. As I stood up to make my way to the bar, I noticed Locket, now back with Alex, whisper something into his ear. He looked away from her and directly at me, his high forehead gleaming from the light. Was it just a coincidence? Again, I had that odd sensation that she knew me. Had I been marked as a *Buzz* reporter?

After fighting my way to the bar, I asked for another Guinness. Just as the bartender, a stocky redheaded guy, slid it toward me, a stool opened up. I decided to hop on and bide my time there. From that position, I could see into the side room and watch the goings-on.

Over the next ten minutes, I perched on the stool and nursed my mug of beer. Other than having to hose down two horn dogs who came on to me, I was left to my own devices in the orange glow from the bar lights.

It just happened that I glanced up at the moment Chris entered the pub with Harper. They stood at the front door, with her shaking her head vehemently and him clearly trying to soothe her. The whole scene bugged me. This was the guy I'd slept with last night, who'd announced he wanted to consume every inch of me. Though I knew he'd been called on to help Harper in her grief, it looked as if they were in the midst of a lovers' spat—he was mad, perhaps, that she'd been flirting with other guys, or she was pissed because he never called when he said he would. I felt that odd little sensation in the pit in my stomach, the kind you get when a guy you've gone to bed with for the first time unexpectedly starts putting on his pants at five the next morning with some story about a very early meeting, which if he doesn't haul butt to could lead to the collapse of not only the World Bank, but possibly even Western civilization. As I watched them surreptitiously, Harper suddenly looked all the way down the bar and made eye contact with me. Chris followed her gaze. His eyes seemed to plead for patience.

"Where'd your date go? He didn't abandon you, did he?"

Expecting to see another horn dog, I spun around to discover Deke's large head four inches from my own. He smelled like sweat, onions, and grease, and he eyed me up and down as if I'd just stripped to my panties. I would have liked to hose *him* down instantly, but it was a golden opportunity for me, my chance to finally learn what he knew about Tom.

"He's talking to Harper right now," I said. "She's pretty upset—about that actor Tom Fain." I figured I might as well jump right in and see what I turned up.

"Oh yeah, that's a real bummer. I'm Deke, by the way. Deke Jacobus. This is Danny De Mateo." He indicated his sidekick with a flick of his head.

"Bailey Weggins," I said, shaking Deke's hand, which felt as thick as a baseball mitt and as rough as plank wood. Danny shook my hand, too. He was tall and wiry, with frameless glasses that magnified his eyes so much, he looked like a bug.

"So you an actress?" Danny asked.

"God, no," I said. "The last time I was on stage I was playing a Pilgrim in a grade-school production. All they let me do was carry a squash." I flashed a little smile at the end, though trying to flirt with these two dudes was about as much fun as licking the inside of someone's shoes.

"So then how do you know Jared?"

"Pardon me?" I said.

"Chris, aka Jared. The guy who's supposed to give Dr. Mc-Dreamy a run for his money." He said the last part sarcastically, which was ironic considering Deke, with his thick, broken nose and greasy, dirty blond hair, was about as dreamy as a Spam sandwich.

"We're old friends," I said. "I know Harper, too. This is just awful for her—I mean, what happened to Tom."

Danny had turned away at this point, to shout an order to the bartender. Deke just let the remark hang there.

"You knew Tom, right?" I said.

"Yeah, about as well as you ever get to know any of the actors on a set."

"But I thought you guys played cards together. Harper said you even went to Atlantic City together."

He stared hard into me with slate-colored eyes. "Harper still has a real thorn in her claw about that Atlantic City trip, doesn't she."

"She didn't like Tom hanging at casinos?"

"That wasn't the prob. Tom had just started dating Harper, but on that trip he brought along this other chick—some actress."

Blythe? I wondered. In the days before she'd become a real pain.

"Was Tom much of a gambler? Do you think that could have anything to do with his death?"

"What are you anyway—a little Miss Marple?"

"Just curious."

"I really haven't a clue," he said, and moved past me, his thick thigh rubbing hard against mine. He and Danny claimed a spot halfway down the bar in the middle of the crowd.

Something was odd. It was clear Deke didn't like discussing Tom, and it wasn't because he was in mourning. I looked down the bar to the front door, hoping to catch Chris's eye again. I thought I spotted the edge of his shirt, but some other patrons were blocking him from complete view and there was no sign of Harper. This was starting to get *really* annoying. I turned and checked out the side room. A few chairs at the *Morgue* tables were empty now, and Locket and Alex were standing, clearly ready to be on the move. Locket glanced through the doorway in my direction and just for a second locked eyes with me, then looked away. Something caught my attention out of the corner of my eye, and when I turned my head, I spotted Amy standing by the door of the garden, gesturing for me to come over. After shrugging off my jeans jacket to save my stool, I headed over there, weaving my way through the crowd.

"What's up?" I asked.

"What's going on with Harper, anyway? I saw her at the end of the bar a few minutes ago."

"She's pretty upset, apparently. She showed up here and Chris is trying to talk her off the ledge."

"I know this sounds rude, but I hope she's going to be able to work next week. We're only two weeks from the premiere."

"I'm sure she'll pull it all together," I said, having no idea whether she could or not. Amy sighed, said good-bye, and wandered off. It took me a second to realize my cell phone was ringing.

"Hey, it's me," Chris said. "Harper's in the ladies' room right now, and when she comes out, I'm going to run her home in a cab. Are you cool with that?"

"Sure," I said, though I was actually sick of Chris playing baby-sitter.

"Do you want to wait here and I'll come back for you?"

"How long do you think it will be?" I asked.

"Not long—maybe fifteen, twenty minutes. She lives straight east of here—around Gramercy Park."

"Why don't you call me when you're done. If it's not too long, I'll stay; otherwise I'll head back to my place. You could come by—if you want."

"Great, I'd love that," he said.

The ladies' room was just around the corner, and before heading back to the bar, I slipped in there, curious. Harper was standing at the sink, staring at her reflection in the mirror.

"Harper, I'm so s—"

"Do you think he suffered?" she demanded, her penny eyes catching the reflection of my eyes in the mirror.

"I don't know—I hope not," was all I could muster. She stomped past me in her cowboy boots, as if my response had irritated her to death.

Two minutes later I threaded my way back to my stool. A pack of girls, all in low-slung pants or minis, shouted to one another nearby as they surveyed the room like falcons. Deke and Danny had slipped off to parts unknown. I continued to sip my beer, trying to decide whether to stay or leave. Was I right to be *this* annoyed? I asked myself. If Chris was just taking Harper home, why not let me ride along in the cab and then head to my place together? Finally deciding to blow the place, I slid off my stool. One of the girls next to me asked if she could have it.

"Sure," I said. But it came out "Sllur." Suddenly it was as if I were watching myself from far above me. And as I watched, the only thought in my mind was, God, you're drunk. Really, really drunk.

CHAPTER 8

The first thing I became conscious of was that it was cool, almost cold, out—and that I was shivering. I crossed my arms over my torso and rocked back and forth to generate heat. Just that small movement seemed exhausting, and I lowered my head, catching it in my hands. I could see my thighs, but my feet, I realized, were in darkness. And there was a taste of vomit in my mouth. I popped my head up. I was sitting on the stoop of a brick town house on a street lit only by the glow from streetlamps and the random lights on buildings. I glanced to the right and then the left, my heart pounding. I didn't have a clue where I was—or how I had gotten there. And from the emptiness of the street, I knew it had to be very, very late.

My first urge was to run, just tear down the street like a bat out of hell. But I was too tired even to move. My arms and legs felt as if they'd been poured with wet sand. I took a deep breath, trying to calm myself—and to think. What was this street, and what was I doing here? Even in the dark I could see that the street was pretty, tree lined, with mostly brick-fronted four-story or five-story buildings. I wasn't in the Village, I was pretty sure—the side streets there were much shorter. And the stoops here weren't high, like the ones on the Upper West Side.

I glanced to the left again. There were several more town houses and a big, white-brick apartment building and then the cross street, a few cars whizzing along it. It was an avenue, but I had no idea which one. Side streets this long might mean Chelsea. *Chelsea.* And then, like a wine stain spreading on a tablecloth, I began to see in my mind the Half King on 23rd Street. I had been there with Chris, and we had been talking to people, and then Chris was leaving and I was alone.

My arm jerked, and I felt clunkily for my purse. It was there, beside me on the cool stone steps. I dug through for my phone, flipped it open, and looked for the time: 3:47. God, I'd arrived at the pub just before nine. I didn't remember leaving. I remembered saying good-bye to Chris and being at the bar. But that was all.

A sound in the street—a scratching noise—startled me. I glanced up to see a rat the size of a tabby cat scoot from under a car and scurry across the road. My head had started to throb, and I fought off the urge to cry. I wanted to run, to get *out* of there. Though the strength was returning to my arms, my legs still felt leaden, and I couldn't imagine how I could get my body to move.

I forced my mind back to earlier. Why had Chris left me? *Harper.* That was it—he'd been taking her home. But he'd been coming back for me, hadn't he? And then I remembered. I'd decided to leave. And I was slurring my words. I'd felt woozy, plastered actually. But I'd had only two beers. And suddenly it hit me like a bloody hammer. Someone had put something into my drink—a roofie, maybe.

Fear overwhelmed me, squeezing my breath out. Had it been

a guy planning to date-rape me? I glanced at my clothes. They weren't disheveled. But where had I been for the past hours?

For an instant, I thought of calling 911. I realized, though, that it might take fifteen minutes for a patrol car to show, and I couldn't bear the thought of sitting alone in the dark here any longer. I flexed my feet several times. Miraculously, they felt much lighter now, and I was pretty sure I was going to be able to move. I shook out my arms and legs, trying to jump-start them.

And then my phone rang. I jerked my hand in surprise, as if the phone were electrified. I knew it had to be Chris. He had said he'd come back for me. He must be crazy wondering where I was.

"Hello," I said breathlessly.

The sound that came through from the other end was ugly and horrible. It was someone laughing, not a man or a woman, but something almost inhuman. Laughing demonically. And then it disconnected.

I sat there almost paralyzed again, staring at the phone. From down the street to the left, I heard a muffled sound from near the parked cars across from the apartment building. Was it the rat? Could someone be down there, crouching behind one of the cars?

I inhaled as well as I could, grabbed my purse, and lunged from the stoop. I began to run in the direction opposite from where the noise had originated. At first, lifting my legs seemed nearly impossible, like fighting an undertow, but after a dozen strides, they found their strength again. As I tore down the street, it seemed as if my heart were beating so hard, it would soon outrun the rest of my body.

Within a few seconds, I could see the traffic light at the end of the street, where it met the avenue. But which avenue was it? Would there be anything open? Would there be cabs? I slowed just enough so I could turn halfway around. There didn't seem to be anyone behind me, but the street was so dark and leafy, it was hard to know for certain.

I stumbled a little when I spun back around, and as I caught myself, a stitch popped in my left side. I slowed my pace, rubbing my side with my free hand, willing the cramp away. As the pain ebbed, I picked my speed back up again.

I was almost at the corner now, and there was a building on the near right side—a small hotel, its ground floor lit up and the front door open. I staggered into the lobby. An older guy, fifty or so, was sitting on a bench just inside the lobby, reading a rumpled newspaper, and his head jerked up in surprise when I stepped through the open doorway.

"I think someone is following me," I sputtered, figuring the "I was slipped a roofie six hours ago and have no idea where I've been since then" excuse wasn't going to make much of a dent with this guy. As it was, he looked as though he wanted me out of his lobby as fast as possible.

He craned his head so he could see behind me, a frown forming on his face.

"Look, miss, we can't help you here," he said in a gravelly voice. "We're just a hotel. You gotta call the police."

"Where am I, anyway?" I asked. "I mean—I know I'm in New York and everything, but what street is this?"

"Twenty-second Street," he replied almost reluctantly.

"That's Ninth Avenue, then?" I asked, tilting my head to the left."

"Yeah. Like I said, why don't you give the cops a call?"

"Sure," I told him. "Thanks for your help. It's nice to know that chivalry is alive and well in Chelsea."

Outside, I glanced up and down the street. There was no one in sight. I hurried the few steps to the corner and stepped onto the avenue. The entire block was empty of cars, the street pavement shimmering red from the traffic light, but several blocks farther down I could see cars bunched up at a light. Shivering, I glanced behind me. No one there. After what seemed an interminable wait, the traffic began to move again. I spotted a taxi with its top light on and threw up my arm. The second the cab stopped, I yanked open the door and jumped inside.

By the time I was back in my apartment, the fatigue had returned, but it was different now—not so much the leaden arm and leg thing, but an overall weariness. I stripped off my clothes and glanced over my body, checking for soreness or bruising. Then I popped two ibuprofen tablets and wolfed down a few stale saltines to help chase away the puke taste in my mouth. What I wanted more than anything was to sleep, but first I grabbed my BlackBerry and punched in the number for Dr. Paul Petrocelli, an ER doctor just outside of Boston whom I'd interviewed once for a story and now used frequently as a resource. I wasn't certain what his current work schedule was, but he favored the night shift. To my relief, he answered his phone. I asked if he had a few minutes to talk.

"Sure, no one's tried to drive through a tree tonight—yet," he said. "You don't sound so good."

"I don't feel so good, actually. I was out in a bar earlier, and I'm pretty sure someone slipped a drug in my drink."

"Were you assaulted?" he asked. His words were blunt, but I heard worry in his deep voice.

"No, I don't think so. I mean, I haven't got any bruises, and there's no sign whatever that I had sex." I had quizzed Paul easily about everything from poisoning to blunt trauma to the brain, but it was awkward to talk to him about my own body.

"So tell me what happened—though I take it you don't remember much."

"I don't remember *anything*. The last thing I know is that I was taking a swig of my beer at the bar, and then all of a sudden I felt completely woozy. A few minutes earlier, someone had called me over to talk, and I stupidly left my beer unattended. The drug could have been slipped in at—"

"Jeez, Bailey, if anyone should realize not to leave a drink on the bar, it should be you."

"I know, I know. Anyway, the next thing I realize, it's after three in the morning and I'm sitting on a stoop in pitch darkness. I had a headache, and I must have vomited somewhere because I could taste it in my mouth. Does it sound like I had a roofie?"

"How much were you drinking?"

"Why?"

"No offense, but it's not uncommon for women to think they've had a roofie when they've actually just overindulged. They assume they've been drugged because they can't remember anything, but what they've actually experienced is an alcoholic blackout."

"Honestly, I only had two beers. In fact, I didn't even finish the second."

"How many hours were you missing in action—give me a rough idea."

"Almost six."

"Did you come out of it pretty quickly—like you were popping awake?"

"Yeah, how'd you know?" I asked.

"I think what someone gave you was GHB. It's different from a lot of date-rape drugs in that the recovery time is shorter—and you just sort of come out of it with a jolt."

"Should I go to an ER and get my blood tested?"

"It only shows up in a urine test, and you have to do it within twelve hours. You still have time, but without any evidence of assault, most ERs won't administer the test for you."

I thanked him for the info and before signing off promised to provide an update later. Based on what he'd told me about my chances of getting tested, I decided that it was pointless to head to a hospital. My phone still in hand, I called up the log. The caller with the demonically evil laugh had rung me at three-fifty a.m. It had said "Caller Unknown," just as it had with the weeper's call on my way back from Andes. Were they the same person? I thought so. And was the caller the person who had drugged me? That laugh had been so knowing. It was as if the person on the other end had been fully aware that I was sitting alone in the dark, terrified, and had chosen to mock me. Even if the person wasn't close by, I sensed he or she knew I was alone and vulnerable. But why exactly was whoever it was doing this to me? Was the person Tom's killer? Did he or she know I was making inquiries?

While I sat there, bone tired with the phone in my hand, something else occurred to me. There were absolutely no calls in my log from Chris. If he had come back to the bar and not found me there, he should have been curious, even concerned—so why hadn't he attempted to track me down? I dragged myself off the couch and into my office to check the light on my phone. No messages. God, why hadn't Chris been worried about my whereabouts? He'd certainly been all fussy over Harper—was something going on with them?

On top of everything else that was happening, I now felt like giving myself a swift kick in the rear. On principle, I was in no way opposed to the occasional romp with a guy I'd never set eyes on again. But I couldn't bear the idea of going to bed with someone who made it *seem* as though it meant something when it really didn't. And then the next day you felt like shit.

I returned to the living room and flopped on the couch, pulling a throw blanket over me. For some reason, the couch just seemed more appealing to me than my bed—more womblike, I guessed—and that's what I needed at the moment.

When I woke three hours later, it was to the light coming through the windows of my living room and my head was still throbbing. I popped another ibuprofen and swung open the door to my terrace so that the fresh air rushed in. Part of me longed to sink into the couch again and spend the day in a fetal position. The emotional hangover I was experiencing from being drugged was almost worse than the physical one. But I now had too many urgent things on my plate to wallow in misery.

After making coffee, I headed for my computer and Googled GHB—or what turned out to be the official name, gamma-hydroxybutyrate, sometimes called "GHB" or "grievous bodily harm." What a perfect term for it. The side effects were just as Paul had described. In low doses, the drug produced a high or euphoric feeling and a loosening of inhibitions. But if you upped the dose just a little, all sorts of bad things occurred: nausea, head-ache, drowsiness, dizziness, amnesia, and loss of muscle control. And with just the right amount, there was a loss of conscious-ness, respiratory arrest, and then last but hardly least, death. *Fun!*

Despite the fact that the drug was illegal in most states, it would have been easy enough for someone to get their hands on it. Apparently, the most frequent users were clubbers, rave party participants, date rapists, strippers, and bodybuilders—who be-lieved it counteracted the negative effects of steroids. According to one site, all you had to do to score some was to walk in a gym and put the word out.

It also would have been simple for someone to slip it to me. It came in clear liquid form, and though it was salty, the taste was easily disguised by alcohol. Especially beer. I'd been drinking the perfect beverage for it. I cringed when I read that consuming GHB *with* alcohol increased the likelihood of death. It was lucky that I'd consumed less than two beers.

And just as Paul had pointed out, the effects of the drug lasted only about four to six hours, burning off quickly toward the end. There was one other fascinating tidbit buried on one of the sites: GHB could cause you to experience an out-of-body feeling. I suddenly remembered the sensation of slurring my words and simultaneously seeing myself from above as I did so.

That was enough research for the time being. Now I needed to get busy trying to find answers about what was going on. Not only was I on assignment for *Buzz* about Tom, but I also now had an urgent personal motive for trying to figure out who the murderer was: Someone was after me—and in all likelihood, it was the killer. I needed to know who it was before he or she did something worse than slipping a date-rape drug in my drink.

After plucking two eggs from my fridge, I scrambled them, made more coffee, and took my breakfast out to the terrace, along with a number two pencil and a black-and-white composition book. Whenever I'm working on a big reporting story, especially one with riddles and plenty of unanswered questions, I find it enormously helpful to jot down my musings in an old-fashioned composition book.

I spent the first few minutes creating a timeline of Tom's story and then fleshing it out with details I'd uncovered—about what Tom had been up to as well as the various players in his life. Then I started jotting down questions, beginning with the big fat obvious ones: Who had killed Tom—and why? Was it someone from Andes? Beverly had said it had been years since Tom had spent much time in the town, so the chances of anyone up there holding a grudge seemed next to nil. What about a stranger, though—someone who had showed up at the house thinking it was empty, only to discover Tom painting the bathroom. Would a burglar set a body on fire? It seemed unlikely.

Though the murder had taken place in Andes, it seemed far more logical to focus on Tom's circle of acquaintances in New York City—particularly people involved in the production of *Morgue.* There was the Nordic warrior and possibly abusive Alex Ottoson. Had Alex learned about Locket's fling with Tom and sought vengeance? He'd been snappish toward Tom during a recent taping, so he might have suspected the truth. But he would have had to know that Tom was traveling to Andes on Saturday, and if even Chris hadn't known, how would Alex have gotten wind of the plans?

And then there was the lusty-lipped Locket to consider. She'd been having a fling—or had *had* one—with a guy who was sleeping with someone else involved in the show. Certainly women *did* kill men in jealous rages, but how annoyed could Locket possibly have been over Tom's relationship with Harper? After all, she had Alex guaranteeing her fame and fortune. That was called having your cake and eating it, too. Plus, if Locket had minded Harper, and had verbalized that fact to Tom, it would have opened the door for Tom minding Locket's relationship with *Alex*. And there could be no way in the universe Locket would back out of *that*. She knew that without Alex's help, all the collagen and Botox in the world probably wouldn't catapult her into prime time.

Of course, she could be such a big diva that she wanted Tom to have the hots for her and her alone, despite her relationship with Alex. And that raised another point: What if Tom had fallen for Locket and had threatened to reveal his affair with her if she didn't dump Alex? Oh dear—Locket wouldn't have liked that at all.

Alex and Locket weren't the only people of interest. I had no good reason to suspect Deke, but I didn't like him. My encounter at the bar with him had seeped back into my consciousness, and the overwhelming sensation was of the nasty vibe he'd given off. And he hadn't seemed at all keen on discussing Tom. I tried to dredge up other elements of my brief conversation with him. I had mentioned the trip to Atlantic City, and he'd volunteered that Tom had brought an actress along—very possibly Blythe. Harper had learned about it, Deke said, and hadn't been happy. If I could reach Blythe, I might be able to discover more about that road trip.

Thinking of Harper nudged something else loose from my memory: what Amy had said about Harper returning to New York on Saturday, not Sunday. Of course, she was now supposedly in deep despair about Tom's death, desperate for Chris's shoulder to cry on, but that didn't necessarily undermine her likelihood as a suspect. In my days as a newspaper reporter, I had covered a case in which the most grief-stricken person on the scene was the killer. She had murdered her boyfriend because he'd been cheating, but she was still desperately in love with him and overwhelmed with a sense of loss.

All four people on my list of possible suspects had been at the pub last night. Any one of them could have slipped the drug in my drink after I'd followed Harper into the bathroom, including Harper herself, who'd departed before me. It seemed that whoever had done it must also be the killer. But why target *me*? Harper knew I was snooping around about Tom. Deke had called me a little Miss Marple. It seemed likely that whoever was harassing me believed I was playing detective.

But unless I wanted to assume the role of sitting duck, I was going to have to continue to play a little Miss Marple. At four p.m. I would be meeting Mr. Barish, which might provide more insight into Tom and his life. And at the book party at Elaine's, there would be more opportunity to study Locket. In the meantime, there were a few other things I could do.

The first was to try to piece together the missing hours of my life last night. At eleven I called the pub, figuring that they probably served lunch and there would be staff on the premises. I knew it wouldn't be wise to go on the offensive, proclaiming that I had been drugged. As a beat reporter, I'd learned that restaurant and bar people have a tendency to clam up and close ranks when they think you've got a gripe. I would have to try a different tack.

"You know the bartender with the red hair who was on last night?" I said after a youngish-sounding girl answered the phone.

"He wanted me to get him a phone number?" I lied. "Can I leave him a message?"

"You mean Rusty?" she asked after a moment's hesitation.

"Red hair? Kind of big?"

"Yeah, that sounds like Rusty."

"Would you mind taking down a message for him?"

I was pretty sure that she *would* mind.

"He'll be in at one today. Do you just want to call him back then?"

"Sure." But I wasn't going to call him. It would be smarter to just show up, let him see what I looked like, and watch his face and body language as he spoke to me. I checked my watch and decided I would set out for there shortly.

Next, a call to Harper. Again, I was going to have to proceed carefully and not box her into a corner about her travel plans the weekend Tom had gone to Andes. After all, she hadn't actually lied to me but had simply led me to believe she'd been in L.A. for the entire weekend. One strategy would be to cover that ground again with her, ask more specific questions, and see if she came right out and lied to me. If she did, *then* I would challenge her.

She answered her cell phone groggily, as if she were lying in twisted sheets, and I suddenly had this horrible image of Chris stretched out buck naked beside her. Had his grief counseling involved a long, sensuous shag, like what he'd offered me in my hour of need? Was that why he'd never called me last night and come back for me?

"Hi, Harper, it's Bailey Weggins," I said. My voice sounded unnaturally high, and I wondered if she could sense the rush of anxiety I'd just experienced. "How are you feeling today?"

"Just great," she answered sarcastically. "Can you call me back later? I didn't get much sleep last night, and I'm really trying to rest right now."

"Okay," I said. "In fact, would it be possible for us to get together at some point today?"

"What for?"

"I just wanted to talk about everything's that happened."

She sighed loudly. "I don't really care to talk about it—it just makes it worse."

"I understand. It's just that there are some details about Tom that I wanted to share with you." It was a cheap ploy, but I refused to allow her to dodge me. I could tell by the pause that it had worked.

"It will have to be tomorrow," she said finally. "There's a book party for Locket tonight and I'm coordinating it."

"The one at Elaine's."

"How do you know about that?"

"I'm actually going," I said. "A friend from work asked me to tag along." I wasn't going to give away that I'd hunted down an invite—from this point on it might be better not to reveal the extent of my snoopiness. "Why don't I look for you there."

"I'm not going to have any time to chitchat," she said almost sullenly. "What exactly do you mean by 'details about Tom'? You make it sound as if there were something bad going on with him."

"I didn't mean to imply that. Why don't I let you get back to bed and I'll see you later."

Harper might not be receptive to chitchat at the party tonight, but I would try to pull her aside for a minute. Tonight would also be a chance to really see Locket and Alex in action. But how was I going to learn more about Deke? Chris might be able to assist me on that one. Just thinking about him caused a pang. I had no idea what I wanted from him or exactly how I felt about him after our randy romp, but I hated how shabbily he'd treated me last night. At some point I was going to have to get in touch because I was dependent on his help in the case, but I felt awkward about phoning him right at the moment.

I nearly lurched to the shower and let the hottest water possible cascade over me. It seemed to wash away some of that slimy feeling that still clung to me from last night. While I toweled off afterward, a long-shot idea popped in my head. Maybe Blythe had phoned home again. She could provide info about the trip to Atlantic City—if she had, as I suspected, been the one with Tom. I decided to call Terry. At the very least, it seemed I should inform her about Tom's murder, which would give her extra incentive to have Blythe call me if she heard from her.

She answered the landline on the third ring, her voice sounding as irritated as when I'd talked to her in the vestibule. I started by breaking the news about Tom.

"Omigod," she said. I had the feeling that the excitement was going to make her weekend. "Blythe is going to die when she hears this."

"You haven't heard from her since I talked to you, have you?"

"No. God, I can't believe it. Do they know who did it?"

"Not that I'm aware of. But as you can see, it's important to have Blythe call me. I need to talk to her." I gave her my cell, home, and work numbers because I imagined the business card I'd handed her the other day had long since been tossed in the trash.

"If I hear from her, sure. What are they going to do about the show he's in?"

"I don't really know. Did Blythe ever mention going to Atlantic City with Tom?"

"Atlantic City? Yeah, she went with him—back in July, I think. She bought this little black dress that she thought would look like something a James Bond girl would wear at the craps tables in

Monte Carlo, but when she came back she said that all the other women were in track suits with fanny packs."

"There was another person on the trip, wasn't there? A guy named Deke?"

"I don't remember his name, but yeah, there was another guy. And he ruined the whole thing."

I caught my breath.

"How?" I demanded.

"He borrowed a huge amount of money from Tom. And then he wouldn't pay it back."

CHAPTER 9

How much money—do you know?" I asked her.

"Oh, it was a lot—like a couple thousand. They were at the blackjack table or the roulette table or whatever, and this guy—like I said, I don't remember his name—asked for a loan. He said he was on a streak and didn't want to lose it by having to go to an ATM. And then later he could only come up with, like, two hundred dollars. Tom and this guy had a big argument, and Tom and Blythe drove back early. The only reason I know about it is because Blythe was so pissed off that this guy ruined the weekend for her."

"Did Tom ever get the money back?"

"How would I know? Do you think that's the killer—the guy who borrowed the money?"

I told her I didn't know, but as I hung up I knew damn well that I now had a possible motive for Deke. If he had never repaid the loan, Tom might have been pressuring him to do so, possibly even making threats about taking the matter to a higher-up on the show. I was going to have to find out more.

For now I concentrated on the best way to extract info about my whereabouts last night. Because I wanted to convince the bartender Rusty that I wasn't a nutcase and troublemaker—and I would probably go directly from the pub to my meeting with Mr. Barish—I chose a blue-and-green Diane von Fürstenberg dress that I usually reserved for brunches at my mother's that involved shrimp salad and flan. As I reached for a jacket in my closet, I realized that my jeans jacket had never made it home with me last night.

As soon as the cab let me off in front of the Half King, I felt the muscles in my stomach tighten. I couldn't recall anything that had happened to me at the pub after around nine-thirty or ten, yet the sight of it made my tummy hurt.

Lunchtime was almost over, but there were still customers loafing at the tables outside, their elbows propped among empty bottles of Pinot Grigio and Saratoga water, their faces tilted to the sun. Once inside, I needed a minute for my eyes to adjust. There weren't many diners inside the pub—just one or two in the front room and, from what I could see, a few at the tables in the back garden. I scanned the bar area. A girl was working back there, a quizzical expression on her face as she surveyed a tab. No Rusty in sight. But just as I was about to inquire at the bar, he came around the corner, hoisting a case of Guinness on his shoulder. I shot a smile in his direction, hoping to start off on the right foot.

"You're Rusty, right?" I asked, stepping forward. He looked about ten years older in the half-light of day.

"Yup, what can I do for you?" he said, setting the case on the pockmarked wooden bar. It was not far from the spot where I'd sat the night before. As he looked up, I saw a flash of recognition in his eyes. He knew he'd seen me before.

"I was here last night with a bunch of people from that new show *Morgue*," I explained, figuring that mentioning the show would give me cred. "We were sitting in the other room, but then later I came out here with a few people and had a beer at the bar."

"Okaaay?" he said, dragging out the word in mock expectation of some kind of punch line from me. He didn't seem in the mood to gab.

"Something happened last night, and I could use your help. I promise it will only take a minute."

"Hey, if there's a problem, you really need to see the manager," he said. "He'll be in at three."

"I'd prefer to talk to you. I promise it will only take a minute."

A Hispanic busboy had emerged from the kitchen and began dragging a broom along the floor. Rusty glanced in his direction and back and then raised a large, freckled hand.

"So shoot."

"Do you remember me?" I asked. "I was down at this end of the bar, drinking a draft beer."

"Yeah, I remember."

"Someone put a drug in my drink, and I just want to know if you noticed anyone around who could have done it."

"Yeah, well, that really *is* something you should be talking to the manager about."

"I don't want to make any trouble. And there's no way the police could do anything, anyway. I think the person who did it might be someone I know, and I figured if you had worthwhile information, I could at least be on my guard with that person."

He sighed, flipped up a section of the bar that was on a hinge, and slid behind it. Effortlessly, he began sliding beer out of the case as if his arms were on pulleys and then dropped the bottles into a cooler under the bar.

"You were by yourself, right? But you talked to a couple of dudes at one point."

"Right. Could one of them have done it, do you think?"

"Don't know. It was pretty crazy here last night. What I do know is that you did seem kind of snockered all of a sudden."

"Did I say anything to you? Did I talk to anyone else?"

"Nothing to me. There were a bunch of girls nearby, trolling for guys, but I never saw you interact with them. You did talk to that black chick—after you made a trip to the head. By the way, you'd left your purse on the bar."

"But I talked to her over by the garden door," I said, lifting my chin in that direction.

"The one I'm talking about came right up to you by the bar— like I said, after you staggered back from the bathroom. Your hair was all wet around the edges then, like you'd dunked your face in the sink."

It must have been Amy. Perhaps something about my behavior had concerned her, and she had come up to see what was the matter. I closed my eyes and tried to conjure up a memory, *anything*. I recalled the sensation of water splashed on my face, but it may have been due solely to Rusty the bartender planting the seed.

"And then what happened?" I asked.

"You split, I guess. The next time I looked, there was someone else sitting on your stool. And no, you didn't leave a tip."

"Do you have any clue what time it—?"

My cell phone rang at that moment, and when I flipped it open I saw to my surprise that it was Chris. I asked Rusty to excuse me so I could take the call. He shrugged a shoulder as if he could have cared less what I did.

"Hey," I said, stepping away from the bar. Now that Chris had finally called, I wasn't exactly sure how to play it.

"Everything okay?" he asked, concern in his voice. Odd question from a guy who had ditched me at a bar the night before.

"Actually, no," I said. "Someone spiked my beer with a date-rape drug last night."

"*What?* Are you okay? Did—did anything happen to you?"

"Nothing bad happened from what I can tell. But there are still a lot of loose ends I'm trying to piece together. I'm at the Half King right now trying to get answers."

"Why didn't you call me?"

"*Call* you? You were supposed to come back for me. And then I never even heard from you."

"But you told me *not* to come back," he exclaimed.

"*What?* When we talked right before you left, you said you'd be back in fifteen minutes."

"But I got a text message from you when I was in the cab with Harper. It said you were splitting and not to come back. After dropping Harper off, I headed home."

My body went warm and liquidy, as if I'd been deboned.

"Read it to me, will you?" I demanded. "I need to know exactly what it says." I didn't use the option on my BlackBerry that saved text messages so I was going to have to take Chris's word for it.

"'Decided to leave, need sleep. Call you tomorrow.'"

I had no recollection of having sent it, which of course meant nothing because I couldn't remember anything past around nine-thirty or so. Yet I didn't think I *had* sent it. First, it didn't sound like me; and second, why would I have texted Chris instead of just calling him?

"I don't think I sent it. Someone may have gone in my purse. They could have overheard me talking to you and then would have seen yours was the last number on my log."

"God, I should have realized something was off. Who could have done it—some guy who was after you?"

I told him that I had to get back to my conversation with the bartender, but I would fill him in later.

"Tonight?" he asked.

"I'm going to Locket's book party. I want to see if I can engage her in a conversation about something other than the absurdity of my name."

"I wasn't planning on going, but since you're going to be there, I think I'll drop by—if that's okay with you. Maybe we could grab dinner after."

"Sure," I said. "I'm really relieved. I didn't understand why you hadn't gotten in touch."

"I never would have just left you there, Bailey. I feel terrible about what happened."

After signing off, I sauntered back over to the bar, where Rusty was wiping his hands on his tight gray T-shirt. He looked pleased as punch that I had returned for another round of Q&A.

"Just one more question," I reassured him. "Any idea what time I disappeared for good?"

"Nope, sorry. My best guess is that it was sometime around ten."

Amy might know, I thought. More than likely she would be at Elaine's tonight, and I'd be able to quiz her.

"Thanks for your help," I said, guessing from Rusty's expression that I'd used up his patience and it was time to leave.

"You know . . . ?" he said as I turned to go.

"What?" I asked, spinning around.

"Never mind."

"No, please tell me."

"Are you sure you didn't just get a little sauced? Sometimes girls get crazy thinking they were slipped a roofie when the truth is they were just pounding back one too many."

"Thanks for the insight," I said sarcastically, and hurried outside.

For the next hour, I combed the streets of Chelsea, starting with 22nd Street. In daylight, the street couldn't have been more charming. The block was lined with old brick buildings, and leafy plane trees ran along the outside of the sidewalk. Not far from Tenth Avenue, I was pretty certain I found the stoop I'd been sitting on the night before, but it could have just as easily been the one next door. A woman approached, pushing a stroller with a towheaded toddler, talking to him in a too loud, singsongy voice.

"That's a *very* smart answer," she said. "You are a *very*, *very* smart boy." I wondered how she'd respond if I suddenly asked: "By any chance did you happen to see me puking my guts out around here sometime last night?"

Systematically I made my way down every block from 25th to 21st between Eighth and Tenth avenues, hoping to jog my memory. Nothing seemed familiar to me. And there was no forsaken jeans jacket lying in a heap somewhere—that would have been scarfed up hours ago. At one point, moving north, I came to the block that Beau Regan lived on. There was no way I was going down there. I was pretty sure I'd never been on that block last night. I felt if I had, I would just know.

Though the skies were now a dazzling shade of blue and the day was as warm as yesterday, I felt overwhelmed with a forlorn feeling. Someone at the bar had not only drugged me, but riffled through my purse, used my BlackBerry to send a text message.

Or *had* they? What if, as Rusty had suggested, I'd simply overimbibed? The draft beer mugs at the pub had been hefty in size, and since I usually drank bottle beer, I *had* consumed a bit more than usual. If I'd been drunk, it was entirely possible that I'd decided to blow Chris off, since his coddling of Harper had started to work my last nerve. Man, it felt as though someone were fucking with my mind. The only thing that kept me from wanting to bawl my eyes out was the fact that Chris hadn't acted like a jerk after all.

At three-thirty, I threw in the towel. It was time to meet Robert Barish. After hiking through Chelsea, I had no energy for the train, so I hailed a cab and headed for East 43rd Street.

The building turned out to be on one of those short, cavernous blocks between Madison and Vanderbilt, just to the west of Grand Central Terminal. It was nearly deserted on the street and in the lobby, too. A security guard in white shirtsleeves sat in the crisp artificial coolness, staring desultorily at the *Daily News*. After motioning for me to sign the visitors log, he told me to take the elevator to the twelfth floor. The building looked like something out of a 1940s film noir—the marble lobby, the brass pointer above the elevator indicating the floors that were being passed. It was 1940s style on the twelfth floor, too, as if the area hadn't been touched in over sixty years. I walked down the wide, empty corridor, half expecting Sam Spade or Philip Marlowe to step out from behind one of the office doors with a frosted window.

Suite 1236 turned out to be all the way down one corridor and then another. It was so quiet on the floor, it seemed as if no one could possibly be here, that Barish had forgotten our appointment, but after I knocked on the door, I could hear the dull sound of footsteps from deep within. A man dressed in gray slacks and a gleaming blue dress shirt swung open the door and introduced himself soberly as Robert Barish. He was about six feet one and formidable looking, but his face was doughy, and there was a gut hanging over his pants, as if he'd stuffed his shirt with a small ham. He looked like the kind of guy who might suddenly turn purple one day on the squash court and be pronounced DOA while he was still in the ambulance

"Hello, Bailey—may I call you that?"

"Of course."

"I appreciate your coming to midtown," he said, leading me

through a small mauve-colored foyer. "I have a conference call with a client today, and I need to have all his paperwork in front of me."

"Are you a lawyer?" I asked. We were now in an open area of about four or five nondescript workstations, making our way to a doorway at the end that opened onto a spacious office filled with blond furniture and photographs of Barish shaking hands with husky men I didn't recognize.

"No, I'm a financial manager. I guide clients on everything from investments to estate planning."

"Was Tom Fain a client?"

"His parents were—not Tom himself. But I'm the executor of the Fains' will, so I had to spend some time with Tom for that reason. We weren't in contact all that much recently, but he was a fine young man, and as you can imagine, I'm devastated by what happened. Why don't you take a seat."

Though there was a sofa and two armchairs at one end of his office, he motioned to a chair on the opposite side of his desk and then skirted behind to his own chair. I felt as if I were on a freakin' job interview and that any minute he was going to start discussing the company's 401(k) plan.

"I finally managed to get hold of the sheriff's office," he said. "I know a bit more than when I spoke to you last night, but not much. You found the body in the main house?"

"Yes, in what I think must have been the master bathroom."

"What can you tell me about how Tom was killed?"

"It was pretty horrible. It appears he was stabbed or bludgeoned—there was a fair amount of blood—and then he was set on fire in the tub."

"Good God!" he exclaimed. "What kind of *animals* live in this world?" He turned right to gaze out the window—a view of nothing but windows of other buildings—and pulled on his chin. There was an oddly monochromatic quality to him: sandy blond hair with a hint of red, yellow brown eyes, a slightly ruddy face. I sensed I would forget what he looked like ten minutes after I left.

"Because the crime occurred upstate, I don't know how much time the police will devote to checking out matters down here," I told him. "I worry this case may fall between the cracks."

"Matters down here?" he said, narrowing his eyes. "What do you mean by that?"

"Well, unless Tom pissed off somebody in a town he rarely went to anymore, his killer had to come from his sphere of acquaintances down here."

"Are you saying that the motive wasn't robbery?"

"If it was, his murder is the biggest case of overkill I've ever seen—if you'll excuse the expression. Why would a burglar need to go to that much trouble?"

He raised his eyes and leaned back in his chair, one of those aerodynamic models that allowed him to put his whole weight on the back.

"Okay, I see what you're driving at," he said. "Any ideas who?"

"No, not at the moment." I certainly didn't feel comfortable sharing my suspect list with him.

"How is it that you ended up in Andes anyway?" he asked.

I explained how I had pieced it together after Chris had requested my help. He listened intently, watching me, it seemed, with a hint of skepticism, as if there were an element of my story that struck him as odd. He could prove to be a valuable resource, and I didn't want to alienate him. I decided to try a little stroking.

"Of course, you're a big part of the reason I found Tom," I said.

"How do you mean?"

"If you hadn't put a fire under the missing persons department, we might not have learned that Tom had headed north."

"Fortunately I was able to pull a few strings. After I learned from this kid Chris that Tom was AWOL and that the cops don't generally take action for missing young males—*despite* what we see on TV—I phoned one of my clients in media, and he made the call to the right person. It didn't get us more than a cursory effort—but at least you took the initiative to follow up on it. I want to thank you for what you did. As horrible as the outcome was, you must feel relieved to have all this behind you."

"Well, I'm not done yet," I said. "I'm still poking around."

"Is that really wise?" he asked. "It sounds like we're dealing with a real monster."

"Well, like I said, I don't know how much time and effort the sheriff's office will give the case down here. Besides, I plan to be careful."

I didn't point out to him that the night before, I'd spent six hours upchucking along the streets of Chelsea with no memory of having done so.

"Well, I hope so," Barish said. He studied me for a few seconds before rising. I'd just been signaled that we were through.

"Actually, I have a question for *you*, if you don't mind," I said hurriedly.

"All right, but I do have that conference call coming up—so if you could kindly make it quick."

"You dealt with Tom about money matters. Did he ever mention that someone from the crew of the show, a grip named Deke, had borrowed several thousand dollars from him and not repaid it?"

"You mean *recently*?" he exclaimed, sounding taken aback.

"No, earlier in the summer."

"Yes, I was aware of that incident. Tom was quite upset about it and called me to discuss whether he had any recourse. I told him that unfortunately he had no legal leg to stand on. Now that I think of it, that must have been one of the last conversations

I had with Tom. It was in July I believe. Do you know if he ever got the money back?"

"Not that I'm aware of."

"That's actually a nice little motive, isn't it?" he said, cocking his head.

"Possibly," I said. Suddenly another question rammed itself against my brain, something I should have thought of earlier.

"There's one other thing," I said as Barish moved toward the door.

"Of course. Why don't we talk on the way out." He led me back through the empty workstations. As I glanced to the right, I saw that there were several offices along the wall, and a young woman, her pale blond hair in a bob, sat in one of them, staring at a computer screen. She glanced up as we walked by. Must be fun to be holed up in an office on Saturdays.

"When you were talking to Missing Persons, why didn't you mention the fact that Tom might be in Andes?" I asked to Barish's back.

He stopped in his tracks and swung around to me. "That's easy to explain," he said, crisply. "Tom had told me he'd *sold* the house. The closing was supposed to be in July. I only found out when I spoke to the sheriff that the sale had fallen through."

"That wasn't something Tom would discuss with you? Or the fact that he was withdrawing money for work on the house?"

"As I said previously, Tom wasn't my client, and he handled his own bank account. As a courtesy, I would occasionally answer a financial question for him—like when he'd foolishly loaned someone money who wouldn't repay it—but that was really the extent of it. Of course, as executor, I keep an eye on the trusts."

"Who gets the money now that Tom is dead?" I asked.

Barish looked at me with what almost amounted to pity, as if he felt sorry for the fact that I was capable of asking such a crude question.

"As you might imagine, I can't discuss such things."

"My interest isn't prurient. I'm looking into Tom's murder."

"Understood," he said, and then offered a tight smile. "Between the two of us, the bulk goes to charity—his parents arranged the trusts that way. And please do understand that I appreciate all your efforts. I hope you will keep me informed." Of course, as executor, some money would go to him.

In turn, I asked to be informed of any funeral plans.

I had thought I'd just hop on the Lex at Grand Central, but as I rode down in the empty elevator, I felt overwhelmed by both fatigue and a weird malaise, as though the hangover from my experience in Chelsea had resurrected itself. I took a cab instead, and as soon as I was home, I poured a hot bath with a huge glob of bath gel and nearly fell into it. I laid a warm wet washcloth over my eyes and tried to clear my brain for a few minutes, but thoughts kept shoving their way in there. Who had killed Tom, and why? And was that person now after *me*? I hadn't learned very much from Barish, but his confirmation of Deke's debt had been important. That and the fact that Tom, a guy known for his live-and-let-live attitude, had been extremely agitated about it. As an old reporter I used to work with once said, money burns a hole in the gut no matter *who* you are.

My guess was that Tom hadn't let the issue die. It might have been uncomfortable for Deke to see Tom on the set, and the situation would have really heated up if Tom had threatened to go to management. Deke looked like a guy with a short fuse and a big temper—I remembered the hostile way he'd rubbed his hard thigh against me in the Half King after I'd tried to pump him about Tom—and I suspected that rather than allowing himself to be guilted out by Tom, he would have felt cornered. And mad. Had he turned violent when Tom had refused to back off? If he was the one who had driven to Andes and killed Tom, there may have been a nice bonus in it for him—the $7,000 Tom had brought with him. I wondered if the sheriff had found it or if it was missing. Maybe Deke had even gotten wind of the fact that Tom had the cash on him, and that had been part of the motive for killing him.

I was nearly positive Deke wouldn't be at the party tonight—I couldn't see him making Locket's list of power players—so I would have to find another way to check him out further. Tonight, instead, my plan would be to speak to Harper, observe Locket and Alex, and also grill Amy, who hopefully had answers about my lost hours. I stared down at my naked body, which had started to go all pruny around the edges. Where *were* you last night? was all I could think. Every time I considered my amnesia, I felt positively morose. Maybe a night with Chris would help chase away my gloom.

As soon as I was dried off from my bath, I called Jessie and asked if she'd be willing to meet about half an hour before the party started so I could fill her in on everything that had transpired. If she was going to be a second pair of eyes for me tonight, she needed to be in the loop. She was game and suggested a wine bar on a side street in the East 80s just a few blocks from Elaine's. The forecast promised cooler night weather again, and I ended up wearing a miniskirt, leggings, and a boxy short jacket over a low-cut top—I figured it said summer and fall at the same time.

Jessie had also opted for a mini and leggings, which made us both snort with laughter as she strutted over to greet me in the small wine bar. I saw that she'd really glammed herself up—coral lips and lots of black mascara. Pieces of her thick brown hair fell with perfect dishabille from a sloppy bun on top of her head.

"You look pretty darn gorgeous for a *book* party," I said. "Are you going to try to help me and get lucky at the same time?"

"I admit it—I'm in the mood for a new man. Though don't ask me *why*. Have you heard the age theory about New York men? They have their chronological age and then they have their New

York age, which is about four to five years younger. You meet a guy who's thirty, but the age he acts is *twenty-five*—and his idea of a good time is telling his buddies about the time some chick gave him road head while he was driving eighty miles an hour."

"Gosh, Chris is only in his early twenties, so that makes him, like, seventeen. Does that mean I could get arrested for sleeping with him?"

"So what's the latest?" she demanded.

I told her everything that had happened since we'd spoken the day before, including the drugging. A couple of times she opened her mouth to ask a question, then shook her head, as if she were too spellbound to break the flow.

"Oh, my God," she said when I'd finished, ending with my futile search for my memory along the streets of Chelsea. "It's like one of those awful good news/bad news jokes. The good news is that you're knocking boots with a total hottie who's starring in a major TV show. The bad news is that you're being stalked, drugged, and possibly marked for death."

"Yeah, and that's why I need your help," I told her. "Flirt your butt off tonight, but I want you to keep your eyes open and your ears perked. I want to know if you see anything weird going on between Locket and Alex. I'll keep my eye on them, but I won't be able to hover for too long."

We strolled into Elaine's at seven-thirty, about half an hour after the party had officially started. There were at least fifteen paparazzi out front, and though a couple of them snapped our picture just in case we might be *somebody*, most lowered their cameras as we walked past, the boredom registering on their faces. I wondered if within weeks Chris would be making his way into events with flashbulbs popping in his face and photographers screaming his name.

Inside, the place was already mobbed. Elaine's, one of those old-style New York restaurants referred to sometimes as a watering hole, is a favorite haunt of both celebs and literary types. The dark walls are crowded with old posters, black-and-white photos, and framed covers of books written by regular patrons. Which, along with the amber glow from the wall sconces, gives a clubby feeling to the place. I squeezed through a group of people bunched up at the door (including Mary Kay!) and cast my eyes around the main room. There was no sign of Chris, but Alex and Locket were stationed farther along to the left by the bar with a dozen fawning sorts ringed around them.

"That's them up there, holding court," I said, leaning into Jessie.

"Yeah, I know," she replied. "I actually used to watch her soap—until her character got kidnapped by terrorists and then decided to become a doctor."

I told her that she was free to patrol if she wanted because I'd take the first watch. We broke apart, and after grabbing a glass of wine from a passing waiter, I headed toward the end of the bar, making sure I didn't catch Locket's eye. She was busy regaling her admirers with a story, and I found a spot not far behind her and Alex, buffered by several other guests but close enough to hear snippets of their conversation.

"I'm doing a luncheon for beauty editors, but Alex thought this would be fun, too. A real old-fashioned book party."

Someone asked her a question I couldn't make out.

"The most important?" she said, rolling one shoulder forward coquettishly. "No sun *whatsoever*. This summer I practically wore a burka in East Hampton, even when I went to the farmer's market."

Alex scanned the crowd, looking bored with the bonus beauty tips, and cupped Locket's elbow as if anxious to change locations. "Ready for another drink?" he asked, almost like a demand.

"Please, darling, yes," she said.

A waiter passed by him with a tray of white wine and

champagne, but Alex shook his head and turned instead to the bartender.

"A glass of Veuve Clicquot," he demanded.

There was a good two-second beat before the connection caught up with me, but when it did, I felt my blood go icy. Veuve Clicquot was the brand I'd spotted in Tom Fain's cottage.

As Locket accepted the champagne glass, Alex grasped her elbow more tightly and began to maneuver her away from this particular thicket of people. I spun around, not wanting them to see me.

Only inches away, and nearly face-to-face with me, stood Beau Regan.

CHAPTER 10

A s if I were seeing Beau for the first time all over again, the words that flashed instantly through my mind were the same ones that had formed that day last summer when I'd met his intense brown-eyed gaze across a hushed reception area: *I'm going to marry that guy.* They were now quickly chased away and replaced, however, with the words *Fuck-face scumbag.* Beau had arrived back in town and never called me. I clearly meant nada to him.

"Bailey," he said, obviously as taken aback as I was. "I— What brings you here?"

"Just trying to pick up a few beauty tricks from Locket Ford," I said. "I hear she has a recipe for an oatmeal-and-apricot scrub that takes about five years off your face." Ha, ha, Bailey, you are so freakin' funny! I felt like screaming. But I couldn't totally fault myself. I was so nervous right then that my tongue felt as heavy as a U-Haul trailer parked in my mouth, and I was lucky I could say anything at all.

"You aren't covering this for the magazine, are you?"

"No, I'm still on the fun and fabulous crime beat for *Buzz*." That didn't really answer his question, but who the hell cared.

Well, I cared, clearly. My heart was beating wildly just from the sight of him. He was wearing black pants and a cobalt blue long-sleeved shirt open at the collar, which looked awesome with his smooth, tanned face. His dark hair seemed a little lighter, perhaps bleached out from weeks in the Turkish sun, and it was longer, brushed behind his ears.

I figured it was my turn to ask how he had ended up at the Locket Ford book bash, but I couldn't summon the energy for any phony cocktail banter. If he wanted to make a stab at it, let him. And he did.

"Her book agent's a pal of mine. I just got back yesterday, and he said he thought this would be good reemersion therapy. I'm not so sure, though."

"Yeah, well, any party where the paparazzi almost outnumber the guests probably isn't going to be good therapy." Oh great, now I was playing Dr. Phil. But I felt incapable of saying anything witty, paralyzed by conflicting emotions. There was the longing to dazzle him blind, making him realize that he really wanted me desperately after all, but also a fierce desire to be my own angel of mercy and extricate myself from the bloody situation.

"Well, it's great to see you, Bailey," he said, his voice low and soft. "I was planning to call you this week. I'd really like to—"

He stopped suddenly, his attention caught by something just over my right shoulder. Before I had a chance to turn to see what it was, I felt a strong, muscular arm enclose me. Biceps like that could belong to only one man. There *is* a God, I thought as the arm pulled me close to the body it was attached to so brilliantly.

"So here you are," Chris said. "I've been looking for you."

"I just got here a minute ago."

I glanced back at Beau. I may have been mistaken, but I

thought I saw a hint of discombobulation in his eyes, a chink in the unflappable manner that he was such a master at presenting to the world.

"Oh, sorry. This is Beau Regan. Chris Wickersham. Chris is working with Locket."

"Are you with the publishing house?" Beau asked. That was funny. I could just imagine Chris calling Locket and announcing, "I've got page proofs for you, Miss Ford. Would you like me to drop by and review them with you?"

"No, we're on *Morgue* together. Do you know her?"

"I don't, actually. I'm just a hanger-on tonight." Beau sounded breezy enough as he spoke, but I could see his eyes scrutinizing Chris, taking in everything about him. "What's *Morgue,* anyway, a new soap?"

"Actually, a new nighttime drama. Listen, would you mind if I steal Bailey away? I've got something important I need to discuss with her." He lifted his arm from my shoulder and combed his fingers in one languorous stroke through the back of my hair. It was the kind of cock-blocking gesture that announced he'd been to bed with me or at least damn well *intended* to be there tonight. One of Beau's eyebrows lifted just a little, involuntarily, I guessed.

"Of course," was all he said. "Nice to see you, Bailey." He turned and melted into the crowd. Chris took my hand and led me to the side room, which wasn't nearly as mobbed as the rest of place. We claimed a corner to talk in.

"Sorry to do that to you," Chris said. "That wasn't the most important conversation of your life or anything, was it?"

"Hardly," I said with the kind of disdain I'd normally reserve for people guilty of cell yell.

"I've just been really worried about you. When you first told me about getting drugged, I naturally assumed some guy did it. But later this afternoon, I started to wonder if it might have something to do with Tom's murder."

"I'm wondering the same thing," I admitted. I filled him in on the details of last night—both what I'd recalled and what Rusty had shared—as well as what I'd learned about GHB. He winced as I described my terrifying experience on the street in Chelsea.

"Jesus, Bailey, this is getting really scary," he exclaimed. "I think it's time for you to back off—I don't want to put you in any more danger."

"It's too late now. If it's the murderer who drugged me and has been calling me, he—or she—knows I'm snooping around. I'm better off trying to figure out who it is before the person tries anything else."

"And from the phone call you couldn't tell whether it was a man or a woman?"

"No, that's the odd thing. Both the laughing and the crying sounded as if they came from some bizarre androgynous creature. Chris, you may be able to help," I added. "It's more than likely that my beer was messed with while you were still in the bar. I drank more than half of it, and I was just fine. Then I went over to talk to Amy, and after that I dropped into the ladies' room to find Harper. Do you remember seeing anyone over by my stool around that time? Because that's when someone must have slipped the drug in."

He scrunched his mouth and thought for a moment, then shook his head back and forth methodically. "I didn't see anything—it was just so crowded in there."

"Amy is my only other hope, then. Is she here tonight, do you know?"

"Yeah, she's here. The last I saw her, she was toward the back of the other room—with Harper."

"Why don't we meet up later. I want to talk to Amy and Harper—and maybe Locket as well. Oh, I nearly forgot the big news." I told him about Alex ordering the Veuve Clicquot for Locket.

"That doesn't necessarily mean she was there—at Tom's place," he said, frowning. "Other people drink that champagne."

"I know—it's just an odd coincidence, and I never like coincidences."

"Well, it might be connected—but not in the way you think. Since Tom had his little fling with Locket, he could have started drinking it himself—because he thought it would impress her."

"Possibly," I said. "But it's worth keeping in mind. One more question. Were you aware that Deke had borrowed several thousand dollars from Tom and never paid him back?"

"You're kidding—are you sure about that?"

"Yes, two people told me."

"What an asshole. I— You know, now that I think of it, I got the sense that things had cooled between the two of them, but I figured it was because Harper kept advising Tom to spend less time with the crew. But there was one night—about a week or two before Tom disappeared—when a bunch of us were going out and at the last minute Deke decided to come. The next thing I knew, Tom bailed with some flimsy excuse. I never connected it to Deke until now."

"I talked to Deke briefly last night, and he seemed hostile."

"Do you think *he* could have killed Tom?"

"It's a possibility. If Tom was threatening to get him canned, he may have decided to shut him up. Maybe he never intended to kill him but things escalated. And Deke was right near my drink last night."

"And guess what? You know how you said gyms are a good source for GHB? Well, Deke is a big bodybuilder."

"I've got to find a way to have more face time with Deke, as unpleasant as that may be. Can you make that happen, Chris?"

"I'll try. You've just got to promise me to be careful."

I smiled, gave his elbow a squeeze, and told him I'd connect with him in about an hour. I made my way toward a corridor in the back that led to another door to the front room. People were really jammed in there now, rich and successful-looking New Yorkers with their heads bobbing in conversation or muscling their way through the crowd in search of someone better to schmooze with. I spotted both Amy and Harper in the back, just as Chris had predicted, but before heading over there, I glanced toward the front. Jessie was standing at the bar with none other than Alex himself and another man. And Beau was in the same vicinity, in a cluster that included a man, perhaps his buddy, and two hot-looking chicks. But his eyes were scanning the room. Was he looking for me? What words had he been about to say before Chris had interrupted our conversation? "I'd really like to . . ." *What?* *Talk* to me? *Get together* with me? *Explain things* to me? I could feel an ache beginning to form in my heart, but I was too wired for it to take over. I had work to do.

Amy had a look of concern in her eyes as soon as she saw me approach her, and I figured she probably thought I was still recovering from a *Guinness Book of World Records*–caliber hangover.

"Got a minute?" I shouted to her above the din.

"Sure. You okay today?"

"Not so much."

"I know, I know. I probably should have made sure you got home okay. But it was so early, I figured—"

"Look, you probably think I was drunk, but I wasn't. Someone slipped a drug of some kind in my beer."

She raised both eyebrows. *"What?"*

"I can tell you about it later, but right now I need answers since I remember practically nothing. The bartender told me you came back over and spoke to me again—after we'd talked by the garden. What was I doing then?"

"Just sitting there. I realized that Harper had left, and I asked you if there was some new development. As soon as you started to speak, I could tell you were . . . well, I thought you must have had a pretty good buzz on. Your hair was kind of wet, and you were slurring your words."

"What did I say?"

"You told me that Harper and Chris had left."

"And then?"

"Nothing, really. I asked if you wanted me to find you a cab, and you said you were going to walk for a while, get some air. Then you left. It was still early, and I figured you'd be fine. No one *attacked* you, did they?"

"No, I'm okay. But if you think of anything else, will you let me know?"

"Of course," she said emphatically. She looked sheepish, and I suspected she had a case of the guilts. Maybe that gave me a chit I could use to my advantage down the road. As for my missing night, it seemed as if I'd never be able to fill in the pieces. I'd apparently gone to the ladies' room to try and revive myself and then later headed outside, where I'd wandered aimlessly, searching for my bearings.

My next target was Harper, but I could tell by the expression on her face as I approached that I was the last person she wanted to chat with tonight.

"How are you doing?" I asked. She was standing next to a woman with a clipboard, and they both appeared to be "on duty."

"This isn't a good time," she said. She was pretty dolled up, in a slinky black cocktail dress and dangly silver earrings, but her face looked fatigued, smudged with bluish circles under her copper eyes, verifying the fact that she *had* tossed and turned last night. If she'd killed Tom, why get all churned up now and not two weeks ago? It might be that the discovery of the body made it finally real. Or she could be wigged out now that the police were on the case.

"When, then?" I asked.

"Tomorrow. Call me tomorrow." She turned back to the woman with the clipboard, offering me a view of her bare back.

I summoned the energy to edge my way through the crowd again, and when I'd progressed about two feet, I felt someone grab my arm. I thought it must be Chris, but when I twisted around, Jessie was wedged behind me with an impish expression on her face.

"Have you *seen* him? Beau Regan's here."

"Yeah, I almost had to call for a defibrillator."

"It took me a minute to realize who he was—I'd just seen him once at that party in the Hamptons. If it's any consolation, I gave him the evil eye for about ten minutes. I think it worked because someone sloshed a glass of red wine on his shirt."

"Thank you. Could you try for a vat of rancid cooking oil next time? That would *really* make my night."

"Don't look, but he's staring at you. That's funny—he has no idea that I know him, and he's just gawking away like an idiot. Do you think the two of you will hook up again?"

"Not likely. Anything interesting going on between Locket and Alex?"

"They seem perfectly pleasant to each other. But if he squeezes her elbow any tighter, it's gonna pop like an egg."

For the next half hour we inched our way around, checking out the scene, with me biding my time for just the right opportunity to approach Locket. It was interesting to play total observer at a party, not worried about meeting anyone or having someone to talk to, but just happy to be the proverbial fly on the wall. I watched people air-kiss, fawn, flirt, fake interest, slug down drinks, and shove their way through the crowd. One woman got her large silver bracelet caught in the zipper of a man's pants, and she went nearly frantic trying to get it off, like a muskrat with its leg in a trap. At one point I figured out that Beau must have left, because there was no sign of him. Chris, on the other hand, seemed to be at the throbbing center, having clearly been dubbed the new It boy. An ever changing group of people ringed him—mostly superslick guys who might have been producers or agents hoping to poach him as a client, and babes—tons of babes. There were both hot young chicks with flat shiny hair, Chloé tops, and $3,000 handbags and so-called cougars—too-smooth-faced, over-forty glamazons who looked hungry for a no-strings-attached romp in the sack with him. Chris remained rooted in one spot, and women were sucked in his direction from every which way, like birds into the engines of a jet on takeoff. If my twinges of jealousy were any indication, I was starting to feel more than lust for Chris.

Unfortunately, Locket also remained surrounded most of the night, and Alex's large pale hand was usually holding her elbow or pressed to her like a Post-it note. At about a quarter to ten, just before the party was due to end, I left the main area and ducked into the bathroom, considering what I should do. Perhaps I needed to enlist Chris to work his way into the phalanx around Locket—with me in tow. But it turned out not to be necessary. As I was rummaging through my purse for a tube of lip gloss, I heard the door open, and before I had a chance to glance up, I recognized the overwhelming scent of patchouli and vanilla. Miss Ford, *Morgue* star and beauty guru, had entered the bathroom. Her eyes went instantly to her reflection in the mirror, so it was a few moments before she realized who was standing alongside her.

"Lovely party," I said. "Congratulations."

"Thank you," she said haughtily, her eyes making contact with mine in the mirror. "My, my—you and Chris are getting to be quite the item."

"Actually, I came with a friend," I told her. I swiped on my lip gloss, buying time while I quickly considered how to maximize the few short moments I would have alone with her. I decided to go for broke.

"It must be hard for you tonight, though," I said, offering a newly glistening but sympathetic smile.

"What do you mean?" she asked bluntly. She was the kind of woman who didn't appreciate people other than herself defining anything about her.

"Well, you have this wonderful celebration for your book, but at the same time you must be grieving over Tom's death. I happen to know that you two were extremely"—I paused for emphasis—"*close.*"

She was a damn good actress, I had to hand that to her, because her face registered no emotion whatsoever, but I saw her eyes quickly skirt the floor, making certain no feet were visible below the doors of any of the stalls.

"Who told you *that?*" she asked as her eyes found mine again in the mirror.

"Someone with real information."

At that moment, two postpubescent actressy types burst into the ladies' room, gawking at a photo on one of their cell phones and giggling like idiots. For the first time, I saw alarm on Locket's face. She wanted to know what I knew, and she wasn't going to be able to find out right now. She swung open the ladies' room door and motioned with her head for me to go first into the small, dark corridor. It appeared that she wanted to resume our conversation there.

But Alex was standing outside, rigid and waiting.

"What's going on?" he asked when it registered with him that we'd obviously been talking.

"Have you met Chris's girlfriend, darling?" she asked brightly, rolling her shoulder forward coyly. "Her name is Bailey, of all things."

"No, I haven't had the pleasure," he said coolly, though I

could see recognition in his eyes as he met my gaze. He snapped his head in greeting rather than shake my hand. I nodded back. I didn't have Locket's acting chops, and I wondered if he could tell by looking at me that we hadn't exactly been chatting about the new Jimmy Choo shoes while we powdered our noses.

"People are waiting for us, Locket," he said. "It's time to go."

He took her elbow yet again, guiding her away. Neither of them said another word to me.

Damn, I thought. It had seemed as if I'd been about to get *something* from Locket—an admission, perhaps, or a *hint* of admission—but thanks to the two Lindsay Lohan wannabes, I'd come away empty-handed.

Eager to reconnect with Jessie, I decided to call her cell rather than try to search for her. As I was punching in her number, I caught a movement in my peripheral vision. I glanced to my right, and there was Beau again. So he hadn't left after all.

"Calling in an exclusive on that apricot scrub?" he asked.

"Yeah, they're bumping a Kevin Federline item for it. Now we'll never know what books are on his night table." Still at the top of my game with the witty comeback. Gosh, I was surprised I hadn't been tapped to do an HBO comedy special.

"How did your summer end up, anyway?" he asked, his eyes quizzical—as if he really *were* curious. Those brown eyes still had the power to blow me away, and I could feel my pulse starting to race again, as if I'd just mainlined a Red Bull. But I felt something else as well: the first swells of anger. Beau had come back and never made contact, subjected me to a DWE—dumping without explanation. And now he was insisting on torturing me with tedious small talk.

"Pretty good, I guess," I said flatly. "I went up to Cape Cod—my mother has a place there. Ate a lot of clams."

"I'm sorry I never sent more than a couple of postcards, Bailey. It was pretty crazy in Turkey. We sometimes worked fourteen-hour days."

"One."

"Sorry?"

"One. You sent one postcard. But that's okay. The thing about getting *one* postcard is that it really lets you know where you stand."

I'd caught him off guard with my sarcasm, and he opened his mouth ever so slightly in surprise. He pulled up the left side of his mouth in a rueful smile.

"Well, you obviously didn't waste any time fretting over it," he said, matching my sarcastic tone.

The two gigglers spilled out of the bathroom suddenly, squealing now, as if they'd just done a few lines of coke in a stall. Before things got any worse between Beau and me, I decided to beat a retreat.

"Well, I'd better go," I said. "Have a nice night."

"You too," he said dryly as I turned from him.

Walking away, I smirked. It was fun to imagine him thinking of just *how* nice a night I would probably have with the star of the show. But as I emerged from the corridor into the main room of the restaurant, my heart sank. Until tonight I'd harbored fantasies that there was still a chance for me and Beau, that he would return from his journey, blow off the Turkish dust from his belongings, and realize that he had missed me horribly. Now I had to face the truth: It was really over.

The crowd had thinned out in just the short time I'd been absent. Obviously, as the first wave of A-listers had moved to the door, others had taken it as a signal that the fun was about to come crashing to an end. To my despair, Chris was at the bar talking to two Bottega Veneta bag bimbos, but as soon as he spotted me, he broke free and made his way to me. Simultaneously, Jessie headed toward me from another direction. I introduced her to

Chris, and I could tell from Jessie's expression that she liked what she saw.

"I ran into some friends from *People*, and we thought we'd head downtown and hear some music," she announced. "Want to come?"

Chris glanced at me with uncertainty on his face. "Are you up for that, Bailey? You've had a pretty rough twenty-four hours."

"Probably not," I told him. "We could grab a bite somewhere—or I could just make you something at my place."

"Really? That sounds pretty appealing."

We said good-bye to Jessie and hailed a cab outside. As we hurtled down Second Avenue, Chris pulled me into the crook of his arm.

"How you doing, anyway?" he asked softly. "Do you really feel up to standing over a hot stove?"

"I think it'll be therapeutic—though I can't make any promises about the quality of the food."

I had learned to cook in just the past few years. During my marriage, I'd been more than game to wrestle with a chicken breast or two in the kitchen, but my ex had been almost rabid about eating out. We were always in a different bistro, brasserie, or sushi bar, and it was only later that I understood why. He'd already begun to accrue his mondo gambling debts, and being on the move made him feel safer, less in the line of sight of guys who wanted to break his legs in two. After the divorce, I'd bought a few cookbooks, and though I was no Giada De Laurentiis, I could whip up a dozen or so dishes pretty well.

My cupboards were nearly bare at the moment, but I had bacon in the freezer, so after we arrived at my place, I cooked a few pieces in the microwave and made spaghetti carbonara. All you need are bacon, eggs, white wine, and Parmesan cheese, but the sauce is dreamy, especially when accompanied, as Hannibal Lecter would say, by a nice Chianti. I served it indoors, with the

terrace door open a crack because the night was indeed cool, finally more fall than summer. I was grateful for the temperature
change, because pasta on my terrace would have reminded me
too much of Beau—and I was having a hard time chasing him
from my thoughts.

"You were really holding out on me last winter," Chris said. "I
had no idea you could cook like this."

"I like to keep a few aces up my sleeve," I said, smiling.

"Oh, is that what you were doing?" he said, leaning toward
me and stroking my hair. "I thought you were just torturing me."

"Not intentionally."

"Speaking of torture, anything else from the party?"

I shared my conversation with Locket outside the bathroom.
"She's definitely hiding something," I said.

"Well, we know she's hiding her fling with Tom," Chris exclaimed, almost in exasperation. "But that doesn't mean there's
more. Just because Tom was drinking her brand of champagne
doesn't mean she drove up there—or—or killed him."

"What makes you so sure?" I said, surprised by his stance.

"I just don't see her doing it. What would be the reason?"

I was about to make the case for Locket as a definite suspect
but decided to back off. Chris didn't seem at all happy with that
as a possibility, and I wasn't interested in any contentiousness. I
moved on to Deke.

"Do you think you can get me in his presence again soon—
like on set?" I asked.

"We're shooting at Chelsea Piers on Monday," Chris said. "I
may be able to sneak you in."

He helped me with the dishes after that, and then we didn't
even bother to sit on the couch and play the seduction game—we
went straight to my bed. The sex was different this time, not the
fierce, bittersweet variety we'd engaged in the other night, but still
amazing. Later, his arm around me, Chris made me laugh with

a story about sharing a bed one summer with his little brother, nicknamed Kicker.

I nodded off right after, with him spooning me, but just after one, my eyes popped open. It had started to rain suddenly, and I could hear the drum of it on the metal railing around my terrace. I closed my eyes again, willing sleep to return, but it was clear within a few minutes that it had no intention whatsoever of doing so.

After slipping out of Chris's grasp, I padded naked out to my kitchen, where I tried milk therapy, night two. Yet even as I swallowed the milk, I knew it probably wasn't going to do the trick. Seeing Beau again was bugging the hell out of me, and the afterglow of sex with a gorgeous guy I really dug wasn't going to ameliorate the situation. What had he been about to say when he'd uttered the words *I'd really like to . . .* ? Thanks to that sarcastic missile I'd lobbed, I'd blown my chance of ever knowing.

As I set the glass in the sink, my home phone rang, startling me. I wondered if it might be the infamous night caller, now with access to my home number, too. I picked it up as quickly as possible, not wanting to wake Chris.

"Is this Bailey Weggins?" demanded the voice on the other end.

"It is." I glanced at the clock: 1:14.

"This is Locket Ford."

I caught my breath in surprise.

"Hello," was all I said. Clearly she was the one with an agenda now, and I was not going to say anything that would short-circuit it.

"We should talk," she said coolly.

"Now?"

"Now isn't good. Tomorrow."

"Okay, when?"

"At four. Meet me at my apartment." She gave me a number on Central Park West.

"Is that in the Seventies?"

But she'd already hung up.

I slipped back into bed a few minutes later, and Chris stirred.

"More insomnia?" he murmured.

"Unfortunately."

"I have a way to help."

"I'd love to try."

"I heard the phone ring," he said as he pulled me toward his naked body, ready for sex again.

I opened my mouth to tell him about Locket's call—and then, for some reason I couldn't define, I thought better of it.

"Wrong number," I said.

CHAPTER 11

This time I slept straight through till morning and woke to the light seeping through the shades on my windows. I felt Chris stir beside me. I turned my head toward the middle of the bed and saw him lying on his stomach, his bare arms folded on the pillow under his head. It felt really good to have him next to me, and I couldn't help thinking of the contrast between last night and the horrible night before.

"Hey, good morning," Chris said. His eyes were still closed, but he offered me a sleepy smile.

"Good morning to you. Are you hungry?"

There was a pause, as if he were deliberating.

"Actually, yes," he said, opening his eyes. "I'm ravenous." By the mischievous look he gave me, I could see that he didn't mean for breakfast. We had sex in the soft, almost autumnal light. I felt a growing connection between us, but I didn't know what the heck we were supposed to do about it. As we lay in each other's arms Chris announced that it was his turn to cook, that if I had more eggs, he would make me an omelet to end all omelets.

After starting coffee, I turned my tiny kitchen over to him. Before long, I could hear him rummaging through the drawers of my fridge.

"There's some cheddar in there somewhere," I called out.

"Found it. I've also located some scallions that have clearly been here since the Clinton administration—but they don't cause botulism, do they?"

"Only heartburn, I think."

As I set the table, I watched him out of the corner of my eye. He had slipped into his pants but not bothered with a shirt yet and had tucked a yellow dish towel into his waistband as an apron. He hummed as he worked, at least when he wasn't exclaiming a triumphant "Yes!" at each successful step in the omelet-making process. There was a totally boyish quality to his effort, as if he were a kid working with a chemistry kit that he secretly hoped would blow up the kitchen. I realized for the first time that the boyishness wasn't because he was barely over twenty-one; it was just the way Chris *was*. Chris would be eternally open and easy and fun—what you saw was what you got. Unlike with Beau, there was nothing that felt elusive about him or maddeningly mysterious.

That's not to say I felt I totally knew Chris. As he set the plates on the table, announcing, "I'm Brent and I'll be your waiter today. We used only eggs from free-range chickens and aged California cheddar," I couldn't help wondering how many other chicks would love to be treated to one of his après amour omelets. That swarm around him last night had been awful. When Chris and I had dated briefly in the winter, I'd been conscious of how good-looking he was and that other women were often devouring him with their eyes, but I'd never felt very discomfited by it. His success, however, was going to ratchet up everything. How would I fit into the picture? Wouldn't Chris want to sample all the bounty

before him, especially all the lithe twenty-two-year-olds? Did I
really want to get involved with a hot young actor who was ten
years my junior to boot?

"You okay?" he asked. "You look kind of perplexed."

"Oh, I was just contemplating the feast I'm about to devour."
I took my first bite. "Oh wow, this is awesome," I said. "You're a
real soup-to-nuts kind of overnight date, aren't you?"

"In a manner of speaking," he said, laughing. "I do like cooking, though, and I want to get better at it—preparing great food
for friends. What I don't want to ever do again is put on a black
tie and serve a meal to people I don't know."

"I think your waitering and bartending days are over. Maybe
the next time you put on a black tie will be for an event like the
Golden Globes."

"You just can't ever count your chickens in this business," he
said. "Guys like Patrick Dempsey and George Clooney did a bil-
lion pilots before things took off for them. Think of how many
times they must have thought, Okay, this is it. And then it wasn't.
And even worse is when you consider the people who did a bil-
lion pilots and *still* didn't make it."

"Are you worried that the show won't take off and you'll be
back making the rounds in L.A.?"

"Oh yeah. I lucked out and got a show right away. But instead
of relishing it, I worry that it came too easily."

I asked him then about the couple of months he'd spent in
L.A., because other than during those brief moments in the bar
last Tuesday night, we really hadn't had a chance to talk about it.
He described the craziness of pilot season, the nonstop auditioning, meetings, and drinks, and the occasional trips to the beach
just to stay tanned through the whole thing. He made me laugh
out loud as he imitated the *Entourage*-style way agents and casting
directors talked. It was one of the first times since he'd been back
that we'd been discussing a topic other than Tom. His disappear-

ance and death had colored so much of our interactions, and it was nice not to be burdened with that for a brief while.

It wasn't long, though, before Tom was rushing my thoughts. As Chris reached the part about auditioning for *Morgue* and his screen test with Locket, I flashed back on what Harper had revealed to me: Tom had nearly nailed the role originally, but after providing the tip about the show to Chris, he had promptly lost the part to him. If Chris ever found out, it would probably be devastating for him.

"Speaking of *Morgue*, I'd better tackle these dishes and hightail it out of here," Chris announced. "I've got a lot of lines to learn today. Alex has a shit fit if you mess up."

"So he's around a lot during shooting?"

"In the beginning, apparently. I hear his MO is to micromanage like crazy, make sure the show's a hit, then finally step back a little."

"Has he ever been really tough on you? Harper said he came down pretty hard on Tom a few times."

"No, thank God. He lit into Tom in front of people, and it was pretty awful. Even the director seemed taken aback."

"Maybe he sensed something was up with Tom and Locket."

"Or maybe *Tom* felt totally awkward because he was banging Locket, and that affected how he delivered his lines."

"That's a legitimate explanation. But in my mind, both Locket and Alex are still suspects. There's motive for both of them."

"To be honest, I just don't see either one of them going to the effort," he said.

This would have been the moment to mention the call from Locket and her insistence that she needed to speak with me, but once again I decided not to go there. For some reason, Chris didn't seem to want to entertain the idea of Locket as a murderer.

"For the show's sake, let's hope they're innocent, then."

"I thought Deke was at the top of your list right now," Chris said, rising from the table. He picked up both our plates and headed toward the kitchen. "Tom had a long fuse, but he wouldn't let you just roll over him. I bet he was furious at Deke about the money. I could definitely see a confrontation happening."

"Yes, Deke is still high on my list. I need to get in Deke's face a little bit and see what his reaction is. I hope you can really get me on set tomorrow."

I heard the sound of running water and dishes being slid into the dishwasher. Chris stepped back into the living room, his eyes lowered as he thought.

"They let people sneak in a friend or relative as long as they don't get in the way. I think I could pull it off. But I'd have to call you later and let you know. I need to enlist one of the production assistants to help me."

"Great. Leave the rest of the dishes. I don't want Alex taking off that gorgeous head of yours."

As he leaned down to kiss me good-bye, a memory surged through my mind: Chris admitting Friday night that he'd snatched the note from Locket to Tom so the cops wouldn't find it. I had urged him to turn it over. I needed to follow up on that, but this wasn't the moment.

"So I'll call you later about the set visit," he said. "I'd love to see you tonight, but I try to hit the sack pretty early on Sundays. Are you open Monday night? If I can get out in time?"

"Yup," I said, experiencing a twinge of disappointment. I was enjoying the sex, the comfort, and everything else that came from being with Chris. "Why don't we talk tomorrow."

"I was thinking of more than talk," he said, grinning, and kissed me again, long and tenderly.

It was just nine-thirty when he left, too early to call Harper without irritating her any more than I already had. I grabbed my tote bag of exercise clothes and headed over to the gym. Thirty minutes on the StairMaster seemed more miserable than usual, but when I was done and showered, I realized that for the first time since Friday, I actually felt completely like myself again. Maybe I'd sweated the last of the drug out of my system.

Before returning to my place, I headed off in search of a cappuccino. On University Avenue, I ran smack into Landon, walking down the street in a navy blazer and lemony yellow tie.

"Are you doing the walk of shame—preppy style?" I asked.

"If *only*," he said. "No, I have a very nasty client who insisted we meet for breakfast early Sunday morning. I was actually going to knock on your door when I got back. What's the latest?"

"Could you handle more coffee? You wouldn't believe everything that's going on—and I could really use your advice."

He agreed eagerly, and we slipped into a small café halfway up the block. I ran through all the developments on the case with him, including my Friday night saga.

"Goodness, Bailey. Oil riggers have safer jobs than you do. You worry me sick."

"I admit that I'm a little bit freaked this time. I feel I've been able to defend myself pretty well in a bunch of situations in the past. But getting drugged is a whole other story. You're completely helpless. That's why I have to figure out who killed Tom. Whoever it is—man or woman—is toying with me. Right now the plan seems just to scare me, but it could get uglier."

"Any ideas who it is?"

"A few. But that's not all I need to talk to you about. Guess who was at the party last night? None other than Beau Regan— back from the sacking of Constantinople."

"Oh dear. How did it feel to see him?"

"Not bad, really. About the same as if someone had just backed over me with their SUV. Honestly, it was this god-awful mix of unrequited love and raw humiliation over the fact that he hadn't called me. If they could only harvest that feeling, it would make a perfect weapon of mass destruction."

"How long has he been back in town?"

"A day or two, I guess."

"Well, that's not so bad. He may have intended to call when—"

"He started to say something about it. He said, 'I'd been planning to call you. I'd really like to . . .'"

"Like to what?"

"I don't *know*. Chris came by at that moment and grabbed me like the Jaws of Life. I'll never know what he was going to say."

"You could call and ask him."

I told him then about the final conversation and Beau's sarcastic barb about my not wasting any time.

"That kind of seals the deal, doesn't it?" I said. "There's no place to go from there."

"Well, what do you want to happen? I thought you had the hots for Chris these days."

"I *do* like him—very much. But I can't seem to get Beau out of my system."

"Then I'd call him," he said, swirling his spoon around in his coffee. "Ask him what he was going to say."

"Isn't that groveling?"

"Yes, but as you know, I do think it has its place in love. Besides, you really have nothing to lose. If he's hoping to connect with you, you'll be giving him a second chance. If he was just blowing smoke up your you-know-what, you're no worse off than if you didn't approach him—except for the dent in your pride, that is."

Later, after our walk home, I mulled over what he'd recommended. It was the kind of advice (permission to call him) that I'd secretly been hoping for, the kind of advice that friends often give because they know it's what you want them to say, but in the end all it does is leave you feeling like an idiot for making contact with a guy who probably couldn't even remember what state you were from. I pushed it out of my mind and settled down to work.

First I tried Harper—yet again—but got only voice mail. I left a message, saying it was urgent that I speak with her. I also tried Sheriff Schmidt's cell and, when he didn't pick up, the office. The woman who answered told me he was unavailable but she would take a message. Last, I called Beverly's antiques store again. She answered the phone grimly. Clearly, Tom's death was still weighing on her.

"The sheriff's department has been around talking to people," she told me. "I know they've spoken to Barry and also the Realtor, but based on the questions they're asking, they're not very far along in their investigation."

"What will happen to the house, do you think, considering there are no heirs?" she inquired.

"I learned that the money in Tom's trust will probably revert back to the Fain estate and go to charity. But I don't know what will happen to anything that was outright Tom's. At his age he may not have had a will."

There was a moment before she said anything else, and I could sense her ruminating.

"It's a shame there couldn't be a way for the play to still be staged, though," she said finally.

"The play?" I asked, curious.

"Tom had written a play, and he was hoping to mount and direct it at a small theater somewhere. He was going to use part of the proceeds from the house to do it."

"Why not just use money he already had? I mean, he was able to come up with plenty of cash to advance Barry."

"Oh, Tom needed more than that to put on a play. Originally he was hoping to get it from his trust, but there turned out to be complications from that."

A question for Mr. Barish, it seemed.

I thanked her for her help and asked her to call me if she heard anything at all—even if it was only rumor.

There was an empty chunk of the day ahead of me before my planned assignation with Locket. I scribbled notes in my composition book—recaps of my meeting with Barish and the party. For the next two hours, I worked on my freelance piece, writing a rough draft on my laptop.

When it finally came time to dress for my trip uptown, I spent more energy than I would have liked selecting an outfit. That's because Locket, I knew, would be checking me out, running her eyes up and down me and then widening them slightly in that way of hers, suggesting that I had a skanky wet stain on the front of my pants. I didn't want to award her any more power than she already possessed. I finally settled on a pair of black slacks, a long-sleeved black sweater, and killer red slingbacks. And the diamond studs my mother had given me after my divorce to make up for the jewelry my husband had pawned for his gambling debts.

As I'd expected, the apartment building she lived in on Central Park West was one of those big, imposing stone edifices that look as though they could survive a massive meteor attack. Her apartment, on the other hand, was far *more* than I'd expected. I'd assumed, of course, that she and Alex lived in something spacious and classy—why wouldn't they? But after she'd ushered me into her gallery-size foyer, I saw that the apartment behind her was beyond sumptuous and seemed to go on forever. The ceilings were easily fifteen feet high.

"A slight change of plans," she announced before I even had a chance to say hello. "Alex just called, and his golf game is over earlier than expected. I certainly don't want him to find you here."

"What if we run out for coffee?" I asked. I was *not* going to let her out of confessing whatever dirty little secret she had planned to spill to me.

"Actually, I thought we could go over to the Central Park Boathouse for a drink. I can give the dog a walk."

She turned and headed down a hallway to the right of the gallery, where it seemed the bedrooms must be. Halfway down, she gently slapped her thigh several times and called out the name Muchi. Why wasn't I surprised by the name of the dog?

As she entered a bedroom in search of what I knew for certain would be a dog no bigger than a head of Bibb lettuce, I edged my way to the back of the gallery and peeked into the living room. It was gigundo, with three different seating areas, fabrics splashed with oranges and gold and pale, minty green, killer views of Central Park, and a floor-to-ceiling limestone fireplace that you could roast a pig in. Through a doorway at the end of the living room, I could see a huge dining room, also looking onto the park, with not one but two huge round tables. This would be tough to have to relinquish.

At the pitter-patter of little feet, I spun back around. The dog was indeed a teacup pup, a fluffy little white thing with coal black eyes that I knew was neither a pug nor a Chihuahua, but I had no clue to the breed and didn't care enough to ask. Locket had tied a Hermès scarf around her head and donned a pair of big round black sunglasses. In her slim yellow pants and crisp white blouse with three-quarter sleeves, she looked as if she were attempting to channel Jackie-O.

After crossing Central Park West and entering the park, we walked about another twenty minutes before reaching our destination—and she didn't say a word to me the entire way. I took her silence to mean that we would wait until we were sitting down— and she didn't have to concentrate on yanking Muchi's nose out of every dog turd that she encountered—to talk. Heads turned as we walked, people either recognizing Locket even behind the headgear or guessing that with so much camouflage going on, she had to be *somebody*.

When we reached the Boathouse restaurant, nearly on the East Side, she steered me to the outdoor café part along the side and then toward a table by the water. There were still a few people rowing boats on the lake, many of them clunkily, as if they'd never used oars before. The lake was that mossy green color of hip waders and almost thick looking, though you could see flecks of orange from the koi. Though the willows and maples bordering the lake drooped from the lack of much rain late this summer, they were still vivid green. The trees in my mother's backyard were probably already tinged with yellow, but there wouldn't be a sign of autumn in Central Park for weeks.

"So what did you want to see me about?" I asked after we'd each ordered a glass of wine and she'd positioned Muchi on her lap—as if she were holding a large powder puff. I'd spent the walk through the park waiting and wondering exactly what she had up her sleeve, and I didn't have any patience left.

"I'd like to know what you were insinuating last night—about me and Tom?"

For all her haughtiness, she couldn't prevent the catch in her voice when she said his name.

"I wasn't insinuating anything," I replied.

She let out a breath, clearly confused by my comment. "Well, it certainly sounded like you were. I have a reputation to maintain, and I can't have people going around making careless remarks."

"Actually, I was calling a spade a spade. I *know* you were involved with Tom sexually."

She still had her sunglasses on, a disadvantage for me, but I could spy her eyes just enough through the lenses to spot the alarm that registered in them.

"How dare you," she said in an angry whisper. A young guy at the next table shot a look in our direction, probably not because he'd overheard her words, but because her whole body had stiffened and her mouth was tight in anger. Muchi seemed to sense her discomfort, too, and raised her itty-bitty snout. I hoped she wasn't contemplating leaping across the table and taking a bite out of my face.

"Locket, let's not play any games," I said. "I know, and you know I know. That's why you wanted to meet with me."

"What is this—some kind of extortion?"

"No, all I want are facts. I know you were in Andes the day Tom died. I want you to tell me what happened that day." I was playing a hunch, based totally on the empty bottle of Veuve Clicquot and the rumpled bed.

"Did you *date* Tom or something? I thought you were *Chris's* girlfriend."

"I'm a *friend* of Chris's—and I was looking into Tom's disappearance for him. Now I'm trying to find out who killed him."

"Just for sport?" she asked sarcastically.

"No, because I'm worried that the local sheriff's office may have a hard time investigating a case that took place up there but has so many ties to New York. Now, tell me about your trip to Andes."

She started to open her mouth, and all I could think was, Bingo. But then a young woman dressed in tennis whites and a visor and carrying a tennis bag barged over to our table.

"Do you mind my asking what kind of dog that is?" she asked. "I want one like that." There was something about her manner that suggested she'd recognized Locket, and I guessed that the dog inquiry was a ruse just to get up close to a legendary soap star.

"It's a Maltese—and they're very ferocious," Locket said in exasperation. The girl looked irritated and plopped down at the table that had just emptied behind us. I hoped I hadn't lost momentum.

"Should I repeat the question?" I asked.

"Why should I have to tell you?" she asked.

"If the answer is satisfactory, I may be able to keep it between the two of us. Otherwise I may have to take action."

She thought for a moment, the fingers of her right hand pressed against those inner-tube lips. They were so ripe, they looked almost edible.

"First you have to tell me how you developed this little theory of yours," she demanded. "If you have information, regardless of whether it's true or not, someone else may have it, too."

"No one else has access to the info I have," I lied. "Of course, that's not to say someone else hasn't learned about you and Tom in some other way. Tom arrived at Andes on Saturday morning, and my guess is that you met him there sometime that afternoon."

Locket exhaled loudly. "All right, I *did* go see Tom that afternoon," she confessed. "That weekend I was staying with some friends of mine about an hour south of Andes, and I drove to Tom's house for the afternoon. But he was very much alive when I left, I can assure you."

"Is there any chance Alex knew about your affair with Tom?"

"Absolutely not," she declared with indignation. But I could tell by the way she stiffened again that the same thought had crossed her mind recently.

"How can you be so sure?"

"He was working that day—in New York. Things are fine with us—he had no idea."

"What about Harper?" I asked. "Could she have figured it out, that you and Tom were lovers?"

She lifted her hand from its spot on Muchi's back and took a sip of her wine, which until now had gone mostly untouched.

"It's possible," she said, setting down the glass. "Harper had started to put more pressure on Tom lately. I could tell from her behavior that she wanted to take the relationship up a notch. But

Tom wasn't ready for a long-term relationship with anyone, let alone her."

"Was that a problem for you—did *you* want to take things with him up a notch?"

She snorted. "You *can't* be serious. I worked my fanny off to get from some no-name town in West Virginia to where I am today, and I'd hardly throw it away for a boy toy, no matter how hot he was between the sheets. Tom was a wonderful diversion for me—and I for him. We provided a certain—*comfort* to each other."

"What about Deke—did you know about Tom's problem with Deke?"

"Deke? I have no idea what you're talking about. Believe it or not, our relationship didn't involve a lot of *talking*. I'm not the kind of woman who needs chitchat."

"So—"

"Look, I wish I knew who killed Tom, but I don't. You asked me to tell you about that afternoon, and I have. I've kept my end of the bargain, and I expect you to as well."

"What time did you leave that afternoon?"

"At around four. I needed to get back to where I was staying."

"What were the last words Tom said to you?"

"Pardon me?"

It was kind of a wacky question, but I wanted to hear how authentic she sounded. It would give me a sense of whether he was really alive when she left.

"You heard me."

"He walked me to my car and said good-bye, and then he kissed me."

"And that was it? Nothing about his plans for the rest of the day?"

"No," she said, but she'd hesitated for a second before responding.

"What?" I demanded.

She glanced around the area. The girl with the tennis visor was reading a magazine. There was just one last boat on the lake, and the people in it were rowing toward shore. Out of the corner of my eye, I saw a turtle surface and poke its head above water.

"I talked to Tom later on the phone," she admitted. "He wanted to be sure I arrived back okay to my friends' house, so I called him. It was about five-thirty."

"There wasn't a record of it on his cell phone."

"I called the house phone. He'd given me the number since his cell phone got such bad reception up there."

"And he said something about his plans then?"

"No, he said he had to get off the phone. Somebody had just driven up."

CHAPTER 12

An editor I used to work with once cut the word *thunderstruck* from a lead I wrote, saying it was not only hyperbolic but antiquated. Yet I don't know what word could have better described how I felt at that moment with Locket. *You stupid, silly, Botoxed, blubber-lipped ninny!* I wanted to scream. She possessed information of crucial importance to the police, and she was just sitting on it to protect her bony ass.

But I didn't scream. I didn't want to do anything to freak her out and thus derail the revelation that was in the process of unfolding.

"Driven up?" I said. "He used those exact words?"

"Yes. He said someone had just driven up."

"He didn't say who it was?"

"No, and I didn't ask. I didn't butt into Tom's business."

"And when you called him, where was he?"

"I don't know. He just said he was working—painting."

"Did he say anything else? Anything at all?"

She paused, foraging through her memory. "He made a strange comment that I thought might be a quote—like from a play or a poem. He said he had to—let me think—'arm himself against some unhappy words.'"

"Sounds Shakespearean," I said, puzzled. Chris had tossed out a line from *Merchant of Venice* when we'd first met, so it would be worth asking him if he recognized it. Alan Carr, however, might be an even better resource.

"Had you ever heard him use that phrase before?"

"No, never."

"Locket," I said as calmly as I could, "Tom may not have offered up a name to you, but this is still a critical piece of information for the police to know. It's evidence that Tom knew the person who killed him—that it wasn't a stranger."

"But the person who stopped by didn't necessarily kill him," she said defensively, almost petulantly. "I heard that the police aren't sure when he died. It could have happened the next day for all they know."

"Aren't we dealing with an awfully big coincidence, then? Tom's holed up for the weekend in a town where he barely knows anyone anymore, and as far as I can tell, you're one of the few people he's informed that he's there. All of a sudden someone drives up, and he tells you that he's about to come face-to-face with someone's unhappiness. That *has* to be just before he was murdered—it's essential that you go to the police with this information."

"I *can't* do that," she exclaimed in a loud whisper, a hint of her Southern roots suddenly creeping into her voice. "There's no way in the world I can let Alex find out I was up there."

"This is a murder investigation, Locket."

The sun was beginning to sink in the sky somewhere behind the buildings that rimmed the park; Locket slipped her sunglasses off her face and dropped them on the table. Her eyes betrayed both worry and anger.

"I bet the next thing you're going to tell me," she said, "is that if *I* don't do it, *you* will."

"No, I'm not going to say that. I don't have to. Because the police are going to have a record of that call, and it's only a matter of time before they contact you about it. I just think it would be a lot smarter for you to take control and reach out to them first."

She caught her breath, started to say something, and then bit her tongue. She took a sip of wine as if she were fortifying herself.

"All right, I'll do it," she announced as she set the glass down firmly. "But I have to pick the right moment. I can't do it when Alex is hovering around me. I'm not shooting any scenes on Tuesday, and that's going to be the best time. I'll call that detective I spoke to—he gave me his card."

Something was cooking in that little brain of hers—something that had eased her worry. I couldn't figure out what it might be.

"And you know what—I don't have to say I was involved with Tom," she added. "I can just tell them I was calling him about something to do with the show—a scene we were shooting."

Oh, so that was it. Well, let her lie about that, I thought. What mattered was that she was going to tell them about the phone call—and the cops were surely smart enough to fill in the blanks.

Locket signaled for the check, and I decided to let her pay since she was Miss Moneybags. After she'd slid several bills from her wallet and laid them on the plate, she looked directly in my eyes.

"You probably think I'm so cold, don't you. But I cared about Tom, I really did. After they decided to cast me as the lead, they tested me with him—for the part that went to Chris in the end. We had a special connection from that moment on."

"I heard Tom came pretty close to landing the part. Do you know why they went with Chris instead?"

"Yes—but you can't say anything to *anyone* about this. They thought Tom was terrific, and they were all set to go with him, but they found out that he'd been in rehab—for an addiction to antidepressants. They just weren't going to take a chance with someone like that. I don't think he ever realized the reason why—*I* certainly never brought it up with him."

"Was Tom going to stick with the show? I heard things hadn't been going so well for him."

"I don't know. He wasn't all that invested in it after he lost the big part of Jared. He wanted to be able to try out for other things."

She glanced at her watch, a white ceramic Chanel rimmed around the face with a couple of rows of dazzling little diamonds, worth many thousands. "Look, I have to get moving," she announced irritatedly. Her tone indicated she'd just managed to reconnect with her inner diva. "I don't want Alex wondering why I took the dog out long enough to circumvent the reservoir twice. Are you weady, Muchi?"

It was pretty clear she didn't want me moseying on back to Central Park West with her, so after she departed with a curt good-bye, I sat for a while at the table, sipping my wine and thinking.

There was a chance, I knew, that parts of her story were a bunch of malarkey. Just as she'd thought nothing about twisting the truth for the cops, it would have been easy as pie for her to lie to me to protect herself. Maybe she really *had* killed Tom, and the whole bit about talking to him on the phone was just a fabrication calculated to add a layer of authenticity to her story. Of course, the phone records, which she'd seemed to have lost sight of, would either back her up or sink her.

I was inclined to believe her. It was one thing to cover her ass by making up a story, but the part about the Shakespearean quote seemed like such an odd element to throw in.

So if Locket didn't do it, who did? Who had pulled up in a car late that afternoon and caused Tom to predict an eruption of unhappy words? Harper could certainly fill the slot. Let's say she came back early from the West Coast, knew about the Andes house, and headed up there. She may even have seen Locket's car and waited for her to depart (God, maybe she'd simply smelled her trail of patchouli), and that could have led to the fight from hell.

Deke was another strong possibility. If Tom had made noises about exposing Deke's dishonesty to management, Deke could have decided to confront him about it. His intent may not have been to kill Tom, just to make him back off, but the situation could have escalated into violence.

And then there was Alex. The fact that he'd been down on Tom lately suggested that he'd picked up a whiff of the affair, or at least of an attraction between his star and the boy toy, and he could have decided to follow Locket when she went out of town that day. But if it had been Alex pulling up in the car, wouldn't Tom have announced that to Locket? Maybe not. He may have not wanted to alarm her until he knew what it was all about.

As I drained the last of my wine, I glanced around me. The outdoor café had nearly emptied, and the last of the boats had been tied up on the shore of the lake. I picked up my bag and headed out of the park, past joggers and bikers on their final lap. I caught the subway at Lex and 68th Street and rode it to Astor Place.

I stopped at the grocery near my apartment and scarfed up a couple of chicken breasts, arugula, and cherry tomatoes in order to make chicken Milanese. Before I let myself into my apartment,

I scribbled a note to Landon on an old envelope I dug out of my purse and slid it under his door. I could feel the early twinges of the Sunday night blues, and sharing a meal with him would help ameliorate things, especially if he provided a bottle of a super Tuscan, something he almost always did when I cooked Italian.

Chris had called when I'd switched off my phone during drinks with Locket, saying that he'd arranged for me to meet him at nine-thirty at Chelsea Piers. He gave me all the info I needed and said he'd see me the next day. Jessie had checked in, too, and I returned the call as soon as I'd dumped my supplies in the kitchen. She wanted to be filled in on anything that had happened at the party after she'd left and, as she put it, the latest developments in the sordid love triangle I now found myself in the middle of.

"I was no whiz at geometry," I said, "but if I remember correctly, by definition you need three sides to make up a triangle. Since Beau has no interest in me, that only leaves two."

"I told you he was gawking at you. These two girls kept trying to chat him up, and he would do this thing of looking off as if he were contemplating some brilliant answer, but he was always looking in your direction, checking you out."

"Well, if there was any chance of ever seeing him again, I blew it." I told her what had happened outside of the bathroom.

"Ouch. But I like what you said about the one postcard. Very funny."

"Do you think there's anything I can do? Landon told me I should just call him and ask him what he was going to say earlier. That I have nothing to lose by doing that."

"*God, no,*" she exclaimed. "Landon is such a wienie to say that. If you go crawling on your belly like a reptile, you look desperate. You need to be a challenge to him, make him want you bad."

"Well, the star of the show wrapped himself around me as tight as a python. Doesn't that make me a challenge?"

"Too *much* of one. Guys don't like challenges they can't surmount."

I sighed. "So are you saying there's really nothing I can do?"

"No, I didn't say that. You have to try what I call the sugar-and-spice strategy—and I suggest it only because Beau appears to have the hots for you—otherwise it would be pointless."

"Okay, so tell me," I demanded.

"Pick a time you don't think he'll be around and call his cell phone. Do *not* talk to him in person. Tell him there's no need for him to call you back, you just wanted to apologize for being a little snippy. Make it light and say something funny. But not directed at *him*, Bailey, okay? Tell him good luck on his project—that you'd love to see it when it comes out."

"How is that sugar and spice?" I asked.

"The sugar part is you being nice, not bitchy like you were last night. The spice part is you being kind of elusive. Not needing him to call back and saying you'd love to see the project when it's finished, which is probably going to be a whole fucking year from now. You've opened the door just enough to let him kick it down if he wants to."

"Okay, okay, thanks," I said, doubtful.

"Just one condition. If you end up with Beau, you have to give me Tad Hamilton. He's to die for."

After I hung up, I didn't give myself time to digest her comments and advice. I tried Harper again but struck out just as I had earlier in the day. I left another message on her voice mail saying I *really* had to talk to her. Then I made the call I was dreading—to Professor Alan Carr.

"Who did this to Tom?" he asked before I could get more than a couple of words out. "Do you know?" It was pretty clear he'd been drinking; he wasn't slurring his words, but there was a sloppiness to them that suggested a few glasses of booze.

"No, but I am going to do everything possible to find out."

"How could someone kill him? He was the world's nicest guy. Tom wouldn't hurt a fly."

"I'm so sorry for your loss."

"Maybe that was his problem. Too nice of a guy."

"How do you mean?"

"He didn't know how to say no to people. Damn, I can't believe it."

"I have a question for you, Professor Carr. Like I said, I'm doing what I can to investigate Tom's death. Shortly before he was killed, he apparently told someone he was arming himself against some unhappy words. Do you know if that's a line from a play—and what it might mean?"

The phone went quiet as he thought, but after a moment I almost wondered if I'd lost reception.

"Profess—"

" 'Be thou armed for some unhappy words.' Baptista says it in *The Taming of the Shrew*."

"What are the circumstances?" I asked. That was one play of Shakespeare's I probably hadn't read since high school.

"Petruchio is sure he won't have a problem wooing Katherina because he's as obstinate as she's supposed to be. Baptista wishes him luck but predicts he's in for trouble. He tells Petruchio, 'Be thou armed for some unhappy words.' "

"Would that line or the play itself have had any kind of special meaning for Tom?"

"He did a scene from it here for a class. Not that particular scene, but he played Petruchio. I remember because he was so goddamn good. And later he told me he did the play in New York. At some off off Broadway place. Or maybe it was just in a workshop."

"But why would he quote that particular line?"

"I dunno. Tom loved Shakespeare. He loved to toss out lines from the plays."

"Speaking of plays, did Tom mention he'd written a play?"

"Yes, it was a great little play he hoped to stage. Do the police have any leads? We're all sick about this."

I revealed that the police weren't sharing much with me, but before I hung up I promised him I would pass on what I knew when I knew it.

Washing the arugula, I considered what I'd learned about the line. If Tom were in the habit of quoting the Bard, he might have used that phrase whenever he was faced with unhappy words in life. But there was a chance it could have a more particular significance. What I needed to do was find out when and where Tom had been in the play. I had turned over his résumé to the sheriff in Andes, but Chris might know about Tom's stint as Petruchio.

As it turned out, Landon never knocked on my door—perhaps he'd gone out early for the entire evening. I tossed one of the chicken breasts in the freezer for another night. I pounded the other one until very thin, coated it in egg and bread crumbs, and began sautéing it in olive oil. I dried the arugula, added the cherry tomatoes, and made a lemon vinaigrette. My kitchen smelled heavenly, and I sipped a glass of cold Pinot Grigio as I worked, humming to another Maria Callas CD. What more could anyone want? In fact, I decided, I could have been in a freakin' documentary about single chicks who cook feasts for themselves, buy their own crystalware, and live their lives to the fullest—knowing all the while that they may want a man at some point but don't *need* one. The problem was, I could feel myself falling into a big ugly slump.

It only got worse as I ate alone on my terrace. It was crisp enough for me to need a jacket, but gloriously clear, the kind of night that would have been nice to share. My aloneness was exaggerated by the sounds of frivolity—some of it probably naked—that wafted over from the open windows of the NYU dorm one block north; apparently, these particular students had not been informed that Sunday night was a time to buckle down, get into their jammies, and prepare for the week ahead.

Consuming my meal, with a wine-to-food ratio that was definitely more on the side of the vino, I thought of how Beau had rescued me two months earlier from the Sunday night blues. I'd been making *spaghetti alle vongole* at the time, and he'd dropped by, sucked down a bowl of it, and then seduced me in my tiny kitchen.

I wondered if Jessie's plan would work if I tried it. There was nothing to lose by calling Beau's voice mail—Landon had been right on that account. If he wasn't interested and didn't respond to my phone call, I'd be in the same exact place I was now. Except why should I bother leaving a coy little message with someone who had treated me so shabbily? That, speaking of the Bard, was the rub. No matter how much I wanted to know what Beau had been about to say, I couldn't bring myself to suck up to him.

Jessie. I loved her, but as I poured myself another glass of Pinot Grigio, I thought of how much I'd hated what she'd said about wanting dibs on "Tad Hamilton." I might still be pining for Beau, but I really, really liked Chris and didn't want to consider him with another chick.

My head was pounding at nine o'clock the next morning as I hailed a cab for Chelsea Piers. In an attempt to stave off any insomnia, I'd polished off most of the bottle of wine and woke with a vein throbbing so hard in my forehead that I could see the movement in the mirror above my bathroom sink.

I'd been to Chelsea Piers a few times over the years. It's a series of buildings constructed on four adjoining piers where the West 20s meet the Hudson River. Back in the early part of the twentieth century, it had been a thriving part of the riverfront, where some of the great ships docked in between their transatlantic crossings. In fact, according to a sign posted there, the *Titanic* had been destined to dock at Pier 59, and hundreds of people gathered there after the sinking, waiting for word of their loved ones. Eventually, the docks fell into disrepair and spent decades just sagging in the Hudson until they were finally rescued and renovated. Now there was everything from a netted-in driving range to a bowling alley to photo studios to restaurants with river views. One large warehouse-looking blue building housed the sets of several television shows that filmed in Manhattan.

Chris had told me the unmarked entranceway was at the corner of the building, and the cab had just overshot it when I yelled, "Stop here!" Slipping inside, I found myself in an empty, grungy area with a carpet that appeared to be stained with everything from gum to diesel fuel. The walls, however, were lined with posters for the shows being shot there, proving I was in the right spot. There was even a poster for *Morgue*. Locket stood boldly in the middle of a small group of people, her brow furrowed in the name of justice. Chris was just to her right, looking hunky but weirdly airbrushed. Following Chris's instructions, I took the stairs one flight up.

On the second floor, I found a seating area with a receptionist engrossed in a Nora Roberts novel. Whereas the entranceway downstairs had been oddly quiet, up here I could hear the sounds of bustling activity emanating from the corridors that shot off in different directions. As I was about to give my name to the receptionist, someone came up behind me and asked, "Bailey?"

I spun around to find a spunky-looking girl with spiky black hair, dressed in cargo pants and a clear earpiece plugged in her ear, stepping toward me.

"I'm Cara," she said once I'd acknowledged that I was indeed Bailey Weggins. "Chris asked me to keep an eye out for you. I can take you to him now."

After securing me a visitor's pass from the receptionist, she led me down one of the long corridors, nodding as she walked to various people we encountered along the way. There were lots of doorways along the hall, which I assumed must be dressing rooms, but based on the spacing between them, they couldn't be very big. A door to one opened, and as a man emerged dressed in a cop uniform, I saw that a fake leather reclining chair ate up most of the narrow room.

"These are the dressing rooms for day players, who have just a few lines," Cara said, seeing me check out the room. "Chris is around this way, with the regulars."

He wasn't in his dressing room, however. After knocking once, Cara entered, and when she saw the room was empty, she motioned me in with her shoulder.

"He said that if he was in makeup, you should just have a seat. Why don't you make yourself comfortable. I doubt he'll be that long."

His dressing room here was larger than the one in the honey wagon, and though one chair was strewn with clothes, the rest of it was orderly—neat stacks of books and magazines, a brand-new looking Bose CD player, and a row of water bottles. There was a Rubik's Cube on a tabletop, and I picked it up, turning it over a few times in my hands.

"Please, take that," I heard Chris say behind me. "It's driving me insane."

"I didn't picture you as a Rubik's Cube man."

"My mother sent it to me when I told her the TV business is all about hurry up and wait."

He was dressed in jeans and a button-down Oxford shirt, and he was wearing a touch of makeup, just as he'd been when I'd visited him on location last week. He leaned down and kissed me hello. "How you doing this morning, anyway?"

"I finally feel as if that drug is out of my system—except I've got this killer headache. I overdid the vino last night."

"Do tell," he said, looking at me quizzically.

"Oh, just me alone on the terrace," I said quickly, "losing track of how much I was imbibing as I watched all the city lights come on." I felt oddly guilty, perhaps because so many of my thoughts had been focused on Beau. And also because I was planning to withhold Locket's revelation. I'd given my word to her.

"Well, maybe I can get out early enough tonight so you won't have to drink alone," he said. He was grinning, but he seemed slightly preoccupied. I knew he must feel wired up about shooting, and the last thing he needed was me on the premises.

"I like the sound of that," I said. "Now, tell me what's happening this morning."

"I'm doing a scene with Locket—in our offices. Cara is going to be your escort. She'll make sure you don't trip over any wires—or accidentally get placed in one of the morgue drawers."

"What?" I exclaimed.

Chris laughed. "When the drawers are pulled out during a scene, there are real people on them—they use extras. They just look a lot more realistic as dead people than dummies do. . . . Look, though it's fine for me to have visitors, you should try to be as inconspicuous as possible this morning. Alex is around, and we don't want him to wonder what you're doing here."

"Will do. Though I'm dying to watch you shoot a scene, my main goal is to ask Deke about the loan—to see how he reacts. Where will *he* be?"

"He'll be around, mostly on the periphery. He's a grip, in charge of scenery. Everything's already set up, but if they decide to change anything, he's got to be standing by, ready to do it."

"I'm not looking forward to chatting with him, but it has to be done."

"Just try to keep it low-key. If Alex gets wind of—"

"I know, I know."

There was a light tapping on the door. After Chris called, "Come in," Cara poked her head inside the room.

"They're ready for you, Chris."

"Okay, be right there." He waited for her to close the door. "Get this—shows *insist* on escorting the stars from their dressing rooms to the set. It makes you wonder if a few actors have panicked over the years and bolted out a side door."

"Have *you* ever had the urge?"

He glanced to the left wistfully and then returned his gaze to me, smiling. "Nah. I mean, there are moments these days, now that success seems within my grasp, that the pressure feels freaking intense, and I wonder if I'll look back with any regrets. But there's no urge to bolt. That's why I couldn't believe Tom had just taken off."

"So do I come with you now?"

"No, Cara will bring me down and get me settled and come back for you in a few minutes."

"Well, break a leg. Just one thing before you go. Do you know when and where Tom performed *Taming of the Shrew*?"

"What makes you ask that?" he asked, his eyes squinted in puzzlement.

"Just a funny little lead I'm pursuing."

"He did so many plays—some at that little theater company I mentioned, but others all over the place." Absentmindedly, he glanced in the mirror along one wall and smoothed down his shirt.

"Does he have an agent I could talk to?"

Chris froze. "An agent?" he asked. "Why would you need to talk to an agent?"

"To find out about the play."

"He didn't have a regular agent—just used a few people free-lance. Look, I better go, okay?"

He left the dressing room seeming even more distracted than when he'd first come in. I realized I probably shouldn't have bothered him about the case right before he'd been about to shoot a scene.

For the next few minutes, I cooled my heels in the dressing room, and then, out of boredom, I stepped just outside the door. A few crew types dressed in jeans and grungy T-shirts ambled up and down the corridor, and then a woman who appeared to be a makeup artist—with a large fanny pack around her waist—sprinted down the hall as if she were answering a code blue. Maybe one of Locket's lips had exploded. I watched her run and as I turned back, I spotted none other than Deke, making his way down the corridor. I saw a flash of recognition in his eyes, but he completely ignored me. As he passed in front of me, he hoisted a can of Diet Coke to his mouth and took a swig.

"Hey, Deke," I called out after him, knowing this might be my only chance. "Have you got a sec?"

"Not really," he said, turning in his tracks and eyeing me surlily.

"It's really important. Really."

"You got exactly thirty seconds. What is it?" He stepped closer to me and let his slate-colored eyes bore into me. I noticed, to my disgust, that he had a bunch of coarse hairs hanging from his nostrils.

"Remember how we were talking about Tom? I found out you borrowed a huge chunk of money from him and then didn't pay it back." I was stirring things up big-time, yet if Deke were the one who'd poisoned my drink, he already had plenty of suspicions about me, and I wasn't going to be any worse off than before.

He kept his hard eyes steady, but the edge of his tongue escaped involuntarily, flicking at the corner of his mouth like an ugly red lizard.

"You really are a little Miss Marple, aren't you?"

"Just trying to help," I said.

"Well, to put it politely, it's none of your f-ing business. But if you *must* know, I paid Tom back the week before he died. Everything was nicey-nice with us."

"Is that right?" I asked incredulously. "So it would be indicated by a deposit to his bank account?"

"He didn't ask me to manage his finances," he said, smirking.

I tried to figure out where to go next, but before I had a chance, Cara called out my name from the end of the corridor and motioned me to hurry with her. I wanted to keep poking at Deke, but it wasn't going to be possible now.

Cara and I double-timed it down the corridor, made another turn, and then descended a staircase. Once on the lower level, she led me to a door with a red alarm light to the right.

"Your cell phone off?" Cara said, stopping.

"Good point," I said, and fumbled for it in my purse. After I'd switched it off, she pushed open the door and we entered a dim, cavernous space bustling with at least thirty people. There were plenty of crew, dressed in the standard uniform of jeans and T-shirts and some with tool belts about their waists, but there were also a few businessy types hovering around the edges.

To my left was a huge three-sided morgue, with gleaming stainless-steel tables, sinks, hanging scales descending from the ceiling, and even, oddly, the smell of disinfectant. Maybe they added that for true verisimilitude, to make the actors really believe they were in the world of death. The only thing not totally real were the windows. Behind each one was a fake backdrop of brick city buildings, though I assumed they would look real enough when you saw them on TV.

With me two inches behind her, Cara proceeded to the next section on the floor, which featured a stage—this one brightly lit—with a shabby-looking bullpen area of a dozen work desks. Chris was sitting on one of the desks, staring into space. Locket stood right in front of him, studying a small white script packet, while a hairstylist used his palm to flatten her flyaway hairs. A few crew members fussed on the set, apparently following the orders of a fortysomething guy standing among them. While the scene in the park had been shot with handheld cameras, this one involved two cameras on dollies.

Cara parked me on the sidelines in a small cluster of crew who at the moment seemed to be just waiting around. There was a large group of people farther down, all sitting on director chairs in front of several monitors. I caught a glimpse of Alex in the mix, but he was involved in a discussion with someone I assumed must be the director. And suddenly there was Deke, too. He must have come from a different direction. Trying to be less conspicuous, I stepped back a couple of feet, deeper into the shadow created by a wall on wheels beside me.

There was a palpable tension in the room, as if everyone were on pins and needles awaiting news of some kind. "Last looks," someone called. The makeup artist I'd seen earlier stepped quickly from the shadow, brushed something onto Locket's lips, and scurried off.

"Rolling," the same person called next. Then, "And action."

Cara tapped a finger to her lips, indicating I should be quiet, and then, concentrating on someone's words into her earpiece, wandered off.

Locket spoke first. "But death occurred before midnight, Jared. The autopsy's going to show that."

Chris shook his head. "But consider how hot the room was," he said. "That changes everything." He seemed so at ease, so comfortable, with all these people around him. I forgot about

Tom and Deke and everything else and allowed myself to be mesmerized by the exchange of lines between the two stars.

Then, without warning, I felt the oddest sensation across the rise of my foot. I glanced down and peered into the shadows. A huge black snake, endlessly long, was slithering over my foot. My breath seemed to freeze in my chest. I fought a scream, I did everything possible *not* to scream, but I couldn't help it. I let out a wail like a banshee and leapt backward.

CHAPTER 13

The snake shot forward, hugging the wall, and then I couldn't see it anymore. I became aware that the low-level hum in the room had ceased in a split second and that the two actors had stopped speaking their lines. I looked up and around. Cara was rushing toward me, and everyone else was just staring at me or craning their necks, trying to pinpoint where the scream had emanated from.

"What the hell's going on?" the director yelled.

I didn't say anything, feeling paralyzed and also hoping that maybe it was just a rhetorical question and that in a few seconds the director would call out, "Rolling" again, or *something*. Then I could simply whisper into Cara's ear about what had happened and slink off, letting her deal with it all.

But the director shouted again—"I *said*, 'What the hell is going on?'"—and that surely meant I was supposed to volunteer an answer. The shock and repulsion I'd felt at the sight of the snake were snatched away and replaced by a feeling of total and complete humiliation. I hadn't felt this embarrassed since fourth grade, when my underpants had slipped to the ground while I was jumping around in my best pink party dress. The feeling got even worse when I finally made eye contact with Chris and saw that he looked completely chagrined—and that the blood had drained from his face, leaving it as colorless as a latex glove.

"I—I'm so sorry," I sputtered. "But there was a huge black snake on the floor next to me. It—it slithered off toward the back there."

At the sound of the word *snake,* people all over the set let out cries of alarm and began sweeping the floor anxiously with their eyes.

"A snake?" the director snapped, slipping off his chair. "There aren't any *snakes* in here." He began walking in my direction, followed, to my dismay, by Alex.

"Well, there was one today," I declared. "I think you should try to find it. It might be dangerous."

"I am absolutely petrified of snakes," Locket announced loudly. "We have to find it—or I can't work."

The director reached the spot where I stood. "What kind of snake?" he demanded. "You mean like a garter snake?" Alex, I noticed, was standing silently behind him, his top lip curled. He had a look on his face that suggested he wouldn't mind seeing a python crush every bone in my body and then swallow me whole.

"No, not like that," I said, trying to sound as calm and sane as possible. "It was at least four feet long, black—with some white markings."

"You're *sure*? And you say it went toward the rear of the set?" He swung his shaven head in that direction, then looked back and posed the question I'd been dreading: "Who *are* you, anyway?"

Oh God, I thought. I didn't want to get Chris in any kind of trouble. "My name is Bailey Weg—"

"*That's* what she saw," a man's voice exclaimed, interrupting. Simultaneously, the director, Alex, and I all turned. Squatting behind me, arms resting on his beefy thighs, was my good buddy Deke. He jabbed his finger at a partially coiled length of black cable on the ground to my left. "That's her snake right there."

"Oh, for chrissake," the director said. He sighed in annoyance and strode back toward his chair.

"That *isn't* what I saw," I called after him, feeling totally sandbagged. "I definitely saw a real snake—with white markings."

"You need to leave," Alex snarled, his voice low but frighteningly firm, like someone squeezing your arm really hard with his thumb. "Right now."

I wasn't going to argue. Nothing I said was going to convince them, and nothing would make me happier than to just get out of there. As for the snake, I didn't care if they all ended up with fang puncture wounds in their asses—except for Chris, of course. At the moment I didn't dare look him in the eye. I lowered my head and walked quickly down the hall, with Cara nipping at my heels. I suspected she was trying to make it appear as if she were taking action like a good PA but didn't know me from Adam. Once we were back near the dressing rooms, though, she gave me a piece of her mind in a loud, rapid whisper.

"I leave you alone for two seconds and you disrupt the whole set. I could get fired."

"And what would *you* have done if some huge snake had slithered over *your* foot? Grin and bear it?"

"*If* you even saw a snake. What would a snake like that be doing in here, anyway?"

"You tell me. Is there any chance it's being used in an upcoming scene?"

"In *CSI* they'd think nothing of having one crawl out of a corpse during an autopsy. But we're a much more realistic show."

"Look," I said, realizing that there was no convincing her,

either, "I'm sorry for creating any problems for you. Will you please tell Chris I'm really sorry, too? I'll give him a call later."

Luckily, a cab was dropping off a passenger right outside the building, and I hailed it. As I leaned back against the leather seat, I realized I could barely think straight.

"You gonna give me the address?" the driver grumbled as he was pulling out onto the West Side Highway. What I felt like doing was telling him to drop me in a bar in the Village where I could pound down a margarita, but I had to show at *Buzz* and finish my story on Tom.

As the cab shot uptown, I replayed the scene in the studio again and again in my head. Was there any possibility my imagination had gotten the better of me? Maybe what I'd seen *had* been the cable, yanked at that precise moment by one of the crew members so that it slid across my foot—and in the dim light just *looked* reptilian. Deke might have even been the yanker himself, eager to scare the bejesus out of me. Originally, I'd noticed him standing far off to the right, but then I'd become spellbound by Chris's performance and had momentarily lost track of Deke's whereabouts.

No, I was almost positive—what I'd seen was a live, butt-ugly snake. There'd been those whitish markings on its back—which the cable didn't have—and I'd observed its head, too, with the snoutlike shape that could trigger primordial fear in just about everyone.

But what was a snake doing on a soundstage? Was it possible that it belonged to Deke and he'd set it loose when he saw me arrive on the set? He looked like the type of guy who would enjoy having a pet that slithered. Or perhaps the snake belonged in the building for a reason unbeknownst to me. Chris would clearly learn more as the day went on and would clue me in later. Thinking of Chris, though, made my stomach knot. Shouldn't he have come to my rescue back then? It would have been such a relief if he'd acknowledged me as his friend and assured the director that I wasn't prone to hallucinations. But everything had happened so fast, I couldn't totally blame him for hanging back, unsure of what to do.

When I arrived at *Buzz*, the place was *literally* buzzing, as if someone had dropped a thousand cicadas on the floor. Monday was always at least a nine on the nutty scale, but it could reach a ten when something really big was happening—for instance, when a star couple split or an A-lister ended up caught with his pants down. This seemed like one of those days.

"What's going on?" I asked Jessie as I parked myself in my workstation. "It seems like all hell is breaking loose." Just as I spoke, I caught a glimpse of Nash in his glass-walled office shaking his head hard as he spoke to Valerie and one of the other deputy editors.

"Apparently Nash is changing the cover story, so people are scrambling," Jessie said. "What's up with *you*? Your face looks kind of pinched, like you slipped a disk as you were walking into the building."

I described my nightmare at Chelsea Piers. Leo, who started off half listening, rolled his chair closer as the tale got juicier.

"A *snake*?" Jessie said after I'd reached the climax of the story. "You've got to be fucking kidding me."

"They say if you dream about snakes, it means you're really horny," Leo said. "Or wait—that you're *afraid* of sex. I forget which."

"I didn't *dream* I saw a snake, Leo," I said, aggravated. "I really did see one." He shrugged and returned to his computer. Jessie, on the other hand, pumped me for more details.

"And what about Chris?" she asked. "Was he there through this whole thing?"

"Oh yeah. And from the look on his face, you would have

thought I was flashing my boobs for a *Girls Gone Wild* video. He looked positively mortified."

"Did you talk to him afterwards?"

"No, because he was shooting. I'll catch up with him later—I'm sure everything will all be okay." But a part of me remained worried.

I needed to tackle my work, but first and foremost I was going on a snake hunt. I Googled big black snakes and found several Web sites devoted to the delightful creatures. It didn't take long to find a species that matched what I'd seen: *Lampropeltis getulus,* better known as the common king snake. It was found in most parts of the southern United States (which, of course, didn't explain what the hell it was doing at Chelsea Piers) and grew anywhere from just over two feet long to almost seven. It was black or dark brown with white or yellowish markings—that often took the form of crossbands or stripes. The good news for the actors prancing around the set was that it was nonvenomous. The king snake's claim to fame: It liked to feed on other snakes, even poisonous ones. Yummy.

After grabbing coffee, I checked in with the art department to review the final layout for the item on Tom. They were using his head shot as the photo along with an inset of a shot that the network must have provided, because he was sitting at his morgue desk, holding out a slip of paper. The entire piece was just a few paragraphs long, short by even *Buzz* standards. Sad, I told myself, to think that a change in hairstyle by Jessica Simpson garnered more ink than Tom's death. But then maybe Tom would have never wanted to possess any real estate in a magazine like *Buzz.*

Back at my desk, I reviewed the text I'd submitted Friday. What I needed was an update on the investigator, and this gave me the excuse to hound Sheriff Schmidt again. I got right through to him this time and explained that I was now calling as a journalist.

"Why didn't you tell me that from the beginning?" he demanded, sounding Miffed with a capital M.

"I'm sorry about that," I said, not wanting to burn any bridges. "But I didn't know that I was going to be writing the story then. I'd been searching for Tom as a favor to a friend, not in any journalistic capacity."

"Well, I don't have much to tell you. We've confirmed that the body is that of Tom Fain, and that death was the result of repeated blows by a sharp object. We are questioning people in the Andes area and, with the assistance of the New York office of the state police, people in New York City as well. At this time, we do not have a suspect."

Something about the tone of his voice made me assume that there hadn't been much progress on the case, though that was a point he would neither confirm nor deny.

"Do you think that Tom could have been killed by someone who worked on the show with him?" I asked, knowing he wasn't going to share but curious as to how he'd respond.

"I'm not at liberty to discuss any of our theories at this point."

I couldn't help feeling guilty as I considered the info I was sitting on—Locket's visit to Tom and her revelation about the unnamed visitor. But I had given my word to Locket that I would let her break the news to the cops. If she didn't do it tomorrow, as promised, then I would have to take matters into my own hands.

There was a piece of information I *could* share with Schmidt, though, and I decided this was the moment. I told him that in the course of doing my research for my article (*slight* distortion), I had discovered that Tom had loaned a crew member several thousand dollars and then had run into difficulty getting it repaid. I'd been reluctant to throw Deke under the bus until I learned more about the situation, but it was clear to me now that the dude was a real creep.

Schmidt didn't comment for a few seconds, though I could discern him breathing.

"We're aware of this matter, yes," he said at last.

I wondered how he'd stumbled onto it. "Oh, Mr. Barish must have told you," I said. He didn't say anything back, making me suspect my guess had been right.

"You don't have anything else you want to share with me, do you?" he asked.

"No, I don't," I said, convinced that my voice had jumped an octave as I'd spoken. He was gonna be mad if come Wednesday I was the one breaking the news about Locket's little sojourn to the Catskills.

"Well, I want to hear from you if you learn anything of significance."

"Of course," I told him.

My item in *Buzz* also gave me an excuse to call Harper again. She could play hard to get with me on a personal level, but as the PR rep for *Morgue*, she would have to respond to the message I was about to leave on her cell.

"Harper, it's Bailey Weggins. We're going to bed at *Buzz* with a short item on Tom's death, and I'm calling to get an official response from the producers and cast of *Morgue*." On the one hand she might not have much interest in crafting the perfect "We are deeply saddened" message for *Buzz*, but as a publicist she wouldn't want an item going to press without her knowing what it said and how it might impact on her—and without her having had a chance to mold it to her liking.

For the next half hour I fiddled with my little piece, incorporating what I'd learned from the sheriff's department and leaving room for whatever Harper coughed up. I called Tom a promising young actor, and my heart ached as I reread those words on my computer screen.

After I routed the piece to Valerie, with a few TKs indicating I was still waiting for more pieces of info, I refilled my coffee cup in the kitchenette. On my stroll back I considered what my next move should be. I'd reported on Tom's death, but I still had to figure out who had brutally murdered him. Deke and Alex were definite contenders, and so, too, was Harper, but right now I didn't have a reason to suspect one more than another.

There was only one possible clue left for me to work with— the line Tom had spoken from *Taming of the Shrew*. I needed to find out more about when and where he'd performed the play and what meaning it held for him. Chris didn't know who Tom used as a freelance agent, but Barish might. I phoned him.

"Actually, I do have a name in my file," he said after I was put through. I could hear a drawer slide open. "Okay, here it is— Buddy Hess." He ran off the number.

"Thanks, I'll follow up. I spoke to the sheriff's office today. I hear you passed on the information about the unpaid loan."

"Yes, I'm glad you reminded me of it. It's definitely a motive, and I want them looking into this Deke fellow."

"I saw him today on set, and he told me that he repaid the loan the week before Tom died. Could you check and see if there's any record of Tom depositing that money in his bank account?"

"Let me see what I can find out, but he may have just decided to use it as a cash reserve."

I also realized that Tom could have used the cash as part of the fund he was pulling together for Barry, the guy doing work on the house in Andes—though I highly doubted the loan had ever actually been repaid.

"Well, thank you for keeping me in the loop," Barish added. "I have a client waiting, so I need to sign off."

"Just out of curiosity," I said before he cut me off, "was Tom trying to mount a play he'd written?"

"Who told you that?"

"A few people mentioned it to me."

"Yes, as a matter of fact, he was. We're not talking Broadway, of course. He would have gone the off off Broadway route."

"I hear part of his motivation in selling the house was to obtain money to finance the play."

"I believe that was his intention, yes."

"But it seems like he already had money at his disposal. Why couldn't he have simply withdrawn money from his bank account for the play?"

"Because it was going to cost more than he had in his day-to-day reserves. Putting on even a minor production is fairly expensive."

"Could he have taken money from his trust fund?"

Barish sighed as if I'd just suggested the earth was flat. "The house was a white elephant, and Tom wanted to unload it anyway. And besides, I'd be derelict in my duty letting Tom dip into his capital. His parents' intentions were for the trust to last Tom for a lifetime. Now, if you'll excuse me . . ."

I looked up Buddy Hess's number and phoned his office. Rather than identify myself as a reporter from *Buzz*, which would guarantee that Hess *wouldn't* pick up, I told the arrogant-sounding woman who answered that I was calling with important information about the murder of Tom Fain. Hess picked up a minute later.

"Who is this, anyway?" he said curtly.

I explained my involvement in looking for Tom and how I was now trying to figure out who had killed him.

"What a damn shame this all is," he said, softening. "Tom was a real sweetheart, and you don't find many of those in this business. So what's this news you want to share with me?"

"Actually," I said, "I was hoping to get a bit of info from *you*. I'm following a few leads related to Tom's death, and I really need your help."

"Isn't that a job for the cops?" he said.

"Yes, but they're upstate and they may not have the resources to devote to this. As you say, Tom was a real sweetheart, and I hate the idea that his killer might not be apprehended."

"Okay, so what can I do for you?"

"Tom was in a production of *Taming of the Shrew* here in New York. Do you know when and where?"

"*Taming of the Shrew*? Sounds vaguely familiar. Maddy, get me a copy of Tom Fain's résumé, will you? You have to understand that I only represented Tom on a freelance basis, so I can't tell you off the top of my head."

"How does that differ from having him as an actual client?"

"A client is under contract. But you don't sign anyone until you're reasonably sure it's going to be good for both of you. There's a big pool of actors I keep head shots on, and when I hear of something they might be right for, I submit their shots to casting agents on a freelance basis. I sent Tom out for a small part on *Morgue,* and they liked him so much they tested him for the bigger role, too. He was *this* close to nailing it, but they pulled out at the last minute, and ironically he ended up with the part he'd first auditioned for."

"I hear he was pretty bummed."

"Yeah, but like I told him, it was still a nice break. He's—he *was* a good actor and a great-looking guy, and I think it was only a matter of time before something else turned up for him. I offered to sign him at that point, but he was suddenly gun-shy. I think he suspected I was partly responsible for him not getting the bigger role. . . . Okay, here we go. He did *Shrew* last February. It was at the Chaps Theatre on West Thirteeenth Street."

"That's the theater where he was a member of the company?"

"Yeah, it's an off off Broadway theater, small, but I do some scouting there. It's a pretty decent group."

"Thanks. By the way, is it true that Tom didn't get the part of Jared because the producers found out he'd been in rehab?"

"How'd you hear that?"

"It turned up in my inquiries."

"Yeah, that was lousy. I tried to make the producer see that it was extenuating circumstances—his parents dying and all that. I could see absolutely no reason for it to become a problem for him again. But they didn't want to take the chance of getting burned."

"Did they do an investigation—is that how they found out?"

"They do conduct background checks, but I had the feeling in this case that someone tipped them off."

I felt goose bumps rise on my arms. "You mean squealed on him?"

"Yup. No one said this was a pretty business. You ever see *Rosemary's Baby*? Her husband makes a pact with the devil so he can land a part. That's tame compared to some of the stuff I've experienced."

After I signed off, I headed for the kitchenette in search of more coffee and then, with my Styrofoam cup in hand, stole into one of the small conference rooms at the far end of the floor. I closed the door and fell into a chair, finally removed from the cacophony of closing day. I felt really weird, but I wasn't sure why. Maybe the events of the past few days were finally catching up with me. Maybe, too, I realized, the more I learned about Tom, the more heartbreaking his whole story became. It seemed as if the poor guy really *had* been cursed: First he loses his parents, then the role of his dreams, and finally his life. Yet his own personality may have contributed in part to his death. Tom was a good guy, kind and generous, yet also somewhat of a pushover—and that trait had on certain occasions conspired against him. He had a tough time saying no to guys like Deke who wanted cash and to chicks who wanted to bed him—from what I'd discovered, Blythe, Harper, and Locket had all been the aggressors.

After chilling for a while, I went back out to the zoo. People were charging around the cube farm, barking into phones, and shouting to one another across workstations. As far as I knew, Tom Cruise had just run off with Paris Hilton, and that was the new cover story Nash was crashing. But I couldn't have cared less.

Just after the first proof of my piece surfaced, Harper called.

"So now you're Miss *Buzz* Reporter, is that it?" she said. Her tone was as testy as her words.

"I've always been a reporter for *Buzz*—you knew that."

"But I didn't know you were covering this story. You were just helping Chris."

"Look, Harper," I said, trying to keep any edge out of my own voice, "I swear I never misrepresented the situation. We're doing a very small story on Tom. Can you give me a quote I can use—just something nice about Tom from the cast and producers."

" 'We are deeply saddened by the death of Tom Fain. He was a wonderful actor and a terrific asset to the show, and we will all miss him.' There—is that it?"

"Actually, no. I want to talk to you about your relationship with Tom totally off the record. I was trying to do that all weekend."

"I really have nothing to say to you. What went on between me and Tom is private."

"Well, my question isn't about the private aspects of your relationship. I'm curious why you implied to me that you returned Sunday night of the weekend Tom disappeared when you actually took the red-eye back on Friday night."

"What the hell difference does it make? We finished up early, and I just felt— You're not trying to imply that *I* killed Tom, are you?"

"Did you know he had a home in Andes?"

"No, though it's none of your business whether I did or didn't. I can't believe what you're hinting at. What possible motive do you think I had? Tom and I were dating. We cared about each other."

"And what if you found out Tom was seeing someone else?"

"What are you talking about?"

"Let's just say you found out Tom was involved with someone else. Like someone on the show. That could make you angry."

It was like throwing a stink bomb. But goading her might be the only way to trigger a reaction.

"Who the fuck are you talking about?"

"No one in particular. I'm just tossing out a theory."

"Look, I gave you the quote, now leave me alone. And I don't want you coming by the set—ever again. Do you hear me?"

"That's not for you to say, is it?"

"No, you're right—it's not for me to say. But Alex doesn't want to see your face again. And I bet Chris doesn't, either. You totally humiliated him."

"I—"

But she had hung up.

Oh jeez, what did she mean by that? I wondered. I had not phoned Chris yet, expecting that I'd be hearing from him, but maybe I needed to do damage control. I called his cell and left a short message, asking him to ring me.

For the next few hours, I hung at my desk sullenly, waiting for my story to clear. I made a call to the Chaps Theatre phone number, but discovered it was only a central box office service. I'd clearly have to stop by. Finally, at seven, I was good to go. Almost everyone else, except for the fashion and beauty writers, was still at their desks, held hostage by Hollywood.

It was dark when I arrived home. After changing out of my work clothes into jeans and a short-sleeved sweater, I headed out for a walk. I wanted to check out the Chaps Theatre, which wasn't far from me, but mostly I just wanted to give my brain a respite from murder and mayhem. I picked up a slice of pizza on University Place and then zigzagged my way north and west. I could tell half a block from the theater that it was closed—no light fell onto the sidewalk in front of it. When I reached the building, I peered through the glass doors into the small, weary looking lobby. One light remained on and lit rows of framed memorabilia of old productions. A sign announced that performances for the current production, a new play called *Coeds from Hell*, ran from Wednesday through Sunday.

I continued to ramble, stopping at one point for a double chocolate ice-cream cone—because I damn well felt like it—and when I left the shop I headed north. I had walked for about ten more minutes, thinking about trips I'd taken and stories I'd written, anything to keep my mind temporarily off Chris and Tom and Locket and Harper, before it hit me: I was making a beeline for Beau Regan's building.

CHAPTER 14

Don't be an idiot, a little voice in me commanded. I felt as if I were watching a horror movie in which the heroine is spending the night in a sagging old house about six miles from the main road and has decided to investigate a tapping sound she's heard in the attic or basement, despite the fact that it's thundering and lightning and the power is promising to go out at any second.

But I couldn't stop myself. What I realized, however, was that I wasn't heading to Beau's in order to try out Landon's or Jessie's tactics for winning him back. He wasn't interested, and nothing I did would change that. The reason for my trip was that I had unfinished business with Beau. On Saturday night, I'd relished delivering my zinger about the postcard, but that hadn't really conveyed how disappointed I was by his behavior. So I would ring his bell, and if he was home, I would apologize for being snippy. And then I would use up five minutes of his precious time to tell him how I really felt. Weren't articles in magazines like *Gloss* always suggesting the importance of closure?

It was eight-thirty when I reached his neighborhood. There was only a decent chance that he was home. For instance, he might have stopped by his apartment for a shower or change of clothes or to pick up a jumbo box of Trojans before heading out for the night. *Or* he might even be there with a chick. Oh God, was it really smart to be doing this? But I just couldn't stop my little legs in their quest. They were like a pair of Disney movie dogs that had been separated from their owner and were crossing the Rockies in order to make it home.

I reached his building and opened the door into the empty foyer. Taking a breath, I pushed the buzzer. Excruciating seconds passed without a response, and I tried again, just for the sheer torture of it. Still no response. With a surprising surge of relief, I turned to go. And then, just as I reached the door, Beau's voice came over the intercom, jerking my body like I'd just stuck a fork down a toaster.

"Yes?" he asked. He sounded sleepy.

"Um, hi, Beau, it's Bailey. I'm down here in your foyer"— *obviously*—"and I was wondering if you might want to grab some coffee—or like a glass of wine."

There was the longest pause, and then it hit me. He *was* with a woman. He'd probably just finished having a *predinner* sack ses- sion and had padded down the hall to the intercom, leaving her flushed beneath his pale gray comforter while he determined who had rudely interrupted their carnal bliss.

"Oh, hi. Sure. But why don't you come up first. I need to put some clothes on."

Fucking great, I thought. He's going to *introduce* me to her.

"I don't want to interrupt anything. I was nearby and—"

"It's not a problem. I was taking a nap, but I'm up now."

He hit the buzzer, and I pushed open the door. My legs felt

wobbly suddenly, not the brave doggies they'd been only minutes before.

Beau had thrown on some clothes by the time I got up there—a pair of blue jeans and a blue-and-white-striped dress shirt, with just one side tucked in. His hair was tousled, and his eyes had that dreamy quality I'd noticed in the few mornings I'd awoken next to him.

"Sorry to wake you," I said, staving off the awkward shift my body was dying to make.

"I'm glad you did," he said. "I've had a little jet lag since I got back. Come on in. Would you just like to have a drink here?"

"No, I don't want to put you to any trouble." I would have liked to stay, to be in that serene space again, *his* space, but it didn't seem like the smartest idea. "I was thinking we could just go in the neighborhood someplace—you know, like a coffee place."

"Okay. Just let me get my shoes."

He wandered off to the bedroom, and I let my eyes dart around his living room like bumblebees. There were piles of papers on the ottoman, as if he'd been going through the mail that had accumulated when he'd been in Turkey. An exotic, musky scent hung in the room, just a slight undertone, and I panicked until I remembered that it was *Beau* who smelled that way.

He came back in less than a minute, wearing a pair of flip-flops. I knew he had to be curious about why I was here, but in that Zen way of his, he gave nothing away.

We walked up toward the avenue, him leading. As we maneuvered around pedestrians and baby strollers, we didn't talk much. I asked if he generally suffered from jet lag.

"No, not usually," he said.

He asked why, since Monday was closing day, I was out of work reasonably early, and I explained that I'd had only a short crime piece to do tonight. Gosh, at the rate our zippy banter was going, people were going to accuse us of trying to top Bogey and Bacall.

When we reached the avenue, I thought he was going to steer me to the little café/bakery where we'd eaten breakfast together once, but instead he nodded toward a storefront restaurant with a dark wood bar and dozens of little votive lights twinkling on every surface.

"We can sit at the bar," he said. "They'll even let you have a cappuccino if you want."

I was dying for a glass of wine, just to take the freakin' edge off, but I thought it would seem as though I'd duped him into a quasi-date— so I went for the cappuccino. As he asked for a draft beer and shifted his body on the stool, I felt his leg brush up against mine. Those slim but muscular legs underneath had on several occasions been wrapped around me brilliantly in bed.

"So how was Turkey, anyway?" I asked, stalling just a moment before plunging into what I really wanted to say. "How did the film go?"

"I'm just starting the editing now, but I think the shooting went well. Aphrodisius's pretty awesome. It wasn't looted by the Europeans the way places like Ephesus were. The days were hot and dusty, so the work was tough, but it was all pretty fascinating."

And there was a girl, undoubtedly. Some archaeology student working on a master's degree, brown as a nut from the sun and absolutely gaga, no doubt, when the hunky documentary filmmaker blew onto the site.

"I'm glad it worked out," I said as the bartender set down his beer. Beau stared at the glass for a second and then looked back at me, his eyes expectant.

"So what can I do for you?" he asked.

Stalling opportunity over.

"First of all, I wanted to apologize for the nasty comment I made at the party. It wasn't really what I intended to say."

"It's nice to know you don't actually harbor any evil thoughts about me."

"I didn't say *that*," I corrected, half-joking.

He raised one eyebrow. "Ahhh."

"Don't worry—I'm not going to bite your head off. I want to be honest, though. I shouldn't have been rude the other night, but there's a reason I acted bitchy. It really bothered me that you just went incommunicado. I would have accepted it if you'd told me before you left that you flat-out couldn't commit. You'd already been candid about your situation. But you left saying that things were still open for discussion. And then I didn't hear from you."

He rubbed at his chin, clearly choosing his words. "I don't have any excuse you'll like, Bailey. Like I told you before, you blew me away when I met you. But I was at a weird place in my life, not really feeling ready for anything serious relationshipwise. I thought Turkey would be a time to think it through. But once I got there, New York seemed like another planet, and I just didn't feel like I was in a spot or a position to make a decision. The longer I waited to try to write you those words, the harder it was to do. I'm sorry that I handled it that way."

"Okay, well, at least now you've explained it, so thanks." My voice sounded squeaky suddenly, and I realized that I was stinging a little inside, as if I'd been snapped by a big fat rubber band. I'd already accepted the rejection by him, but this was the first time I was hearing it verbalized.

"I hope you're not always going to view me as some giant rat," he said.

"No, I don't think I implied that." My cappuccino arrived, and I took a sip, then licked the foam off my lips. "I just feel it was unfair of you to make me sit around waiting rather than letting me know where I stood. End of lecture."

He cocked his right eyebrow again. "Actually, the other night it didn't look as if you'd waited all that long."

"Just because I spent time with another man doesn't mean it hurt any less not to hear from you."

"What's his show about again? Hard bodies finding dead bodies?"

"Sort of," I said, smiling. "It's about the New York City Morgue."

"Where does one meet an actor if you're not in the business? At the gym?"

My, my. He seemed hot and bothered. Was the unflappable Beau Regan actually flapped?

"We met over a year ago," I said, ignoring the little dig. "And then recently he asked for my help with a friend of his." I gave him a brief overview of the Tom situation, of finding the body and trying to figure out what in the world had happened.

"That sounds horrible," he said. "Any leads?"

"A few that I'm checking out."

I glanced surreptitiously at my watch. It seemed time to high-tail it out of there. I'd said what I needed to, and now the last thing I wanted was for the night to dissolve into idle chitchat between us.

"Well, I should go," I said. "I'm sure you've got things to do, too."

"Ready if you are," he said, reaching for his wallet.

"No, no, I asked you," I insisted, riffling through my purse.

"I'll tell you what," he said. "We'll have a drink one day, and you can pick up the tab that time."

"Oh, is this the 'Let's try to be friends at least' part of the conversation? Why don't we aim for 'Let's be *friendly*' instead—in case we bump into each other at another Locket Ford party? That seems like a more realistic goal."

"Okay, if that's how you'd like it," he said, and offered what seemed like a rueful smile.

Suddenly we were out on the street. I felt a weird sinking sensation as I realized that it was definitely over, that *this* was the last time I'd ever be with Beau.

"I don't know what good it will do for me to say this, but I hope you'll be careful on this story," Beau said. "It sounds pretty scary." He didn't know the half of it—I hadn't told him about the drugging or the phone calls.

"Of course, yes. I'll be careful. Well, good-bye. Take care."

"Good-bye, Bailey." He leaned forward and kissed me lightly on the cheek. I caught the full force of the musky scent he wore. I turned quickly and strode off, wondering if he stood on the sidewalk watching me or if he was already hurrying home, glad to have his closure-over-cocktails experience with me behind him.

By the time I was two blocks away, I felt close to blubbering. But I didn't let myself. If Beau couldn't recognize the brilliant connection he had with me, then I couldn't help him. And I had Chris—Chris, who made me laugh and seemed so caring and protective and wasn't some freakin' mystery man.

I fished my cell phone out of my purse, wondering if I'd missed a call from him. There wasn't any word. "Chris," I said, leaving another message, "I'd love to catch up with you. Please give me a call."

Back at my place, I poured a glass of wine and took it over to the couch, where I leafed through a stack of magazines and newspapers that had accumulated on my coffee table over the past couple of days. There was a hurricane watch along the coast of Florida that I'd been completely oblivious to.

At ten-thirty, when I was on my second glass of red wine and gnawing at a block of cheddar like a rodent, Chris finally phoned. I felt a rush of relief when I heard his voice.

"Sorry not to call earlier," he said, sounding less than his usual delighted-to-talk-to-me self. "I worked a lot later than I expected. I don't think we can get together."

"Okay," I said, wondering still why he hadn't let me know, at least. "About this morning. I really feel awful about that whole incident. I hope it didn't embarrass you—or throw you off your game with the scene you were doing."

"God, what was that all about, Bailey?" he asked, his voice rife with irritation. "I told you that you needed to keep a low profile."

"What was that all *about?*" I said. "A huge snake shot across my foot, and as far as I knew, it was poisonous."

"Deke said what you saw was a cable."

"Deke is an asshole, and I'm surprised you'd believe anything he said." I took a breath, telling myself to take my annoyance down a notch. "I looked the snake up, and it was a common king snake. I'm wondering if they might be planning to use it in an episode."

"No, there aren't any episodes that involve a snake."

"Well, there's got to be an explanation. I am absolutely positive it wasn't a cable."

"Sorry to sound so testy. Locket was jittery to begin with this morning, but once you yelled that thing about the snake, she could barely focus—and then Alex turned into a real tyrant after you left."

"Okay, well, I just wanted to check in. Try to explain what had happened."

"Did you accomplish anything while you were there? I mean, I know it wasn't long, but—"

"I spoke to Deke again. He claims he repaid Tom the money the week before he died, but I seriously doubt it. Anything new on your end?"

"Not really. Everything just felt kind of off today." There was a pause, as if he were taking a slug of a beer. "Look, I better hit the sack. I've got a six a.m. call tomorrow."

God, this was amazing. At the rate I was going, there was a

chance I'd set a land record for being rejected by the most hunky guys in one twenty-four-hour period.

"Good night, then," I said.

"It's gonna be a pretty crazy week for me, but maybe we could get together Wednesday or Thursday. How's your schedule look?"

"I'm fairly open this week."

"Okay, I'll give you a ring tomorrow."

He had sounded more like his normal self toward the end of the conversation, but not a hundred percent. Was his coolness all due to what had happened this morning?

Feeling glum, I crawled into bed and plotted out the next day. I would check up on Locket to make sure she'd made contact with the police. I'd try to determine if there was any way that Deke had indeed repaid the loan and that Tom had planned to use it in his down payment to Barry, the contractor. The Chaps The-atre wouldn't be open until Wednesday, so I would have to wait until then to pursue the *Taming of the Shrew* lead. I still had several suspects, glaring brightly, but no way to learn if one of them really *was* the killer. I'd done my best to provoke them, but the only one that had coughed up anything worthwhile was Locket—and I wasn't a hundred percent sure she'd spoken the truth about every aspect of her visit to Tom. If I were a cop, I'd be able to check on key info—Harper's whereabouts on Saturday, for instance, after she'd taken the red-eye back from L.A.; Deke's bank account, to see if there was any record of him withdrawing cash to repay the loan. But I didn't have those options. I was running out of stones to overturn, and I had no idea what to do next.

I fell asleep in just a wife beater and panties, a book on my chest, and was jarred awake by the sound of my cell phone ring-ing on my bedside table. I peered at the clock as I reached for it clumsily: 12:02.

There was only silence. I felt a pinch of fear, remembering how the caller from hell liked to use silences.

"Hello," I said again hoarsely.

And then there it was, that awful laughter I'd been subjected to before.

"Who is this?" I asked stupidly, knowing there wouldn't be an answer. And then the caller was gone.

I scooted up in bed, my back against the headboard, feeling freaked. There'd been that same undertone of evil to the laugh. And also that same asexuality. For the life of me, I couldn't tell whether the voice belonged to a man or a woman.

After climbing out of bed, I paced my living room. On the two previous occasions, it had seemed as if the caller had had an uncanny sense of where I was and what a vulnerable state I'd been in, almost as if the person had been following me. And each call had come at such a consequential time. What did the call tonight mean? I wondered.

Just as I tucked myself back into bed, my cell rang again. Grabbing a breath, I answered the call. It took a second to recognize the voice: It was a Manhattan cop named Caleb Hossey, who used to give me tips regularly when I was covering crime for *Get* magazine.

"You still covering the celeb crime stuff?" he asked, chomping on food as he spoke.

"Yeah, what have you got?" I said, scooting up in bed again.

"Got a DOA in Central Park. Celebrity. I don't know her from Adam, but a bunch of the guys here do—Locket Ford. Soap star."

My hand flew to my mouth in shock. "Omigod. Do they have a suspect? What were the circumstances?"

"Don't know. Might be a sexual assault or a mugging gone bad. The report just came in around eleven-thirty, and I thought of you."

"Where was it, exactly?"

"Near the boat pond, closer to the East Side. Enter the park at Seventy-second Street and just look for the camera crews."

I thanked him profusely for the tip. By the time I hung up, I was almost shaking. I hadn't liked Locket one bit, but the fact that she'd been murdered was horrifying. There was a chance, this being New York, that a stranger had assaulted her as she'd walked that little powder puff pooch of hers through Central Park. But my mind immediately leapt to a more likely scenario: that someone she knew had followed her into the park and murdered her, someone who had gotten wind of the fact that she was planning to share a pivotal piece of information with the police tomorrow. I felt a surge of worry, wondering if I'd made a huge mistake in not forcing her to go to the cops immediately. The delay might have cost Locket her life.

And surely it was the *killer* who had called me. The timing was just too perfect to think otherwise. Something else gnawed at my mind, but each time I tried to grab hold, it slipped away.

I called Nash immediately on his cell phone and told him the news, as well as my suspicion that Locket's death could be related to Tom's.

"This is big. How soon can you get up there?"

"I'm five minutes from hailing a cab. What are the chances of getting anything in the issue?"

"I'm here now, and there's still time to have the art department tear up the cover and put Locket's picture on the roof. Lemme think—we can drop some of the fashion, so you've got at least one spread to play with, and we'll want to move the stuff about the actor into this story. As long as we ship everything by eight in the morning, we're okay. And of course we're going to want to break this on the Web site."

I threw on a pair of pants, sweater, and jacket. As I dashed from my apartment building, I glanced up and down 9th Street.

Was there a chance the killer was watching me, just as I'd sensed Friday night? The street appeared nearly empty, though.

There were plenty of cabs tearing down lower Broadway, so I hailed one and had the driver turn down 8th Street and head back uptown. Chugging a Red Bull with one hand, I called Chris on my cell with the other. Not surprisingly, his voice mail picked up. There was a slim chance he knew already, that someone from the show had phoned him, but more than likely he was fast asleep and wouldn't learn the grim news until morning. My stomach sank as I considered what a wrench Locket's death would throw into the production of *Morgue* and how that might impact Chris's career. Would they write her death into the show and try to salvage it? Or would they just scrap the whole show? I wanted to offer as much support as possible to Chris. I also, selfishly, wanted to find out what he knew about Locket's last day on the face of the earth.

I had the cab let me off at East 72nd Street, near two or three TV vans with satellite dishes on their roofs. There were fewer vans than you'd expect, but the murder had gone down at an awkward time for the TV stations, when they would have already sent their crews home for the night. The ones who usually showed up at late night crime scenes were freelance camera guys who a reporter friend of mine liked to call "the ghoul squad." Some of them even kept traffic cones and yellow police tape in the trunks of their cars so that if the cops had cleared out before they arrived, they could re-create the scene for their camera.

I entered the park and headed west. I wasn't far from the Boathouse café where Locket and I had stopped on Sunday. Seeing the vans made me think that there'd be lots of activity in the park, but as I hurried along the rambling sidewalk scattered with leaves, I suddenly found myself alone. Ordinarily, I'd never be so stupid as to go into Central Park by myself this late, but here I was. I paused and looked around me anxiously. Get a grip, Bailey, I told myself. Far off through the trees to the left, I saw flashes of white, which I assumed were the police lights. I broke into a jog and made my way in that direction.

The scene I emerged onto had that eerie quality that crime scenes always have—the overly bright lights like a movie set and the hum of the generator overpowering the quiet of the night. Yellow police tape had been strung around a wide area, and there were a bunch of cops congregated inside—forming almost a human shield around the body. I spotted only the tiniest sliver of a white sheet up against a cluster of large bushes, yards away from the path. I winced as I thought of Locket lying there dead, that lovely white skin possibly bruised and battered. Why had she gone off the path? I wondered. Had she let the damn dog wander in the darkness? Had she been lured there by someone she knew and then strangled or bludgeoned?

The crowd rimming the yellow tape wasn't huge—a few dog walkers, a handful of reporters, several camera crews—but it pulsed with a nervous energy. Standing on the periphery was a reporter from Channel 5, nearly sixty, who I used to bump into regularly when I was covering the crime beat for *Get*. He had once dispatched reports from the Middle East in tan safari jackets, but after losing his hair and his stamina ten or so years ago, he'd ended up as a local reporter, covering murders, water main breaks, and elderly women found dead in their apartments from heat exhaustion.

"Hey, Stan," I called out, strolling toward him. He greeted me with his typical warm but weary smile.

"What took you so long?" he asked. Though he'd kicked the two-and-a-half-pack-a-day habit a few years back, he still had a hoarse smoker's voice. "You don't have access to up-to-the-minute police info at that slick little rag you work for these days?"

"No, but I can tell you what kind of shoes Nicole Richie had on tonight. So give me a fill-in, will you?"

"Well, as I guess you heard or you wouldn't be here, it's Locket

Ford lying over there. She was apparently out walking her dog—on the late side, I'd guess—and someone nailed her. Not sure if we're talking rape or not—the ME's people have been in there for a while, but no one's saying anything yet."

"Who found her?"

"Another dog walker. Heard Locket's dog whimpering over by the bushes and went to investigate."

"Has her boyfriend shown up yet?"

"Alex Ottoson?" He shook his head. "My news desk says that they haven't been able to locate him yet. That's usually a bad sign. You know about the other death, don't you? I wouldn't be telling you this if you were with Channel Four, but someone else on the show got knocked off lately. Just a small-time actor, but still . . ."

"Yeah, thanks, I did hear about that," I said vaguely. "Are the police saying they might be linked?"

"No, but our assignment editor mentioned it to me. Ironic, isn't it—the show's called *Morgue?*"

"Yeah, I'll say. I'm gonna wander around a little. I'll check back with you later, Stan."

I pulled my reporter's pad from my purse and moved along the border of the police tape, trying to manage a better glimpse of the body, jotting notes about the scene. I found one of the freelance photographers *Buzz* uses and arranged for him to contact the photo department about selling shots of the scene. I also approached each of the six people with dogs, thinking one of them may have been the first on the scene, but they all admitted they'd arrived only later. Suddenly, the cops reconfigured their positions inside the cordoned-off area, and I caught a full view of the body, Locket's tiny frame draped in the death sheet, a chunk of her blond hair sticking out at the end. Seeing her body that way made me feel like puking into the bushes.

Had she died because of what she knew? If only I'd pressured her to go to the police *sooner*. I wondered if *Alex* had killed her. Locket may have decided to 'fess up to him, knowing that he might learn the truth anyway once she spoke to the police. He would have been furious to find out about Tom. But if he hadn't known about Tom until tonight, that would mean he wasn't *Tom's* killer. Could there be two separate murderers? It just seemed too far-fetched.

Once again, a vague thought gnawed at my brain, but this time I finally grabbed it. When I had talked to Harper on the phone earlier, I had goaded her, implying that Tom had been involved with someone else, someone on the show. Perhaps she had known Tom had cheated, had killed him in a fight about it, but had never been exactly sure who his other lover was. I'd given her the hint she needed. And then she might have gone looking for Locket.

CHAPTER 15

For the next fifteen minutes nothing much happened, though more reporters arrived, as well as several additional camera crews, unshaven guys with rumpled hair who looked as if they'd been called out of bed by their news desks. The crime scene people shuffled about looking for evidence, the ME investigators poked around alongside them, and in terms of excitement, the whole thing ended up being one notch above waiting in a line at the DMV. Of course, if I was a good citizen, I would have called over one of the cops and announced that I had important information to share. But if I did that, I'd be spending the next two hours talking to the cops instead of doing my job.

Since there was a lull in the action, I called Harper. She answered on the second ring. Was that because she'd been up dealing with the horrible mess for a while now—or because she was the creator of the horrible mess?

"Yes," she demanded, sounding wired.

"It's Bailey. I take it you know about Locket."

"God, don't you ever go away?"

"I'm covering the story for *Buzz*. Can I get a statement from you?"

"It's horrifying and sickening. There's nothing more I can say." Though she was wide awake, clearly she hadn't had time yet to cook up the perfect canned statement with the people at the top, and she wasn't seasoned enough to do a great job just winging it. Harper was probably in over her head on this one.

"What about Alex?" I asked. "I've heard that the police can't find him."

"That's absolutely not true. He was out with friends tonight. And now he's talking to the police in his apartment."

"What will they do with the show? Will they have to scrap everything they've shot so far, or will they write Locket's death into an upcoming episode?"

"That will all be determined over the next few days. I've got to go."

"Some people are saying there's a *Morgue* curse. What comment do you have on that?"

It was a cheap shot, but Nash might want something on the curse angle, and I didn't want to return empty-handed.

"That's fucking ridiculous," she said. "There is absolutely *no* curse. This show is going to be a huge hit." Then she disconnected. She had sounded extremely wigged out, but it was impossible for me to tell whether that was due to guilt or stress over everything that was going down.

"Who you talking to?" It was Stan behind me. I liked the guy, and he'd given me the fill-in, but I was hardly going to offer up Harper's name and number to him.

"Just my boss. I have to file something before too long. Do you think they'll make a statement?"

"From what I hear, not tonight. I'm probably going to pack

it in myself before long. At this point there's not much to run with, is there? Unless you know something from your end about Locket's personal life? You get all that kind of dirt at *Buzz*, don't you? How were things between her and this Alex Ottoson guy?"

"Locket wasn't exactly the kind of A-lister they keep tabs on at *Buzz*. Now, if she'd been living with Jude Law, that would have been a whole different story."

I made another sweep around the periphery, watching the cops work, eavesdropping on conversations among crews, taking a few more notes on the scene. Eventually one of the cops from the press office gave us some info "on background only." The victim was Locket Ford. EMS pronounced her dead at 23:14. They would await the medical examiner's cause of death at the postmort. I phoned Nash and told him I'd be coming in soon. I would have preferred to stay at the scene, just in case the cops did make a statement, but it was almost two a.m. and I needed to start writing.

As I was planning my exit, I spotted Stan with his camera crew starting to make their way from the scene, and I scurried over in that direction. I hated feeling like a scaredy-cat, but I had no interest in walking through the park alone. I followed about twenty yards behind, not so close to be obvious but close enough to feel safe. One stretch we traveled was absolutely desolate—nothing but black trees and bushes and the intermittent puddles of light from the streetlamps along the path.

When I tore into *Buzz* fifteen minutes later, there were more than a dozen people hanging around the bullpen—a deputy editor, a couple of production guys, the art director and a designer, a copyeditor/fact checker, and a few reporters. Nash spotted me immediately through his glass door and jumped from his desk.

"Bailey, get in here," he called from his doorway. "And everyone else, too."

We all crowded into his office, congregating near the round

conference table. People seemed tense but also giddily excited. Though they were used to breaking stories that required pulling all-nighters, they generally involved celebrity breakups or DWI arrests, not homicide.

"Tell us what you've got, Bailey," Nash said, shoving his reading glasses on top of his head, "and then we'll put it all in play."

I filled everyone in on the fairly meager details I'd learned about Locket's death.

"That's enough to work with," Nash said. "We've got shots of the scene and plenty of pix of her." He nodded toward one of the staff reporters. "Bethany's done all the background on Locket. She's writing the sidebar—and she'll help you fill in any blanks you have about her brilliant career in soaps. I'd write long, and that's what we'll post on the Web site. Then we'll trim it back for the magazine. Try to get me something in thirty or forty minutes, okay? I'm gonna work on the cover."

I nodded, but as people hustled out of the office, I hung back.

"Why do I smell a Bailey Weggins bombshell?" Nash asked, staring me straight in the eye as I stood planted in the middle of his office.

"It's pretty big—and it's going to ruffle some feathers," I told him. "On Sunday, Locket admitted to me that she had been having a fling with that young actor who was murdered, Tom Fain. She was at the house in the Catskills several hours before he was murdered."

"Holy shit. Bethany told me Ford was living with Alex Ottoson. Do you think he found out about the affair?"

"I don't know. If he found out, it makes him a suspect in both deaths. If he didn't know, learning the truth in *Buzz* is going to piss him off. That's what I mean about ruffling feathers."

"Why would Locket Ford tell *you* what was going on?"

"Because I stumbled on some information, and I told her

I'd figured it out. She was afraid that if I went around looking for proof, it would cause more problems for her than if she just 'fessed up."

"Okay, I better get the lawyers on the phone and run all this by them. How do you see working your personal conversation with her into the piece?"

"I'll just be very up front about it. 'In an exclusive interview, Ford told this reporter'—that kind of thing."

"Okay, get going. And I hope you're ready for your close-up—because you're going to be doing a hell of a lot of press this week."

I grabbed a cup of coffee first, though I was pretty sure I could have survived without it: I was being powered by a high-octane mix that could have given crack cocaine a run for its money—it was a blend of agitation, grief, a fierce desire to make a mark with my story, and a big splash of fear. I'd mentally outlined my story during the cab ride to *Buzz*, so as I soon as I sat at my computer, I started writing. Though questions about the murder kept dragging at my brain—Had Alex murdered Locket because she'd confessed about Tom? Had I inadvertently goaded Harper into killing Locket?—I knew I couldn't include them in the story, and I had to shove them aside so they didn't slow me down.

I spent just over a half hour pounding out the article. I broke the news about Locket's relationship with Tom right at the end of the opening paragraph and then, after offering the few known details about her death, circled back to her revelation and how it might mean the two deaths were linked.

I'd told Nash my piece was going to ruffle Alex Ottoson's feathers. But the police were going to be bent out of shape, too. I was sharing info in my story that I hadn't yet offered up to them. Not everything, though: I was *not* going to spill the news about Locket's phone call to Tom and his comment about the person heading up the driveway. It would have been great to be able to include that stuff, but those details would be critical to the official investigation, and just because Locket hadn't had the chance to go to the police with them didn't mean I could run with the info. As soon as I had a chance today, I needed to share what I knew with them.

There were other feathers that might get ruffled, too: Chris's. He'd brought me into this whole business as a friend, and he'd confessed his discomfort when I'd morphed into reporter. Now I was taking things one step further: I was exposing the affair, something Chris had obviously wanted to keep under wraps. That's why he'd snatched Locket's note to Tom. Of course, with Locket dead, there was no reason now to safeguard her privacy. I knew I'd done the right thing for my story. But I was worried Chris would feel I'd betrayed his trust. We'd literally clung to each other after Tom's death, and I'd liked that clinging. After Chris learned what was in my piece, however, he might be pissed enough to blow me off. Maybe I should have realized that his job and my job were never going to be simpatico.

Though we had until eight to get the piece out the door, we ended up finishing before four—with the exception of the production guys, who stayed behind just in case I called in an update. Nash walked out with me, hammering out press details on his cell with someone in the PR department.

"Great news," he said to me as he snapped his phone shut, "you're on the seven o'clock hour of the *Today Show*."

"The *Today Show today*?" I exclaimed, trying to keep my eyes from bugging out of my head.

"Yeah, a car will pick you up at six, so it's probably best just to stay up. Our PR people are suggesting what they call an even-break strategy—giving the story exclusively to a few places—the *Today Show*, CNN, a few radio stations. You can crash later this morning."

Thank God I was too wired to feel sleepy or freaked about

the TV appearance. I'd done both television and radio for previous articles, and though I didn't relish the day ahead, I knew I could handle it without breaking into a cold sweat.

Back at my place I showered, dug out a little purple suit I hadn't worn in a year, and used about a quart of volumizer when I styled my hair. Then I plopped down on the couch with a cup of tea.

I must have dozed off because the next thing I knew I was being roused from my sleep. I'd had a dream, an ugly one. There'd been a snake in it, the size of an anaconda, and then later an interminable train ride in the darkness. I rode in a near empty car that rocked back and forth. I was filled with anxiety because I wasn't sure where I was supposed to disembark. When a noise jarred me awake, it felt as if I were surfacing from the bottom of a lake. With a damp hand I slapped at what I thought was my alarm clock buzzing until I remembered I was on the couch, and that it was my cell phone that was going off. I fumbled for the phone and flicked it open. Chris's number was on the screen.

"Oh, Chris, there you are," I said hoarsely as I checked the time: 5:15. "Are you okay? I've been so worried about you." What I didn't add was that I was feeling guilty, too.

"You've heard, then?" he said.

"I'm covering it for *Buzz*, so I was up in the park late last night after word leaked out. This must be awful for you."

"One of the producers just woke me and told me the news. I've got to see you, Bailey. This is awful. Can I come over? Needless to say, we're not shooting today."

"Believe it or not, I've got to leave here at six. But why don't we meet in the coffee shop in my building. They're open all night."

"Okay, see you in ten minutes."

After gulping down a glass of OJ, I went online and skimmed through the reports on Locket. I hadn't missed much while I was sleeping. The police had released a sheet saying Locket had been stabbed numerous times. And that was it. A few of the news sites mentioned my report. Some had a more polished statement from Harper than the one she'd given me, and there was also a comment from a network suit, declaring that they were determining what to do with the show but that for now their thoughts were focused on Alex Ottoson and Locket's family. Alex was reportedly sequestered in his apartment and not making any statement. Last, I checked the *Buzz* site. Already people all over America were sipping coffee and discovering the bomb I'd dropped.

Chris was already in the near-empty coffee shop when I arrived, staring gloomily into a coffee cup, his long legs stretched out sideways from the table. I felt a terrible stab when I saw how dejected he looked. He rose from the table at the sight of me, and we hugged each other tightly. It was a relief to have those arms around me. But I dreaded having to disclose to him that I'd busted the Locket-Tom affair. From his tone on the phone, I was pretty certain he hadn't heard yet.

"I was desperate to talk to you last night, but you didn't pick up your cell phone," I explained as I sat down. "I wanted to tell you the news myself."

"I had my cell phone near my bed, but I guess I didn't hear it when you phoned last night. After I hung up with the producer, three different reporters called. God knows how they managed to get my cell phone number. There was no press outside my building this morning, but I bet it's only a matter of time before the vultures descend in force."

Oh boy. I was technically one of those vultures.

"This has got to be such a nightmare for you," I said, stroking his hand.

"Yeah, I feel sick about Locket," he said, laying his hand over mine. "*And*, I'm ashamed to admit, I'm worried about what all of this means for me and the show."

"Don't be ashamed, Chris. Your world got turned upside

down today, and that's a totally legitimate concern. Any inside word about what the network might do?"

"I've talked to a few people already, and according to the rumor mill, at least, they're going to write Locket's death into the show and find a new female lead."

"That makes a lot of sense," I said after ordering a cappuccino. "It would be crazy to bail after all they've invested."

"Yeah, but that could very well happen. With two actors on the show murdered, the network's got to feel the show is tainted, and they may want to bag the whole thing."

"Well, it's awful to say, but they may feel this actually works to their advantage. There's going to be a hell of a lot of morbid curiosity."

"You said you're covering the story—do you know anything yet about how Locket died?"

I explained how little info I *did* have and asked if he'd managed to glean any details from his end.

"Nobody seems to know anything. I got through to Harper once, but she was like a maniac and had nothing to offer. The papers are saying it might be a botched robbery, but of course everybody at the show is wondering if Locket's death is connected to Tom's."

"I'm pretty sure it has to be," I said. "Right before I found out she'd been killed, I got one of those awful phone calls again—the person laughing like someone gone mad. And I still couldn't tell if it was a man or a woman. It's as if they had called to announce what they'd done—to brag about it."

"Have you told the police?" Chris asked.

"Not yet—but I will today. There's something else I need to share with them, too. On Sunday, Locket *admitted* to me that she'd been having a fling with Tom—and also that she'd been with him in Andes the Saturday he disappeared. What's even more amazing is that after she left, she called Tom to check in and he mentioned that a car was just pulling up in the driveway." I quoted the line of Baptista's that Tom had used.

"So that's why you asked me about *Taming of the Shrew* yesterday."

"Yeah, exactly."

"But why not tell me about this before?" Chris said, his voice hardening. He stared at me so intensely that his green eyes seemed to penetrate mine. "I thought we were being completely open with each other."

"I couldn't tell you because I gave Locket my word I wouldn't say anything until she'd had a chance to go to the police," I said, feeling my cheeks redden. Chris had never seemed this miffed at me about anything—and he didn't know the half of it. "I planned to fill you in as soon as I could. Locket said she had Tuesday off and was going to call the cops then."

His shoulders relaxed as he seemed to accept my explanation. "Are you thinking that someone found out she had info and killed her before she could go to the cops?" he asked.

"That's one possibility. Another is that she spilled to Alex— knowing he was probably going to find out anyway."

"That's a piece of news he wouldn't have been pleased to hear."

"Did you see any interaction between the two of them yesterday?"

"He was curt with her through most of the day, but like I told you last night, he was a real tyrant yesterday, and *nobody* was spared. Something was definitely eating at him. At first I thought it was because of the whole snake incident, but it lasted too long for that.

"And hey, by the way," he added. "You were right. There really *was* a snake."

"Do tell," I said.

"One of the ADs told me they found out that a snake had

escaped from a cage on some kind of vet show that's also shot in the building. Sorry I didn't just take your word for it, Bailey. I—"

"Don't worry about it," I said, relieved that things seemed back to normal with us. "Talk to me more about yesterday. Did you see Locket interacting with anyone else in a way that might be significant? Like with Deke, for instance."

"No, not Deke, though something weird was going on with him. He seemed to be on his cell most of the day, and one of the ADs finally complained to him. But Locket had a tiff with Harper. I couldn't tell what the problem was, but they were barking at each other in a corner."

"What time was this?"

"Late afternoon. Why?"

"She avoided my calls all weekend, but I finally got her on the phone yesterday to ask her why she let me think she'd returned to New York on that Sunday night rather than Saturday. She was all pissy and defensive, so I goaded her a little. I said something about the possibility of Tom having an affair with someone on the show. I'm wondering if she may have confronted Locket about it."

"Well, they weren't clawing each other's eyes out, but their voices were raised."

"So what this all means is that there's still no clear suspect. I've got one or two small leads to follow up on—like the *Taming of the Shrew* stuff—but if they don't lead anywhere, I'm at a dead end."

I took a long sip of my cappuccino. It was time to break the news about my story, and I needed fortification.

"There's something you need to know, Chris," I said. "I had to include the information about Tom's affair with Locket in my piece."

"*What?*" he demanded, his face pinched in agitation.

"I know you wanted to keep it private, but it's a critical part of the story."

"But why does the world have to know about it? All it does is sully Tom's name and Locket's, too."

"The affair explains why the two deaths are probably linked. And like I told you, I'm going to be filling the police in on this today—I *have* to—so the news on this will come out anyway."

"And so what does this mean for me? Are you going to tell the cops I took Locket's note from Tom's apartment?"

"You haven't told them about it yet?"

"No—no, I haven't. I just haven't wanted to open that can of worms."

"They're going to wonder exactly how I learned the truth about those two, but I won't say anything about the note. I'll—I'll tell them that I heard rumors about the affair and that I bluffed with Locket, hinting to her that I had evidence when I really didn't. But I still think it's essential for you to turn in that note. Chris, it was one thing to be protective when the affair didn't seem to have anything to do with Tom's death, but now it looks like it may have—and Locket's, too—and you have to be forthcoming. It might help catch Tom's killer."

Chris stared at the table, massaging his forehead with his hand.

"Chris, talk to me."

"Okay, I'll go to the police. You've got a point. But I just hate all this *Buzz* stuff. One minute you're helping me, and the next thing you're turning it all into a story."

"I see what you're saying. But I never knew the situation would blow up this way. There's one thing you've got to know. I may be covering this story, but first and foremost my goal is still to find out what happened to Tom."

"Am I going to end up in a *Buzz* story?"

"God, Chris, of course not," I insisted. "I'd never do anything to hurt you."

He sighed. "Okay, I guess I'm just going to have to trust you."

My cell phone buzzed in my purse. It was Nash on the line.

"You up with your hair combed?" he asked.

"Yup."

"Then you need to call the PR folks. They've got a pretty big plan for you."

I promised I would and signed off.

"Look, unfortunately I need to get moving," I told Chris. "But let's stay in touch today, okay? I promise to do a better job of keeping you in the loop."

"I'd appreciate that."

Outside the coffee shop, Chris and I lingered awkwardly on the sidewalk. Please kiss me good-bye, I thought. I don't want any more friction between us.

"Promise me you'll be careful," he said. "This is all really scary."

"Promise. And let me know if you hear anything about the show."

As if he'd heard my mental pleading, he leaned down and kissed me tenderly on the mouth.

"When this is all over, I'm going to whisk you off to Jamaica for a long weekend," he said. "We'll listen to Bob Marley songs and drink lots of rum."

I beamed at him, happy that things were straight between us. "That sounds divine."

But as I watched him cross Broadway, I saw from his profile that his face was scrunched in consternation. He had a lot on his mind right now, of course, but I wondered how much of his agitation had to do with my breaking the news about Tom and Locket.

From that point on, the day moved like a bullet train.

I felt jittery as I sat on the *Today Show* couch in my purple suit with my hot pink lips, compliments of the makeup artist, but once I was talking and just describing what I knew about the case, my fears slipped away.

Later, while I waited for the car to take my PR escorts and me to CNN, I called the Central Park police precinct and told the desk cop that I had information that was pertinent to the investigation of Locket Ford's death. I was transferred to a detective who urged me to come in immediately. I said I had work obligations, and though he pressured me, I stuck to my guns. Nash would strangle me if I blew the press bonanza.

After a blitzkrieg two hours, I was dropped off at home, told I could rest, but that I needed to begin round two in the early afternoon. I slept for two hours and then bolted awake, knowing how much I still had to do. I checked with my contacts in the police and ME's office for more info on Locket (she definitely hadn't been sexually assaulted; there were no suspects yet). My cell phone was clogged with calls from reporters I knew (including Stan, who chided me for holding out on him). When I checked in at *Buzz*, I was told my phone had been ringing off the hook.

I was back on the press bus by one for *Court TV* and a couple of live radio shows. By three-thirty I was finally done for the day.

Still in my suit and slingbacks, I headed north in a cab for the Central Park precinct on the 86th Street transverse, rehearsing my remarks in my head. I'd decided not to raise the idea of Harper as a suspect until I had more facts. I would, however, share what I knew about the loan to Deke.

I waited only a couple of minutes on a folding chair in a small entrance area before being summoned by a detective named Mark Windgate, a good-looking African American, mid-thirties, who was dressed neatly in a khaki blazer and blue-and-tan tie.

"You've been a busy lady today," he said as I took a seat, in a tone that indicated he knew all about my *Buzz* story and the press I'd been doing—and he was none too pleased. "The next thing you know, Greta Van Susteren's gonna be out of a job."

"I'm sorry I wasn't able to stop by before now," I said as apologetically as possible. I'd learned with cops that it's always best not to become defensive.

"*Sorry?*" he nearly shouted. "And are you also sorry that you released critical information to the world at large before giving it to us, possibly screwing up our investigation?"

I fought the urge to squirm like an earthworm tugged from the ground.

"My boss insisted that I do the press as part of my job," I explained lamely. "I got here as soon as my last interview was completed."

"And why not inform us on Sunday, after Ms. Ford reportedly told you about the affair?" he asked, arms folded tight against his chest.

"Because I felt that it was *her* obligation, and she swore to me she was going to contact you on Tuesday."

He eyed me warily as he used four fingers to smooth his thin mustache again and again. Finally, he let his hand drop. "Have you asked yourself how things might have turned out differently if you *had* come to us immediately?" he asked.

Ouch.

"Look, I promise to cooperate every step of the way going forward," I told him. "And I have something very important to share, something I didn't think was appropriate to put in my story."

"Let's hear it."

I told him then about Locket's call to Tom, the arrival of the visitor to Dabbet Road, and Tom's line from *Shrew*.

He took notes as I spoke, his face blank. I knew he must find the revelation about the visitor crucial, but it was impossible to tell how meaningful he thought the line from Shakespeare was.

Then the questions started. He came at my conversation with Locket from several different angles, clearly hoping to extract info I might have forgotten to mention or didn't realize was significant—about the affair, about the mystery visitor—but there was nothing to add. Sure enough, he asked why Locket would have been so candid with me, and I told the fib I'd promised Chris I would. When we'd exhausted that subject, he had me backtrack, describing my trip to Andes. That gave me the chance to raise the phone calls I'd begun receiving on my return and the incident at the Half King.

"And why not contact us about *that*?" he asked.

"I had no proof I'd been drugged, and it may have been unrelated. As for the phone calls, I thought they could be pranks. It wasn't until the call last night—timed so perfectly to Locket Ford's death—that I was sure they were really connected."

He jotted down my cell phone number, saying they would make an attempt to trace the calls.

By the time we were done, I felt wiped, and the back of my cute little suit was damp with sweat. As he walked me to the front of the precinct house, his manner softened.

"So, we've got an open line of communication now?" he asked, holding open the door for me.

"Absolutely. Any update on the case, by the way?" It didn't hurt to try.

He smirked, mildly amused at my chutzpah. "Not that I can share with you. And I don't want to read a *word* about the phone call we discussed. It's essential that it be kept under wraps for now."

"Fine."

"And last but not least, you need to be careful, Miss Weggins. The killer knows now that Ms. Ford spoke to you. If she was murdered because of information she was privy to, the killer may suspect you have that information in your possession now."

Not that I'd taken my situation lightly up until then, but hearing him put words to the danger made my fear harden like a boulder in my gut.

Out on the 86th Street transverse, I checked my voice mail. Two requests from the relentless PR department for me to do additional shows tomorrow, a call from Nash asking if I had updated info for the Web site. Just as I was about to return calls, my phone rang.

"Is this Bailey Weggins?" asked a pompous, vaguely familiar voice.

"Yes, who's calling?"

"Alex Ottoson. I want to see you."

I probably shouldn't have been surprised.

"Okay. Where—and when?"

"My apartment. Now. Central Park West at Seventy-fourth Street. How long will it take you to get here?"

"I'm actually only fifteen minutes away."

"There's a horde of paparazzi out front, so you need to use the service entrance around the corner. A few of the jackals will probably be positioned there as well, but my assistant will be waiting."

Alex had of course read the *Buzz* Web site or been told about it and wanted to grill me on the subject of Locket's fling with Tom. This would be the perfect chance for me to take a measure of him, yet it wasn't going to be a pleasant situation. As I picked up my pace along the park, my eyes roamed the large dusty bushes off to the left, not unlike the one Locket had been killed near. It would have been so easy for Alex to follow her as she walked the dog—or catch up with her at a spot he knew she'd be. She would have been surprised to see him, but not necessarily alarmed. And he could have bashed in her head before she even knew her life was in danger.

There *were* paparazzi by the service entrance, as it turned out, about five of them, but the assistant, a slim Asian woman dressed in a black tunic, leggings, and pointy black ankle boots, was waiting just outside the door and whisked me by them. She led me up a flight of back stairs and then around to the front lobby. She said nothing at all to me as we rode the elevator and then only, "Please follow me," after she'd unlocked the apartment door. I trailed behind her through the gigundo living room and down a long corridor lined with closed doors, a different route from the one Locket had taken when I'd visited her. The place was totally silent, tomblike, like a space belowground. At the very end of the hall, the assistant rapped on a door, and through it we heard Alex's muffled voice announce, "Enter." As I stepped into the large spare study, the assistant faded back into the recesses of the apartment.

Alex was sitting at a sleek black desk, with absolutely nothing on it but a phone. He wore a crisp white cotton shirt, long-sleeved, and a camel-colored cashmere sweater was knotted around his neck. Kind of spiffy for someone in deep mourning. He didn't rise, and he didn't offer me a seat.

"I'm very sorry for your loss," I said.

"Let me cut right to the chase," he said bluntly. "I want to know everything Locket told you about her relationship with Tom Fain."

"I'm under no obligation to share with you what Locket revealed to me."

"But you didn't hesitate to reveal to the world that she was having an affair with Tom Fain."

"She was about to go to the police with that information. It wasn't going to be a secret any longer."

"Was she in love with him?" His voice cracked slightly when he spoke, releasing a soupçon of pity in me.

"I don't think so," I admitted. "She said she never wanted to jeopardize her relationship with you."

"Lovely," he said, his voice thick with sarcasm. "And why, might I ask, would she share all this information with you?"

"I'd been looking into Tom's death—not as a reporter, but because I'd found the body and wanted to know what had happened to him. I heard a rumor about her and Tom, so I confronted her. Were you aware of what was going on?"

"I had my suspicions, but no proof. Locket was quite the master of deception, and she could cover her tracks brilliantly. She visited some old friends the weekend Fain apparently died, and when I called they told me she'd gone antiquing. She even returned with several eighteenth-century silver serving spoons just to drive home the point."

"Where were *you* that day?" I asked. If he was going to cut to the chase, so would I.

"Off the record—with a young lady. As I was last night."

Oh, nice. Mr. Pot calling the kettle black.

"Have the police given you any indication of what they think happened to Locket?" I asked.

"All I know is from the doorman. She left to walk the dog about nine. I assumed she'd stopped by a friend's. Now if you'll excuse me . . ."

I wondered if I was supposed to see myself out, but when I turned toward the doorway, I saw that the assistant was back, hovering. Had a bell under the desk summoned her?

"Just one question," I said to Alex as he reached for the phone. "How did you find out that Tom Fain had been in rehab?"

"If you must know," he said, "Chris Wickersham's agent in L.A. told us, though of course we had it verified."

The news almost knocked the wind out of me. It had been *Chris* who had sabotaged Tom. The thought sickened me.

On the other hand, was it such a surprise? Perhaps I should have guessed the truth when Locket had told me what happened. I knew Chris was driven. He wanted fame and glory—what actor who heads for L.A. doesn't? I'd even understood why he hadn't come to my rescue on the set—because it might hurt his standing with the director. But betraying Tom was in a whole other league.

By the time the cab pulled up in front of my building, I felt miserable. I hobbled to the door in my wrinkled suit and scuffed slingbacks and offered Bob, the doorman, a pathetic hello.

"You just missed her," he said.

"Who?" I asked, confused.

"Your sister-in-law. I let her into your apartment like you asked."

"Like I *asked?*" I exclaimed, feeling a charge of adrenaline. "What do you mean?"

Bob stared at me, his eyes widening in alarm beneath the brim of his brown cap.

"You called me an hour ago. And told me to let her in."

CHAPTER 16

I paused for a split second to gather my wits, then charged across the lobby and around the corner to the elevator bank.

"Is everything all right, Ms. Weggins?" Bob called out behind me.

"I don't think so," I yelled back. "I never called you today."

My heart was thumping hard as I rode the elevator to the fourteenth floor. I *hadn't* called Bob, and for all I knew, one sister-in-law was in the Caribbean with my brother and the other was in Boston coping with her addiction to the Crate & Barrel catalog. That meant someone had phoned the lobby impersonating me. And that person apparently had shown up and spent time alone in my apartment.

I'd no sooner stepped onto the floor than the door of the other elevator slid open and Bob darted out.

"I got the porter to watch the door. Are you saying you weren't the one who phoned here this afternoon?"

"No—and my sisters-in-law aren't in New York now. What exactly did this person say when she called?"

"Just hi, that it was you, Bailey, and that you wanted me to let your sister-in-law use your apartment while she was between planes. We're supposed to get written notes on stuff like that, but it was so clearly you who was calling. I wanted to do you the favor."

He pushed back the brim of his cap, and I could see that his forehead was glistening with sweat. Poor Bob—he probably suspected he was going to get canned before the day was through.

"The woman who showed up here—what did she look like?" I asked. "And how long did she stay?"

"To be honest, I didn't get a great look. She was on the tall side, maybe five eight or nine, though she may have been wearing heels. She had on big sunglasses and some kind of hat—like a fedora. And oh, her hair was peeking out a little from the top—it was blond. She stayed about thirty minutes. Like I said earlier, she left about fifteen minutes before you got here."

"And you're sure it was a woman?"

"Huh? You mean could it have been a guy dressed up like a woman? I—I don't think so."

"Okay, we better check my place now," I said, glad Bob was with me. I had no idea what I was going to find there. Had it been trashed? Booby-trapped?

"You better be prepared for the fact that you may have been robbed," Bob advised. "She certainly didn't take your TV out of here, but she might have stolen cash or jewelry."

But when I stepped into my entranceway with Bob at my heels and glanced around, nothing at all seemed amiss. We moved with trepidation from the living room to the kitchen and then back through the living room to the bedroom, the bathroom, and my tiny office. There were no rifled drawers, no cabinet doors flung open. And my small cache of jewelry, the pieces my ex-husband hadn't managed to pawn, was still tucked in a nest of my thongs.

"Is anything missing?" Bob asked nervously.

"No, not that I can see."

"Then what did she want?"

"I don't know, Bob. I don't know."

"Do you want me to call the super?"

"That may not be necessary. Let me get settled in and I'll take a closer look around. If I find anything wrong, I'll let you know."

Bob departed looking totally chagrined, his collar wet from flop sweat. I didn't fault him for what had happened. But that didn't mean I wasn't freaked.

After I'd stripped off my suit and kicked my heels into the closet, I searched through my bedroom again, mostly through drawers, and I did the same in my office. My papers seemed in order. My laptop was in the exact spot I'd left it. Why had she come to my apartment? Who *was* she? She had to be a good actress or mimic—after all, she had managed to imitate my voice well enough that my doorman had assumed it was I.

There was an even more chilling question to consider. Was the mystery visitor related to the murders? If yes, it narrowed the field. It certainly couldn't have been Deke disguised in a hat and sunglasses. Or Alex. But it might have been Harper. Or possibly someone in league with the murderer. Or maybe it didn't have anything to do with the killings at all. But then why would someone go through the whole ruse and spend a half hour in my apartment the day after Locket's murder?

I pulled on a pair of tan capris and a black jersey top and returned to my office. I called Detective Windgate and described on his voice mail what had happened. I asked him to call me the first chance he got, and I also left a message for Nash saying that there were a few new developments, but nothing that couldn't wait, and

I'd fill him in tomorrow at the office. Then I made calls to some of my contacts, coming up with nothing new.

By this point, my stomach was grumbling and my whole body ached from fatigue. I phoned Landon, hoping he was up for company because the thought of spending the next hours alone in my apartment gave me the willies. Ever so faintly, I heard his phone ring through the wall in my office, again and again until his machine picked up. It looked as though I were going to be on my own with whatever sorry provisions I could locate in my fridge.

On my way to the kitchen, I checked my terrace door, making certain it and the windows were still bolted. I started to relax just a little, realizing that no one was going to be able to gain entry.

Practically limp from hunger and exhaustion, I foraged through my freezer for a pork cutlet I had vague recollections of having tossed in there and finally discovered it, lying rock hard beneath a sleeve of frozen bagels. As I turned with it toward the microwave, my eye caught a flash of silver in the sink. Lying in the otherwise empty basin was a steak knife with a wooden handle. It was from a fancy set I'd received as a wedding gift, from some relative who had wrongly envisioned my ex and me savoring thick sirloins together for the rest of our lives on earth. I hadn't noticed it earlier when Bob and I had done our sweep, but then I hadn't looked there. I was sure I hadn't put the knife in the sink. I hadn't, in fact, used those knives in ages. The blade looked cold and menacing lying there by itself.

In all likelihood, the intruder had left the knife there. Had she used it to open something? I didn't think so. I thought instead that the knife was a message: *I can hurt you if I want to, just like the others.* Perhaps it was even a promise.

I backed out of the kitchen, leaving the knife where it was, and left another message for Windgate, this one even more urgent. Though I no longer had the same appetite, I ordered a deep-dish pizza over the phone. While I waited for it to arrive—and for

Windgate to make contact—I sat at my dining table with my composition book and began to write. Having a pencil in my hand gave me a small feeling of control.

I started by jotting down Bob's description of the woman, and then I wrote a single name: "Harper." *She* was about five nine, maybe five ten, the height Bob had assigned to the intruder. Her hair was short, but there were definitely pieces long enough to peek out from under a hat. And, I suddenly remembered, she had planned to be an actress once. Chris had told me that when he'd first come to me about Tom.

I certainly had every right to consider Harper a prime suspect. She'd led me to believe she'd been in L.A. that weekend, but she had actually rushed back, presumably because she had a bad feeling about Tom. She could have begun to suspect he was cheating on her—and she may have killed Tom without ever learning who the other woman actually was. When I'd hinted yesterday that it might be someone on the show, Harper might have convinced herself that it was Locket and confronted her in the park.

I'd become so preoccupied about my intruder that Alex's revelation had escaped my mind temporarily—but now it popped into my brain like a sunken object finally shooting to the surface of a pond. Chris had cost Tom the part in the show, all because of his own fierce ambition. I imagined how it had probably happened: Tom had called Chris and told him about being cast in the show and suggested to Chris he get in to see the casting director. Chris had auditioned, had inferred somehow that everything wasn't totally nailed down yet with Tom, and told his agent to leak the info about rehab.

The revelation made me both angry and sad. Angry because Chris had derailed Tom's career. Was that why he'd wanted me to find Tom—out of wretched guilt? And sad because I really cared about Chris. I'd liked going to bed with him, I liked the way he made me laugh, I even liked his freakin' omelet with aged cheddar. And now I could see he wasn't the guy I thought he was. It would have been nice to call Chris for comfort tonight, to possibly spend the night at his place away from the nasty steak knife, but there was no way I'd do that after what I'd learned about him. I realized, in fact, that I had never heard from Chris this evening, despite the fact that when we'd had breakfast together, he'd implied we'd talk later. Tomorrow I was going to force him to tell me the truth.

As I sat staring at a blank page of my notebook, my pizza arrived, and no sooner had I paid for it than Windgate returned my call. I explained the whole situation about the intruder. When I was done, there was only silence on his part.

"Are you—" I started to say.

"Could it be a woman you know personally—someone from your own life?" he interrupted, his voice neutral. "A woman who's trying to get back at you for some reason? Maybe she thinks you stole her boyfriend, for instance."

"You mean a stalker?" I asked, trying not to sound as exasperated as I felt. "God, no, I don't think so. There's been no indication that anyone's obsessed with me. And I've never stolen anyone's boyfriend."

"Okay, okay, just sit tight, then. I'm going to send an evidence collection team over to lift fingerprints. And I want you to be extremely careful, is that understood?"

As relieved as I felt that the police were taking the intrusion seriously, I was ready to crawl into bed and pass out. Now I was going to have to hang around my living room while guys brushed the surfaces of my apartment with fingerprint powder.

The smartest move, I decided, was to try to grab a catnap before the cops arrived. I took two bites of pizza and staggered over to the couch. Cell phone in hand, I sprawled out on the length of it. As soon as I'd closed my eyes, my cell rang again.

"Did I catch you at a bad time?" a voice asked. It was Beau Regan.

Yeah, I'm in the reverse cowgirl position with a dude, and it's kind of hard to talk right now was what I was tempted to say, but instead I just muttered something about eating take-out. I couldn't even muster the gumption to lie and imply I was having a fabulous time.

"I heard about Locket Ford. You said she'd worked with that actor who died—whose death you were looking into. I wanted to make sure everything was okay with you."

"Uh, that's nice of you to call. To tell you the truth, I'm pretty sure the two deaths are related."

"That's what I wondered. Are you doing all right? You're not in one of those hot spots you love to gravitate toward, are you?"

"Actually, I—" My voice caught, much to my chagrin. "Someone got into my apartment—and I think it might be the killer. The police are supposedly on their way to look for prints."

"What do you mean, it might be the killer? What happened, exactly?"

I ran through it quickly for him. My voice caught again during part of my story, and I felt ridiculously wimpy. The last thing I wanted to do was make Beau think I was a "boo-hoo" kind of girl in need of rescue.

"Bailey, you can't stay there tonight," he said, my efforts apparently a failure. "I hope you're not planning to."

"I'm sure I'll be okay," I insisted. "It's not like this person has a key. I don't want to put out a friend on such late notice." I wondered if he was curious why I wouldn't bunk down with my "hard body."

"Why don't you stay at my place," he said, his voice gentle.

My breath froze in my chest, like a paralyzed nerve.

"You could have the couch," he added. "Or I could. I just

don't like the idea of you staying alone there. Remember, I was the guy who put the ice pack on your bruises last July."

I was about to say no, *really* I was, because from the moment I'd left Beau on the sidewalk in Chelsea the night before, I had felt as if I were finally moving away from him mentally and no longer wondering if there was a snowball's chance in hell for us. Staying at his place, even if only on the couch, would surely set me back.

But I also knew how freaked I felt and how much I didn't want to be in my apartment contemplating 101 things someone could do with a steak knife. So I said yes.

While I waited for the evidence collection team to arrive, I zipped my laptop into its case and packed an overnight bag with the only other suit I owned. The cops finally showed at around eight-thirty. After explaining the situation to them and giving them the lay of the land—as well as letting them take my fingerprints—I beat it out of there. When they departed later, the door would lock behind them automatically. In the lobby, I arranged for the night doorman to go up to the floor after the police left and make sure the dead bolt was on with the key they kept to my place. Though I'd felt wasted earlier, my body had been totally recharged by adrenaline.

Only a day had passed since I'd seen Beau last, but now he looked far more rested. He was wearing tan cords and a yellow crewneck sweater, and his feet were bare. My tummy started to go all weird at the sight of him.

"I opened a bottle of red wine, thinking you might need it," he said after walking me into the living room. "And I have a huge chunk of Stilton cheese my mother sent home with me."

"Just what the doctor ordered."

While he put things together in the kitchen, I sank into his sofa and took the chance to study the living room. The pile of papers that had been strewn about yesterday was now cleared away, and everything else was pretty much as it had been earlier in the summer: the sleek black leather furniture; the primitive-style rug in blue, black, and orange; the striking black-and-white photos of the Far East lining the white walls. There were several new photos, though, of what I assumed must be ancient streets in Istanbul, propped against the base of a wall. It made me nervous to prowl every inch of the room with my eyes—I'd once found a pink Daisy razor in the shower of a guy I was gaga for, squashing any hopes for eternal love, and I hated the thought of discovering bread crumbs from some chick here—but I couldn't help myself.

"So your mother sent you home with a wedge of *cheese*?" I said as Beau carried in a wine bottle, two glasses by their stems, and a plate with crackers and the blue-veined Stilton.

"Wedge isn't quite the right word," he said, pouring a glass of wine and handing it to me. "Wheel, I'd say. I went up there for dinner the other night—they wanted to check me out after I got back, perhaps hoping two months in the Turkish heat had convinced me to stop making documentary films and start a hedge fund. And as I'm leaving, my mother has the housekeeper hand me a shopping bag of food. I could win a bloody Oscar for a film someday, and my mother would still be asking me if I had enough clean clothes for the week."

"You seem to take it in stride," I said.

"Years of practice. So tell me more about the intruder. What makes you think she could be the murderer?"

I took a long drink of the wine first. It was an excellent-tasting Bordeaux that was probably noted for being redolent of things like plums and tobacco and saddlebags. Interesting, I thought, that he'd opened such a great bottle.

"I suppose there's a chance it's unrelated," I said. "The detective I've been dealing with even posed the idea I could have a stalker unrelated to the killings—someone who's convinced I'm after her man, for instance. But I just don't see it. It would make everything that's happened so coincidental."

I described the calls I'd received and also the incident at the Half King.

"Bailey, it's clear you're really in danger," he said. "I'm glad you came to your senses and decided not to stay at your place."

"Well, I appreciate your offer. It's horrible how something like this can leave you feeling so miserable in your own home."

He took a sip of wine and leaned back into the sofa, one leg crossed over the knee of the other, and just stared at me with those intense brown eyes. He had an uncanny ability to be *still*, to sit in one position without shifting or flexing or sweeping his hand through his hair. And he could hold your gaze until it became unbearable and you were forced to look anywhere but his eyes. I met his gaze awkwardly for a second and then glanced away, taking another long sip of my wine. I realized suddenly that my cheeks were hot—and not just from a combo of the Bordeaux and my own distress. It was due to lust, pure and simple. I'd kept it at bay yesterday, but now that I was all alone with Beau in his apartment, it felt unstoppable, like trying to contain an oil spill in the Atlantic.

"Why not stay with your actor friend?" he asked finally. His voice was even, as if he were simply curious, asking, perhaps, why I'd chosen Verizon over T-Mobile.

There was no way in hell I was going to describe what I'd learned from Alex Ottoson, the revelation that would create an irreparable rift between Chris and me.

"It's not like he's my steady boyfriend or anything," I said. "I just figured he had plans tonight."

"Sounds like a kind of casual thing." Again, perfectly even.

"Well, yeah, I guess. I mean, it's not some big exclusive deal."

"I thought you preferred exclusive," he said. An eyebrow went up this time.

"I wanted things to be exclusive with you and me. But that had to do with how I felt about you. I— Look, why are you asking this stuff, anyway?"

"*Why?*" he said, setting down his glass. He straightened up and looked me dead in the eye again. "To be perfectly honest, I don't really like thinking of you with that actor."

"Oh yeah," I said, unable to resist smiling. This was really very funny. "Why? You think I'll go all Hollywood?"

"Yeah, maybe," he said, smiling back. "You'll buy one of those yappy little dogs and carry it in your purse."

"And have Paris Hilton as my bff?"

"I think you know where I'm headed, Bailey," he said, serious now.

"No, honestly, I don't," I said.

"I don't like the idea of you in bed with another guy."

I couldn't believe how this conversation was unfolding.

"Well, what is it that I'm supposed to do about that?" I asked.

"Don't go to bed with him."

"Isn't that pretty unfair on your part? I believe they call that having your cake and eating it, too. Because you want to go to bed with other women."

"I know I told you that I didn't feel ready for any kind of steady relationship. But I realize I was wrong about that."

"So what are you saying, then?"

"I'd like to give it a shot," he said, his voice soft and smooth. "You and me. I want a relationship with you."

I nearly gulped. Here was the declaration I'd been yearning for and had given up on ever hearing. It was coming totally out of the blue, like the wheel of a plane that snaps off midflight and plunges to earth.

"Gosh," I said. "I'm just—I just wasn't expecting this."

"I know I didn't stay in touch, because things were kind of

crazy in Turkey and I didn't know what I wanted and didn't know how to say that. But as soon as I was in New York and had my head on straight, I realized how much I'd missed you and that I did want to be with you. I had every intention of calling you, but after I saw you at Elaine's, I figured you weren't interested anymore."

"Nothing's changed about my feelings," I said. And I knew for certain nothing had.

I'd let my eyes wander because I felt so flustered that I could barely even *meet* his gaze this time, and after a moment my eyes fell on the large ottoman. I flashed on the night he had laid me down on it, pulled off my dress and underwear, and covered every inch of me with his mouth. I blushed, a rush of blood to my cheeks so fast that it felt like a firecracker going off—and when I turned back, I could tell he knew what I'd just harkened back to.

He grinned. Then he leaned toward me and laid his right hand on my left thigh. Underneath, through the fabric of my capris, I felt my skin turn hot. He slid his hand up the length of my thigh and then moved it to the space between my legs. With his thumb he began tracing the seam of my pants, back and forth, back and forth, until I could feel myself trembling.

"Well, since we're both on the same page, why don't we go to bed and remind ourselves of how good it is between us," he said, grinning.

My tongue felt so numb, I could barely talk. So I didn't. I just let things unfold. He reached for my right arm and pulled me toward him, kissing me softly on the mouth and then, after a moment, more urgently. I closed my eyes and let myself just savor the taste of him. His tongue slipped into my mouth, and he began to run his thumb more firmly back and forth between my legs. It was almost unbearable.

I leaned into him, kissing him back deeply. His hand moved from my groin to the buttons on my cardigan. With one hand he unbuttoned the entire sweater and pulled the sides apart. He took my breasts in both his hands, and then reached behind me, unhooked my bra and pulled it down. Now his hands were on my bare breasts, kneading them, caressing them, using his thumbs to circle my nipples in that same deliberate, intoxicating motion he'd used between my legs.

"So what do you say?" he said, pulling back but with his face just inches from mine. "Shall we go to bed?"

"Yes. Though I thought you were partial to ottomans."

He laughed. "Oh, did you like that? Well, why don't we try again—with a variation this time."

As he said the word *variation*, I felt a shot of red hot lust run through me. He worked off my sweater and bra and tugged my pants down. Then he laid me on the ottoman, facedown this time.

"I promise this will take your mind off everything—and you don't have to do a thing."

"Seems awfully selfish," I muttered.

"You'll have a chance later to return the favor."

He began to rub my back with sensuous, hypnotic strokes. One hand worked its way up my neck, and his strong fingers kneaded my scalp over and over again. Then slowly his hands made their my way down my back and my butt, massaging, caressing. It was pure bliss just to surrender, to think of nothing but the pleasure of what was being done to me—and by whom. Slowly he eased off my thong, and I heard it almost silently touch the rug. By the time he slipped two fingers inside me and began to move them rhythmically in and out, I had lost track of my own name.

It took me only seconds to climax once he entered me, and then I just let myself concentrate on Beau's quickening breath, him filling me as he thrust powerfully inside me, and the sounds of his groans as he came and relaxed his weight into me.

Afterward, he poured us each more wine, and we took it

with us to the bedroom, where we had sex again, and finally I could hear his gentle breathing beside me. I was totally, utterly exhausted, but I knew within minutes that sleep had decided to elude me yet again.

I lay still for a while, as still as Beau was, trying to just let go, to ignore that prickly feeling of awakeness, but eventually it overwhelmed me. I couldn't believe I was going to be dogged by insomnia again. I tried gradually relaxing all my major muscle groups, but it was as futile as blowing on a burn.

"You okay?" Beau whispered. He'd been lying on his stomach, but now he turned on his side and spooned me.

"I guess I'm too wound up to sleep. Would you mind if I rummaged through your fridge?"

"Be my guest. There's a quart of milk in there. Isn't that supposed to be good for insomnia?"

"Yeah—or chopping one's head off."

I made my way to the kitchen, a sleek, smallish space with lots of stainless steel, brightened by a large abstract painting of red and gold. As I opened the fridge, I let my eyes explore the few things tacked on the door—a take-out menu from a sushi restaurant, a photo of a small girl splashing in the ocean who I assumed might be a niece. Next to the fridge on the counter was a white ceramic bowl with two oranges and papers that appeared to have been thrown there during a cleanup mission. Another take-out menu, this one from a Mexican restaurant. A Con Ed bill. And one of those small cards that accompany a floral arrangement: "Welcome home, Beau. I missed you."

CHAPTER 17

Oh fuck, I thought. Was this the Daisy razor moment I'd been dreading? Please let it be from his mother, I pleaded in my mind. After all, the kind of mother who forces a wheel of cheese on you is also the kind of mother who would send flowers upon your return home from a long trip. But, of course, it *could* be from a chick.

I wondered if Beau had been honest with me earlier, if he was really ready to forsake seeing other women and date me alone. I worried that a surge of testosterone had prompted him to bullshit me into bed with him. Guys were brilliant at deceiving chicks when they wanted to pants them. But I had no reason right now *not* to believe Beau.

For the first time all night, I thought of Chris—and experienced an accompanying twinge of guilt. It's not as though we'd pledged to have an exclusive arrangement, yet there had been this implied sense of getting into something special. But what did it matter now, anyway? As far as I knew, he'd totally misrepresented himself to me as a person, allowing me to believe that he was Tom's friend and had never had anything but Tom's best interest at heart. That was totally affecting how I felt.

I took my milk into the living room, where I unzipped my laptop and set it up. I assumed, rightly, that Beau had wireless service, and I went online, checking Web sites for updates on Locket—nothing yet but endless speculation—and e-mails. There was a message from Nash, which he'd assumed I'd read on my BlackBerry—saying he'd heard I was continuing to handle the press well and that there'd be plenty more tomorrow. There were also e-mails from the PR team, detailing my responsibilities for tomorrow. Oh, goody. I had my suit with me, of course, and I'd do what was required—but I also needed to find the time to talk to both Chris and Harper as soon as possible. There were loose ends to tie up as well: I still wanted, for instance, to determine if Deke had actually repaid (fat chance) the loan to Tom. Certainly Deke wasn't the person who had prowled around my apartment, but he may have convinced some chick to do it for him. And I needed to get to the Chaps Theatre.

After dashing off a few replies, I felt suddenly ragged, almost shaky with tiredness, as if the day were finally catching up with me. It seemed as if the sheer power of my fatigue was going to be able to defeat my insomnia. Before staggering back to the bedroom, though, I Googled "stalker." Detective Windgate had piqued my curiosity with his question. I couldn't imagine who from my own universe might have suddenly decided to stalk me, but I wanted to at least consider what Windgate had suggested. Though I'd recently investigated the subject for a piece on a celeb with an obsessed fan, I wanted to look at the information again and see if it sparked an idea.

Experts broke stalking down into categories. The types that showed up most often in films and pop literature were love obsessional—what some experts called "intimacy seekers"—and erotomania stalkers. Intimacy seekers are obsessively in love with their victims, a person they may have once been involved with or just know casually (think Alex Forrest in *Fatal Attraction*). They know their love isn't reciprocated, so they begin a campaign to win over the person—e-mails, letters, gifts. Erotomanic stalkers, on the other hand, are completely delusional. They believe the object of desire loves them back, though in many cases the two have never even met. Everything the victim says and does is interpreted in some way to support the delusion.

The harassment I'd experienced—the nasty calls, the knife in the sink, possibly (but not necessarily) the drugging—didn't bear any resemblance to these types of stalking. But it did fit under the umbrella of predatory or resentful stalking. That was stalking done to cause distress to the victim or frighten her silly, possibly out of a desire for revenge. Was there someone out there who was mad as hell at me over a perceived injustice on my part? I *hadn't* stolen anyone's boyfriend, at least not that I knew of. But could this be someone I'd covered in a story once—a criminal now at large or the girlfriend of a criminal? Or even an individual I'd written about in a human interest story? It was possible that some woman who had eagerly agreed to an interview had experienced negative ramifications from her moment in the limelight and now resented me for exposing her.

But surely if either of those scenarios was what was going on, there would have been an initial tip-off—an angry letter or call, for instance, or a warning from a source of mine that the person wanted to make trouble.

Totally wiped by this point, I snapped my computer closed. With my last reserve of energy, I checked my voice mail. There were a ton of calls—everyone from Landon, to reporter pals looking for info, to my mother congratulating me on my press blitz but chiding me for not letting her know what I was up to.

And there were two calls from Chris. "Where are you?" he asked almost plaintively in one. "I'm going nuts here, and I need to talk to you," he said in the other message. I felt such a weird mix of guilt and anger hearing his voice.

This time when I hit the pillow, sleep overtook me almost instantly. The next thing I knew, Beau was sitting right next to me, touching his hand to my shoulder. The room was filled with a sooty light that meant it was still very early or raining outside.

"I believe your public awaits you," he said, grinning.

"What time is it, anyway?"

"Ten of seven."

"Shit. I set my internal alarm clock, but I guess I was so zonked I never heard it."

"I figured I'd better wake you—I can hear your cell phone buzzing like crazy in your purse."

"Oh God, I better get going."

He ran his hand up just behind my ear, his open fingers firmly stroking my scalp. "I had to resist jumping your bones. I figured you needed the sleep."

I smiled groggily. "Rain check, then. Do you have an iron? I never took my suit out of my bag."

"I'll dig it out for you. I think it still works."

I checked my voice mail—the PR chicks wanting to make sure I was on schedule—and hopped into the shower. It was my first shower at Beau's, and as I dried off with a huge bath sheet, I glanced around the lovely white-tiled bathroom, with its clean, sparely covered surfaces, and tried to imagine myself here on a regular basis. How many nights a week would I sleep over at Beau's? Was it really going to happen? On the one hand, it felt like my destiny to be with him, yet at the same time it seemed like such an elusive concept.

While Beau took his turn in the shower, I chugged coffee and ironed my suit, using the kitchen counter as a makeshift ironing board. I allowed my eyes to be tugged back to the "welcome home" note again. Give it *up*, for God's sake, Bailey, I told myself. The man redefined the phrase *Ottoman Empire* for you last night, so you have every right to believe he's smitten. But as I chased my doubts away, I realized that something else was gnawing at me, some elusive thought that I couldn't snatch. It was not unlike what had happened to me the other night after I'd learned about Locket's death. Only later in the park did I realize that it had been my subconscious jostling me, trying to suggest that I may have goaded Harper into realizing Locket was the other woman. I wasn't sure if my brain was trying to tell me something about Beau or the murders. Hopefully if I were patient and bided my time, I would eventually learn what was nudging me.

Beau walked me to the elevator and suggested, to my relief, that I spend tonight there, too. He was going to be editing late into the day in his studio but we agreed that I'd call him around seven-thirty and we could grab a bite after that. I figured it would be smart to let a day or two pass before seeing him, but I craved being with him again. And I had about as much desire to be in my own apartment tonight as I did to be riding the Lex at four in the morning.

On my way to my first interview I called Windgate, and this time I reached him, not his voice mail.

"Did the crime scene people turn up anything at my place?" I asked.

"It's too early to know anything about the prints we found around the kitchen. But smudging on the knife in your sink indicates that the last person who used it wore gloves. Which means we probably won't turn up anything from any other surface."

"I gave some more consideration to your stalker question," I said. "But I can't think of anyone who might be holding a grudge. This has to be related to the murders."

"I tend to agree. I've put surveillance on your place in case this person shows up again. I want you to let me know if anything out of the ordinary happens."

"Absolutely," I said. His comments had sent a jolt of fear through me, though I felt a soupçon of comfort knowing that the police would be keeping an eye on my building. Oddly, I also experienced that nudging sensation in my brain again. I made a hard grab for the thought, but it escaped my grasp once more.

"And I want you to be extremely careful," he added. "You should talk to your super about security in the building and watch your back when you're out. This person is extremely dangerous."

I wondered if I should volunteer Harper's name. But I didn't want to create trouble for her and taint her reputation if she wasn't the killer.

"I hear you. By the way, is there anything you can share with me about the case in general? There's got to be some kind of update." I was hoping he might be inspired to cough up a tidbit in light of how cooperative I was being.

"There is one thing I'll share," he said after a pause. "There was no sexual assault. And Miss Ford's purse was still on her, with three hundred dollars in it."

"What about Alex Ottoson? Is he still a person of interest to you?"

"I can't comment on that."

After signing off, I immediately phoned *Buzz* and dictated a rough update on Locket to one of the deputy editors so it could be posted on the Web site. Then, with a lump in my throat, I phoned Chris.

"Bailey, where've you been?" he said, his voice thick with concern. "It's like you've been off the grid for the past twelve hours."

"I'm sorry," I told him. "I—I've been juggling so many balls. I've had to cover the story and also do a ton of press."

"Did you go to bed last night and just turn off your phone or something? I tried your home phone about twenty times."

"I only managed about an hour of sleep the night before, and I was zonked," I said, skirting the need to tell the lie. "How are you, anyway?"

"Okay, I guess. I mean, I feel sick about Locket—we all do. But it's sounding, at least, as if the show is safe. They had a big meeting with all of us, and though they were vague about details, they told us to be prepared to start shooting Monday—and that they'll somehow write Locket's death into the show. My agent told me that they're auditioning every actress over thirty in Hollywood for the new part. For all I know, I could end up starring with Meg Ryan."

I forced a laugh at his Meg Ryan line, but just hearing him mention his agent had made my stomach knot.

"So as grim as things are, my part seems relatively secure," he added. "At least by Hollywood standards. And I have the rest of the week off, thank God. Do the police know anything more—about Locket *or* Tom?"

"All I know is that Locket wasn't assaulted sexually and she apparently wasn't robbed. By the way, have you seen Harper since we talked yesterday?"

"She was in the meeting we had, offering tips on how to blow off the press, which by the way were staked out around my apartment this morning. Are you still thinking Harper may have done it?"

"Things just keep pointing to her. Didn't you tell me that she once wanted to be an actress?"

"Yeah, but what does that have to do with it?"

"I'll tell you more later. Look, Chris, there are some other things I need to talk to you about. Is there a time when the two of us could meet up later?"

"Is something the matter?"

"I just want to talk face-to-face."

"Sounds pretty ominous." He sighed heavily. "Like I said, I'm off this week, so you name the time."

I suggested six-thirty, figuring that would give me time to finish my press rounds and also swing by *Buzz*. He proposed we meet at his apartment in TriBeCa.

"I can't believe you haven't seen it yet," he said. "It's just been so crazy."

I finished the call just as my cab pulled up in front of the Fox News building. Two members of the PR team were waiting outside for me, both looking as brisk as a spring breeze. This kind of press coverage was a big deal for them, proving that *Buzz* could break hard news rather than simply offer up exclusives on which celebs were sneaking into the trailers of their costars.

Shortly after we were shown to the green room, I was led to makeup. As a solemn woman dabbed at my face with one of those little white wedges, I deliberated on what my strategy should be with Harper. The chances of her taking a call from me or returning a message were next to nil—she'd already indicated just how *unfun* she found talking to me and that I was persona non grata as far as folks at *Morgue* were concerned. I decided I had no choice but to flush her out. Once my face had been painted and my hair sprayed from a can the size of a subway car, I slipped into the corridor and tried Harper's number. "Harper, it's Bailey, and I need to talk to you ASAP," I said. "I *know*—so let's talk."

Maybe *that* would get a rise out of her.

For the rest of the morning, I zipped around in a town car with the PR twins, going to several TV and radio stations. Some of the interviewers tried to drag me into the speculation game—one guy, I swear, would have asked me who I thought killed Natalee Holloway if we'd had the time in the segment—but I stayed with the facts I'd presented in my article and didn't proffer any theories. The older of the PR chicks told me she thought I was doing great, but it would be super if I could smile a bit more. *At which point?* I wanted to ask. *Like when I describe the blood-spattered bathroom I found Tom's charred body in?*

We were done by one o'clock, and the girls told me to keep the car for the rest of the afternoon. I directed the driver to *Buzz* and told him I'd be several hours.

Nash was chomping at the bit for an update.

"At this point, I don't have anything more than I gave to the Web site," I told him. "It's a high-profile case, and everybody's being pretty tight-lipped."

"Who do you think did it?" he asked, peering over his black reading glasses at me.

"Someone who knew her, that's for sure."

"But *who*?"

"I'm not sure."

"Like hell you're not. Tell me what you're thinking."

"Let me dig just a little deeper."

He shook his head in mock disgust. "Bailey," he called as I was walking toward the door.

"Yeah."

"You look damn cute in a suit. When this is over, I'm buying you a celebratory dinner."

Oh great, that's all I needed.

Back at my desk, I brought Jessie up to speed on everything that was going on, leaving out my night with Beau. I wasn't sure why exactly, because I liked her and trusted her and had shared lots about Beau with her. Was it, I asked myself, because I didn't want her to go all pouncy on "Tad Hamilton"?

For the next few hours, I trolled for info about Locket's death, did several more radio interviews from my desk, and kept checking my BlackBerry to see if Harper had responded to my goosing—but there was nothing from her. When I had a spare moment, I called Beverly, something I'd never gotten around to doing yesterday, and asked her to call Barry and determine the exact amount that Tom was due to advance him.

At around five, I finally headed home, almost cross-eyed with fatigue. I still had the town car at my disposal, and I took full advantage, telling the driver to drop me right in front of my apartment building. It was nice to play Cat Jones, my former divalike boss at *Gloss*, but there was an additional advantage to sitting behind those tinted windows: I felt safe, something I doubted I was going to experience at home. I had called Bob from the office and made certain he had warned the other doormen to be extra cautious. I probably should have involved the super, too, but I was loath to throw poor Bob under the bus for failing to follow all the rules earlier.

My door was still double-locked, a relief, and I pushed it open slowly, letting my eyes search through the foyer into the living room. They fell finally to the floor, and I jumped. Just inside the door near my feet was a plain white envelope marked "Bailey." But on closer inspection, I saw that the handwriting was Landon's. There was a note inside, saying he was home and to drop by no matter what time I returned or who I'd "dragged home" with me.

After checking through my apartment and cleaning off surfaces smudged with fingerprint dust, I knocked on Landon's door.

"Dear Lord, Bailey, how could you go totally incommunicado at a time like this?"

"Sorry, sorry," I said as he ushered me into his apartment. "It's been absolutely insane, and I've had to do all these interviews. You didn't catch any of them, did you?"

"Yes, last night. It was on a news show, but they were showing a clip with you from earlier in the day. It took me about sixty seconds to realize it was you because I've never seen you in a *suit* before. You looked stunning, by the way. Do you want an espresso?"

"No, I've got to split in a minute to meet up with Chris. So you know all about Locket's murder, then?"

"As much as I can know from being forced to buy the *New York Post* rather than talk to *you*. I hadn't realized when you first told me about her that she was a former soap star. She wasn't on one of those shows with a title like *One Life to Live*, was she? That would be ironic."

I shot him a mock withering look. "That was not her show, no."

"Well, who do you think did it? Was it a simple mugging that escalated?"

"No way. I'm almost certain that she was killed by a non-stranger who followed her into the park—and that it somehow ties into Tom's death. But there's so much more to tell you. And one thing that's pretty serious."

I described the intruder's visit to my apartment. Landon had gone almost ashen by the time I reached the part about the steak knife in the sink.

"That's absolutely horrifying," he said soberly. "Weren't you nervous staying there last night? You should have called me."

"Well, I was on the verge of doing that, but then lo and behold, Beau Regan phoned and basically announced he wanted to go steady with me."

"*What?* That's—but—but what about Chris now?"

"That's a whole other story, and I need to have about two hours with you to take you up to speed on everything. But let's get back to my intruder. The police are going to be watching the building, and the doormen know to be careful, but can you keep an eye out, too? She was about five nine, average weight, blond hair."

"What time did this all happen, anyway?"

"About six-thirty."

His jaw slackened. "Good God, I was here then. I *heard* her."

"What do you mean, exactly?"

"I was sitting at the desk in my bedroom, and then I heard you—or what I *thought* was you—going through your closet. Your closet, you know, backs up against mine. There was a fair amount of activity in there, so I just assumed you were reorganizing. I was dying to talk to you, so after the noise quieted down I called your home phone, but there was no answer. I assumed I'd just missed you."

I could feel goose bumps on my arms and neck.

"Oh boy," I said. "I wonder what the hell she was doing in there. Look, I better check it out before I meet up with Chris. But I promise to call later."

I opened the door of my apartment, feeling even more wigged out than I'd been earlier. Using a flashlight in addition to the overhead light in my closet, I pawed through my clothes, half expecting another nasty leave-behind, but I didn't find anything. I made another discovery, though. Two of my tops were missing. Though there was a chance they were hanging in a plastic bag at the dry cleaner's, I didn't think so.

It was now almost time to meet Chris. I scrubbed off the layers of makeup I'd worn for my interviews and changed into jeans. The renewed dread I felt about the intruder blended into my dread about meeting with Chris like two water spills converging on a glass tabletop, and it was hard to know which one was worse. As I was swiping on lip gloss, Beverly called me back.

"I have the information you requested," she said. "Tom was going to advance Barry exactly seven thousand dollars."

"Ummm. Okay, thanks."

"Do you mind my asking why it's significant?"

"I was just trying to piece some information together. Someone who borrowed money from Tom claims he paid it back, and

I thought if he had, Tom might have included the cash in his payment to Barry. But he took out exactly seven thousand from the bank."

"I'm sorry I couldn't be more helpful. I wonder what will happen to the house now."

"The parents' financial manager, Mr. Barish, will most likely get involved."

"Mr. Barish? Ugh!"

I froze. "Why do you say that?"

"Tom was upset with him. He wouldn't let Tom handle his money the way he *wanted* to. When Tom wanted to mount the play, for instance, he told this Barish fellow that it was something his parents would have wanted for him, but Barish wouldn't advance him the money. I almost mentioned this when I was telling you about the play, but I hate to tell tales out of school."

That would explain why Barish hadn't had much contact with Tom in recent weeks. Interesting that Barish had not given even a hint of the tiff. I had only his work number, and when I tried him after signing off with Beverly, no one picked up. I left a message asking him to call me immediately. As I broke the connection, I realized that there'd been no word from Harper. Clearly my message hadn't flushed her out as planned.

Leaving my building, I glanced up and down the street. There was no one skulking about, at least from what I could tell. Up the block, two men sat in the front seat of a dark blue car, and I wondered if they might be the police—but they seemed deep in conversation, oblivious to my presence.

By the time I was headed in a cab toward TriBeCa, it was six-forty-five, and by the time I reached Chris's place I was nearly thirty minutes late.

"Hey," he said as he swung open the door. "I was worried—considering everything that's happened."

"Sorry, I should have called," I told him. He leaned down and kissed me on the mouth, and I instinctively jerked my head away ever so slightly.

"Are you about to blow me off, Bailey?" he asked, eyes quizzical after he'd pulled back to look at me.

"No, no, I—I just need to talk to you." I was suddenly a jumble of emotions, the dominant one being anxiety. I was going to demand the truth from Chris, but I wasn't looking forward to hearing it.

He turned and walked into the apartment, expecting me to follow. It was a large loft-style studio apartment, really nice, with high ceilings, exposed water pipes, big windows, and pumpkin-colored wood floors. The kitchen, dining, and living areas were all one room, and a small staircase led to a sleeping area. The only furniture was four bar stools by the kitchen counter and a large cranberry-colored sofa—and there wasn't a lick of art on the walls.

"Great place," I said.

"Yeah," he replied, smirking. "If you love the really, really *spare* look. I just need to spend a day at Pottery Barn. Maybe this is finally the week to do it."

"Well, it takes time to pull things together," I said, a hopelessly dull observation that reflected how freaking awkward I felt.

"I've got a great white wine," Chris said, striding toward the counter. "Why don't we go up to the roof. There's a kind of terrace-garden thing up there."

That wasn't at all what I was up for considering the topic of conversation we were about to embark on—plus, I was supposed to talk to Beau at seven-thirty—but I didn't know how to refuse. After Chris pulled a white Burgundy from the fridge and filled two glasses, I trailed him back through the apartment and up a flight of stairs from the hallway to the roof garden. It was simple but well done, with several boxed trees and weatherproof teak tables and chairs. The lights had come on in the buildings all around us, and in some of the windows I could see people moving about, but we were the only ones on the roof. A light wind lifted my hair from the back, making me shiver.

"So what's on your mind, Bailey?" Chris asked. "Something's clearly eating at you."

I wandered over to one of the tables, and Chris followed behind me. We both took seats. As I stared across the table at him in the waning light, I felt a swell of sadness. Up until now, I'd allowed myself to be mostly angry about what he'd done, but it was more complicated than that. I cared about Chris, we'd had sex together, we'd forged a bond because of Tom—but I'd discovered that he'd done something morally reprehensible. It meant that he wasn't the guy I'd thought he was. And there didn't seem to be any way I could forgive him.

"There *is* something bothering me," I said after taking a sip of wine for fortification. "I found out that it was your agent who leaked it to the show that Tom had been in rehab."

"Who told you that?" he demanded, sounding shocked that I knew—but not surprised at what I'd said.

Suddenly something clattered behind me, and instinctively I spun around.

"It's just the wind rattling one of the planters," Chris said.

"Someone in the know told me," I said, turning back. "So please don't try to deny it."

"I won't deny it," he said, his voice hard. "My agent told Alex Ottoson—and that's how Tom got knocked out of the running for the role I ended up with."

"I can't believe it," I said. "Part of me was hoping that you *would* deny it, that it hadn't happened that way."

I rose from the table, just wanting to get the hell out of there. Chris reached out and grabbed my wrist.

"No," he said. "You're not leaving."

CHAPTER 18

What?" I said sharply. "I'll leave if I damn well please."

"You can't, Bailey. You have to let me tell you the whole story."

He relaxed his grip, and I tugged my hand away.

"You mean, you had a good reason for what you did," I said sarcastically. "That your success was more important than Tom's?"

"No, it didn't happen like you think it did. I swear."

To my utter amazement, tears began to well in his eyes.

"Okay, shoot," I said, sitting down again.

"When I tried out for the part of the morgue desk assistant, Tom supposedly already had the part of Jared, the one I have now. I hadn't tried out for that myself because it looked like I'd been cast in another pilot for the season. When that pilot fell through, it seemed I'd be *lucky* to get the assistant part and so I agreed to read for it. Plus, my agent kept saying maybe they'd expand the part once they saw my test. He asked me about Tom at the time—like, why he hadn't heard much about him. It seemed purely out of curiosity—a 'Who *is* this guy?' kind of thing. I told him about Tom doing mostly theater and how he went off the radar for a while after losing both parents. I mentioned the rehab just in terms of explaining the low profile.

"Later, when they ended up giving *me* the big role, my agent told me that it was because they'd rethought the part a little, and I was more the physical type they now had in mind. I felt like shit, but Tom seemed to take it in stride. Then late this summer, this lackey who works for my agent spilled the story to me. My agent had apparently told one of the producers under Alex about the rehab. I couldn't believe it. I told my agent to try to fix it, but it was too late."

He heaved out a long, sad sigh and let his head drop into his hands.

"Is that the truth, Chris?" It *sounded* real, but how could I be sure? He was a goddamned actor, after all.

"Yes," he said, looking back up. "I'm as ambitious as the next dude in this business, but there's no way I would have hurt Tom."

"Why didn't you tell Tom the truth once you found out?"

"I couldn't bear to. Plus, I was afraid if he learned what had really happened, it would send him into a tailspin and he might even start using drugs again. This is partly why I was so crazy to find him. I thought maybe he'd heard what had happened from someone else and just bolted because of it."

In the dim light of the terrace, I saw Chris clench his fists on the table.

"Now, of course, I could kick myself for *not* telling him. If Tom had known what had really happened, maybe he would have just bailed on the show. And he and Locket wouldn't be dead."

I felt an emotional jab as I watched his face, faintly illuminated by the two wall-mounted lights. I'd accepted Alex Ottoson's words as the truth. I'd allowed my anger to bloom without ever first asking for Chris's side of the story—and I'd used the info as a reason to sleep with Beau with a clear conscience.

"Chris, I think you probably made the right judgment call at the time. Tom *could* have gone into a tailspin, and he might have bagged the part—which would have been a lost opportunity for him."

"I was looking out for myself, too. I didn't want to rock the boat. It's the same reason I took Locket's note. I didn't want to make any waves that would affect the show."

"Have you called the police yet about the note?"

"No. But I will. I swear."

I took a long sip of wine as I gathered my thoughts.

"Why don't we grab some dinner?" Chris suggested. "We could do take-out here if you want."

"Um, gee, I'd like to, but I still have a few leads to follow on the case." I wasn't lying. I needed to swing by the Chaps Theatre before I met up with Beau. "Maybe we can get together tomorrow sometime."

"What kinds of leads? Are you still thinking Harper might have done it?"

"Yes, she's a definite suspect, but I'm just trying to turn over every stone regardless of whether they seem directly connected to her or not. What I'm hoping to find out tonight is whether that line Tom used from *Taming of the Shrew* meant anything."

"Just be careful tonight, okay? Promise me."

I opened my mouth to tell him about the intruder but decided against it. He seemed pretty shaken up by our discussion, and I didn't want to make things any worse.

"Promise. Look, I better fly now."

Downstairs, by the elevator, Chris hugged me and kissed my

forehead. It was a relief, knowing the truth now, but I also felt like a heel.

"Tomorrow, then?" he asked.

"Absolutely," I said.

As soon as I was on the street, I tried Beau. To my chagrin and annoyance, I reached only his voice mail. True, I was phoning later than I was supposed to be, but why wouldn't he be available?

I gave the cabbie the address to the Chaps Theatre. As I sank into the saggy leather seat, my thoughts raced back to Chris. He hadn't betrayed Tom after all. He *was* the same person I'd always thought he was. Though we certainly hadn't gone to bed with any promise of exclusivity, there'd been an undeniable connection between us, and if he knew what I'd been up to last night, he'd see it as a real breach of trust. I felt the flames of ho hell licking at my ankles. Speaking of which, what the hell was I going to do? Beau was the guy I'd been pining for, and now, finally, I had him, and the thought of that made my heart pound like crazy. But I also felt an attraction to—and bond with—Chris. I had tried chasing him from my brain after the revelation from Alex, but he was there again, after our talk tonight.

The theater was all lit up, and I felt hopeful of finally picking up what I needed. But as I tugged at the door, I found that it wouldn't budge. I glanced at my watch: 8:25. The lobby was empty, and from this angle, at least, I couldn't spot anyone in the box office. I leaned my head toward the door and pressed my ear against the glass. I was pretty sure I heard the rustling sound of muffled laughter from an audience. My guess was that the door had been locked after the last stragglers had arrived, perhaps so the box office person could hit the restroom or take care of another duty in the theater. I would just have to wait until signs of life appeared. There was a small café diagonally across the street, and I headed for it. While I was stepping off the curb, my cell phone rang. Beau, I figured.

But my guess was wrong. The number was unrecognizable. I answered and discovered Harper on the other end. The pheasant had finally been flushed from the woods.

"Do you want to explain that cryptic message you left me?" she demanded.

"I think you know what I was referring to," I said.

I'd wondered if my message might infuriate her, regardless of whether she was guilty, but what I'd never imagined was what happened next. Her voice caught in her throat as if she were about to cry.

"Do you have something *against* me?" she asked quietly. "You keep hounding me, and I don't know why."

"I don't have anything against you. I just want to know the real story."

It sounded as if she choked back a sob. Was it all a damn *act?* I wondered.

"Let's talk, then," she said. "Do you want to come to my place? I don't feel like traveling far. It's supposed to rain tonight."

Not on your freaking life, I was tempted to say. There was no way in hell I was going to be alone in an apartment with her.

"You're in the Gramercy Park area, right?" I asked. "Why don't we meet at the bar at the Gramercy Park Hotel. Twenty minutes from now."

She sighed as a way of agreeing to the location, and I flagged down a cab. I wanted to be sure I was there ahead of her, safely in my seat in the bar.

The Gramercy Park Hotel is on Lexington Avenue, just where it meets the legendary park. The hotel had been totally refurbished into an extravagant, enchanting place with two bars, each opening onto the other. I went to the larger one in the back, a cross—with its velvet armchairs, high, wood-beamed ceiling, sawtooth chandelier, and massive stone fireplace—between Barcelona, a medieval gallery, and *Citizen Kane*.

I found a chair by the fireplace and plunked down, scooting it slightly so I could see the door. Was this going to be it, I wondered, the moment I learned the truth? Was Harper unraveling enough to finally spill everything? Or was this a trap set by a woman so wily that she'd been able to hoodwink my doorman?

Harper was late, and as the minutes ticked by, it occurred to me that she might not be coming, that this was indeed a trap of some kind. But at nine-ten she finally stepped through the doorway dressed in jeans, black boots, and a black turtleneck sweater. She looked spent, like someone who'd been trying to rescue people from rising floodwaters for several days. Her skin was splotchy and broken out, suggesting she was a major stress mess, and there were deep blue and yellow circles under her eyes, like old bruises. Either her grief was getting the better of her, or she was being eaten alive by guilt.

"Would you like a glass of wine?" I asked, pulling over a chair for her. I had ordered a glass of wine myself but was taking baby sips so my head would be clear.

"I'll take care of it," she said, and after flagging down the waiter with a quick whip of her hand, she asked for a single-malt Scotch on the rocks. She wasn't messing around.

I didn't say a word, just waited. She'd indicated earlier that she wanted to talk, and I sensed that the best strategy was to just bide my time—and create a vacuum of silence that she would feel overwhelmed to fill. After her drink arrived, she opened her mouth.

"This is off the record, okay? I agreed to talk to you, but I have no intention of finding myself in that Web post of yours."

"Okay," I said.

She took a deep breath. "Believe it or not," she said, "I really don't respect myself for what I did. I wish I could take it all back."

Oh boy. Was she about to confess to me that she was the murderer?

"Why don't you start from the beginning," I said softly.

Elbows tight against her body, she pressed the tips of her fingers to her mouth, as if trying to prevent the words from escaping. Her penny eyes began to gleam with water. Gosh, I was bringing half of New York to tears tonight.

"Okay," she said, dropping her hands to the table. "I know I was the pursuer in the relationship, but from what I could tell, Tom came along willingly. Right before he disappeared, however, he suddenly seemed to cool down toward me—he was vague about plans, just sort of wishy-washy. I suspected there might be someone else, but I didn't have any proof. Of course, now, thanks to your blog or whatever it is, I know *exactly* what he was up to. I have to hand it to Locket—I never thought she was much of an actress, but she disguised her fling with Tom brilliantly."

The last line was delivered with total scorn, and she took a slug of her drink afterward, as if it would cool down her anger.

"The weekend he disappeared, I'd planned to stay in L.A.," she continued, "but when Tom said his trip to the Hamptons got scrapped, I decided to take the red-eye back. I told him I could now see him earlier than Sunday, but when I arrived home there was a message on my machine saying he'd made other plans for the weekend. I was furious at him for taking off. And that's why I did it."

What? I wanted to scream. But I sat there nearly motionless, an expression (I hoped) of knowingness on my face, as if I knew the truth but was giving her the chance to put it into words.

She took another sip of Scotch and straightened her back.

"I called Alex and used the excuse that we should have lunch that day to review the sweeps PR strategy. But Alex knew what it was all about. He'd been giving me these looks for weeks. So after lunch we went back to his place—Locket was away for the weekend—and fucked each other's brains out."

Oy. So *this* was the info she thought I was privy to. I hadn't seen it coming at all.

"So you're saying the last time you ever spoke to Tom was that Friday night phone call?" I said, pretending not to be nonplussed by her revelation.

"That's right. Up until yesterday, I felt eaten up by guilt. I kept thinking that if I'd convinced Tom to be with me that weekend—and I hadn't ended up with Alex—he might still be alive. Of course, then it turns out Tom had been with *Locket* that weekend. But I'm still disgusted with myself for sleeping with Alex."

"Were you also with Alex Monday night?" I asked, remembering Alex's alibi.

"Yes," she said sullenly. "He came back to my apartment with me after a meeting. I kept thinking that maybe if I *felt* something for the man, I could excuse myself for what I'd done, but it's just not possible. I can't imagine what Locket saw in him."

"Do the police know?"

"They do *now*. Alex gave me as his alibi. I bet it took about two seconds for him to decide to offer me up."

"Was he unhappy in his relationship with Locket? Is that why he cheated?"

"Do you think he lay in bed with me sharing all his deepest feelings? Alex's idea of being self-revelatory is to tell you he once had arthroscopic surgery on his knee."

"What time did he leave your place on Monday?" I asked.

"Around eight-thirty."

"And what time did the two of you split up that Saturday?"

"Midafternoon. *Why?* You're not suggesting Alex killed Tom and Locket, are you?" She straightened her back again. "Or that *I* did?"

It was still a possibility. Locket hadn't gone out until nine, which meant either one of them could have spotted her going into the park—and followed or joined her. The trip to Andes took two and a half hours. If they'd split in the afternoon, either would have had time to drive there that Saturday.

"I'm not suggesting anything," I told her. "I'm just trying to learn the truth. I hear you had a heated discussion with Locket on the set the other day—after I'd hinted Tom had been seeing someone besides you. Did you confront Locket about that?"

"Hardly. Like I told you, I had no clue about their relationship. If you *must* know, Locket was miffed because I wasn't helping more with her book PR. I told her it wasn't in my job description. You really think I might have killed her, don't you?"

"No, I'm not saying that, Harper. But I do have reason to believe the killer might be a blond woman who has acting skills. Someone who can impersonate people and even make her voice sound like a man's. Any ideas?"

"Oh, great. So now you're implying Tom was seeing someone *else?*"

"It's possible the killer is a man, and this woman is simply in cahoots with him. Does Deke ever have anyone like that around? Or even Alex?"

She looked as me as if her wheels were spinning but shook her head. "No one comes to mind."

Surreptitiously, I glanced at my watch. I needed to make my way back to the theater. I thanked Harper for her help and signaled for the check.

"I need to know," she demanded. "How'd you find out about me and Alex? Does everyone else know?"

"The police let it slip," I lied. "I'm not aware of who else knows at this point, but you better be prepared for the fact that news may leak out on the set."

It had started to drizzle when I left the hotel, and it took me forever to hail a cab. My clothes were damp and spongy by the time I collapsed in the back of one. I checked my phone and saw that Beau had finally called—I had turned off my cell phone before entering the hotel so there'd be no interruptions. I wanted to call him back and firm up our plans for tonight, but first I needed time to think.

I hadn't suspected anything between Harper and Alex, but it wasn't tough to accept it. What I couldn't be sure about, though, were her claims of innocence. She was a former actress and now a professional spin doctor, and that meant she was probably a damn good liar. Maybe the whole point of her confessing to me about the booty calls with Alex was to deflect my attention from the bigger crime she was guilty of.

But if she wasn't the murderer, who *was?* There was still Deke hovering in the wings. I wondered if he had a chick in his life, someone who would be willing to play havoc with my mental state by making scary phone calls and going through my steak knives. Maybe Chris would know.

As the cab pulled up in front of the theater, I could see movement in there. An overweight woman with long, lank red hair and thick black-framed glasses (the "I'm hip and live downtown" style) was screwing the cap back on a Pepsi bottle on a small table, left over obviously from intermission. I tried the door and this time it opened.

"May I help you?" she asked gruffly. "The box office is closed."

"I just wanted to see if I could get some information. My name is Bailey Weggins, and I'm curious about a play you did a year or so ago."

"I'm a member of the company—I can probably help you. My name's Natalie."

"*Taming of the Shrew,*" I said. "I want to check who was in the cast."

She crinkled her eyes curiously but then cocked her head in

the direction over my left shoulder. "We did it at the end of the winter. The program's up there on the wall someplace."

As she resumed her cleanup, sliding cookies from a paper plate into a plastic tub, I crossed to the other side of the small lobby. It was a shabby space, stuffed with a few worn armchairs and scarred café tables.

From the cheaply framed programs on the wall, I could see that the theater had done an eclectic mix of productions: some of the classics like *Julius Caesar, All's Well That End's Well,* Anouilh's *Antigone, Six Characters in Search of an Author,* and then a range of contemporary stuff by playwrights unknown, with kooky titles like *Hearts Too* and *Black as Day.*

It took only a second to find *Shrew.* While some of the other programs featured illustrations or photos, this one was fairly simple, with just a border and the words set in a kind of Elizabethan-style type. My eye went instantly to Petruchio and then followed the line to the opposite side of the page: Tom Fain. In that split second, Tom seemed alive, and I felt a gigantic stab of remorse. I dragged my eye down to Katharina and then followed that line. When I saw the actress's name, I gasped. Suddenly it felt as if someone had grabbed me hard by the back of the neck. It was *Blythe* who had played the role. The play had run last February— ten performances. That may have been when Tom had first met Blythe. Was *she* the mystery visitor in Andes? Had Tom quoted Baptista to Locket because it was Katharina herself who had driven up that day?

"Everything okay?" the woman behind me asked.

"Did you know Tom Fain?" I said.

"Of course," she said soberly. "We all did. He was part of this company."

"I'm a friend of a friend, and I'm looking into his death. Is there anything you could tell me about him that might be significant?" I wanted to know about Blythe, of course, but I sensed it was smart not to tip my hand with someone in the theater group.

"No—other than the fact that the guy was a real sweetheart. He was the only actor I ever met who asked questions about *you*. Why so interested in *Taming of the Shrew*? What would that have to do with anything?"

"I'm just following up every lead possible. Was he friends with anyone in the company?"

She pulled off her glasses and turned them around, examining the lenses—for *what*, a smudge? Her eyes seemed much smaller without the lenses in front of them.

"He had a few buddies," she said, sliding the glasses back on. "And he used to date Blythe Hammell, the girl who played Katharina. She's just sick about what happened—as you can imagine."

Every muscle in my body froze.

"Oh, Blythe's around?" I asked as casually as possible, but my voice seemed muffled to me, like the dampened sounds of laughter emanating from inside the theater. My mind was reeling. "I thought she'd gone to Miami."

"She went somewhere south for a while—she had a part in an independent movie down there. But she came back when she heard about Tom."

"And you had a chance to talk to her."

"She dropped by yesterday. She wants to do another play. She thinks it will help take her mind off things."

"Is she a good actress?" I said.

"Blythe? Oh, she's brilliant. The problem with Blythe is that she's a bit of a maniac. The reason she isn't any further along in her career isn't because of lack of talent—she just doesn't realize that you're only entitled to be a *diva* after you've made it."

"Will she be around again?"

"Yeah, but I don't know when."

"She looks like she's on the tall side," I said, thinking of the visitor to my apartment.

"*Tall?*" she said, her tone indicating that her patience was now wearing thin. "I *guess*. She's probably five eight or nine."

She glanced at her watch and gathered up a batch of empty soda liters in her arms. "I need to finish up here. Is there anything else?"

"A cell phone number for Blythe," I blurted out almost desperately. I forced a smile. "I'd love to touch base with her—she might know something."

"You'll have to talk to the manager. He should be around the office tomorrow." She rattled off a number that I hurriedly entered into my BlackBerry.

"I know you're busy, but just one more thing," I nearly pleaded. "Is there a cast shot somewhere—from *Taming of the Shrew*?"

"Over there," she said, indicating another wall.

I hurried over there. Tom was dead center in the shot, his hair very short at the time. Standing next to him was a woman with thick black hair.

"Is this Blythe?" I asked. "With the black hair?"

"Yes, but she doesn't actually look like that," she said. "Blythe's really a blonde, but she's a master with wigs."

Oh, I bet.

When I stepped outside a minute later, I discovered that it was teeming now. Ducking under an awning, I hit Beau's number.

"There you are," he said. "I was worried about you."

"There's a new development," I blurted out. "I'll fill you in when I see you."

"Can you come over now? I want to hear everything."

"It's raining absolute buckets out here. I have to find a cab home first and then one to your place. It may take me forever to get there."

"Why don't I meet you at your place. That means only one trip for you—and it's usually easy to find a cab around here."

I thanked him for the offer and sloshed my way toward Fifth Avenue. A taxi came hurtling down the street, spraying water with its wheels, but as soon as I stepped into the street, a cab poacher leapt out a few yards ahead of me and shot up his hand. It was fifteen minutes before I managed to hail one successfully. I was soaked to the bone by the time I finally threw myself into the back of it.

As soggy as I was and as shivery as I felt, there was only one thought on my mind: Blythe. She was an actress, reputedly a brilliant one. Now I knew why I'd felt that jostling sensation in my brain: The stuff I'd read online about stalker behavior had clearly lined up in my subconscious with the memory of all those cards and notes Blythe had sent to Tom. Although theoretically her behavior was within the realm of what your average red-blooded girl might resort to in the desperate days after being kicked to the curb, it also hinted at a possible obsession. Perhaps Blythe had never gone to Miami at all. She may have been aware of the house in Andes and shown up there that Saturday afternoon. Tom, not knowing how dangerous she was, would have seen her arrival as more of a nuisance. He may have called to her from the window when she emerged from her car, told her to come up to the bathroom. At the time, her intention may not have been to kill him, just make him see reason. When he hadn't, she could have attacked in a frenzy.

Why kill Locket, then? Perhaps she'd actually seen Locket leave Tom's place in Andes and had decided she had to die, too, once an opportunity presented itself. Or maybe she suspected Locket knew something about Tom's murder. But how would she have gotten wind of that?

As I climbed out of the cab in the rain, I glanced anxiously around the area in front of my apartment building. You'd have to be crazy to be out on a night like tonight, but whoever had talked their way into my apartment—Blythe or not—might very well *be* crazy, and I was worried that she'd be back at some point.

Even before stripping off my sopping wet clothes, I did a full under-bed-and-in-closet inspection of my pad—slightly overboard, perhaps, but I knew if I didn't, I wouldn't feel totally safe. The place looked exactly as I'd left it—no daggers lying about tonight. Once I was in dry jeans and a sweater, with water heating for tea, I grabbed my composition book and furiously jotted down notes and questions to myself. Should I go to the police immediately? It was hard to imagine them wanting to investigate Blythe simply on my hunch. A whole bunch of cutesy Hallmark cards spelled heartsick chick, not necessarily dangerous stalker. And the line to Petruchio was hardly a definitive link. Since Tom liked quoting the Bard, you could argue that he might have used that line to refer to *anyone* he was about to have an unpleasant conversation with, not simply someone who was in the play with him. I needed to gather more info before I approached Windgate with my theory.

If Blythe was planning to spend more time hanging around the Chaps Theatre, that could provide me with the perfect opportunity to come face-to-face with her and initiate a discussion. But in order to find out when she'd be there, I was going to have to proceed delicately, or someone might tip her off that I'd been making inquiries. If she were indeed the killer, she would be easily spooked.

The hapless roommate, Terry: That was another avenue to pursue. If Blythe was back in town, she may have made contact and revealed her whereabouts. I tried the number, and Terry picked up on the third ring, sounding as if she'd long since crawled under the covers for the night.

"I'm so sorry to bother you," I told her. "It's Bailey Weggins again."

"I *just* got to sleep. And I've got a presentation on rolling benefits to do tomorrow."

"I'm sorry, but it's really important."

"Yeah, well, actually I was going to call *you*, but I lost that slip of paper with your number. Blythe is back in New York."

"You *talked* to her?" I exclaimed.

"Yeah, she called me. She swears—and I mean *really, really* swears—that she's going to pay me back everything she owes me. According to her, she made a nice chunk of change from the movie she did."

"Is she planning to move back in with you?"

"No, and she won't tell me where she's staying. She won't even give me her cell phone number."

Damn, I thought. "Does she know about Tom?"

"Yes, I told her, and she said she'd already heard. And it was weird—all she said was that she felt sorry but that he wasn't really all that nice of a guy."

"Have you any idea what she's up to?"

"Now that her movie is done, she says she wants to get back into *theater*." She said the word *theater* in a fluttery, mock highfulutin way. "She practically told me to expect to see her as a presenter at the Tonys next year."

"But did she say anything *specific* about her plans, about what she's going to be doing over the next few weeks? Any auditions, for instance?"

"Well, I think she's doing stuff with this theater company she's a member of. It's in the Village. I know she's going there tomorrow afternoon because she said that afterwards she was going to drop by the apartment here and pick up some stuff she left behind. I told her she'd better have a check with her—for the *full* amount she owes me."

"Did—did you mention me, by any chance?"

"I gave her your message—I mean, that's what you *told* me to do. I thought maybe you'd have already talked to her."

"Why?" I asked. There was a stirring of the hairs on the back of my neck.

"Because she seemed to know who you were."

CHAPTER 19

"Did she *say* she knew me?" I asked.

"Not in so many words. I could just tell that she did. What's going on now? Is she in some kind of trouble?" She asked the last question eagerly, as if nothing would please her more than learning that Blythe was under suspicion for something like running a giant Ponzi scheme.

"She may be. But you can't let on to her about it."

"I *knew* it. My mother was so right about her."

"What time is she supposed to come by your place tomorrow night?"

"Around six or seven. You aren't going to send the cops here, are you? If the super sees them, he could decide to evict me."

"No, no. I might drop by the theater, though, just to ask her a few questions. I know the theater. Did she say what time she's going to be there?"

"I think around four. She's meeting a few people to talk

about a play. You know, maybe I should show up there, too. Then I'm guaranteed to see her."

"But you don't have any leverage if you go by the theater," I said hurriedly. "You've got her things at your place, and you can ask for the check before you hand them over to her." I was scrambling to talk her out of it because Terry would be a major fly in the ointment if she tried to lobby for money from Blythe at the precise time I was attempting to extract info.

"I guess," she said.

"Just do me one favor, Terry. When you *do* see Blythe, it's best not to get into any kind of confrontation with her tomorrow, okay?"

"Okay, okay. Now let me get back to sleep."

I hung up and leaned back into my sofa. So tomorrow, if everything went as planned, I would have the chance to meet Blythe. Would asking her a few questions really give me any sense of whether or not she had killed Tom and Locket in a frenzy of sexual jealousy, of whether or not she was the one who had left a steak knife calling card at my apartment? I didn't know, but that was all I had to start with. My strategy, I decided, would be to tell her that I wanted to interview her for my story for *Buzz* since she and Tom had once dated. I would watch her, listen to her. And see if she gave anything away.

About fifteen minutes later, after I'd wolfed down a grilled-cheese sandwich and tried to decompress, Beau arrived. He was wearing this amazingly sexy black trench coat, damp on the shoulders as if he'd had a hard time finding a cab after all. His hair was wet, too, and his skin was glowing. I had this one totally Harlequin romance moment in which I thought, God, he's here, he *chose* me. I had been convinced that would never happen.

As soon as he'd peeled off his trench and hung it over a dining table chair to dry, we both collapsed on the couch. He said he was dying to know what the new development was. I carefully laid out my theory about Blythe.

"If you're right, it's absolutely chilling," he said. "There's something totally film noir about it. You half expect Blythe to be played by a young Barbara Stanwyck."

"But do you think I could be right? I have no proof whatsoever."

"Let me play devil's advocate. What if Blythe actually *was* making a movie in Miami during this time? Is there some way you can check on that?"

"The roommate didn't have any details. I could certainly find out from *Buzz* if a major studio was shooting a film in Miami recently, but there's no way to know about minor indie films—or grad student projects."

"So where's she been living all this time? And how's she been getting around? She'd need a car to get up to Andes, and according to the roommate, she's always broke."

"We know she's a conniver and extremely manipulative. I'm sure she's managed to mooch off other people—even borrow a car from someone."

"It's pretty clear why she might kill Tom. But why Locket? Just because she'd been sleeping with Tom?"

"That's what I'm assuming for now."

"Why not Harper, then, too?"

"Well, Harper *could* be in danger. Or maybe Harper never struck Blythe as much of a threat on a romantic level. Or maybe Locket was killed because Blythe thought she might know something about the murder."

Beau pushed himself off the couch and paced the room for a few moments, thinking.

"You got the first phone call on the way back from Andes. How would she have known you went there?"

"I've thought about that," I said. "I'm wondering if she may have been hanging around the property and saw me drive up. In fact, she could have been staying up in Andes for a good chunk of this time. You know, it's true that killers often revisit the scene. She may have wanted to know exactly when the body was finally found, so she was keeping an eye out for any activity."

"That's really scary to imagine," he said, plopping back onto the sofa and slipping an arm around my shoulder. "That she was there and may have been watching you."

"But you know, you just made me think of something," I said. "How in hell did she get my cell phone number?"

"Would they give it out at *Buzz* if she called there?"

"Not to just some stranger calling. But she's such a damn good actress—for all I know, she called pretending to be my mother and said she'd lost it. But—but that would mean that on the Thursday I drove up there, only *one day* after I started looking into Tom's disappearance, she'd already gotten wind of the fact that I was, as they say, on the case. How could she have possibly known so quickly?"

"Here's another scary thought," Beau said. "What if she's ingratiated herself with a friend of yours, pretending to be someone else?"

"That's a possibility," I said. "But—you know, as I'm talking about it, the whole theory is starting to sound a bit far-fetched. Maybe I'm completely off base here."

At that same moment, though, I felt something tug yet again maddeningly at my subconscious. I would just have to give it time to surface.

"Have you talked to the police about her?" Beau asked.

"I haven't yet because I felt I needed more proof. And now that I've discussed it with you, I see that I've really got to sort more of it out before I go to them."

"Promise me you won't do anything that's potentially dangerous. If Blythe did commit the murders, she's obviously a real psycho."

Sharing my plan to drop by the theater tomorrow afternoon suddenly seemed like a bad idea.

"Okay, I promise not to hotdog it," I said. "Look, do you feel like a drink or anything? I haven't even offered you one."

"You know what I feel like on such a rainy night? Sharing a bath. Any interest?"

"That sounds like a perfect idea."

While the tub filled up, I lit some candles in the bathroom and poured us each a few splashes of brandy. We set the glasses on the floor by the tub as we slid in. Beau positioned me between his legs, and he spent a good ten minutes massaging my shoulders and neck, working his thumbs into all the tight knots there. It felt delicious, and for a little while, at least, all my thoughts about murderous machinations slipped away.

Before Beau and I went to bed, I ducked into the kitchen and called Harper. I hadn't ruled her out as a suspect, but at the same time I didn't want it on my conscience if anything happened to her. Her voice was low and tight when she answered, suggesting she'd been crying.

"Are you okay?" I asked.

"What do you need *now*?" she asked, not bothering to answer.

"Remember how I mentioned that Tom may have been killed by a blond woman? I now think it might be a girl he was dating before you. There's a possibility she became obsessed with him."

"*Who?*"

"An actress named Blythe Hammell. Did you ever hear of her?"

There were several seconds of silence.

"There *was* an actress," she said finally, "but I never knew her name. He apparently took her to Atlantic City with him just after he and I started dating. Deke derived some pleasure in spreading that around. I was furious, but Tom told me that he'd booked the trip with her weeks before and wanted to honor the commitment. He swore that was the last time he was ever with her."

"Well, like I said, I think she became obsessed with him—and she was convinced that he was in love with her, too. It's what they call erotomania. She may have killed him in a frenzy once she confronted him and realized he didn't care at all. And then she may have been so consumed with sexual jealousy that she killed Locket, too."

"Do the police know?"

"I need to gather a bit more evidence before I present this idea to the police," I said, my voice low. "I'm going to drop by the Chaps Theatre late tomorrow afternoon because Blythe is reportedly going to be there. But I wanted to let you know so you'll take precautions. If Blythe really is the killer, she may be crazy. You could possibly be a target, too, because of your relationship with Tom."

"I can't bear any more of this. I went into PR because it seemed more *sane* than acting."

After I'd signed off, I went back into the bedroom. Beau was propped up on a pillow, the sheet pulled up just to his waist.

"Getting a little glass of milk to help you sleep?" he asked.

"Hopefully, I'm tired enough that I'm not going to need it tonight. I had insomnia really bad a year or so ago, and I dread it coming back again."

"Were you going to bed thinking about your work? That could keep *anyone* awake."

"Actually, it was just after I got divorced. I wasn't sorry it was over, but it's the sort of thing that weighs on you no matter how much you swear you won't let it. I love how all these actresses today rebound so quickly. Two weeks after they announce they're separated, they're dating someone like George Clooney and claiming they've never been happier. We mere mortals require a longer rebound phase."

"I don't know anything about that part of your life."

"Bailey Weggins, the Dark Years. I'll save it for a day when there is absolutely nothing else in the world to do."

"What did your ex do for a living, anyway?" Beau asked.

"His day job or night job?" I said, smirking. "He was a lawyer—criminal cases. I met him on a story I was doing. But it turned out he was also a compulsive gambler who had loan sharks pursuing him with tire irons, and it took me way too long to figure that out. At first I thought he must be having an affair, and then I even wondered if he might be gay. I should have been asked to turn in my press credentials for being such a lousy reporter when it came to my own life. But look, let's save the gory details for another time. You told me last night that I'd have my turn to focus attention on you. Why don't we try that tonight?"

"As long as I can leave the light on," he said, laughing. "This is something I'd like to watch."

We made love in the light and then again in the darkness. It was a little different from the other times we'd been together—slower, more languorous, but just as intoxicating. As relaxed as I felt, my mind went crazy as soon as my head hit the pillow, with thoughts about the murders ricocheting from one side of my brain to the other. I kept replaying everything I'd heard about Blythe, wondering if she was indeed the stalker-killer. I also contemplated how I should handle her if I *did* get the chance to talk to her.

For a few minutes, I thought of Chris, too. I'd believed the worst of him and had told myself that I never wanted to be with him again romantically. I'd gone to bed with Beau assuming that it was over with Chris. But Chris wasn't guilty of the crime I'd thought, just of being as ambitious as the next person in his business. I was thrilled that Beau had decided he wanted to make a go of it with me, but that meant I was going to have to break off my relationship with Chris, and the odd thing was, that made me sad. As I'd realized last night, I still felt an attraction to Chris. What a mess.

Overwhelmed by that mess, I fell asleep after only about thirty minutes of brain burn. I awoke the next morning to the distant ringing of my cell phone in my purse. It was one of the PR twins, rattling off the drive-time radio shows I needed to do. While I conducted one interview over the phone in my office, Beau showered. We ended up with only a few minutes together, chugging coffee at my dining table.

"You're great on radio," Beau said. "I overheard it."

"I'd much rather be *asking* the questions, but of course these days if you're press, you have to *do* press, too. Nash told me that he actually looks for staffers who are *mediagenic*. I should be writing off my highlights on my income tax."

"Ah, another secret I've managed to procure before leaving. It's only a matter of time before I figure you out, Bailey."

I laughed, but his remark gave me pause. I probably *did* hold back with him. But it was in part because *he* was a mystery of sorts. He didn't seem closed off, but his quietness at times, the way he had of studying me without saying anything, left me with the sense that I just didn't know what was really going on behind his eyes at all times.

"When do you plan to speak to the police today?" he asked.

"Soon," I said. "I'll probably call them right after you go." My legs were crossed beneath the table, easing my guilt slightly.

While he slipped into his trench coat, Beau mentioned that a friend from out of town had called a few days before and asked if he could crash at his place for the night.

"It's the last thing I need since I'm just catching up after Turkey—plus I'd really like to be with *you*—but he's too good a friend to say no to. Can we skip tonight and spend the weekend together?"

"That sounds nice. I just have to stay a bit flexible because of doing press, that sort of thing."

"Call me today and let me know what's happening. I want to be sure you're safe and sound."

The kiss he gave me was long and intense, and my heart was pounding as I shut the door. A week ago, I had given up hope of ever being with Beau again, but now everything had changed. I had no choice but to let Chris know things were over with us. Yet I couldn't stand the thought of doing that.

After pouring another cup of coffee, I made several calls to contacts I had in the police department to see if there had been any break in the case, but I heard the same word from each source: No definite suspects, no arrests. Though Alex Ottoson initially had been a person of interest, one source acknowledged that he'd produced an alibi that had checked out. I wondered if the news about Harper had started to leak out.

I really wanted to see a good photo of Blythe before I showed up at the theater, but I didn't want to tip off the theater manager that I was coming by—in case he told her. It suddenly occurred to me that she might have a Web site. I found it under her exact name, but the words *Under Construction* were all that came up on screen.

Going over my notes, I realized that this would be a good time to try Barish again, since I hadn't heard back yet. A young woman answered. When I said my name, she hesitated, as if she'd been told to be on the alert for a call from me. She asked me to hold and then came back a minute later announcing that Mr. Barish would be with me shortly. I wondered if she was the same woman I'd seen in the office on Saturday.

The man who picked up the phone a minute later was the

nice and friendly Barish, his first comment an apology for not returning my call.

"September is a very busy time for us. We're coming up on the final, final deadlines for filing all tax returns. What's going on with the case? I heard the news about Tom and the Ford woman."

"I have one piece of news. The amount Tom was going to advance the handyman was exactly the amount he withdrew from the bank. So if Deke gave him a few thousand dollars that week, Tom did something else with it."

"This Deke fellow seems very suspicious to me. I hope the police are taking him seriously as a suspect."

"I wouldn't know. Any word on when Tom's body will be released—so that a funeral can be arranged?"

"They keep promising any day. Was that your urgent question?"

"Well, I was interested in learning when the funeral will be. But I had another question for you. Were you and Tom on speaking terms during the last weeks of his life?"

"I beg your pardon?" he demanded testily.

"I've been told that things were strained between the two of you—that Tom didn't like the way you were dealing with him on money matters."

"What in the world would make you say that?"

"Tom said as much to people."

"I was very fond of Tom, but as I told you, he was not my client—his parents were. And it's—correction, it *was*—my fiduciary duty to make certain, as his parents desired, that Tom's financial future was protected. That meant saying no to the occasional whim on his part."

"But—"

"I'm not at liberty to say any more. The Fain family finances are a confidential matter. And they don't involve you at all. Now, I must get back to my work. Good day."

As I listened to dead air, I realized that I'd hit a nerve of some kind with Barish. Why was he being so defensive? I wondered. Had Tom stopped speaking to him simply because of the play, or was something else going on? What if Tom had discovered that Barish was guilty of an impropriety with his money? My fingertips suddenly felt icy. I had never once considered Barish a suspect, but maybe I'd been stupid not to look at him that way. Barish had certainly known about the house in Andes.

I would have to find a way to look into the matter, but today there was Blythe to contend with. I glanced at my watch; it was just before noon. Based on the facts that Terry had shared, I figured my best bet was to show up at around four-fifteen. If I was too early, I might arouse suspicions. If I was too late, I might miss her.

So that meant cooling my heels for the next few hours. I made more calls to my sources, perused online sites, drank coffee, left a message for my mother saying I was alive and well, paced around my apartment, and pushed aside thoughts about the freaky state of my love life.

At three-thirty, I finally threw on a trench, grabbed an umbrella, and departed for the Chaps Theatre, figuring that if I saw a cab, I'd grab it, but otherwise I would walk. There was only one word worth using to describe the day, weatherwise: raw. The sky was low and bruised looking with clouds, though at the moment it was spritzing rather than raining, which in some ways was even more annoying. No matter how I positioned my umbrella, water sprayed at my face.

I could tell even before I reached the theater that I was out of luck. No light fell from the windows onto the sidewalk. I tried the door anyway. It was locked. I rapped several times on the glass just in case, but it was totally dark inside, and it was clear no one was there. Damn.

But that didn't mean Blythe wouldn't eventually show—it was still relatively early. I jumped a large puddle just off the curb and dashed diagonally across the street toward the café I'd noticed the other night. After ordering a cappuccino, I positioned myself at a table by a window in the nearly empty room. From this far down the street, I had no view of the door of the theater, but if someone turned on the lobby lights, I'd be able to see the reflected glow on the slick sidewalk.

For the next fifteen minutes, I sipped my drink distractedly and peered outside. Nothing happened. Once I got up and checked outside, just to make sure I hadn't missed anything. The waiter shot me an aggravated look when I returned, as if he thought I'd been attempting to skip on the $3 tab or was waiting to do a coke deal in the street. I paid the bill and waited some more.

Minutes later, I glanced up and saw that the sidewalk directly in front of the theater was now gleaming with light. I willed myself to stay calm, but as I punched my arms frenetically through the twisted sleeves of my trench coat, I could tell how anxious I was.

It had started to really rain, and I dashed down the street, not bothering to open my umbrella. When I peered in the glass door of the theater, I saw that the lobby was empty, but I heard the faint sounds of music. I knocked on the glass a few times. No response. I tugged at the door, and to my surprise it opened. Inside, I could hear the music better now—it was some kind of rock, playing from around the back of the theater to the left.

I decided not to announce myself by calling out a hello. That would likely bring someone to the lobby, who would then go back and explain my presence to anyone else who was there. It just seemed smarter to catch Blythe unawares. I snuck over to the double black doors to the actual theater and quietly opened one a crack. The lights were down, except for one floor lamp with a bare bulb standing forlornly on the stage toward the front. A friend had once explained to me that in the theater world there used to be a superstition that if the theater was left totally dark at night, it might become haunted, so a "ghost light" was always left burning on stage to discourage any spirits from taking up residence. It's a practice that's followed even now.

Though the bare bulb created only one circle of light, I could see some of the pieces that made up the spare set: two twin beds with pink bedspreads, two desks, a shag area rug. It must be, I realized, where the coeds from hell spent their nights.

I eased the door closed again and decided to follow the music. To the left of the box office was a corridor that seemed to lead to where it was coming from. I made my way past two doors, each marked RESTROOM, and a small kitchen with a light burning. On the countertop were several liters of soda and a few Tupperware tubs with cookies inside, obviously the refreshments for tonight's intermission. Next door was an office, darkened, and then the corridor veered to the right. This seemed to be the official backstage area. The music was growing louder.

I heard a creak behind me suddenly and spun around.

"Hello?" I called out. The hallway, up to the bend, at least, was empty. "Is there anybody here?"

There was no reply. I waited a moment but heard nothing. I proceeded on.

The first room on my right was a narrow, shabby makeup room. Mirrors lined one of the long walls, and on the counter sat five identical white plastic wig heads. No humans, though. I kept going. I passed a messy storage room filled with props, a vacuum cleaner, period furniture, and large plastic tubs stuffed with what I assumed were costumes and more props, and then finally the room where the music was coming from. It appeared to be a dressing room. More mirrors, odd chairs strewn about, two stained, beige Victorian-style clothing forms without a stitch on, and a radio/CD player. Snow Patrol was singing "Chasing Cars." But there wasn't a soul in sight.

As I turned away from the doorway, I heard another noise. Above me. It seemed to be the sound of a chair scraping—and then footsteps—on the second floor. That, apparently, was where people had gathered. I hurriedly retraced my steps along the corridor toward the front of the theater. As I stepped into the lobby, a woman with reddish-brown hair and dressed in a baggy beige sweater and black pants emerged from the doorway on the far side. I started to open my mouth to explain my presence, then realized it was Terry. Crap, I thought.

"So you decided to come after all," I said, barely able to contain how less than thrilled I was with this development. Terry offered a self-satisfied smile, as if she were the brightest bulb in the box. She didn't have a hat on today, so I had a closer look at her reddish brown horsehair. It was about the weirdest color I'd ever seen.

"After I talked to you, I decided I was stupid to wait around for Blythe to bring the money to me," she announced. "I knew she might never show. So I decided to come here, just like you. And guess what? I got the check." She tapped her big brown shoulder bag for emphasis.

"So Blythe is here now?" I exclaimed.

"She's upstairs. But she's not staying long, so if you want to see her, I'd hurry."

"Where exactly is she?" I asked, starting to move.

"In the office on the second floor. You just follow the hallway and take the first set of stairs up, and there's a door at the top. You go through into a little hallway, and then there's another door to the office."

"You didn't tell her I called, did you?"

"No, I *said* I wouldn't, didn't I?" she proclaimed petulantly. She turned away and crossed the lobby, heading toward the exit.

"Is Blythe alone?" I called out to her back.

"No, one of the other theater geeks is with her."

Good. I certainly didn't relish the idea of being alone with her in the theater.

I made my way through the door Terry had come through and followed the hallway. This passageway was narrower than the one on the other side of the theater, though it eventually widened nearer the stage. I peeked through a curtain to the stage, lit eerily by the bare bulb. That was where Tom had performed, I realized, dreaming of one day being a star.

To my right was a set of stairs—just one flight with a landing at the top—that was clearly the one Terry had referred to. There was no light at the top, but there was enough light from the hallway for me to see my way up. I climbed the stairs, my ears pricked. From where I was now, I could no longer hear the music, and the theater was totally hushed.

The door to the left at the top was black metal, scuffed and dirty, with a bolt beneath the handle that had been drawn. Odd to have a bolt on this side, I thought. What were they keeping up here, anyway—Mr. Rochester's first wife? I put my ear to the door and listened. There were no sounds of conversation or activity, but then Terry had said I needed to go down a hallway before I reached the office. I paused for a moment, thinking. Something was gnawing at my mind again, but it felt totally unformed.

I reached for the handle and yanked, and after pulling open the door, I automatically lifted my foot to take a step forward. As I peered ahead, I saw that rather than a hallway, I was looking at a wall of cottony grayness, lit from below. In a second that

seemed to last forever, I realized that the space I was stepping
into was only air.

My mind yelled for me to pull back, but it was too late. I
pitched forward, scrabbling with my hands for something to
grab hold of. As my left leg slipped off into nothingness, my
right hand found something hard and metallic above me to
grasp. A half second later, my right leg followed the left into the
abyss below. And then I was dangling.

My brain seemed to split in two. Part of it thrashed in complete terror and confusion over what was happening to me. The
other observed it all calmly, as if I were watching a documentary
called *Girl Falling off Edge*. I realized that I had stepped through
a doorway that opened onto a space high above the stage. I had
grabbed a metal chain across the doorway and was now hanging
by my right hand. If I let go, I would fall and possibly die. At the
very least, I would break my neck.

Straining, I reached with my left arm upward as high as I
could and managed to grasp the metal chain with that hand, too.
I was suspended now like someone holding on to a trapeze, fac-
ing the doorway, with a grid of black stage lights just off to my
left. The chain, I could see, had been strung across the door as
a final but pathetic barrier. The real protection against someone
falling, the bolt on the door, should never have been undone.

"Help!" I screamed. "Help me!" I tried to maneuver my
right leg back up onto the landing, but I was hanging so low
that it was impossible. I steeled myself to take a look below. My
stomach turned over at the sight of the stage floor and the ghost
light below. The drop was easily fifteen feet.

"Help, help!" I screamed again. As my body dragged on
the chain, the links cut painfully into my palms, and my arms
started to ache. I didn't know how much longer I could hold on.
Suddenly, I heard the sound of footsteps. Someone was coming up the stairs to the landing. The person was moving slowly,

like someone old and tired—or someone deliberately taking her time. Please, I begged in my mind, don't let it be her.

But it was. As the footsteps reached the landing, I craned my neck back and saw Terry looming above me, a snicker on her face. But it wasn't Terry, of course, under that hideous wig. It was Blythe.

"Oh dear," she said. "I should have told you to watch that first step. It's a killer, isn't it?"

CHAPTER 20

Help me up, will you?" I pleaded. "Don't make things any worse for yourself."

"You know what?" Blythe said. "You are *absolutely* right. What was I thinking?"

And then she hoisted her big purse above her head and brought it down as hard as she could on my hands.

My knuckles stung from the blow, but I didn't open my hands. From sheer terror, they remained glued to the metal. But I knew Blythe wasn't going to stop at one measly swipe from her handbag.

I glanced down to the stage floor again. There was a chance, if I let myself drop straight down, feet first, like someone jumping from a diving board, that I might only break an ankle or a leg, but the thought of just letting go was terrifying. As Blythe brought up her purse again, ready for another strike, I glanced to the left. Hanging from the light grid was a long, thick rope, some kind of pulley, it seemed, connected to the lights. I mentally measured the distance to it. If I could scoot across the chain, I might be able to swing my legs out and grab hold of the rope with them. But I couldn't let on to Blythe what I was up to.

The second blow was even more forceful, and I had to fight the urge to both scream and unclench my hands from the chain. As Blythe stepped back, plotting her next move, I inched my hands quickly down the chain. There was a groan from the door frame as the screw on the right side protested the strain. Blythe might not even *need* a next move. There was a chance that the chain would just be ripped from the door, and I would end up hurtling to the stage below.

"Now, now, be careful," Blythe admonished as she heard the sound. She couldn't keep the delight off her face.

I was within reach of the rope finally—or at least my legs were. There was no way I would be able to use my arms in the process, so I was going to have to grip as tightly as possible with my thighs. But first I needed to find momentum. I looked up toward Blythe, my neck aching from the angle I was holding my head.

"The cops are coming," I told her, trying to shift her attention. "They're going to meet me here."

"That's not true, and you know it, Bailey," she said in an exaggerated chiding tone. "You're trying to tell me a *really* big lie—and I don't like that."

"Do you think I'd come here alone? Of course I called the cops. I told them to meet me at the theater because you were going to be here. They know all about you."

She made a *tsk-tsk* sound. "Do you think any woman who has her apartment decorated in shabby chic style like you do—that is *soooo* nineties, Bailey—would be smart enough to call the police? I know you didn't. I've seen you—and you like doing things all by your little self."

She straightened up and flicked her head back and forth in a maniacal gesture of disagreement. The door frame groaned again, louder this time. My arms were starting to quiver. If I was going to move, I was going to have to do it now.

I slung my eyes to the left. In one swift move, I thrust my left leg and then my right one over and coiled them around the rope, and then as I did so, I drew the rope closer to my body. Out of the corner of my eye, I saw Blythe pull back, startled, unsure of what was going on. Reaching as far as I could, I grabbed the rope with my left hand and pulled myself over there. As I let go of the chain, I heard it snap from the door frame. Two seconds later it reached the stage floor with a loud thwack.

I was now hanging perilously from the rope by just my left side, like some Cirque du Soleil performer. "You little bitch!" Blythe screamed at me. With the help of some muscle memory from a gym class fifteen years ago, I managed to lift my torso fully toward the rope, clenching it with my other hand.

For a few short seconds, I just hugged the rope. My body was nearly trembling with fatigue, and my legs stung from rope burn. I needed to keep moving, though. I'd outsmarted Blythe for one brief moment, but if she reached the stage before me, it wouldn't do me any good.

Loosening my grip slightly, I began to slide down the rope, trying to ignore the burning sensation on the insides of my arms. I craned my head to the right to see what Blythe was up to. She was on the landing, watching me, but as soon as our eyes met, she spun around, and I could hear her clattering down the stairs I'd come up earlier. I loosened my grip to increase my speed downward toward the stage floor.

Without warning, the light grid, which was attached to the rope, rammed against the ceiling. I hadn't realized that the rope was a pulley to raise and lower the grid. The rope jerked in my hands, and before I knew what was happening, I had lost my grip.

I hit the floor hard, collapsing in a heap, and in the same instant, my right ankle made a popping sound. Pain shot through my foot like a loud scream.

I lay on the ground long enough to gather my strength and then struggled up to a standing position. I wasn't sure if I'd broken or sprained my ankle, but it hurt like hell. I looked all around me. At any second, Blythe was going to come charging through the door at stage left. The best escape route for me would be stage right, but even then she could easily catch up to me. I swept the stage with my eyes, looking for a makeshift weapon. Leaning against the dresser by the fake wall at the back was a field hockey stick. I limped across the scuffed stage floor and grabbed it.

Something was weird, though. Blythe should have been down the stairs by now. Was she going to try to ambush me somewhere else in the theater as I tried to escape? All I knew was that I had to get out of there.

I staggered across the small stage, toward the door that I knew led to the corridor lined with makeup and dressing rooms. Suddenly Blythe appeared in the doorway, ten feet ahead of me, her hands behind her back as if she were about to present me with a fun birthday surprise. She'd obviously gone down the stairs and circled around to the other side of the theater.

"Ahh, I should have known you played field hockey, Bailey," she said, her eyes wide in mock fascination. "Even with all those hip little clothes of yours, I could sense you were a preppy at heart. By the way, I hope you don't mind—I took a few of your tops when I was over at your place the other day."

"Blythe," I said, trying to sound calm, "why don't you stop this now and make it better for yourself."

"Oh, you want me to believe that not killing you will make it *better* for me? Bailey, I keep getting the feeling you don't think I'm very smart."

"Oh, I think you're *very* smart. And very talented. You totally fooled my doorman, you know."

"Please, that hardly deserves an Oscar. Sure, I imitated your voice, but that doorman of yours has a brain the size of a lichee nut."

"How'd you nail my voice?"

She smiled coyly. "I heard you at the Half King. I was standing right by you at the bar the whole time."

The pack of girls next to me. There had been one hanging off to the side, and that must have been Blythe.

"So you put the drug in my beer—and texted Chris?"

"If you say so."

"What have you got against me, anyway?"

"You got all snoopy, Bailey. Coming around my apartment, leaving me all those messages, bugging poor Terry."

"Where's the real Terry, anyway?"

"She said she was going away on a long trip. You know, the health insurance business is *hopelessly* boring."

I wondered if Blythe had killed her, too—weeks ago.

"Tell me about Tom, will you?"

"Bailey, if I'm not mistaken, you're doing that stalling-for-time thing. I really don't have the patience for that."

"I want to hear your side of the story—really. You drove up to Andes to see him?"

"Do you know, Tom never told me he had a place there? Maybe he secretly wanted to surprise me when he got it all fixed up. But I'd been doing a little research on Tom, and I found out about the house. Needless to say, I was very, *very* disappointed to see he was there with another woman, someone who was not only beneath him, but a very bad actress as well. And did you *see* that woman's lips? She looked like a hippo."

"So you killed Tom out of jealousy?"

She snickered. "No, Bailey," she said firmly. "I broke *up* with

Tom that day. And I could see by his reaction that if he couldn't be with me, he didn't want to live. He pleaded with me to put him out of his misery. Thank God I'd found that axe out by the barn."

"Why the fire? Was Tom dead by then?"

"I'm not *cruel,* Bailey. Of course he was dead. I just couldn't look at his face anymore. FYI, paint thinner is an excellent accelerant."

"And then you went back to your place—not Miami?"

"If you say so. If you must know, one night I even stayed at Tom's for old time's sake. I promised him I would." That explained the light left burning.

"What—"

"Who do you think you are—Oprah? I'm getting really tired of answering all your questions."

"Just tell me about Locket," I said. I was trying to keep my voice easy, casual, despite my fear and the blinding pain in my ankle. "Why her? She wasn't a threat anymore now that Tom was dead."

"Locket was another snoopy dog, just like you. I could tell she knew something—she was talking to you about it."

"You—you were the girl in the visor?" I said, stammering. "The one who asked about Locket's dog at the Boathouse?" It had to be, I suddenly realized. The girl had seemed so intrusive.

"Oh, Bailey, you think you know all my tricks, but you don't."

With that, she pulled her right hand out from behind her. It clutched a black-handled butcher knife with a glistening blade about eight inches long. My body felt leaden with fear.

"Don't you know the police will figure this out?" I told her. "They'll know you were here today."

She laughed too loudly. "But you see, Bailey, I have my own private key to the place, and no one knew I was coming except you." She laughed again. "And Terry, of course. But like I said, she's not available for comment these days."

I tightened my grip on the hockey stick, sensing that she was done talking and was going to take some kind of action now. Turning my head slightly, I calculated how long it would take her to catch up with me if I made a mad dash toward the door on stage left. Only seconds because of my ankle. As I turned my head back in Blythe's direction, she made her move, lunging toward me with the knife.

I raised the hockey stick and whipped it across her body as hard as I could. I had hoped to dislodge the knife from her hand, which didn't happen, but she reeled back in pain from the blow.

"You little bitch!" she screamed. "How dare you do that to me?"

She shifted her grasp on the knife and raised it above her head in a stabbing position. And then she lunged once more.

I swung the hockey stick at her again. But just before contact, Blythe raised her free arm and managed to grab the stick. She jerked her arm to the right, and the stick went sailing out into the theater. It bounced and clanged over the backs of several seats.

"Oops," Blythe said, and formed her face into an expression of grossly exaggerated glee.

I shot a glance to the set on my right. There was nothing else there that could help me, just the beds and dressers and pink shag rug. I started to back up, careful not to edge too close to the end of the stage, my ankle hurting so much that I could barely think over the pain. On my fourth step back, I bumped into the ghost light, just behind me and to my left. It rocked slightly and then steadied itself.

Blythe puffed up her chest, ready for another strike. And then she charged. Taking one more step backward, I grabbed the lamp with both hands. It was sturdy but lighter than it looked, probably made of hollow metal. Like a little kid holding a light saber,

I swung it as hard as I possibly could. Suddenly the lightbulb went out as the cord was yanked from the socket; a moment later, in total darkness, I felt the lamp make full contact with Blythe's body.

There was a thud and a burst of air from her lungs. I could hear the scuffing sound of her shoes as she staggered on the stage. Then, suddenly, I realized she was airborne. A second later, I heard her crash hard into the seats below the stage.

I squinted, trying to see. A little bit of light was coming from the corridor off stage left, the one with the stairs I'd taken. I dropped the lamp, and with my hands out in front of me, I staggered off the stage in that direction.

Once I was in the corridor, I could finally see again—there were wall sconces burning along the way. Dragging my right leg, I made my way as fast as I could down the corridor, retracing the steps I'd taken earlier. Approaching the lobby, I heard movement out there. My heart stopped as I wondered if Blythe had quickly managed to right herself and hurry up the main aisle of the theater.

But as I peered out into the lobby, I could barely believe my eyes. Detective Windgate was standing out there, along with a small man of Asian descent.

I limped into the lobby, and Windgate pulled his head back in surprise.

"What in God's name is going on?" he demanded. Both men glanced down at my bum leg, searching for the injury.

"Blythe Hammell is in there," I blurted out. "She tried to kill me with a knife, and I knocked her over, into the seats. She must be hurt—but I don't know how badly."

Windgate shot his partner a look of exasperation and turned back to me.

"You stay right here, do you hear me? If I find out you moved a muscle, I'm going to arrest you."

"Okay," I said meekly.

"Which is the best way to get there?" he asked brusquely.

"I'd go right through there," I said, pointing to the double doors that opened into the theater.

As I collapsed into one of the saggy old armchairs, they stepped across the lobby and with guns raised swung open the doors cautiously. The light from the lobby poured into the theater. It was still fairly dim in there, but they would be able to see where they were going,

"She's probably in one of the front two rows," I called out in a loud whisper. I watched as they made their way down the aisle.

It didn't take long for them to find her. I heard one of the cops talking, and then Blythe began ranting, though I couldn't make out anything she was saying. At least I hadn't killed her. That would have been a real mess.

I kept my word and didn't move a muscle, which would have been difficult to do anyhow considering the sorry state of my ankle. Now that I had a chance to look, I could see that it was swollen up as if I had a tennis ball under my skin.

About five minutes later, Windgate came sprinting back up the aisle into the lobby. Just as he arrived, two cops in uniform rapped on the glass door to the lobby. Windgate motioned them in and told one of them to assist "Detective Kwong" and the other to search the premises.

"Do you know if there is anyone else on-site?" he asked me.

"No, but they've got a show tonight, so people should be arriving before long to set up. What made you come here, anyway?"

"You can thank the PR director for the show—Harper Aikins. She got a phone call from someone who claimed to be you but didn't seem familiar with a conversation that the two of you had engaged in. She thought it might be this woman Blythe since you'd worked her into a frenzy on the subject. Miss Aikins called me and said you planned to come here to meet Blythe. You know, I made it very clear to you that you needed to watch your back."

"But until tonight I just wasn't really sure that Blythe was the killer."

"How bad are you hurt?"

"It's just my ankle. Hopefully it's only a sprain."

"I've got two ambulances coming. Until they arrive, we need to find a place to talk."

I told him about the dressing rooms, and after I'd reassured him I could make it back there, he helped me hop to the closest one. I took a seat on a small bench while Windgate went into the kitchen for ice. He returned two minutes later with a chunk of cubes in an old dish towel, which I laid carefully against the swelling. Windgate dragged over a chair and sat next to me.

"I'm going to hold off on the questions for a minute," he told me, his voice firm. "Why don't you start with your version of events."

"*My* version?" I said. "That sounds like you're entertaining another one."

"Miss Hammell claims you lured her here and tried to kill her."

"You can't possibly believe that," I exclaimed. "She's the one who lured *me* here and tried to kill *me*. And she's the one who murdered Tom and Locket. She *admitted* it to me."

Windgate eyed me skeptically, stroking his mustache methodically. I couldn't tell if he was really suspicious of what I was saying or was just acting that way to scare the pants off me—and make sure I coughed up the entire story.

"Blythe also happens to be a very good actress who's going to tell you a pack of lies," I continued. "She's the one who talked her way into my apartment after pretending to be me on the phone. She's also been impersonating her roommate, Terry. For all I know, she killed Terry, too."

I was talking too fast and sounding way too defensive, but I was suddenly overwhelmed by the idea that Blythe could manipulate this whole situation and possibly land me in trouble.

"Okay, relax," Windgate said. "I want to know exactly what you've been up to since the last time we talked—when you promised me you'd be careful and behave yourself."

Figuring he didn't mean *everything,* I skipped any mention of ottoman sex and related how I'd come to the Chaps Theatre to follow up on the clue from *Taming of the Shrew,* how Blythe had tricked me into going through the doorway after obviously undoing the bolt beforehand, and how I had been forced to defend myself with the lamp like a Jedi warrior after she'd tried to attack me with a knife.

"So you're saying that you came to this brilliant conclusion about Blythe Hammell as the killer because of a line from Shakespeare?" Windgate asked doubtfully. He folded his arms against his brown tweed jacket and leaned back in his chair.

"It wasn't any kind of brilliant instant conclusion," I said. "I'd just always wondered if the quote from *Taming of the Shrew* meant anything, and I decided to check it out. When I saw Blythe's name on the cast list for the play, I realized there was a chance that *she* had been the visitor in Andes that day. You'd prompted me to think about stalkers, and I suddenly saw that maybe Blythe had done more when Tom dumped her than send a bunch of silly cards. Maybe she'd become obsessed with him. But I really wasn't sure of any of it. I thought if I talked to Blythe, I'd get a feel for what she was like. If something seemed off, I was going to call you immediately."

"What do you mean, she's been impersonating her roommate?"

"She showed up here pretending to be her roommate, Terry, just as she had when I first went by her apartment. You've got to try to figure out where Terry is. Blythe may have killed her."

"At what point did you realize 'Terry' was actually Blythe?"

I thought for a second.

"Unfortunately, not until I slipped off the ledge. But on a subconscious level, I think my brain had been figuring it out over the past few days."

"You gonna tell me how?"

The cold from the makeshift ice bag was beginning to sting, so I lifted it off and set it onto the counter next to me. My ankle was not only obscenely huge, it now had turned several ugly shades of green and purple.

"One thing that kept nagging at me was how the person who was making the crank calls to me had managed to get hold of my cell phone number—and how he or she knew to call me so soon after I found Tom's body last week. Once I started focusing on Blythe, I didn't think she could have my number. But I'd given my cell phone number to *Terry* that day, after telling her I was going upstate to look for Tom. She told me she had no way to reach Blythe, so theoretically Blythe didn't have it. But *Terry* did.

"And then there was Terry's hair. It was this really weird color, and on some level I guess I realized it was a wig."

He flicked at his mustache.

"How is she, anyway?" I asked.

"She may have a concussion and a broken bone or two. I'm not really sure at this point. But speaking of that, I'd better check on things. If I leave you here, are you going to be okay?"

"Yes, but while you're gone, can you look for my purse? It came off my shoulder as I fell."

He didn't return with my purse, but a patrol cop did a few minutes later, and then shortly after that, before I had a chance to dig out my cell phone, two EMS workers arrived. The guy who examined me said he thought it was a sprain, not a break.

"Then I don't really need to go to the ER, right? I could just nurse this at home."

"Yes, you have to go to the ER," said Windgate, sticking his head through the doorway. "It's protocol. I will call you tomorrow morning at nine o'clock. Understood?"

"Yes, absolutely."

I felt foolish being carried out on a stretcher. By now there was a crowd outside, rubbernecking. As the EMS workers loaded me into the back of the ambulance, I saw another stretcher being carried out of the theater. Blythe lay on it, motionless in her baggy Terry clothes. The wig had fallen off her head, and her long blond hair was matted tightly to her scalp. Just having her that close to me made my pulse race again.

After a short ride with no siren, the ambulance deposited me at St. Vincent's, a hospital in the Village a few blocks west of my apartment. The last time I'd been in the ER had been to remove a pebble lodged in the corner of my eye, and I'd waited four hours to be put out of my misery. But catastrophes seemed on the light side tonight, and it wasn't long before I was ushered into the examining room. A doctor ordered an X-ray of my ankle, and after that I found myself sitting on a bed in a curtained-off area, listening to a man on the other side of the droopy green fabric deal with a world-class phlegm problem. Nearby, a baby began to cry, and its mother gently tried to shush it. Even I, who had yet to experience any maternal yearnings, knew that repeating "Shhh" over and over again to a wailing baby was about as effective as reading it Dante's *Inferno*.

Despite the noise, I needed to call Beau. I had resisted phoning him from the theater because I hadn't wanted to make Windgate wonder what I was up to, but I was dying to share tonight's awful saga with him. I yearned for a shoulder to cry on. Though I had come out of the confrontation with Blythe with just a sprained ankle, I felt badly shaken. When he didn't pick up his cell phone, I tried his home number.

To my shock, a woman answered. I'd had Beau's number on speed dial, so I knew there was no mistake.

"Is Beau there?" I asked hesitantly. I wondered if it could be a cleaning lady, except she sounded far too arrogant to wield a Swiffer.

"He's not home yet," she said. "May I take a message?" There was a trace of amusement in her voice, as if she'd detected my awkwardness and damn well liked it.

CHAPTER 21

Great. The night was going quickly from sucky and nightmarish to *Texas Chain Saw Massacre* caliber. I took a breath and reassured myself that there had to be a reasonable explanation for why a smug little chick was answering Beau's phone. We'd been going steady for forty-eight hours, so he'd hardly be cheating already.

After torturing myself for a minute, I sat back up and called Nash. I dictated an update on the murder investigation for the Web site and told him I would report back when I knew more.

"Where are you, anyway?" he asked. "It sounds like a bus station."

"Sort of," I said. He'd know soon enough about my ankle when he saw me struggling with crutches tomorrow.

As I started to put my BlackBerry away, it rang in my hands.

"Bailey, are you okay?" It was Chris, rushing his words out before I'd barely said hello. "Harper called me all worried."

"I'm okay, but I almost wasn't. It was *Blythe* who killed Tom—

and Locket. She tried to kill me, too, tonight—at the Chaps Theatre. I'm over at St. Vincent's with a sprained ankle."

"I'm coming there right now."

"Chris, you don't have to."

"Look, I may not be a doctor, but I practically play one on TV. I'll be there in ten minutes, fifteen tops."

I didn't fight him. It was going to be awkward with Chris and me, but he was entitled to know everything that had transpired with Blythe. And I felt so lousy, it would be great to have someone for support right now.

There wasn't much time to think about it, anyway, because a few minutes later a different doctor parted the curtain and walked in. He was dressed in corduroy pants and a navy wool sports jacket—tall, sandy haired, and good-looking. A resident, I guessed.

"The good news? It's only a second ligament sprain," he said briskly. "That's not super serious. The bad news is that you're going to have to stay off it for about three weeks."

He wrapped my ankle in an Ace bandage, gave me prescription ibuprofen for the swelling, and told me that I needed to follow the RICE strategy: rest, ice, compression, and elevation. The hospital would supply me with crutches.

Chris arrived just as I was trying out the crutches—and doing a pathetic job at it. He placed his hand on the back of my head and kissed my forehead.

"Are you ever going to forgive me for getting you into this?" he asked, his eyes worried.

"My book tour isn't until November, and my volleyball career ended with college, so there's no harm done."

"Thank God for small favors."

"Chris," I said over the sound of the still-wailing baby, "in all honesty, I don't regret any of this. Though I never met Tom, I *cared* about him. And I'm glad I found his killer."

While I waited near the door of the hospital, Chris hunted down a cab. When we arrived at my apartment, there seemed to be no question that he was going to help me upstairs.

"Do you want a cup of tea or something?" he asked after he settled me on the couch with my leg elevated.

"Brandy," I said. "Make it a double."

"Is that going to mix okay with your pain medication?"

"I don't care. I just want to pass out."

Chris clearly decided to ignore that request because I heard him fill the teakettle. While he worked in the kitchen, I called the manager's number at the Chaps Theatre on my cell. A woman answered who I thought might be the redhead I'd seen the night before in the lobby stuffing cookies into Tupperware containers.

"This is Bailey Weggins," I told her. "I'm the woman who was attacked in the theater today. Do you have a minute?"

"Well, when we arrived at six, the cops told us they wouldn't let us put on the play tonight, so basically I have all the time in the world."

"There's something I need to know. I fell through a door fifteen feet above the stage. Why in the world is that there?"

"Oh God, I heard," she lamented. "I don't know how that happened—we always keep it bolted."

"But why is it there?" I repeated. "Does it have something to do with sets you use?"

"No, that's not it. This was once an apartment building, years and years ago. That was a flight of stairs that went to the second floor—long before the stage was there."

After I hung up, I leaned my head back against the couch, suddenly feeling close to tears. Chris emerged from the kitchen carrying two mugs of tea.

"To you, Bailey," he said, raising his mug after handing me the other.

"Gosh, Chris, it was just last Tuesday that you called me. I can't believe all that's happened since then."

"Thanks for what you said earlier. About not being sorry you did this."

"I meant it."

"So tell me what happened tonight from beginning to end, okay, including how you finally figured it all out."

I'd provided highlights in the cab, but now I went through the whole awful saga in detail.

"How did you manage to think straight during all of it?" he asked. "If you hadn't, you might be dead now."

"From pure adrenaline, I guess. And the sheer desire not to want to go splat on the stage. Thank God I used to be decent on ropes during PE."

"Is Blythe *sick*—I mean, crazy?" he asked.

"Screwed up, certainly. Crazy, maybe. In hindsight, did Tom ever say anything that pointed to the fact that her feelings for him had morphed into an obsession?"

"Well, like I told you in the beginning, I thought Blythe was a bit of a wack job, but Tom seemed to view her as more of a nuisance—he wasn't the type to get all hot and bothered by it. And then all of a sudden she went off the grid. The calls stopped—and as we saw, the cards and letters stopped, too. She didn't seem to be an issue anymore."

I took a sip of the hot tea and thought for a moment.

"You know, I told the police that Blythe may have killed Terry, but now I'm not so sure. I'm wondering if Blythe actually *is* Terry."

"What do you mean?"

"That maybe they're one and the same person. Blythe could have created this alter ego for herself—to help her out of sticky situations. When people came looking for her because she owed them money or whatever, she could just trot out Terry. Or maybe she created her after she killed Tom—so that she could lay low but keep an eye on things at the same time."

"God, that's insane. What about Harper? And Deke? They're in the clear?"

"Well, I'm pretty sure Deke never repaid the money he borrowed from Tom, but that may be the worst of his crimes. And Harper? She actually helped save my butt tonight. She told the cops where I was. The one guy I'm not fine with is Barish. It seems Tom had a falling-out with him, and I wonder if he could be up to something funny about the trust. I may call my family lawyer tomorrow and just see if there's any way to check him out."

The ice pack the hospital had given me was warm and Chris went off to the kitchen to empty an ice tray. After he'd positioned a plastic freezer bag of cubes on my ankle, he straightened up in front of me.

"Well, look, probably the best thing for you right now is to get to bed. Are you going to be okay on your own here?"

I didn't want him asking to stay because that would be awkward as hell, but it also felt weird that he didn't *want* to. My mixed emotions clearly registered on my face.

"I don't know what's going on with us, Bailey," he said. "I thought you had a pretty good sense of me, yet you somehow thought I'd been a total dickhead to Tom."

"I don't think that anymore. I'm sorry I thought that."

"Well, there's still something off between us."

"It's nothing you did, Chris." I said. I dreaded where the conversation was going, but I didn't have any choice. "There was someone I was seeing before I reconnected with you, and I honestly thought it was over between him and me. But he came back to New York, and now I'm not so sure."

He shook his head in frustration. "Is it the guy who was at Elaine's?" he asked.

"Yes."

"Christ."

"I'm sorry, Chris," I said plaintively. "I've really felt so good about the time we've spent together—despite how it came about. But I—"

"You don't have to explain it. I'm going to get out of here."

"Chris—"

"There's nothing more to say, Bailey." His face set. "I appreciate all you did. I'm just sorry how it's ending. I would have really liked to be with you."

I couldn't believe how sad it was to see him go out the door.

I laid my head back on the couch again. I was really close to blubbering, and I almost didn't hear my cell phone go off. If my purse hadn't been on the coffee table, I wouldn't have caught it in time.

It was Beau on the other end—with restaurant sounds all around him.

"What's going on?" he asked. "I thought you were going to give me an update."

"I did try to call," I said, sounding as pissy as I felt by this point. "Some girl answered your phone, so I didn't bother with a message."

"A girl? Oh damn, it was my friend Jason's girlfriend."

"What?"

"Remember I mentioned I had a friend from out of town visiting? He's staying at my place with his girlfriend."

"Why would she feel she had to answer your phone?" God, we'd been together two days, and I was turning into a nag and a shrew.

"Because she's a troublemaker. I really like Jason, but I'd be thrilled if he dumped her. Tell me what's going on. Have you talked to the cops about Blythe?"

I sighed, feeling weary. The explanation made sense, but even with Beau's promise of commitment, I kept wondering about him.

"They arrested her."

"Do they think she definitely did it?"

"Yes, she's admitted as much."

"Are you okay, Bailey?"

"Yeah, just tired."

"I wish I didn't have these plans tonight. Can we get together tomorrow?"

"Sure," I said. "Let's talk tomorrow."

I couldn't believe I hadn't told him about the attack and my ankle and everything else. But the combination of pain in my ankle and his friend's bitch of a girlfriend had left me too annoyed to want to talk.

I hobbled to the bathroom, wriggled out of my clothes, and splashed warm water on myself, just to feel cleansed of the whole experience tonight. As I raised my head from the basin, I flashed myself a little smile in the mirror. In spite of my sorry state, I felt pretty pleased with how I'd coped tonight. I'd rescued myself from a precipice and fought off a killer. Granted, I'd probably looked a little ridiculous swinging that lamp like Obi-Wan Kenobi, but what mattered was that I was alive—and that I'd found Tom's killer.

Tom. The thought of him still made my heart swell with sadness. His easygoing nature, his willingness to trust, his susceptibility to any girl who wanted to mount his hot bod, had conspired against him, but in no way had he deserved his fate. I thought suddenly about his play. Maybe I could try to locate a copy and see if it could still be produced.

I pulled down an extra pillow from the closet and wedged it under my comforter toward the end of the bed. Bone tired, I crawled into bed, turned off the light, and elevated my ankle as best I could on the pillow.

It seemed like a joke that I was sleeping alone. If I'd swallowed my annoyance at Beau and confessed what had happened, he would have surely left his friends at his place and flown over here.

Yet for some reason I'd held back. Something about my encounter with Chris had made me hesitate.

What it came down to, I realized, was that I didn't really know what I wanted. I was crazy about Beau. Yet I had hated seeing Chris walk out of my apartment tonight. I dug him, I really did. Okay, he was ten years younger and involved in a business in which guys not only were horribly self-absorbed but routinely fell in love with their fake-titted costars, and yet he seemed to love my company and making me laugh. Beau, who I'd pined for, had finally come round, but he always seemed so damn mysterious, so hard to read.

As I laid my head on my pillow, I realized I had no idea what I was going to do.

But there was one thing I could be grateful for. I was so freakin' tired, nothing would keep me awake tonight.

PROSPECT FREE LIBRARY
915 Trenton Falls St.
Prospect, NY 13435
(315) 896-2736